NAUTILUS

CRAIG WEATHERHILL

NAUTILUS

A sequel to Jules Verne's
Twenty Thousand Leagues under the Seas
and
The Mysterious Island

Craig Weatherhill

2009

Published by Evertype, Cnoc Sceichín, Leac an Anfa, Cathair na Mart, Co. Mhaigh Eo, Éire. *www.evertype.com.*

A catalogue record for this book is available from the British Library.

ISBN-10 1-904808-40-9
ISBN-13 978-1-904808-40-4

This novel is entirely a work of fiction. The names, characters, and incidents portrayed in it are the work of the author's imagination. Any resemblance to actual persons, living or dead, events, or localities is entirely coincidental.

Set in Fournier MT and *Fournier Le Jeune* by Michael Everson.

Frontispiece photo and illustration on p. 156: Craig Weatherhill.

Cover design by Michael Everson. The photo is of a Palau nautilus (*Nautilus belauensis*), taken off the island of Palau, Micronesia, © 2007 Lee R. Berger. Provided under the Creative Commons Attribution ShareAlike 3.0 License. Available from commons.wikimedia.org/wiki/File:Nautilus_profile.jpg

Printed by LightningSource.

Contents

This book is dedicated to the creative and visionary genius of Jules Verne (1828–1905), a great Breton; and to the extraordinary dedication and courage of *Greenpeace*, *The Earth Trust*, *Sea Shepherd* and all those other groups and individuals who strive against all odds to make this planet a better place.

Dramatis Personæ

Lincoln Island 1880–1884

Captain Cyrus Harding, US Army Engineers
Thomas Ayrton, seaman
Herbert Brown
Captain Robert Grant, British steam yacht *Duncan*
Lord Glenarvon, owner, S.Y. *Duncan*
Prince Dakkar of Bundelkhand, India (a.k.a. Captain Nemo)

Deep Watch

Seán McKenna (Éire), captain, MV *Aurora*
Alan Tregenza (UK), mate, MV *Aurora*
Robin McLeish (UK), engineer, MV *Aurora*
Ross Jourdan (Canada), electrician, MV *Aurora*
Dr Carla Schumann (USA), medical officer, MV *Aurora*
Deanne Fischer (USA), diver, MV *Aurora*
Christian Janssen (Denmark), crew, MV *Aurora*
Madeleine Duvall (France), crew, MV *Aurora*
Paul Calvert (UK), crew, MV *Aurora*
Colin May (UK), crew, MV *Aurora*
Sir Robert Maynard, managing director & founder, Deep Watch
Brian Conran (Northern Ireland), captain, MV *Zephyr*

Ketch Greyhound (Krakatau)

Brian Challoner
Susan Challoner
John Reynolds

Greenpeace

David Falco (USA), captain, MV *Atlantis*
Anders Kristenberg (Sweden), mate, MV *Atlantis*
Scott Peterson (USA), crew, MV *Atlantis*

United Kingdom Government

Prime Minister of Great Britain and Northern Ireland
Sir Henry Williamson, Secretary of State for Defence
Gerald Calloway, Secretary of State for Trade and Industry
Malcolm Gallaher, Home Secretary
Nicholas Parnell-Whyte, Foreign Secretary
Christopher Knowles, Shipping Minister
Gilliam Allardyce, Treasury Minister

Ministry of Defence (UK)

Admiral James Garvie, director, Dept. of Naval Intelligence
Captain Michael Rochester, chief-of-staff, Dept. of Naval Intelligence
Commander Donall McEwan Lindsay, naval intelligence operative
Maureen Strangways, secretary to Admiral Garvie
Commodore Roderick Browning, commanding officer, RNAS Culdrose
Lieutenant Commander Charles "Baggy" Oxford, intelligence officer, RNAS Culdrose
Lieutenant Commander Richard Priest, captain, HMS *Challenge*
Lieutenant Commander Peter Jordan, first lieutenant, HMS *Challenge*
Lieutenant Colonel Vernon Byrd, Parachute Regiment
Brigadier Neil Anderson, Ministry of Defence

United States Navy

Commander Randall C. Hayes, captain, USS *Appalachian*
Lieutenant-Commander Paul Vylander, executive officer, USS *Appalachian*
Lieutenant Emilio Garcia, sonar officer, USS *Appalachian*
Admiral Walter Greene, US Naval Command
Captain Byron Fraser, captain, USS *Denver*
Lieutenant Commander Ed Martens, executive officer, USS *Denver*

The Sentinel newspaper, London

Andrew Saunders, editor
Ian Neale, staff reporter
Barrington Hobbes, freelance investigative reporter
Karen Marshall, freelance reporter

The Pyramus Group

Managing Director of the Pyramus Group
Harvey Walterson (USA), director
Dr Thierry Lefèvre (France), director
João Valdera (Portugal), director/legal representative
Isao Mifune (Japan), director
Edson Enriques (Brazil), director
Hans-Dieter Wolf (a.k.a. Jürgen Krabbe and Abel Klein), enforcer
Captain Michael Ryecart. MV *Dogger Bank*
Captain Franz Schiller, MV *Emperor*

London

Dr Melvyn Hunter, naval and maritime historian
Anne Collinson, Lloyds of London
Neville Franklin, Treasury official

Lisbon

Vice Admiral José Marcelo Torres, Portuguese Navy (retired)
Captain Félix Saldanha, Portuguese Army Commandos

Marseille

Marcel Duvall
Hélène Duvall

Japanese hunter-killer submarine Honshu

Captain Honshiro Takamura, commanding officer
Commander Samu Tsuboi, executive officer
Sub-Lieutenant Hideki Kansai, sonar officer

NAUTILUS

"It is killing for the sake of killing. I am perfectly well aware that this is a privilege reserved for mankind but I do not approve of such murderous pastimes. In killing decent, inoffensive creatures like the southern Right whale or the Bowhead whale, people like you, Mr Land, commit a reprehensible crime. Your colleagues have already depopulated the whole of Baffin Bay and they will wipe out an entire class of useful animals. Leave the poor cetaceans alone!"

Captain Nemo
Commander of the Nautilus
The 14th of March 1868

Prologue

Tombstone of a Legend

24 March 1884
Southern Pacific Ocean
1500 miles E of North Island, New Zealand

The granite rock jutting from a vast and empty ocean measured just thirty feet long by twenty wide, its highest point barely ten feet above a sluggish Pacific swell. The nearest land, the tiny Tabor Island, lay more than a hundred miles away and yet, incredibly, six men and a dog lay on the rock's rough surface. All were desperately weak, their lives slowly ebbing with each hour that passed.

Captain Cyrus Harding, technically still a United States engineer even though it had been four years since he had set foot on American soil, found strength from somewhere to crawl to a small, diminishing pool of rainwater where he pressed his cracked lips to the cool liquid. Beside him, his dog whimpered, its eyes pleading.

"Easy, Top." The engineer's voice was scarcely more than a whisper forced from his throat. "Easy, boy. Come on now." Harding helped the suffering Anglo-Norman hound to the water where it took a few feeble laps before rolling onto its side, panting heavily. The man's reddened eyes turned to his prostrate companions, suddenly frightened that one or more of them might have died in the night. To his immense relief, all were still breathing.

The sun had risen. Not a single cloud punctuated a crystal clear sky. Harding could not believe that after all they had gone through, the hardships they had endured, survived and conquered, he was looking at the dawn of their last day on earth. Their meagre provisions had run out and they had nothing from which they could even fashion a simple fishing line and hook. Now, water to drink was scarce. It had not rained for three days and the summer sun would soon be beating down on them without mercy. Without a vestige of shelter, and as strong as their will to live might be, Harding knew that none of them stood a hope of surviving the rigours of the day to come. Barring some unforeseen miracle, it was over for all of them.

He glanced at the rock that had become their final refuge. It seemed impossible that sixteen days ago a large island had stood here—an island which had been their home for four years and which had destroyed itself in a cataclysmic volcanic eruption just hours before the planned launch of the boat they had been building for months.

Pondering the cruelties of fate, Harding rolled onto his back. Behind his closed eyes, the events of those four years flooded back into his mind.

It had all begun on the 19th of March 1880 when he and four of his present companions had left Richmond, Virginia, in a pioneering attempt to fly a balloon across the American continent to California. Harding had not actually intended to bring his dog which, at the moment of take-off, had slipped his leash, evaded his minder and leapt like a gazelle into the balloon's basket to join his master.

It had been the most damnable possible luck for the adventurers to have then been overtaken by one of the greatest storms in living memory, a demented tempest that drove the helpless balloon a third of the way around the globe before dumping it in tatters on an uninhabited island in an uncharted part of the mid-Pacific ocean.

Harding himself should have died that night after being swept from the deflating balloon into a raging sea within tantalizing sight of land. The fact that he had survived, to be found by his companions three days later, was inexplicable. Even more perplexing was the fact that the unconscious Harding had been found under natural shelter more than a mile inland. As the engineer now knew, that had been simply the first of a series of baffling mysteries that would not be solved for three and a half years.

The five men had been cast ashore with nothing but the clothes on their backs but it soon became clear that this island, rich in woodland, streams and wild life, contained everything they would need in order to survive. That the island was volcanic in origin was obvious from the thousand-foot cone that dominated its landscape. Thankfully, from their point of view, close inspection showed that the volcano had been quiescent for centuries.

The ingenuity of the colonists, as they began to see themselves, was put to the test and not found wanting. Harding himself was a man of prodigious scientific talent, the others willing pupils with their own unique qualities. Over the months and years to come, the five Americans tamed and exploited the island's natural resources to an astonishing degree. Perhaps the finest achievement of them all had been the construction of an electric telegraph linking a farm corral in the island's interior to the converted system of caverns they called home, five miles away on the eastern sea cliffs.

The sixth man, whose barely breathing form lay beside Harding on the rock, had joined their company eighteen months after their arrival. Thomas Ayrton, a Scot, had been marooned on Tabor Island in 1870 by Lord Glenarvon, owner of the British steam-yacht *Duncan*, for the crime of piracy. He had finally been rescued by two of the Americans in the *Bonadventure*, a small sailing boat they had managed to build but, in that twelve-year period, the man had been living more like an animal, his mind unhinged by sheer prolonged solitude. Only careful, sensitive treatment marshalled by Harding had restored both Ayrton's health and reason. Now fully repentant of his evil past, the Scot had proved his worth to the Americans time and again.

Harding opened his eyes and turned his head to study Ayrton's heavily bearded face and recall the mysterious message in a floating bottle from which they had learned of Tabor Island's existence and the plight of the marooned man. The puzzle here lay in the fact that Ayrton himself had never sent such a message, and that the *Bonadventure's* return had been aided by a beacon that had blazed out from the heights of their own island—a fire that none of the Americans had lit.

Mystery piled upon mystery. Dangers and difficulties continued to rear up, events that even their own considerable talents could not overcome, only to be averted by the hand of some unseen, miraculous power.

As the months and years passed, so the list of these baffling enigmas grew. Convinced of another human presence on the island, the colonists searched every inch of it, finding nothing but a lead bullet in the body of a three-month old peccary and the corpses of a vicious group of privateers that had invaded their island and placed their lives in peril. The bodies had been found on a riverbank with no indication of what had killed them, except for a small, angry red mark on the skin of each man. Harding vividly remembered the sight of the pirates' ship being blown out of the water by a tremendous explosion that could not be explained.

Even more astounding had been the case of the teenager Herbert Brown. Callously shot by the privateers before their own inexplicable demise, he had sunk into a raging fever and would certainly have died but for the uncanny appearance by his bedside of a box containing quinine sulphate, the only medicine that could have—and indeed did—save his life.

By this time, even the colonists' cool, practical minds had begun to view this unseen guardian in supernatural terms.

It was to be three and a half years after their arrival on the island they had named in honour of Abraham Lincoln, and with the greatest of all disasters lurking in the wings, that the castaways' guardian spirit decided at last to reveal itself.

Following directions sent via their own telegraph, the colonists crossed the island in storm-wracked darkness to the wild northwestern cliffs where they discovered and entered the huge sea-cavern that pierced the island's very foundations. What they found within was no supernatural being, no god-like spirit, but a man, a frail seventy-year old man, on the verge of death and surrounded by the secrets of an existence that beggared belief.

For eighteen years, this man had shunned human society, sickened to the core by appalling personal tragedies and by the inherently savage nature of mankind. Of royal stock, this enigmatic, brilliant man had mastered achievements that visionaries could only dream of. Once he had been accompanied by a score of associates who shared his horror of the "civilized" world. Now only he remained alive.

The old man had come to Lincoln Island ten years earlier to await death. Now, seismic forces that had since constricted the mouth of the cavern had ensured that he could never leave it. After six years of peaceful solitude, the arrival on the island of castaways had greatly disturbed him but, even so, a sense of human compassion drove him to save the life of Cyrus Harding.

After that, curiosity overcame his desire to be left alone. As time went by, his secret observations of these men, their honest bonds of friendship and determined co-operation, began to convince him that these were people able and worthy enough to reconcile him with that humanity he had rejected. A desire to make his peace with mankind began to overwhelm him. Aware of his own approaching end, and of impending natural disaster, the time to do so had finally come.

Cyrus Harding's recollection of that day was photographically clear. The flooded cavern—the existence of which he had never even suspected—was immense. It stretched more than half a mile under the island, its inner end taking the form of a breathtaking chamber a hundred feet high. The rugged arches of a cathedral-like roof rested on vast columns of volcanic basalt and spanned a luminous lake three hundred feet across and of unknown depth. What particularly stayed with Harding's mind was the fact that all this was not only clearly visible, but illuminated by brilliant white rays of light pouring from the unbelievable object in the centre of the lake.

Their benefactor died that same night. Harding remembered the dazzling light fading by degrees in the untold depths of the water as he and his companions silently watched from a small boat. The light beneath the water caused dancing, dappled patterns to flicker on the cavern walls, their crystals glittering like the fabulous gemstones of an Aladdin's Cave until, eventually, the unearthly light descending into the abyssal depths became untraceable and darkness reclaimed the cavern.

The dead man's wishes had been carried out to the letter and, as Harding lit a lantern, he felt an overwhelming sense of loss, just as he felt it now as he and his companions waited for death on a barren, ocean-bound rock. From that moment on, they could expect no more miracles.

Harding recalled that as the boat was rowed back through the vaulted passages, the faint sting of sulphur in his nostrils and barely discernable growlings deep within the rock were reminding him of the old man's final warning.

After centuries of slumber, the volcano that had given birth to the island was reawakening. Awesome pressures, relentlessly building deep within its vast magma chamber, had found themselves confined by the ancient plug of solid lava in the volcano's vent. Harding had been made horribly aware that the eruption, when it finally came, would be violent beyond imagination.

The dying man had instructed him that the flooded cavern's inner chamber was, in reality, an older, redundant, vent of the volcano. At its innermost end, only the frailest curtain of rock stood between it and the active vent. In time, that thin barrier was bound to fail and the results would be catastrophic.

The man who had died at one o' clock on the morning of the 17th of October 1883, with the word "Independence" on his lips, had known precisely what the failure of that rock wall would mean. He impressed upon Harding that there was no earthly hope of preventing the inevitable. Nor would there be any hope of rescue. Lincoln Island lay far from any shipping lanes and featured on none of the available charts. Their only hope lay in the boat they had just begun to build, a boat large enough to carry all six of them the fifteen hundred miles of unpredictable ocean to New Zealand's eastern shore. It would take them a good six months to complete that task, provided the volcano was of a mind to grant such grace.

Fear had gripped the six men when, on the 3rd of January 1884, a huge, hat-shaped cloud of smoke and steam spewed from the volcano's peak and, over the next three days, its activities were to slowly increase.

At this point, Harding took the decision to re-enter the flooded cavern and inspect its rear wall. He remembered how his stomach had twisted with horror at what he'd found there. Almost overwhelmed by the stench of sulphur, he watched as vapour hissed from a series of expanding cracks in the rock face, some extending to within a few feet of the water. Harding again recalled the words of the man who now lay at peace at the bottom of the cavern's black waters. The old man had been right. The danger—a terrible danger—lay right there before his eyes.

After that, the six men worked both night and day, battling to complete the boat that was now their only hope of survival. On the night of the 24th of January, a massive explosion rocked the entire island. Daylight revealed that the mountain they had christened Mount Franklin had blasted away a good third of its height. The new, enlarged crater now tilted eastward and rivers of glowing lava bore down upon everything they had laboured so hard to achieve—their roads, bridges, mills, crop fields and livestock. Nothing could halt the heartbreaking destruction and, within days, devastating pyroclastic flows had reduced the island to a barren, smoking wasteland. Its clear, flowing rivers shrivelled and dried and, of its once extensive forests, nothing but blackened stumps remained.

For a while at least, the colonists were safe, protected from the lava and the worst that the volcano could throw at them by a deep freshwater lake and the bluff that contained their cavern home. Harding then estimated that another eight weeks were needed to complete the boat.

Lying on the isolated rock, Cyrus Harding reflected upon how cruel fate had been. On the 8th of March, they had made the decision to launch the boat the following morning, even though its upper planking had yet to be caulked. Destiny decided otherwise.

On that very night, Mount Franklin's violence turned to catastrophe. Titanic forces tore apart the skin of rock between its roaring vent and the inner end of the flooded cavern. Unchecked, the sea poured into the molten depths, instantly converting to vastly greater volumes of superheated steam than the volcano could ever hope to resist. Lincoln Island blew itself out of existence in a stupendous explosion heard as far away as New Zealand and Tahiti, rivalling that which had destroyed Krakatau the previous year.

That the castaways survived was a miracle in itself—in Harding's opinion, the final cruelty that deprived them of instant death and condemned them to a long, lingering one. At the very moment of the cataclysmic blast, all six men were on the beach, racing to stock the boat with enough provisions to last them for the long journey. Time and the volcano defeated them, hurling all six and their dog into the protective cushion of the sea while all else met with utter destruction.

On the sea-washed ledge of rock—all that now remained of Lincoln Island—Cyrus Harding squinted painfully at the rising sun whose merciless heat would surely, this very day, kill them all. There was still no sign of any cloud that might offer even the slightest hope of protection, only a dark smudge above the southwestern horizon.

Beside him, Ayrton stirred, incredibly finding the strength to haul himself onto his knees and then to his feet where he swayed with weakness like a drunken man. He raised a trembling arm, pointing at the distant smudge and the tiny but solid speck beneath it.

"It's the *Duncan*!" The Scot's voice was barely a croak. "My God, Cyrus, the *Duncan*!"

Just a few hours later, food, drink and fresh clothing had restored a sizeable amount of strength and vigour to the rescued men. A fair-haired, pleasant-faced officer, little more than thirty years of age, pushed his way through the throng of sailors around them and addressed Harding.

"Captain Robert Grant of the British steam-yacht *Duncan*," he introduced himself. "I trust you gentlemen feel a little stronger? My first officer has told me your tale and I must say that to have survived such an ordeal, you must be the most remarkable of men."

"That we have survived is down to you, Captain," Harding responded. "We are more than grateful, believe me. If you hadn't found us, we would not have lived to see the sunset. That much is certain. What I can't understand is how that came to be. No one knew we were here and, in any case, nobody sails these waters."

"Lord Glenarvon, the owner of this yacht, required me to recover Thomas Ayrton from Tabor Island. It was considered he had served a long enough sentence for his crimes."

Harding stared at the captain, uncomprehending. "But Tabor Island is a hundred miles from here. Lincoln Island was uncharted. What made you head for this position?"

"We came to find you," Grant told him simply. "All of you. Tabor Island was deserted but we found the note you left there, presumably when you took Ayrton away to your own island."

"Note?" Harding's eyes held those of the captain. "But we left no note on Tabor Island."

Grant frowned and handed the American a sheet of vellum. Harding stared at it, unbelieving, his spine gripped by sudden fingers of ice. The message it bore was simple:

Lincoln Island, 150 degrees 30 minutes W; 34 degrees 57 minutes S; the present residence of Ayrton and five American colonists

God in Heaven! Harding instantly recognized the bold, rather Gothic handwriting as that of the man he had laid to rest five months earlier. *Even after his own death he saves us yet again! How can this be possible?*

"Captain Harding?" Ayrton's Scottish burr broke into the engineer's shocked train of thought. "What shall I do with this?" A sizeable, heavy coffer was clutched to Ayrton's chest.

"My God, Ayrton! You saved that?" Harding could not believe it. The coffer held a fortune in pearls and diamonds, a parting gift from the man who had seemingly reached out from beyond the grave to perform yet another miraculous deliverance. Harding whirled on Captain Grant.

"Sir, fourteen years ago, your Lord Glenarvon marooned a criminal on Tabor Island. In his place now stands a man whose penitence has replaced all past misdeeds with unflinching loyalty, honesty and courage. A man whose hand I am proud to grasp and call lifelong friend. The Ayrton punished by his Lordship has long since gone. The one you see before you now ranks among the best of men and I trust that every person will respect and treat him as such."

Harding paused, momentarily drained by the strength of his declaration.

"Tell me, captain," he said in a quieter voice. "Are we still at… where Lincoln Island stood?"

"We are just leaving, Captain Harding."

Frail as they were, the rescued men made their way on deck together at the *Duncan's* stern. They stared, white-faced, over the steam-yacht's fantail at the ledge of rock now slipping away astern—the tombstone of a legend.

During his years on an island that had gone forever, Cyrus Harding had performed incredible deeds with nothing but the application of a cool, clever mind, skilful hands and the wholehearted cooperation of his companions. What he had seen during those last hours in the life of an enigmatic genius had made him feel primitive by comparison. How utterly humbling it had been to stand among such god-like achievements, now lost for all time.

God-like? No, the man had not been a god. Just a man, a mere mortal who had now relinquished his hold upon life but whose eyes had beheld so much that no other living person had ever seen. The dead man had been a seeker of peace. He had found it within his extraordinary existence but not within the turmoil and torture of a mind forever scarred by the horrors of his past.

Only a man… how had it all been possible?

Cyrus Harding knew that, in a sense, his private thoughts were flawed. The spirit of the man who lay in an unfathomable tomb was indeed immortal. *In truth,* he told himself, *I can never imagine, even for a moment, that the world has seen the last of him—or of his wonderful creation.*

Chapter 1

LEVIATHAN

1

22 February 2014
Northern Ross Sea
Antarctic Ocean

As idle as a painted ship upon a painted ocean... Seán McKenna smiled ruefully to himself as he realized that his thoughts pulled from *The Ancient Mariner* had been uttered out loud. The words were pretty apt, he reflected, except that on a night as dark as this one, the painting of both ship and sea were blacker than tar.

The Irish skipper of the Deep Watch vessel *Aurora* peered through the windshield from a darkened wheelhouse as if to confirm his opinion. He saw nothing but his masthead light and his own ghostly reflection in the glass created by the soft glow from the binnacle. It was unusual, he thought, to have total blackness in these latitudes at this time of year. He mentally cursed the heavy cloud cover that was the cause of it.

"Just so long as we don't go shooting albatrosses," he muttered.

"Come again, skipper?" Deanne Fischer's soft Californian tones broke into McKenna's doleful train of thought.

"Nothing, Dee. Just thinking aloud."

"Quotes from Coleridge? In Antarctic waters? That's just asking for bad luck," she commented. "Would a mug of strong coffee help to dispel the gloom?"

"Mine maybe," McKenna said. "Any chance of a cure for the pitch darkness out there?" He relaxed suddenly and gave her a wide grin.

"Coffee sounds great, Dee. Could you rustle one up for Alan as well? The poor bugger's standing watch outside and he's going to need a fair bit of thawing out."

He smiled again as the strains of an acoustic guitar filtered up the companionway. "What's the below-decks entertainment tonight?"

"Dubious as usual," Deanne replied. "Ross on guitar to Rob McLeish's shanties, the moralities of which are in serious decline."

"Tell Robbie from me that if *The Harlot of Jerusalem* gets past the first line, he'll be swimming back to Auckland."

"You're a hard man, skipper," Deanne laughed. "It's as well he has broad-minded crewmates and that Mam'selle Madeleine's grasp of English isn't quite up to the niceties."

"I blame it on Robbie's Royal Navy upbringing," McKenna said. "There isn't a whole lot for off-duty submariners to do except to team up and sing bawdy ballads. After all, it's not as if they can sit and gaze out of the window, is it?" He shrugged. "Well, maybe I won't make him walk the plank just yet. He's too good an engineer to waste."

The tall, tow-haired Irishman settled back in his bucket seat as Deanne went back below. He checked his course bearing and dialled up his position on the SatNav before entering its reading in the log. His big hands rested lightly on the helm.

McKenna was content enough, despite his concerns about the zero visibility. There was a good crew on this ship who had mixed well in the week or so since departing Auckland harbour. The engineer and king of the shaggy-dog shanties, Robin McLeish, was an old friend as was the mate and navigator, Alan Tregenza who, at that moment, was standing watch out on the open bridge wing in the biting cold of an Antarctic night. This was the sixth voyage the three of them had made together and they had long since meshed into an experienced, efficient team.

The rest of the mixed international crew were strangers apart from the tall Dane, Christian Janssen, who had been on McKenna's last trip, and the black Canadian ex-boxer, Ross Jourdan, now the ship's electrician. Five years earlier, Jourdan had come within an ace of becoming the WBO World Heavyweight Boxing Champion before retinal damage had forced him out of the ring.

All had sailed on Deep Watch missions before except for the young French girl Madeleine Duvall, and even she had found no problem in settling in. All in all, McKenna reflected, a good-humoured bunch that cheerfully knuckled down to their various shipboard duties. He couldn't recall seeing a gloomy face since leaving Auckland.

But that will come, he thought grimly, if we don't find the rogue whalers before they find the whales. And the bastards are out here somewhere. The intelligence had been passed through to Deep Watch by its big sister organization, Greenpeace, which had none of its own vessels currently handy in that part of the globe.

McKenna had seen it all before—the ships, companies and nations who held not a shred of regard for internationally binding whaling embargoes, the Antarctic Sanctuary, the alarming depletion in the whale population on which so many other species depended, or for world opinion on the matter. Not as long as there were profits to be had. His own eyes had more than once beheld the gouting life-blood and bloated carcasses of the earth's largest and, arguably, most intelligent creatures, their innards horribly mangled by the appalling barbarism of explosive-headed harpoon projectiles. Time and again, he had seen the toughest of men reduced to helpless tears of grief by such heart-rending sights and, in McKenna's view, the greatest obscenity was the convenience of ill-defined "scientific reasons" usually cited to justify the mass slaughter.

Governments the world over had signally failed to halt the killing, preferring instead to leave it to volunteer pressure groups like Greenpeace and Deep Watch to act on behalf of the helpless, or to be convenient scapegoats if things went wrong or became politically embarrassing. It was a hard burden to bear.

The tactics of organizations like McKenna's were mostly passive ones. Breakaway groups like Paul Watson's Sea Shepherd had taken things a stage further by reinforcing the bows of their ships with tons of concrete to enable them to ram or sideswipe pirate whalers or nuclear waste carriers when all else failed. McKenna smiled at the thought. Watson had never been a man to be pushed around and God help anyone fool enough to try.

The Deep Watch vessel *Aurora*, 130 feet in overall length and grossing 305 tons, was a converted deep-sea trawler built at Kingston-upon-Hull in 1976. With a top speed of thirty knots she was the fastest of the three vessels currently owned by the environmental group. However, and as McKenna reflected, she lacked the strengthened hull that was desirable for polar expeditions. The biggest danger, especially on a night like this, was floating ice, hence the need for a constant watch and the *Aurora's* present five-knot progress.

The door on the port side of the wheelhouse slid open and a figure muffled to the eyes in an orange exposure suit stepped over the sill. He slid the door shut behind him to keep out the deep chill.

"The iceman cometh," McKenna commented as the exposure suit was stripped off and neatly stowed in a corner. Alan Tregenza, a stocky man with soft, dark eyes and a shock of black hair, shivered as he adjusted the roll neck of his thick oiled-wool sweater.

"Don't even joke about it, Seán," he said, slumping into the vacant seat beside the skipper's chair. He kneaded his groin gingerly, widening his eyes in mock alarm. "This exposure to cold could gravely endanger my prospects of ever becoming a father. You wouldn't believe how bloody cold it is out there. So much for the Antarctic summer."

"Never mind, son. Hot coffee's on the way."

"No rum?"

"Not just yet. Perhaps we'll see some off at the end of this watch."

Tregenza drew out an impressive hunter watch and studied it mournfully. "That's a whole two hours away. You're a hard man, Seán."

McKenna looked injured. "That's twice in two minutes I've been called that. I'd be changing my name to Bligh if he hadn't been a bloody Cornishman like you."

"And one of the finest navigators in history," Tregenza retorted lightly. "Almost up to my standard, I'll have you know. Even so, that was a low punch, Seán. Be ashamed of yourself." He gave himself a brisk rubdown and shivered again. "I hope Colin and Paul remembered to bring their winter woollies." He referred to Colin May and Paul Calvert, due to stand the next watch and currently asleep in the fo'c'sle cabin.

"Anything to see out there?" McKenna asked him.

"You jest. It's as black as hell's gates. No moon, ten-tenths cloud, not so much as a star to steer by. On the plus side, we have a flat calm sea, negligible wind and no lights anywhere, not that I'd expect any."

His skipper nodded gratefully. "Unusually calm for this part of the world. What worries me is the possibility of ice. We're as blind as a bat."

"This need for a visual watch is a bloody pain," Tregenza thumped the lifeless radar screen. "Why the hell did the boss insist on kitting us out with new radar? There was nothing wrong with the old one. Six days use and this piece of technological garbage ups and conks on us. Waste of time and money, if you ask me."

"I've been on to Auckland about it," McKenna said. "Not that it'll do us any good. It's all a bit late. The boss was adamant that the old one had to go. It was twelve years old when all's said and done."

"At least the damn thing worked. This one was supposed to be the last word in radar technology. Says a lot for the state of the art. Has Ross managed to take a look at it?"

"Took the guts out, then put it all back," McKenna told him. "There's not a thing he can do with it. That's the problem with microchip technology. If it screws up, you've no other course but to send it back to the factory."

"Which tends to create a slight problem when you're in the middle of the Ross Sea," Tregenza observed.

"Even so, Rob Maynard swears by it and says he's going to install it on all Deep Watch boats," McKenna said. "He even has it on his own yacht."

"Probably owns the company," Tregenza commented sourly.

Sir Robert Maynard, philanthropist, entrepreneur and one-time British envoy to the United Nations, was one of the United Kingdom's richest men. Now a UNESCO delegate and always having harboured deep concerns for the plight of the world's environment, he had dipped deep into his personal fortune to found Deep Watch in 1994. Now, Deep Watch offices existed in ten countries and the organization's daring campaigns against the polluters, the rain-forest destroyers and the whalers had earned them a healthy regard from both the public and its sister organizations.

The promised coffee arrived and Deanne left the two men to it. A grateful Tregenza curled his hands around the steaming mug, savouring its life-restoring heat. He took a cautious gulp that nonetheless seared his tongue, then got up and walked across the wheelhouse in the hope that movement might help to thaw out his limbs. Thankful that, at least, the demister was still working, he peered out of the starboard windshield.

With a sudden, urgent movement, the mate set the mug down and stared out, his nose pressed against the cold glass.

"What is it?" McKenna asked sharply.

"Not sure. I thought I glimpsed some white water. I wouldn't expect to see any of that in a millpond like this, unless it was ice. Can't see anything now. No… wait a second. There it is again."

McKenna left the helm and looked out. For a moment he could see nothing in the darkness, then, just briefly, caught the merest glimpse of a dim flash of whiteness. The Irishman slid the door open and stepped outside, wincing at the sudden, painful bite of a polar chill that felt as though he had fallen into a basket of needles. His breath frosted in front of his eyes and he swept the cloud aside impatiently.

This time, there could be no mistake. It was no great distance away, a faint, flickering vee, only just discernable in the black night. To Seán McKenna, it resembled a…

"Oh, my sweet Christ!" he breathed aloud and, in that instant, his eyes registered its speed of approach. McKenna leapt back into the wheelhouse, diving frantically for the helm and reaching for the siren lanyard.

"Jesus, Alan, it's the bow-wave of a ship! A bloody *ship*—coming right at us! And the bastard's showing no lights!"

Tregenza briefly wondered why any ship should be approaching from the south. There was nothing down there but a frozen waste… but the thought lasted no more than half a second as McKenna desperately heaved the wheel hard over. The siren squealed thinly in the night.

Why us? McKenna asked himself. *Why us? We never even saw a bloody albatross, let alone shoot one!*

Despite the turn of the wheel, despite the despairing bleat of the siren, the shattering, side-on impact took the *Aurora* forward of amidships, tearing the converted trawler clean in half. Thrown clear across the wheelhouse by the sheer force of the collision and the sudden tilt of the ship onto its port side, Tregenza briefly glimpsed his ship's killer in the loom of the masthead light. Before he could even begin to believe what he saw, the light itself went out, the mast snapping off at deck level and toppling over the side. He twisted his face away, throwing his arms up for protection, as the windshield suddenly starred, shattered and burst inward.

To both himself and a stunned McKenna, everything became a confusion of blurred images and sounds, a whirlwind of shattered glass, screams of terror from below and the awful, eldritch screech of rending metal, the last cry of their dying ship.

The severed bow section of the *Aurora* sank like a stone, carrying the still sleeping forms of Paul Calvert and Colin May to their cold, silent graves ten thousand feet below. Within minutes, the rest of the mutilated ship followed to everlasting oblivion on the floor of the Ross Sea, leaving nothing on the surface but scattered flotsam.

In the darkness of the Antarctic night, the wake of the *Aurora's* killer cut a barely visible path northward, uninterrupted and unconcerned, just as though nothing had happened.

2

27 February 2014

Extract from The Sentinel *newspaper, London*

HOPE FADES FOR DEEP WATCH CREW

Reuters, Auckland, New Zealand: 26 February

"INTERNATIONAL concern for the crew of the Deep Watch vessel Aurora *deepened today when wreckage spotted yesterday in the northern Ross Sea by a long-range reconnaissance aircraft of the Royal New Zealand Air Force was recovered by the oceanographical survey ship* Erebus.

"The location of the tragic find was just north of the Antarctic Circle and close to the last reported position of the Aurora, *from which no word has been heard for four days. The wreckage has been positively identified as belonging to the Deep Watch vessel.*

"An upturned Zephyr inflatable dinghy, its sides bearing the ship's name, was recovered some miles to the north-west in waters often made hazardous by icebergs.

"A Deep Watch spokesman today confirmed the Aurora's *crew to have been: Seán McKenna, 38, of County Mayo, Eire, captain; Robin McLeish, 55, of Edinburgh, Scotland, engineer; Alan Tregenza, 31, of St Ives, Cornwall, mate; Dr Carla Schumann, 30, of Denver, Colorado, USA, medical officer; Christian Janssen, 32, from Aarhus, Denmark; Deanne Fischer, 26, of Santa Barbara, California, USA, diver; Paul Calvert, 30, of Northampton, England; Madeleine Duvall, 19, from Marseille, France; and Colin May, 28, of Aberystwyth, Wales.*

"In addition, the world of sport mourns the probable loss of Ross Jourdan, 36, of Montreal, Canada, the former boxer and World Heavyweight championship contender, who served as the ship's electrician.

"The cause of the Aurora's *loss remains a mystery…"*

A flood of baying reporters and cameramen surged around the forlorn figure of Sir Robert Maynard as he emerged from London's Deep Watch office off Tottenham Court Road. Drawn and haggard as though he had not slept for several nights, he flinched away from the barrage of flash bulbs and microphones being thrust into his face.

Mentally steeling himself, Maynard picked out one question from the unrelenting babble of shouted queries.

"Sir Robert, what caused your ship to sink? Was it ice? Was she unseaworthy?"

"The *Aurora* was not unseaworthy," he answered firmly. "In fact, she was refitted, inspected and fully certificated as seaworthy just six months ago. A collision with ice can't be ruled out at this stage but, in my view, it's unlikely."

He held up a hand in an attempt to halt a fresh deluge of questions. "Seán McKenna was an experienced skipper well acquainted with polar waters. The ship did report a problem with her on-board radar but Seán would have been meticulous about mounting adequate watches at all times.

"No appreciable ice was seen by search planes or by the *Erebus* within a thirty mile radius of where the wreckage was found. Weather and sea conditions were unusually calm. Nonetheless, the amount and type of wreckage indicates a complete break-up of the ship. The reason for it remains unknown."

"Ian Neale of *The Sentinel.*" This from a solidly built reporter shouldering his way through the crowd. "Sir Robert, will there be an investigation into the loss of the *Aurora*?"

"There will, of course, be an inquest and I will be pressing for a thorough investigation. After all, one has to bear in mind that

Greenpeace's *Rainbow Warrior* was sunk by members of the French secret service in Auckland harbour in 1985."

"You suspect foul play, then?"

"No, I don't suspect it but neither can it be ruled out, Mr Neale. The *Aurora* was in the Ross Sea in response to reports that a Japanese whaling fleet was in the area, hunting schools of fin whales in direct contravention of the recent international whaling ban and the Antarctic Sanctuary Agreement. The Japanese authorities have, in the recent past, made veiled threats but that is all I can say at this moment. Only a thorough investigation can give us any real clue as to what happened and that will be both difficult and hugely expensive. The depth of sea in this particular area is in the order of ten thousand feet."

Neale had no chance to get in a further question, finding himself being pushed aside by a woman from the BBC, accompanied by her cameraman.

"How do you feel about the loss of your crew, Sir Robert?"

Maynard stared at her. *My God*, he thought, *why is that whenever a tragedy occurs, reporters always feel compelled to ask the same bloody stupid question?* Inwardly wishing that a bolt of lightning would scatter her atoms all over the street, he composed himself as best he could and gestured at the building behind him.

"I have just left an office full of people in tears," he said coldly. "The *Aurora's* crew were friends to all of us. In particular, I will greatly miss Seán McKenna who has been a personal friend for many years."

At this point Maynard paused, his voice breaking. Tears were welling in his eyes and he removed his rimless spectacles to wipe them away with the back of a hand. Cameras whirred, clicked and flashed to capture the perfect picture for tomorrow's front pages.

He swallowed hard. "I don't think it takes a great deal of effort to imagine how I feel," he said. "Especially in view of the fact that the official search has now been called off."

The two men descending a short vertical ladder into freezing darkness were more than glad of their protective clothing and thick insulated gloves. In these temperatures, bare flesh would have frozen to the naked metal with excruciating and dangerous results. Their breath clouded and froze in refrigerated air.

The beams of their torches picked out a railed landing and a downward flight of steps. Their footsteps rang on expanded metal grating, echoing eerily in the confined space. At the foot of the steps, a heavy door, its edges sealed with rubber, opened with difficulty into a room some sixteen feet square with carpetted floor and oak veneered walls. Frost rimed the large oak dressers that stood against the walls, and the solid table in the centre of the room. Both men instinctively knew that no one had set foot in this place for years, if not decades.

A second door led into a room of similar size but lined throughout with bookshelves. Rank upon rank of leather-bound volumes rose above beautifully upholstered couches to a high ceiling. Again, a table stood in the centre of the room while papers and magazines, all of them white with frost, lay scattered on the carpet around it. The leader picked one up, shone his torch onto it and frowned at its date of issue.

They moved on to a third door, again with airtight sealing around its edges. It took the combined efforts of them both to persuade it to move but the long unused hinges finally yielded to their persistent strength. Their torch beams played into the dark void beyond.

Both men felt their breath catch in their throats.

The room beyond the door was vast, maybe thirty feet long, twenty wide and sixteen high. Its ceiling was delicately ornamented with gilt arabesques while the walls dripped with rich tapestries and paintings in ornate frames. The thick carpet was a deep wine red. Curved leather divans were ranged about a central group of glazed display cases that surrounded a colossal shell six feet across.

The two men stepped into a deep-frozen treasure house. The light from their torches glinted from glass dials mounted on the far wall as the speechless explorers moved closer. The shorter man stopped abruptly, clutching at his colleague's arm and pointing his torch into a corner of the room.

On a couch lay the body of a man. It was impossible to tell how long he had been dead as the still, deeply frigid air within the hermetically sealed room had kept him perfectly preserved. The white, marble-like skin had nothing of the leathery quality of mummification and still seemed to be supple. The closed eyes and strong, proud features were serene in the tranquillity of death. The beard was as white and luxuriant as the hair that fell across the dead man's shoulders and both had retained the lustre of health. The arms and long-fingered, artistic hands lay crossed on his chest. The body was held in place by buckled straps while the rich blankets that must once have covered him lay crumpled on the floor.

The taller man gazed at the pale, placid face of the corpse then turned to play his torch on the wall-mounted dials and the central display cases. Above these stood an ornate pediment that, like much of what he had seen in these rooms, was classically Victorian in style. The pediment bore a curious gilded legend: a stylish capital letter within an ornamented circle and, beneath it, a brief caption in Latin.

A chill deeper than the one pervading the room crept through the tall man's veins and prickled the hair on the nape of his neck. A slow realization—one that he dared not believe—began to dawn on him. Few men had ever seen what he was seeing now but, somehow, he knew this place. He even felt that he knew the dead man. Possibilities began to take root in his mind. *Christ, it would be audacious, but do we dare?*

The room rocked slightly under a sudden but not entirely unexpected tremor.

Time is running out, the tall man thought. *I have to decide… I must decide now.*

3

25 March 2014
Sunda Strait, Indonesia

Four miles deep, the Mentawai-Java Trench is an immense gash in the floor of the eastern Indian Ocean where the Indo-Australian tectonic plate gradually slides under a southern spur of the Eurasian plate. As it slowly drives, melting, into the earth's mantle, the rocks above it superheat, building pressures that force magma up towards the surface. Here it forms the great chain of volcanoes that give rise to the long line of islands dominated by Sumatra and Java. Between these two major islands, in the Pelat Sunda—the Sunda Strait—there lies the wreck of the most notorious volcano of them all.

Millenia ago a huge andesite cone forced its way above the surface of the sea to a height of more than six thousand feet. The ancient *Javanese Book of Kings* tells that this volcano, then known as Kapi, all but destroyed itself in the early sixth century, a disaster that changed the history of the world and an eerie preview of what was to happen nearly fourteen centuries later.

Kapi's exhausted magma chamber had collapsed, leaving a vast, submerged caldera six miles across. Fragments of its shattered rim showed above the sea as the steep-sided islands of Rakata, Rakata-kecil or Verlaten, Sertung and the strangely named Polish Hat. Over the years, Rakata developed an active cone of its own that spat ash and lava for centuries.

Eventually, Rakata fizzled out but the old volcano was far from finished. Two further cones, Perbuatan and Danan, forced their way up inside the ancient caldera, breaking the surface of the sea, then merging with Rakata and each other to form a new, highly volatile island fifteen square miles in extent. In 1680 a vicious eruption left the island scorched and barren but ensured an uneasy silence for the next two hundred years.

On the 20th May 1883, Perbuatan and Danan violently awoke. Their combined explosions were heard a hundred miles away in Batavia—modern Jakarta. Ash clouds billowed fifteen miles into the air then, like a tired sleeper awakened from a nightmare, the volcano quietened once more and went back to a fitful slumber.

A month later saw greater violence and, this time, the volcano showed no desire to return to dormancy. Both its active cones shuddered and roared until late August by which time it was in a terrifying rage. At 1 p.m. on the 26th August, the first of four shattering blasts spat an immense ash-laden cloud sixteen miles into the atmosphere.

The fourth, final and biggest explosion occurred at 10 a.m. the following day, a colossal blast equivalent to ten thousand Hiroshima atom bombs. It was heard three thousand miles away across the Indian Ocean and launched huge volumes of ash to the incredible height of 48 miles.

Five cubic miles of rock vanished from the map, not blowing into the atmosphere but falling inwards as the weakened roof of the vast, and now empty, magma chamber beneath the volcano collapsed to leave a water-filled basin a thousand feet deep. Only a third of Rakata remained, its dead cone ripped cleanly in half so that its old vent and radiating dykes lay exposed in cross-section. The islet called Polish Hat completely disappeared and not a trace remained of either Perbuatan or Danan.

The tsunamis spawned by the volcano's collapse swelled to a height of 120 feet, killing thirty-five thousand people on the coasts of Sumatra and Java. By the next day there was nothing but a deathly hush. The expelled ash fell over a vast area. At close range, it buried Rakata-kecil and Sertung under two hundred feet of choking greyness.and the contaminated air gave the entire world spectacular sunsets for three years.

In January 1928, increasing subterranean activity forced a new and growing cone above the dark waters of the caldera between the former positions of Perbuatan and Danan. An offspring of the twice-destroyed giant, it was fearfully named Anak—"child of"—Krakatau.

"But do we have to anchor right under it?" Susan Challoner's wide blue eyes gazed up at the smoking thousand-foot cone with open apprehension. She could distinctly hear the awesome sound of the volcano's belly like the throbbing of some vast underground engine and could just as easily picture the titanic forces that powered it.

Brian Challoner, her father, laughed easily. "Oh, it's quiet enough. It'll be a long while before it's able to repeat its 1883 performance." He waved a hand at the surrounding islands with their lush, regenerated coatings of jungle. "The old caldera gives good shelter. I vote we stay over for the night and go on to Jakarta in the morning."

"Is that wise?" John Reynolds, Susan's fiancé, looked concerned. "Malaysian waters are notorious for piracy. The local pirates have a virtually free rein and they don't give a tinker's damn who they kill. The authorities gave up trying to control them years ago and a place like this strikes me as tailor-made for them."

"John, I've never looked over my shoulder in my life," Challoner declared stubbornly. "I'll be damned if I do it now on account of a bunch of gook amateurs. In any case, anyone fool enough to come picking on us will find themselves on the business end of Ol' Samuel." A relic of the old soldier's service days, Ol' Samuel was Challoner's treasured long-barrelled Navy Colt, named by the old man after Samuel Colt himself.

At the age of sixty-eight, Challoner was still the proud warrior of his younger days. A widower from Boston, Massachusetts, his natural posture was still ramrod straight in spite of the fact that he was a dying man. He had survived the most vicious of wars in Vietnam but it was the work of an unseen enemy that was leading him towards final and inevitable defeat—cancer of the lymphatic system.

Typically, Challoner refused to go down without a fight. Knowing there was no cure in his particular case, he declined what he saw as the pointless ordeals of radiotherapy and chemotherapy, preferring to battle through to the end on his own terms.

He had also refused point-blank to hide the facts from his twenty-nine year old daughter and her fiancé. Instead, he broke the news as soon as he himself had learned the truth and then delivered the bombshell of announcing what he intended to do with the rest of his limited life.

"Live," he'd declared. "Live as never before. Sail around the world... visit places I've never seen and always wanted to."

Krakatau had been one of those places on his list.

Chartering the *Greyhound*, a sixty-foot ketch with a three-man crew, Challoner then cajoled and argued until Susan and John Reynolds finally agreed to go with him. It was during this period of persuasion that Challoner revealed the deepest wish he had left; to see the pair of them married in Hawaii where his own wedding had taken place thirty-five years earlier. Both were so stunned and delighted with the idea that all arguments against the voyage effectively ended at that point.

Now, all six of the *Greyhound's* complement were lounging in the open well-deck drinking wine and looking past Rakata's 2,600 foot half-cone at a sunset no less magnificent than those that had followed in the wake of Krakatau's stupendous eruption. Above them, the volcano's monstrous child rumbled and throbbed awesomely. To Susan Challoner, it was a brooding threat and deeply sinister.

"Ever see the old movie?" her father asked. "*Krakatoa—East of Java.*"

Reynolds nodded. "Saw that when I was a kid. Corny as they come and looked nothing like this place but it did have some pretty good effects. The eruption scenes were great. The worst thing about that movie was the title."

"Oh?" Challoner shot him a questioning look. "What was so wrong with it?"

"Check your charts, Brian. It's *west* of Java!"

They came at dawn, twelve desperate, ruthless men in a converted Arab dhow that skimmed across the calm waters of the caldera under its great triangular sail. Her diesel engines lay silent as she moved in on the *Greyhound* like a ghost.

That the Malaysian pirates did not reach the ketch unseen to slaughter her occupants in their bunks was purely down to John Reynolds's complaining bladder. Not wishing to wake up the others by using the heads and operating the noisy pump-flush, he gave in to the demands of his body and crept up on deck in the eerie pre-dawn light to relieve himself over the side. Only when he turned to go back below did he spot the dhow's silent approach.

His shout of alarm was immediately answered by a bullet that took a three-inch chunk out of the gunwale mere inches away. Reynolds dived for the deck as the distinctive crack of an old Lee-Enfield rifle echoed across the water. A moment later alarmed voices and thudding footsteps sounded below. One of the crewmen, wielding a huge gutting knife, came bowling up on deck only to be greeted by a hail of bullets. He cried out, cursing, as one scored across the top of his right shoulder and immediately scuttled for cover, flattening himself to the deckboards beside Reynolds.

The dhow was coming in bow-first. At least eight of her crew, armed to the teeth with rifles, hand guns and wickedly gleaming machetes, stood poised on the forepeak in readiness to board the helpless ketch. The vessel was barely twenty yards away when Reynolds heard calm, unhurried footsteps coming up the companionway from below.

As the white-haired and barechested figure of Brian Challoner appeared on deck, grey-faced and gaunt from the ravages of his illness, the sun rose, bathing him in a rosy, unearthly glow. Ever the proud soldier, the old man stood resolutely erect. Reynolds felt an urge to yell a warning to get under cover but he was as mesmerized by the extraordinary vision of the old man as were the bandits on the dhow, none of whom had made the slightest move to open fire on him.

The strange tension was broken by a rough voice from the dhow, calling across in a language Reynolds could not understand. Other voices joined in with cruel, mocking laughter and Reynolds risked a peek above the gunwale. A large, unshaven figure on the pirate vessel's prow, grinning widely to expose an uneven set of badly stained teeth, pointed derisively at Challoner, then drew the shining blade of a machete across his own throat. The message was unmistakeable.

Brian Challoner provided his own response, slowly raising the Navy Colt in a rock-steady hand. A shot rang out from the dhow, the bullet passing cleanly through the fleshy part of Challoner's left thigh. Only a sudden widening of his eyes betrayed any reaction. The old soldier did not even move, no sound escaped from his tightly compressed lips. The Colt remained steady as Challoner increased pressure on the trigger.

The gun boomed out. As its deep echoes cracked around the caldera, Reynolds saw the pirate's face collapse in on itself. The back of the man's head sprayed a sickening, bloody mixture of bone and brain over his companions as he reeled back into them. Reynolds seized the chance of the momentary confusion to launch himself at the old man, dragging him under cover of the wheelhouse and, at the same time, bawling to Susan and the rest of the crewmen to stay below. The veteran gasped as Reynolds's rough handling brought the pain of his wound to him for the first time and he angrily pushed his future son-in-law away.

"Out of the way, John!" he rasped. "Give me a clear field of fire. God damn it, Ol' Samuel's the only firearm we have. Without him, these bastards'll cut us to ribbons."

Christ, Reynolds thought, *but the old man has guts!*

Challoner's eyes, alight with pain and battle-rush adrenalin, suddenly flicked past Reynolds's shoulder. "Dear God in Heaven!" the old man gasped.

Reynolds twisted around to look and, for a moment, his blood ran cold.

Astern of the *Greyhound*, something was streaking towards them across the calm waters. All that Reynolds could see was something resembling a bow-wave, the parted water sheeting up to a tremendous height and totally obscuring whatever was creating it. Above the babble of Malay voices on the dhow and the deep-throated rumbling of the volcano, a high-pitched whine came to his ears. It was all happening so quickly, so unexpectedly, that he only had a second to realize that the thing was headed directly for the dhow and at a speed he could hardly believe.

There was a tearing crash. Timber groaned and splintered as the centre of the pirate vessel sagged and collapsed. The dhow's mast sheared off ten feet above the deck and came crashing down. Reynolds flinched as the heavy spar crushed the skull of one man like an eggshell and shattered the spine of another. Men began to scream.

Torn in two, the dhow was breaking up and sinking. Those of her crew who still lived struggled in the water, their arms thrashing wildly. Frantic cries began to bubble and Reynolds realized that few of them could swim. He turned to Challoner but the old man had read his thoughts.

"Not a goddamned chance, John." Challoner turned to the crewman. "Tony, get the engines started and take us the hell out of here." Then, to Reynolds again, "If we take even one of them on board, John, we'd be dead at the bottom of the Sunda Straits by noon. Let the bastards stew. They can either take their chances with the sea or with the volcano. I don't much care which. Either way, they'll have a better chance of living than they'd ever give us."

The *Greyhound's* motors took them rapidly away from the scene of carnage. Shocked into a state of unnatural calm, Susan Challoner took charge of running medical repairs. Slitting open the leg of her father's jeans, she began to treat the wound and to tie a makeshift tourniquet around his upper thigh. In spite of the now searing pain, Challoner's eyes followed the peculiar double wake, now smoothing, of the thing that had sunk the pirate dhow. In the distant gap between the islands of Sertung and Rakata-kecil something spouted hugely like a monstrous whale. Then, it was gone.

Whatever the answer to the mystery might be, there was a glow within Challoner he had not felt for years. His wound, however painful, held no worries for him. It was clean, no arteries had been severed and, besides, he'd suffered far worse in Vietnam as his three Purple Hearts testified. Susan's treatment would suffice until he could be properly fixed up in Jakarta. As for his crewman, his wound turned out to be little more than a superficial graze.

They had got off lightly. He knew how lucky they had been but it saddened him to think that he would probably never live to find out just what or who had saved their lives. Perhaps the answer would never be known, an unexplained enigma of the sea like the *Mary Celeste* or the Great Sea Serpent.

Still, there were compensations. If he hadn't been sure of it before, he knew now that he still had the inner strength to fight his cancer long enough to see his daughter married in Hawaii. Only then could he die happy. After all these years, Brian Challoner had once again been called into combat duty and had not been found wanting. He knew for certain that even though the unconquerable scourge of cancer would deprive him of life, it would never take away his right or his ability to be a man.

4

8 June 2014
South Atlantic Ocean
300 miles SE of St Helena

Balaenoptera borealis—the Sei whale—is one of nature's most graceful creations. Its tapered head and long slender body, dark grey on the back, white beneath from belly to jaw, cleaves the oceans of the world with streamlined ease. The southern Sei whale can attain a length of 70 feet, a weight of 30 tons, and is recognized by the central ridge running from snout to blowhole and the tall sickle-shaped dorsal fin set two-thirds of the way back along its spine. It is also the fastest of all whales, capable of speeds in excess of 38 knots.

The Sei pod under David Falco's anxious gaze was showing nothing of that turn of speed. Instead the twenty undulating backs of both adults and juveniles were travelling at a leisurely pace, relaxedly puffing their ten-foot plumes of saturated vapour into a soft breeze and blissfully unaware of approaching danger. To them, a ship was just a ship, a fellow traveller on the deep. None of them had reason or experience to think any differently.

Falco, the East Coast American skipper of the Greenpeace vessel *Atlantis*, knew better. From the bridge of his ship he glared across at the Japanese whale-catcher with a mixture of anxiety and anger. The harrassment of the *Izu-shoto* by members of Falco's own crew was beginning to border on the reckless and, if his hair had not already been prematurely grey, he was convinced that their antics would soon have made it so.

The *Atlantis's* two Zodiac inflatables, each powered by Mercury outboards, buzzed around the whaler like angry wasps, daring and dodging the cannon-jet high-pressure hoses being trained on them by the whale-catcher's crew and, to add worry to worry, Falco was aware that the gracefully arching backs of the whales were less than half a mile away. His knuckles whitened as he gripped the rail, muttering through clenched teeth. "Go on, get the hell away from here! Can't you see what's going down? Move, damn it, move!"

"Too trusting, Dave." Anders Kristenberg, Falco's Swedish first mate, shrugged his shoulders. A sad look haunted his already mournful eyes. "They know vessels only as harmless acquaintances, albeit noisy ones. How can we expect them to grasp the concept of human barbarity when there is none among their own kind?"

The Swede paused, staring across at the whale-catcher and pointing urgently at two figures moving purposefully along the catwalk leading to the harpoon gun mounted on the forepeak. Falco reacted, putting his fingers to his lips and letting rip with a piercing whistle that shrieked out across the water. A face in the nearest of the inflatables turned to the Greenpeace ship, saw the pointing fingers and looked up at the whaler's bow.

The Zodiac shot forward, outstripping the *Izu-shoto* in an effort to put itself between the harpoon gun and the unsuspecting whales, now just a few hundred yards away. The Japanese gun-aimer took no notice, instead focussing his attention on his selected and ever-nearing target. When fired, the harpoon would fly dangerously close to these madcap Western protesters—he knew that, but his orders were clear. His finger tightened on the trigger.

One of the figures in the inflatable suddenly stood up, raising one arm high and waving wildly. The movement caught the gunner unawares and he realized, with added surprise, that the crazy figure was a woman, her long blonde hair flying in the breeze. In the same split second, he fired.

The surprise had been just enough to spoil his aim. As the lunatic figure fell back into the Zodiac, the bulletting harpoon missed her by mere inches but flew wide of its intended target, pitching harmlessly in open water twenty yards left of the chosen whale. The Japanese gunner cursed fluently as the Zodiac waggled cheekily in front of him, oblivious to the danger that was half a second away.

The harpoon cable crashed down across the stern of the Zodiac, tearing the Mercury engine from its mountings. The Zodiac's crew, miraculously unharmed, looked on aghast as the powerful motor cartwheeled, whining, through the air to hit the waves and be lost in eight thousand feet of ocean. The inflatable bounced hugely, its occupants hanging on grimly, and stopped dead in the water.

From his vantage point on the *Atlantis*, Falco breathed a massive sigh of sheer relief that could be heard on the deck below.

"Christ, but that was close! Bloody little fool damn near got her head taken off."

"But she made him miss!" Kristenberg added.

"And the whales have got the message, Andy. Look at 'em go!" He allowed himself a smile of satisfaction. "I think we can safely assume we've ruined the whaler's day. Let's go pick up the Zodiacs… and mark off another outboard against expenses."

Falco made to move away but Kristenberg held him back. "David, the whaler… what in hell is she doing?"

Belching black smoke from her stack, the *Izu-shoto* had put on full speed, turning slightly to port. Falco felt the blood drain from his face.

"Oh, no, he can't be serious. Christ, Andy, this isn't happening… the mad bastard's going for the Zodiac! He's aiming to run her down!" Shaking with helpless rage, his fist pounded the rail. Below him, he spotted a member of his crew aiming a Camcorder.

"Film it, Pete!" Falco shouted down. "Whatever happens, film it all—every second of it. TV networks all over the goddamned world can have it. So can the courtrooms!" *Not that it'll do those poor devils in the Zodiac the slightest bit of good*, he thought, staring white-faced as the whale-catcher bore down on the helpless boat, intent on an act of cold-blooded murder. Behind him, he heard the mate bellowing futilely into a radio mike. David Falco found himself praying for a miracle.

And his prayer was answered.

Under the whale-catcher's stern, the sea erupted into colossal bursts of foam. The *Izu-shoto* lurched heavily as a massive impact slewed her nearly ninety degrees from her course. Falco clearly saw the whaler's rudder torn away and tossed through a confusion of spray as though it were made of cardboard.

For a second time, the ocean boiled and heaved. Falco caught the merest glimpse of an immense blackish back then gasped aloud as tremendous twin plumes of glistening water and vapour, set close together, shot a hundred feet into the air before drifting away and dissipating on the breeze. Then, it was gone. The ocean settled and there was nothing to be seen but a gigantic eddying swirl in the water.

Stunned, Falco gaped at the stricken whaler as it wallowed helplessly. The rest of his crew stood like statues with stupified expressions.

"What the hell, Andy?" Falco said. "What sort of whale attacks ships? It was deliberate, either an act of retaliation or a conscious attempt to help our people out. I can't think of any other explanation. And that blow… the sheer size of it!"

The Swede gazed out at the disabled whale-catcher and a deceptively silent sea, calmly sifting through his own considerable knowledge of the world's cetacean species. There was something in Kristenberg's quietly controlled voice that sent shivers through Falco's spine.

"The biggest blows of all the whales belong to the Fin whale, Bryde's whale, the Sperm and the Blue. Those can send plumes as high as thirty feet. Whatever we just saw blew three times that high.

"And, David, the Blue is the biggest whale of them all. As far as is known, the biggest creature ever to have existed. There are Blues well over a hundred feet long. Now, I had only a glimpse of that thing but, I'm telling you, what I saw was twice the size of any Blue whale."

Falco stared at him. "But you just said that the Blue is the largest creature of all time."

"As far as we know, and we don't know it all. Let's face it, the ocean's a big place. We know less about it than we do about the surface of Mars. A whole lot less. And that also goes for what might live in it." The Swede paused uncomfortably. "A couple of days ago, a French cargo ship south of Cape Town reported a pod of about thirty whales. They didn't identify the species."

Falco nodded, wondering where all this was leading. "I remember you telling me when the report came in."

"But I didn't bother giving you the whole story, David. To be honest, I put it down to someone's idea of a joke, so I let it pass. Now, I'm not nearly so sure."

"Go on."

"They said that the herd was accompanied by a whale of a different type and much, much bigger. They estimated its length at around two hundred feet."

Falco sat down heavily, a strange expression on his face. "Andy, did you ever hear tell of the legend of Leviathan?" he said slowly.

"The great monster," Kristenberg said. "The giant of the sea... oh, now, just wait a minute!"

Falco gestured out at the crippled whaler. "Then you explain it."

Chapter 2

The Hunt

⟵ 5 ⟶

23 December 2014
London, UK

The Right Honourable Sir Henry Williamson MP, Her Majesty's Secretary of State for Defence, settled deeper into the luxuriant red leather upholstery of a comfortable armchair and adjusted his copy of *The Times* with a crisp snap of paper.

The exclusive surroundings of Wyatt's provided him with the perfect sanctuary, not just from the endless daily stream of civil servants, lobbyists and telephone calls, but also—and especially—from Lady Beryl Williamson.

From Sir Henry's point of view, it had been a tragic day when, after twenty years of more-or-less happy marriage, his good wife had become so utterly bewitched by Margaret Thatcher that even Lady Beryl's own character had irretrievably adopted the stubborn stridency and domineering personality of Britain's first woman Prime Minister. Not even the years since Thatcher's downfall had made the slightest difference.

As a result, life in the Williamson household had become strained to say the least. When Thatcher had been finally dethroned (Sir Henry lived in constant fear of Lady Beryl finding out the part he'd played in that event), Williamson secretly rejoiced in the vain hope that her influence over his wife would diminish and die.

Instead, the situation worsened. It was if Lady Beryl was as determined as Baroness Thatcher herself that her spirit would live on regardless. As Sir Henry had unwisely confided to a friendly newspaper proprietor: "It's as though the bloody woman was still in power, except that it's my household she's ruling whilst inhabiting the body and soul of my wife. It's like being trapped in an old horror movie."

And, of course, his off-the-cuff remark had been plastered all over the front page the following day. Sir Henry's need for a secure bolthole increased tenfold and he thanked God for Wyatt's.

One of the great exclusive gentlemen's clubs of St James's Street, Wyatt's had been founded in 1815, Waterloo year, and the wonderful paintings gracing its walls depicted scenes and personalities from that historic campaign. Pride of place at the head of the famous marble staircase was held by Francisco de Goya's portrait of the club's founder, General Sir Thomas Wyatt, himself a central figure of the Napoleonic Wars.

Wyatt's was housed in a four-storey edifice that had been designed and purpose-built by John Nash. Originally a gaming club for cavalry officers, it still retained its gambling heart in a magnificent room that took up much of the first floor. In an establishment whose doors never close to members, bridge, canasta and baccarat in particular were played around the clock, often for astronomically high stakes. It was rumoured that a pre World War II Duke had lost his entire estates on the gaming tables of Wyatt's.

Sir Henry, though, was not a gambling man, preferring instead to use the club to relax or to avail himself of its legendary catering. For the peace and quiet he sought, the reading, chess and drawing rooms of the second floor were his favourite retreats. There, a man could study, read, drink, smoke or socialize in wholly informal surroundings.

And only a man could do so. In an age of political correctness, the famous clubs of St James's Street are among the last establishments to hold out against the onslaught of feminism and to retain their old-fashioned values of chauvinistic masculinity. No woman had ever crossed the threshold of Wyatt's, for which fact Sir Henry was truly grateful.

The old standards and practices have never been neglected at this famous old club. Even the newspapers are still fastidiously ironed before being laid out for the clientele and the heating throughout the building is kept at a constant seventy degrees Fahrenheit (coinage excepted, the metric system has never been allowed to invade the club's traditionalist world). Sir Henry appreciated the pleasant warmth even more than usual as he listened to the hail lashing against the tall, eighteen-paned sash windows, original features of Nash's architecture that had been lovingly maintained over the years. Far better, he thought, than those flat, lifeless plastic monstrosities breaking out all over Britain like a bad rash.

Williamson set his mouth grimly. Perhaps these soulless replacements were symptomatic of modern society. In so many places, plain unadorned ugliness was replacing things of beauty. In exact parallel, he thought, the sparkle and vibrancy that had once epitomized the British people was all but gone, to be replaced by the sort of grim-faced greyness one used to find behind the old Iron Curtain. The one-time caring, pull-together spirit of the country had, it seemed, been tossed aside in favour of greed, selfishness and mutual contempt. Sir Henry recalled a foreign commentator's recent remark about the UK's current crime wave and the travelling thugs posing as football supporters in which the writer had described the British as "the Brutish people".

What in God's name had happened? Williamson had never been able to work it out. In an age when ordinary folk had access to so much more than ever before, why were they so discontented and resentful? He could recall the nineteen-fifties when less than half the nation's households had television and two-car families were rarer than millionaires, yet people seemed so much happier. He sighed heavily. What more did people want? Or was that the problem? That the more they had, the more they craved?

A solidly built man in a dark grey suit eased himself into an armchair facing Sir Henry and the Defence Minister looked up into a familiar face.

"You look as gloomy as the weather outside," remarked Gerald Calloway, Secretary of State for Trade and Industry, "if I may say so."

"No, you may not bloody well say so." A twinkle of the eye removed any venom from Williamson's retort. "If you must know, Gerald, I was just thinking what an ungrateful shower the great British public is. In old Macmillan's words, they've never had it so good but it seems to me that the more they have, the more they moan and groan about what they don't have. Only they don't whine about it any more. They snarl. Just take the crime figures. God above, even the Attorney General's own son got mugged the other day, for forty quid. Forty quid! By a thug wearing a patent leather coat worth at least four hundred. It simply makes no sense at all."

"I know exactly what you mean," the younger man agreed. He pointed at Williamson's empty glass. "Fancy a refill?"

"Thought you were never going to ask," the Minister of Defence grinned, looking up to catch a steward's eye. "Large rum, please, Gerald. Woods, neat."

"Trust an old Navy man," Calloway grumped, then, as the senior steward approached, "Ah, thank you, Burridge. Large neat Woods for Sir Henry, White Horse and water for me."

Calloway waited for the drinks to be served. "So," he finally said, studying Williamson's lined, weather-beaten features. "Why all the world weariness?"

"Oh, pressures of work, you know, Gerald. Brings other concerns closer to mind." He glanced up from his drink, suddenly grateful for a sympathetic ear in surroundings he could guarantee to be secure. It was an unwritten, but rigidly observed, rule that nothing confidential uttered within the walls of Wyatt's ever went outside them. Which, Sir Henry thought, was more than could ever be said for Westminster and Whitehall.

"Bloody weather doesn't exactly help," he continued heavily, eyeing half-melted hailstones sliding down the windowpanes. "Hardly uplifts the soul to pinnacles of rapture, does it? Then there's the onset of old age. That comes more readily to mind in winter and this one's my seventieth."

Gerald Calloway gazed patiently at his senior colleague, content to remain silent and let the old fellow get it all off his chest.

"I have Beryl driving me wild. Thatcher's been out of office for donkey's years but no one seems to have informed my good wife. Strutting and pecking around the bloody house. God's teeth, the woman's even had her hair styled like Margaret's. If she had to select a role model at all, why the hell couldn't she have chosen someone less—"

"Dictatorial?"

Williamson shot him a cold glance. "I was going to say 'authoritative'." He noted his colleague's rueful smile, relaxed a little and chuckled. "Could have had worse influences, I suppose. Michael Foot, for instance. The damn woman would have had me kitted out in corduroys and donkey jackets." He grew a little more serious. "To cap it all, I've just spent the entire afternoon having my ear bashed by the First Sea Lord about terrorism and piracy on the high seas and when was I going to authorize some action to deal with it?"

Calloway sat up slowly. *Ah*, he thought, *now we have it. This is what's really stung the old man.*

"Bloody foreign whalers and a few freighters get their rudders ripped off, or so they claim," Sir Henry went on. "But by what? Nobody seems to have the slightest clue. Some say it's a big black whale, others claim to have seen a bright moving light in the water and one or two postulate an apparently suicidal submarine. No one's managed to get a clear sight of the thing and the tabloids are having a field day with it. An avenging sea monster. Something from outer space or the Twilight Zone. Piloted by Elvis Presley, I shouldn't wonder.

"Seriously, Gerald, what the hell can I do about it? Who or what would I be authorizing action against? The thing hasn't been identified, always assuming that it even exists in the first place. For God's sake, no one can agree on whether it's animal, vegetable or mineral. Nobody's claimed responsibility for these attacks and, more importantly, none of these incidents has occurred within British waters. We could go running to the NATO chiefs but not until we have some definite idea of what we're looking for."

Williamson halted his flow of words to take a mouthful of rum, thankful for its familiar bite on the linings of his cheeks and throat and the warmth of its path to his stomach. For a moment, the winter world outside seemed to take a step away.

"It would seem," said Calloway, "that we have something in common."

"Oh, how so?"

"Well, in my case, it's Lloyd's of London. As if they haven't had enough problems in recent years, they're scared stiff of a rush of claims from the owners of the damaged ships, and live in mortal dread of someone being sunk by this thing. They're already threatening to increase their premiums, so now I have the shipowners and the CBI battering my door down, as well as the Chancellor who is getting pretty hot under the collar. All this could escalate into massive price rises, inflation heading skyward, Prime Minister going completely pear-shaped, and so on."

"Good God above, Gerald! I had no idea." Sir Henry was genuinely shocked and mentally projected Calloway's scenario to a logical and not very attractive conclusion.

"That's not the half of it," Calloway went on. "The Prime Minister had planned on spending a quiet weekend at Chequers. He ended up spending most of it with the Japanese and Norwegian ambassadors who are incensed about their whalers being attacked."

"Serves the buggers right," Williamson grumbled. "Shouldn't be whaling. Damn it, both countries were signatories to the International Whaling Treaty and the ten-year moratorium, albeit under protest and a hell of a lot of pressure. Bloody brass neck to come complaining. Why come crying to us, anyway? What makes them think it's any responsibility of ours? As I recall, the incidents with whalers took place off the Azores and down in the South Atlantic—hardly our preserve. Greenpeace must be delighted."

"Speaking of which," Calloway broke in, "the PM's also had Sir Robert Maynard on his back again, demanding for the umpteenth time an investigation into the loss of his Deep Watch vessel in the Antarctic back in February. British-registered vessel after all," he added in response to Williamson's questioning look. "The coroner's inquest in New Zealand registered an open verdict on the deaths of her crew through insufficient evidence to account for the sinking.

"Personally, I can't for the life of me see why Sir Robert's pushing so hard. His ship went down in ten thousand feet of water and it's hardly likely she'll ever be found."

"Perhaps you'd like to ask him yourself." Sir Henry inclined his head towards the tall figure crossing the room in their direction.

Sir Robert Maynard, founder and director of Deep Watch, cut an impressive figure, his trim build testifying to a fanatical obsession with personal fitness. His beautifully cut blue worsted suit was a trifle lightweight for winter wear. Now in his mid-fifties, Sir Robert's immaculately groomed head of silver hair accentuated a deep tan, and lively blue eyes smiled through square rimless glasses.

"Just discussing things maritime, Bob," Williamson boomed. "Come and join us. Drink?" he offered.

"Thank you, Henry, I will," Maynard responded. "Vodka martini, I think. Good to see you, too, Gerald." He shook hands with them both and

Williamson again caught Burridge's eye to order a further round of drinks.

"How did you fare with the PM?" Calloway asked.

Maynard shook his head. "Got no further than I did last time. Oh, he's sympathetic enough but argues that, with such a lack of tangible evidence, there's little to gain from setting up a further Inquiry. Budgetary restrictions preclude getting a deep-water submersible out there and, God knows, that's a pricy enough venture in local waters, let alone a remote spot like the Ross Sea. To be honest, it looks pretty hopeless. I'd put up the funds myself for a search but there's no deep-diving submersible available anywhere for at least twelve months.

"I don't know what more I can do, but I lost ten good people when the *Aurora* went down. I'd try any channel open to me to get at the truth of what happened out there. At the very least, it would put a stop to the endless speculation and chair-bound 'experts' suggesting it was Seán McKenna's fault. I won't have such an ill-informed stigma attached to his memory.

"Anyway, enough of my troubles. Which particular maritime matters are creating problems for two such eminent Ministers of the Crown?"

"The case of the mysterious ship-crippler, if you hadn't already guessed it," Williamson answered. "Everyone's pushing the government to take action, but against what?"

"Since that incident in the South Atlantic in June," Calloway observed, "all these attacks on whalers and freight carriers have taken place in our half of the North Atlantic. On this side of the pond, we're still seen as the senior power in NATO, so everyone's running to us for protection. Even the whaling nations."

Maynard reacted sharply. "When they're flying in the face of the whaling ban? They've a bloody nerve!"

"Well, it's all got me thinking lately," Calloway said. He drew out a diary from an inside jacket pocket and opened the front cover. A Mercator map of the world was spread across both pages. "Bob, could there be a link between these episodes and the sinking of the *Aurora*?"

"In what way?"

"It's a bit of a long shot," Calloway confessed, "but take a look at this." He produced a pencil and drew a small cross on the map in the area of the Ross Sea. "February, the *Aurora*. Now March, when a giant whale was reported off the Tasmanian coast and, in early June, a similar sighting south of Cape Town. Only days after that, the business between Greenpeace and a Japanese whaler south of St Helena." He drew three more crosses. "Then, incidents off the Azores and, more recently, the North Atlantic." Again he sketched in the rough locations and finished with a line linking them all up. "Do you see? An apparent progressive sequence right across the Indian Ocean and up into the Atlantic."

Maynard studied the map. "You make an interesting point, Gerald. Are you saying that whatever's attacking these ships might have sunk the *Aurora*?"

Calloway shrugged. "I can only say that it's possible, but the dates could be significant."

Maynard went quiet for a moment, again following the pencil line on Calloway's map and staring pointedly at a circle the Minister had drawn to cover the area of the North Atlantic incidents. "And now it's camped here," he said thoughtfully, tapping the map with a well manicured fingernail.

"Reminds me of the war," Williamson said. "The U-boat packs and how the buggers used to lie in wait out there for our convoys."

Maynard looked up sharply. "Are you seriously suggesting that these are submarine attacks?"

"I haven't a clue." Sir Henry shook his head. "I can't imagine torpedo strikes so accurate that they just take rudders off and leave the rest of the ship unharmed. No torpedo is that precise."

"What about deliberate ramming?" Calloway said.

"Be serious, Gerald," Williamson hooted. "There's not a submarine in the world that can take a single ramming action without sinking itself, let alone a whole series of them. They're designed to withstand pressure, not impacts."

"A one-off, then," Calloway persisted. "Purpose designed, perhaps privately built?"

Sir Henry was emphatic. "Not a ghost of a chance. Allied Intelligence is fully aware of every submarine built by every nation and there's precious little that goes on in private enterprise that industrial spies don't know about, either. No one could possibly build such a thing in secret, not in this day and age. Technology's made the world a damn sight smaller and more public place than it ever used to be. Everyone knows everybody else's business, no matter who or where they may be. These days, Gerald, a secret submarine development of any kind is an absolute impossibility.

"Let's face it, we're all groping in the dark and it remains a mystery, at least for the moment."

"For the moment?" Gerald Calloway regarded Sir Henry quizzically. "Am I to infer that you're planning something?"

"Perhaps. It was something the First Sea Lord and I were discussing earlier. Oh, we could stick the odd warship out there but that's pretty hit and miss at best. A more surreptitious approach might be a better option."

"MI6?"

Williamson snorted derisively. "Do me a favour, Gerald. That isn't even funny. After the cock-ups and internal wranglings of the last twelve months, I wouldn't trust Six to see the Queen's corgis across the road.

"No, I've just the fellow in mind. Experienced seaman, experienced operative. Outstanding record and did some impressive solo stuff during that problem in the Med last year." He smiled at Calloway's cocked eyebrow and sideways glance at Maynard. "Oh, don't fret, Gerald. Through his United Nations and UNESCO appointments, Sir Robert has an even higher security clearance than you have.

"The man I have in mind is one of Jim Garvie's team in Naval Intelligence. Name of Lindsay. Commander Donall McEwan Lindsay."

6

North Atlantic Ocean
820 miles WSW of Cape Clear

"Captain to the bridge." Commander Randall C. Hayes, captain of the FFG-7 Class frigate *USS Appalachian*, groaned softly and eased himself off the cot on which he'd so far managed all of ten minutes rest. He reached out for the telephone handset.

"Captain here. What's the problem?"

His Executive Officer's voice responded. "We have a distress signal, sir."

Hayes felt the need for sleep give way to his responsibilities of command. "How far away?"

"Twenty miles north-west of our current position, sir."

"Very well, Ex-oh, I'm on my way up."

In spite of his fatigue, Hayes's flagging spirits rose a little. At last, something constructive to do. There was no doubt in his mind that the last three weeks had been the most tedious experience of his entire career. NATO exercises in European waters were seldom the most exhilarating activities and the one his ship had just completed, code-named Crackdown, had been by far the worst yet. It had proven to be a complete bore dictated by desk-bound British admirals who had long since forgotten the smell of the sea and the roll of a deck under their feet. Men like these were not so much the heirs of Nelson as products of modern bureaucracy, automatons plotting predetermined combat actions that were predictable in the extreme, years out of date and wholly disregarding of the latest technological advances.

Throughout the entire three weeks, the United States frigate, the long-hulled version of her class with a length of 455 feet and highly manoeuvrable at speeds up to thirty knots, had been required to plough through a whole series of rigidly governed course patterns within prescribed grid squares while British and French submarines registered "kill" after "kill" upon her.

Hayes had not even been permitted to use the latest hardware and counter-attack manoeuvres and the sudden twangs of active sonar pulses on the *Appalachian's* hull—each one representing a torpedo hit—would, he felt, haunt him for the rest of his days. He utterly failed to see the slightest benefit from such an exercise. *As if any hostile navy would stick to rules and grid squares, for Christ's sake!*

His own Commander-in-Chief, Admiral Walter Greene, presently enjoying the comforts of the *Appalachian's* well stocked wardroom, had been equally frustrated by the unrealistic constraints of the exercise, even in his official role as on-board observer. Greene, never the most tactful of men, had been heard to dub the whole thing "a goddamn waste of time, money, ships and men" and, at the debriefing session held aboard *HMS Invincible* (*damn fool name*, Hayes thought savagely. *How would the smug bastards live that down should she ever get herself sunk?*), Greene had muttered darkly about "wiping the stupid grins off those Limey faces" in next year's exercise on the American side of the pond.

Hayes was particularly aggrieved about the demoralizing effect the exercise had inflicted upon his crew. Greene, he decided, was right. It had been a thorough waste of time, money, ability and training.

In addition to it all was the appalling timing of the exercise. Hayes thought of his already demoralized crew facing Christmas at sea while their European counterparts whooped it up in their home ports. He had already made up his mind to fight tooth and nail for extended shore leave for his crew from the moment they docked in the *Appalachian's* home port at the Norfolk Naval Base in Virginia. He was almost grateful to the vessel in distress for providing them with a respite from inaction.

"What have we got?" Hayes said as he arrived on the bridge.

Lieutenant-Commander Paul Vylander, his Executive Officer, handed him the signal sheet. "Bulk carrier, the *Dogger Bank*. British owned, Liberian flag."

After his thoughts about *HMS Invincible's* name, Hayes almost laughed aloud. Only the Brits could name a vessel after a shipping hazard. A flag of convenience ship. Hayes could almost picture the faults she was bound to be riddled with.

"Her skipper's not a happy man," Vylander commented. "Name of Ryecart."

"Okay, patch me through to him, will you, Paul." As he gave the instruction, Hayes felt, rather than saw, his officers stiffen before hearing Vylander sing out: "Admiral on the bridge!"

"As you were, gentlemen. Let's skip the formalities, shall we? I'm strictly a passenger on this trip." Admiral Greene was a stocky, pugnacious little man, half a head shorter than Hayes's rangy six feet, with grizzled, short-cropped hair and darting black eyes that missed nothing. "Permission to come onto the bridge, captain?"

"You have it, admiral." Hayes gave him an easy grin. On land, Greene had a reputation for prickliness. He loathed the office-bound position that had come with his promotion and his transformation on the all-too-few occasions he could step aboard a ship was a sight to behold. People either liked Walter Greene or they loathed him; the former invariably consisted of those who had shared a sea trip with him. Hayes enjoyed the admiral's company, the way he took a keen interest in the running of the ship, often seeking a chance to contribute but always taking care not to interfere.

"A Mayday call, I gather?" the admiral said.

"Yes, sir," Hayes answered. "British bulk carrier. I'm just getting linked up to her captain."

"Mind if I eavesdrop?"

"Be my guest, admiral."

Vylander interrupted. "Captain Ryecart on the line, sir."

"Put him on speaker, would you?" Hayes lifted the handset. "*Dogger Bank*, this is the United States frigate *Appalachian*, currently twenty miles south-east of your position. Randall Hayes commanding. What is your status, captain? Over."

"Captain Michael Ryecart, *MV Dogger Bank*," the deep voice boomed out from the bridge speaker. "Good to hear from you and thank God you're a warship. Maybe you can do something about this."

Hayes frowned. "Can you clarify, captain?"

"Glad to. We've been rammed astern. I've lost one screw and all steering. I have power but we're all getting a little tired of steaming around in circles. We're taking in a little water around the shaft seals but the pumps are coping."

"You did say 'rammed', Captain Ryecart. By whom?"

"You tell me. We saw nothing until the moment we were hit. Even then, all we could see was a bloody big swirl of water."

"Could it have been a whale?"

"Not unless the bugger was armour-plated. We all heard the collision. Felt it, too. Whatever did this was rock solid. Had it been a whale, there'd have been bits of it everywhere after hitting our screw, but there's nothing. Not even a hint of blood in the water."

Hayes knotted his brow, perplexed. An ensign handed him a signal from the radio shack and he scanned it briefly. "Good news, Captain Ryecart. As you've probably heard, an ocean-going tug en route from the Azores to Lisbon has diverted and is on her way to you. ETA, twelve hours. I will attend until she arrives." He turned to Vylander. "Paul, what's our ETA to the casualty and her bearing?"

"At present speed, sir, one hour on a bearing of three-one-oh."

"Very good. Let's put her through her paces, shall we? Make your course three-one-oh and make turns for thirty knots."

"Three-one-oh, thirty knots, aye, sir."

Hayes got back to Ryecart. "*Dogger Bank*, this is *Appalachian*. Be with you in four-oh minutes."

"Many thanks, *Appalachian*. We'll put the kettle on. *Dogger Bank*, out."

Walter Greene's face seemed carved from stone. "Another ramming. I make that ten in the last three months. No one knows who, what or why. The victims are whalers and freight vessels, and the tactic's always the same. The renegade goes for rudder and screws, meaning to disable rather than sink, but the reason and the means of achieving it has everyone beaten hollow. And no one ever sees anything tangible."

Hayes smiled tightly. "I have heard something of this, admiral, but didn't realize how many incidents there've been. Maybe, sir, if the attacker's still in the area, we might get to have some fun with her."

Greene nodded thoughtfully. "Randy, will you give your okay for me to contact NATO Europe? I'd like to see if they're game to us taking some positive action if the chance arises. I know for a fact that they're sick to the back teeth with complaints about these attacks but, up to now, they've been chasing a will o' the wisp. What do you say?"

"I say yes, admiral. It'll be exactly what this crew's been crying out for, and you carry the clout to get us that clearance. Go right ahead, sir."

7

Falmouth
Cornwall, UK

Barrington Hobbes raised the collar of his coat against the night chill as he waited for his ageing dog to squat down and pee in the gutter. He used the moment to gaze out over the hundreds of lights mirrored in the calm waters of what, to his mind, was one of the world's finest and most underused deep water natural harbours.

Christmas was in the air and the full, rich sound of a Cornish male voice choir welled out from the Harbour Bar of the Greenbank Hotel that Hobbes had left a good deal earlier than he normally did. Christmas had the guaranteed effect of drawing out astonishing numbers of people and, even at this early evening hour, the bar had become packed, hot and loud. Hobbes had a natural aversion to crowds and noise. He wondered, as he did every Christmas, where all these people hid themselves for the remainder of the year.

Having emptied her bladder, the old dog looked up at him with her usual doleful expression and Hobbes trudged away up the hill towards home. Christmas was far from being his favourite time of year. It brought back too many painful memories. He lived alone and there was no one close with whom he could share and enjoy the festivities, having been cruelly robbed of wife and child ten years earlier by the same appalling car crash that had effectively ended his own career.

Once, his name had been legendary in worldwide journalism. As an investigative reporter, his record stood alone. Hobbes's trademarks had been the courage to tread where lesser hacks feared to venture, and never once resorting to petty sensationalism, distortion of the facts or contrived copy. The diverse armouries of the powerful and corrupt could never deter him from his chosen target and the more power his crooked adversary wielded, the more of a challenge he considered it to be.

Then, ten years ago, he had stepped on one powerful foot too many. To this day, no one but Hobbes knew the full facts of the case he had been striving to crack open and publicly expose. A late night journey down the M5 motorway with his wife and five year old daughter had taken him straight into the jaws of a carefully laid trap—a trio of identical juggernaut lorries which combined to box him into an inside lane before coldly swatting him off the motorway embankment at seventy miles an hour.

He never saw his wife and daughter buried. Six months in intensive care, his life hanging by a thread, and a further two years of convalescence saw an end to his illustrious career. Physically and mentally, Hobbes was a broken man. It was to be a further two years before he could walk without the aid of sticks or crutches and, even now, his shambling, limping gait was a permanent reminder of the night that had shattered his life.

Justice had never been brought to bear, nor had it even come close. Eyewitnesses to the crash suffered sudden, unexplained and apparently permanent losses of memory or, in one case, simply disappeared. Two of the juggernauts' registration plates, incredibly retained by Hobbes's remarkable memory even at the moment his Rover sailed from a fifty-foot embankment, were claimed by the police to have never existed in the central records at Swansea. Eventually, the case was consigned to gather dust on a back room shelf: out of sight, out of mind.

At that time, Hobbes had been within a whisker of identifying the man at the top of an evil organization, the spider at the centre of a wide, tangled web of corruption and deceit whose influence even seemed to reach into the very highest offices of power. He knew that the half-hearted investigation into the slaying of his wife and child had been nothing more than a measured exercise in illusory enquiry, a process of going through the motions for its own sake.

Forced into premature retirement, Hobbes returned to his roots, purchasing a small, end-of-terrace cottage high above Falmouth harbour and just a few minutes walk from where he had been born forty-eight years ago. The abilities of his astute mind had never deserted him and a slow, steady stream of local, minor investigative commissions brought a supplement to the generous pension provided by his old London newspaper, *The Sentinel*, enough to cover his modest needs.

Even so, and although his old leads had long since gone cold, he harboured a deep-seated hope that, one day, he would unearth the man who had destroyed his life.

Hobbes still hankered after the excitement of a major investigative assignment and the port in which he lived, home of the closest ship repair yard to the Western Approaches, had recently become linked to the baffling series of incidents at sea which whetted the old appetites. The sea and its many unsolved mysteries had fascinated him since childhood and, now, an entire series of maritime riddles were occurring, enough to provide plenty of fuel for the popular press and work for the Falmouth ship repair yard. The entire waterfront was buzzing with speculation as to who and what was deliberately disabling ships out in the Atlantic Ocean or, for that matter, why.

Barrington Hobbes followed the events keenly, collecting every shred of newsprint about them that he could find. He had even taken photographs of the latest victim, the *Margarita Sanchez*, a bulk carrier that lay in dry dock little over a mile from his own house, but could find nothing to improve upon the suggestions that ranged from the intriguing to the downright ridiculous.

Before this spate of strange events, there had been another that the newspapers had apparently forgotten. Hobbes could never forget it. He had lost one of his closest friends on the Deep Watch ship *Aurora*, inexplicably lost in the Antarctic: its mate, Alan Tregenza. Hobbes had known Tregenza for years and followed his rugby-playing exploits. Those had peaked with a Cornish cap and a place in a County Championship winning side at Twickenham before he'd joined Deep Watch on a permanent basis. The *Aurora* had made Falmouth her home port four years ago and Hobbes had spent enjoyable visits to the local bars with Tregenza and the *Aurora's* Irish captain, Seán McKenna. Their deaths still remained a mystery.

Puffing from the steep climb,Hobbes paused to catch his breath even though his house was just yards away. His eyes narrowed. There was a light in the downstairs study and the storm-porch door stood ajar. Certain that he had turned off all but the hallway light and closed that outer door, Hobbes cursed his habit of not locking up whenever he left the house.

He moved urgently but quietly, easing open the front door and slipping the dog's leash from her collar. The study door was open and Hobbes took a cautious look inside. There was no one there but a scrapbook had been taken from a shelf and left open on the worktop. He took a closer look. The open pages carried reports that he had collected about the *Aurora* tragedy and this coincidence with the contents of his recent thoughts disturbed him even further.

A low *wuff* of enquiry from the dog caused him to glance round. The animal stood in the hallway, her nose pressed close to the gap under the living room door. The dog's head cocked this way and that and she whined softly. Hobbes drew a stout walking stick from the hallstand and threw the door open, gripping the stick in a mixed gesture of aggression and self-protection.

The old dog padded into a room lit only by the glow of a coal fire burning low behind its guard. A dimly visible figure sat calmly in a chair by the fire, stroking the dog's head as it laid its muzzle on the stranger's knee.

"Hallo, Rusty, I've heard all about you. Fine guard dog you make." It was a soft, female voice. Puzzled, Hobbes relaxed a little and lowered the stick.

"And who the hell might you be?" The question came out less aggressively than it was worded.

"Mr Hobbes," the woman said. "I apologize for barging in uninvited but the door was open and it's cold outside."

Hobbes grunted a non-committal reply and turned on the light. The intruder was young, twenty-three or so, he guessed, attractive with curling brown hair worn short. Her dark eyes were large and Hobbes noticed the shadows beneath them. There had been a deal of pain there, he thought.

"I'm Karen Marshall," she said. "We met once, at a rugby club dinner in Camborne a couple of years back. You knew my fiancé."

"Fiancé?" he asked guardedly.

"Alan… Alan Tregenza."

"Karen!" Hobbes was suddenly flustered and embarrassed. "I didn't recognize you. I'm sorry… I might have offered a better welcome."

She gave a short laugh. "It wasn't your fault. I shouldn't have breezed in unannounced."

"You're a journalist, aren't you?" Hobbes said. "*Western Gazette*. I've read your work and it's pretty good, if I may say so."

"Thank you, kind sir," she said good-humouredly, "but it's not a patch on what you used to produce. I work freelance but the *Gazette* commissions me more often than anyone else. I'm still waiting for a breakthrough to the national press."

"It'll come," Hobbes said. "So, what brings you here? I'm old news if it's an interview you're after."

She bit her lip, switching her gaze to the carpet in front of her. "I came to ask for your help, Mr Hobbes, in connection with the *Aurora* and Alan's death."

"Miss Marshall, I haven't been active in journalism for ten years," he reminded her.

"But you do have all that experience," she persisted. "You don't lose that overnight, not ever. You know exactly how to recognize a lead, follow it and keep it under wraps."

"Go on." Hobbes felt his natural curiosity taking over.

The girl produced a padded envelope from her coat pocket and drew out an object. She passed it to him, wordlessly, and Hobbes examined it. It was a handsome hunter watch, complete with chain and gold-plated. The dial bore Roman numerals. Hobbes turned it over and squinted at the copperplate inscription on its back:

Master Mariner Holman George, July 21st 1938

"That watch," Karen said quietly, "was hand delivered to the *Gazette* early this morning. The desk staff said it was brought in by a tall man with a foreign accent. As you can see from the envelope, it was addressed to me, by name, and marked: *Personal and Confidential*."

"I'm not following your drift," Hobbes said.

She looked up, her eyes large in her face. "That watch belonged to Alan's maternal grandfather. It was Alan's lucky charm. He took it everywhere, Mr Hobbes. Everywhere.

"Even to the bottom of the Ross Sea."

8

North Atlantic Ocean
830 miles WSW of Cape Clear

The *Dogger Bank* was a massive, ugly vessel of some 75,000 tons gross and close on seven hundred feet in length. It had taken the *USS Appalachian's* twin gas turbines and single screw just forty-two minutes to reach her. Commander Hayes took his vessel round the bulk carrier's stern to view the damage.

"Good grief!" Admiral Greene, standing by Hayes on the open bridge wing, stared at the tangle of metal. "Her entire rudder's gone! Starboard screw bent all to hell. Short of a torpedo, what in the name of God could have done that?" His eyes scanned an empty, darkening horizon as Captain Ryecart's voice issued from the speaker.

"Good to see you, *Appalachian*. Thanks for attending. My condition remains the same and, as you can see for yourselves, I'm going nowhere. Thankfully, weather and sea conditions are forecast to remain fair."

"Roger that, *Dogger Bank*," Hayes responded. "We'll stay within visual range of you but I'm in the mood to mooch about some in case whatever did this to you is still in the area. If they are, you'll get to see some fun. I've received authorization from NATO to search, engage and take any action I deem necessary."

"Music to my ears, *Appalachian*. Let's hope you do find something… we'll have the best seats in the house. Good hunting and good luck. *Dogger Bank*, out."

Hayes handed the conn to Paul Vylander and headed for the ship's combat centre. This lay abaft of the bridge and contained the communications, sonar and radar booths. The sonar officer, Lieutenant Emilio Garcia, was a tall, raven-haired man with looks as Latin as his name suggested.

"Emil, give me a full radar and sonar search of the area," Hayes instructed. "Let me know the second anything turns up."

Garcia acknowledged the order, raising an eyebrow. "A test run, sir?"

"Not this time," Hayes said. "You should be pleased to hear that. Tell me about the slightest blip, the smallest noise. I want your team on full alert."

The sonar officer grinned happily as Hayes turned away. "You've got that, sir."

Admiral Greene was waiting for the captain as he returned to the bridge, catching his eye and indicating the wreckage of the bulk carrier's steering gear.

"Strikes me, Randy, that the *Dogger Bank* took a heavy glancing blow from the port side," he said, "judging by the way all that scrap metal's bent toward the starboard. As the ship was on a westerly course, would it stand to reason that if whatever hit her carried on its own course, it might be somewhere to our north?"

"Fair shot, Admiral," Hayes responded. "It's also the best we have. Let's give it a try. Helm, steer three-six-zero. Keep our speed down to five knots to give sonar a fair chance. Let's just see if anyone's lurking about."

The helmsman was repeating Hayes's order as Emil Garcia's voice came out over the speaker. "Bridge, sonar. We have a surface radar contact."

"Already?" Hayes snapped. "Where away?"

"Bearing two-seven-two, sir. It's a transient signal, weak and intermittent, range ten thousand yards."

"Anything on sonar?"

"Nothing yet, captain. Too much wave scatter."

"Keep on it."

Hayes grabbed a set of binoculars and went out on the open bridge wing to scan the sea. Greene went with him.

"Light's fading fast," Hayes commented. "I don't see a sign of anything. Are we looking for a ghost here?"

"If radar only gets an intermittent signal," Greene mused, "then maybe whatever we're looking for lies low in the water, hidden in the troughs for much of the time."

"Submarine?"

Greene shook his head. "We'd see her fin. The wave heights aren't that great."

"Hold on, Admiral, I have something. Long and low. I can't make out any definite features in this light. Here, sir, take a look."

Greene aimed the glasses where Hayes indicated. "Nothing yet… wait. Yep, got her. Black, long and low, just as you say." He snorted derisively. "Randy, it's a goddamn whale."

Hayes stepped back inside and raised Garcia. "Emil, we think we see a whale. Is your radar contact a biologic?"

"No, sir." Garcia's response was definite. "Signal's not that weak. This has to be metallic."

"Has it, now?" Greene broke in. "Then she's either a sub or a capsized wreck. I can't imagine all these ships have been hitting a wreck."

"Not unless the wreck was travelling at a rate of knots all over the North Atlantic," Hayes commented. "Just what the hell are we looking at here?"

Greene had the glasses back to his eyes. "Hey, didn't we both agree the thing was featureless?" He didn't wait for an answer. "Well, it ain't now. I can distinctly see a pair of small projections, fins or something. Probably four, five feet high. They definitely weren't there just now. Jesus!"

Greene suddenly pointed as two columns of water and vapour shot vertically from the unidentified object. A faint but powerful *whoosh* reached their ears as the object slid smoothly beneath the waves. The two men looked at each other and made for the sonar booth at the run.

Hayes didn't wait for formalities. "Give her a ten-second burst of active sonar pulses, Emil. Yankee-search her." Garcia hit the button, grabbed a set of headphones and listened for the strong returns. "Metallic for sure," he said.

"Then we do have a sub," Hayes breathed. Sonarman First Class Leroy Johnson interrupted him.

"Sorry to break in, sir, but I have a passive signal. Faint, real faint. A sound signature like nothing I've ever heard before. Very quiet engine noise, easy to miss but definitely not nuclear. There's no trace of coolant circulation." Johnson studied the "waterfall" display above the console. "I can't figure this out, sir. She has to be either nuclear or diesel-electric but the patterns are all wrong for either. I can't tell what this is."

Garcia peered over Johnson's shoulder. "I have to concur, captain. This is like nothing I've ever encountered either."

Hayes pondered this. If experienced sonarmen like Garcia and Johnson couldn't identify the signature, then he had a real mystery on his hands. Hayes hated mysteries.

"Give out a challenge on the Gertrude, Emil," he said. Gertrude was a term used by the US Navy for an ultra-low frequency underwater telephone. "Tell him to blow his tanks, surface and stop engines, or we will open fire."

Garcia waited for the prolonged moments it took to get a response over this system. "No response, sir," he said finally.

"Try it again."

"Still no response," Garcia told him after a similar length of time.

Hayes gritted his teeth. "Okay, we've tried the polite approach," he said. "So now we take the gloves off. Patch me through to Weapons, will you."

"Weapons," a speaker responded. Hayes picked up a handset.

"Weps, this is the captain. Torpedo and gunnery crews to stand by, immediately. This is not a drill, repeat, not a drill. I want a single Mark Four-Six torpedo loaded and ready to fire on my command. Quarter charge. I say again, quarter charge only. I'm putting the ship on general quarters. Await my orders. Captain, out." Hayes got on to Vylander to order general quarters.

Greene gave him a keen look. "Quarter charge?"

"Yes, admiral. I don't want her destroyed, just damaged enough to force her up. Emil, do you have her?"

"Estimated depth, five hundred feet, heading away at around eighteen knots. Bearing, two-seven-five Magnetic. We're lucky, sir, the inversion layer's either deep or non-existent. A shallow one and we might have lost her, she's so quiet."

Hayes got back to the Weapons Officer. "We have target bearing two-seven-five Magnetic. Range…" he glanced at Garcia's display panel. "Eleven thousand yards. Fire One!"

"Torpedo away, sir."

"Emil, we'll be on the bridge. I want a running commentary on this."

Back on the bridge, Hayes and Greene scanned a darkening sea through the windshield. Garcia's voice cut in over the speaker.

"Bridge, sonar. Torpedo on track. Doppler shows target accelerating to twenty-five knots and going deep. She's down to an estimated eight hundred feet. No doubt about it, sir, she knows there's a fish on her tail. Torpedo at full forty-five knots, eight thousand yards from target and closing."

Hayes gazed ahead, mentally visualizing the 12.7 inch Mark 46 torpedo streaking after its prey, acoustic sensors seeking out and homing in on its target. *Show me the exercise that can prepare for this*, he thought with a certain satisfaction.

"Ever had to open fire in anger before?" Greene asked him.

"Just the once. Persian Gulf, '02. I was a Lieutenant on the *Perry* in those days. We took out a fast Iraqi MTB off the Kuwaiti coast with the three-inch. Bracketed him with the first two, blew him clean out of the water with the third."

"Bridge, sonar. Target's taking a wide turn to starboard. Accelerating to forty knots. Torpedo still on track."

"Fast son of a bitch," Greene commented.

"Target still making his turn," the Sonar Officer continued. "Depth still eight hundred. Coming out of his turn. Captain, she's headed directly for our starboard side."

"How close to her is the fish?"

"Estimate two thousand yards and closing."

"Listen out for any sign that she's flooding her tubes. The bastard might be thinking of taking a crack back at us."

"No trace of her doing so, sir. She's slowing slightly. Thirty-five knots. Target now five thousand yards off our starboard side. Torpedo is still locked on and armed, fifteen hundred yards, still closing."

"Can't keep her speed up," said Greene at Hayes's shoulder. "That's something at least."

"Damned if I can figure out her game," Hayes responded. "If she's not flooding her tubes, why head for us? She's far too deep to be thinking of ramming us. Sonar, any change?"

"Yes, sir. She's slowed again. Down to thirty knots now. Torpedo's just a thousand yards behind her." Garcia paused, reading off the data.

"Target speed dropped again. Twenty-eight knots. Torpedo closing fast... seven hundred yards. What the hell's she playing at? It's almost as if she's inviting the fish to hit her. Target now three thousand yards off our starboard side, still at eight hundred feet.

"Torpedo now at three-fifty yards. Almost simultaneous signal... wait! Captain, she just stomped on the gas. Accelerating like hell! Back to thirty-five... Christ! *Forty*-five knots!"

"Impossible!" Greene shot Hayes a disbelieving look. "No submarine's capable of that. Who the hell *is* this?"

Garcia's voice tensed. "Hull-popping noise. She's coming up. Some other noise as well... sounds like hydraulics. She still hasn't flooded tubes. Coming up fast, real fast. Captain, she's at three hundred feet and *still* doing forty-five!"

"Jesus Christ, she'll fly at this rate!" Hayes said. "Ex-Oh, stand by to take evasive action."

Admiral Greene gasped out loud. Hayes stared, spellbound, as scarcely a mile away the sea exploded upward into the twilight. A sleek black shape, streaming white water, rocketed up through the immense burst of spray, its sharp nose angled steeply at the sky. Beneath it, a pale track streaked through and faltered as the soaring spindle began to fall back, almost in slow motion, to bellyflop in a stupendous eruption of foam. The torpedo track straightened as its sensors picked up the beat of the *Appalachian's* own engines and, the same time, the thunderclap of the submarine's impact with the water stung Hayes's ears.

"Oh, my God!" he said hoarsely. "She's turned our own torpedo back onto us. Helm, full left rudder—do it now! Give me flank speed!" In the same breath, he turned to the intercom. "Weapons, hit the torpedo's self-destruct!"

"There's no response, sir."

Beside him, the admiral muttered quietly, "Holy Mother of God!"

Almost mesmerized by the torpedo's fast approaching track, Hayes tried one desperate last gamble. "Weapons, turn the Gatling on that fish!" *And for Heaven's sake, don't miss!*

The 20-millimetre Mark 15 Gatling's staccato clatter filled the air as its bullets stitched the water ahead of the closing torpedo. Hayes felt his fingers gripping the rail like a vice. At quarter charge, the fish would only cause superficial damage to the double hull of a submarine. The

Appalachian's paper-thin plating was a different proposition altogether. He could see his career going down in tatters… the Navy captain who sank his own ship….

Just two hundred yards away, the sea fountained massively. The *crump!* of the explosion was ear-splitting, its blast wave heeling the ship to port. Hayes, still braced, let his pent-up breath go in a long sigh of utter relief.

"Well done, gentlemen," he said into the handset, wiping sweat from his eyes. "Damn fine shooting. Sonar, where's the target?"

"Gone away, captain," Garcia replied, strangely using the English hunting term. "Heading zero-eight-zero at twenty knots and going deep. And I mean deep, sir. The signal's lousy. There's an inversion layer way down, but she's under it and I'm losing her. If you're ready for this, sir, I last logged her at five thousand feet."

Five thousand feet?

Randall Hayes stared out over the darkening ocean swell, his eyes glazed but picturing in his mind the dark enigmatic shape that had broached like a gigantic whale over the *Appalachian's* torpedo track. His mind's eye examined the featureless spindle. Even at first, he had seen nothing but a smooth shape on the surface. Then Greene had seen two small items of apparent superstructure. Garcia had heard hydraulics. Could it be that this sub had retractable components? Perhaps even including the diving planes… Hayes could not remember seeing any when she breached the surface.

A speed of forty-five knots, faster than even the quickest known submarines, the discontinued Russian *Alfa* Class nuclear-powered attack vessels, which had been capable of forty at a push. The capability of diving to five thousand feet, a good thousand feet deeper than any other ocean-going submarine could attain. Again, it had been the titanium-hulled *Alfas* that could dive the deepest.

Until now.

And—totally unheard of—a submarine that could repeatedly ram large ships without sustaining damage to herself, always assuming that she had been responsible for disabling the *Dogger Bank*. Her presence in the same waters was hardly coincidental.

My God, the Pentagon's going to love this!

Hayes thought on. Why in hell hadn't she retaliated? Why hadn't she fired off a torpedo in reply? She'd had every opportunity but hadn't even flooded her tubes. Instead, this uncanny renegade had used all her capabilities—and at considerable risk—to turn the *Appalachian's* torpedo back onto its originator. Hayes could make no sense of it.

He scanned the horizon in silent thought, taking in the lit-up silhouette of the stricken *Dogger Bank* three miles away, then gazed down into the dark, opaque waters of the Atlantic as though his eyes could penetrate their enigmatic depths. He felt suddenly cold.

Just what are we dealing with here? And, more to the point, who?

9

Falmouth
Cornwall, UK

It took a lot to render Barrington Hobbes speechless but the revelation of the hunter watch in his hand had done it. For two or three minutes he did nothing but stare at Karen and the watch in turn until he finally found his voice.

"But this can only mean that someone's found the wreck and been down to it," he breathed. "But who…?"

"And how?" Karen said. "Think of it. An operation like that would have to be massive."

"And expensive," Hobbes said. "Hugely expensive. The Ross Sea isn't exactly the Solent. It's remote, it's hostile and it's deep. Alan's watch could only have been retrieved by a deep-water submersible, one of those with remote controlled grab arms. They don't grow on trees and they certainly don't come cheap. Nor do the surface support vessels they need.

"In any case," he added after a moment's thought, "an expedition like that couldn't be kept quiet, but there's been not a squeak about it. It would have generated a lot of excitement in whatever port they embarked from. The Press would have latched on to that straightaway, but there's nothing. Someone must have gone to a heap of trouble to keep it all under wraps, but why would anyone want to do that? In any case, who could have had the financial and practical means to pull it off?"

"The only person who springs to mind," Karen said, "is Sir Robert Maynard, the guy who runs Deep Watch. He has money coming out of his ears but I know for certain that he's campaigned for months to persuade the government to fund and organize a salvage and an investigation. So far, without success. That rules him out. What's more, I've also found that every submersible in the world that could do the job have been tied up on other projects. None have been available for at least a year."

"Then I can't see how it was done," Hobbes frowned.

"Alan's watch wasn't all that was in the package," Karen said. "What do you make of this?" She handed him a photograph, in full colour and evidently a computer print out from a digital camera.

The picture was crystal clear, even though it had been taken underwater. The camera had, it seemed, been aided by powerful lighting that revealed a dozen or so heavy looking drums. Some of these lay on their sides, others stood at crazy angles, but all were partially embedded in the soft ooze of the ocean floor. More than a few were badly dented and a wispy dark cloud was seeping through the cracked seal of the nearest canister. On its side was a symbol, an underlined triangle with thick blue sides, the left side being separated from the baseline by a narrow gap.

At the head of the photograph was a brief printed heading: *Great Sole Bank. Toxic chemical waste. 12. 12. 2014.*

Hobbes put the picture down, went to his study and returned with a folded Admiralty chart of the Western Approaches. He spread it out on a table and located the Great Sole Bank 220 miles west-south-west of Land's End, close to the brink of the Continental Shelf. The chart soundings showed that a general depth of some eighty fathoms ran westward from the Scillonian batholith all the way to the Bank which had thirty-five fathoms of water over it. Further to the west, the ocean floor fell steadily to the precipitous continental slope, beyond which lay the Biscay Abyssal Plain at a mean depth of 2,500 fathoms.

He studied the photograph again, pursing his lips thoughtfully, and wondered how the picture had been taken. Thirty-five fathoms, in open ocean, would mean another substantial diving operation with hard suits or submersibles except, as Karen had already pointed out, no submersibles were available. Again, there had been no word of any such operation and Falmouth, with its deep harbour and ready facilities, would have been an obvious base.

Both the photograph and Alan Tregenza's watch testified to the inescapable fact that deep diving operations had been carried out on opposite sides of the globe and, as both items had been packaged together, by the same people.

Hobbes's puzzlement deepened. What was the implied link between the watch from the depths of the Ross Sea and the leaking canisters out on the Great Sole Bank? Not to mention a thought he didn't dare voice in present company—who the hell could have known that a presentation watch to one Holman George was Tregenza's good luck charm, or the connection between Tregenza and Karen Marshall?

It was a rare thing for Barrington Hobbes to be utterly baffled but this had him completely stumped. He started to feel the old excitement of his journalistic days flooding back and he realized, with a rush of pleasure, that the old appetite for getting his teeth into mysteries had not deserted him after all.

The girl spoke as he looked up. "Whoever's behind this must have known my connection with Alan," she was saying, echoing his own thoughts. "They also knew that I was a journalist who might have the means—and certainly the motive—to dig deeper. The watch, the photographs… they're clues of some kind, if only I knew what they're clues to.

"Mr Hobbes, my own experience is pretty limited. Yours, on the other hand, is vast. And you were Alan's friend for a good number of years. Will you help me?"

Barrington Hobbes was no longer listening. There was a strangely haunted expression on his moon face as he again studied the picture of the dumped canisters. Again, he crossed to his study and drew out the photos he had taken of the crippled *Margarita Sanchez* in her Falmouth dry dock scarcely a mile away. Wordlessly, he shuffled through them, stopped and examined a print through a magnifying lens.

Taken through a powerful zoom, the picture clearly showed the vessel's cargo neatly stacked on the dockside. Among crates and containers were pallets of drums stacked three-high. He brought his eye closer to the lens. There it was, printed on the sides of the drums. The very same symbol.

Hobbes's head began to swim, his mind desperate to push back against the flood of appalling memories forcing their way to the surface, whirling him back ten years to a car, a motorway and three lunatic lorries. Little Rebecca asleep in the back. Paula's frightened voice….

Barrie, what are they doing? They're crazy! Oh, God, he's swerving at us! No! Barrie! BARRIE!

The awful shuddering impact as the truck sideswiped him. The eldritch screech of rending metal and shredding tyres. Two registration plates, as clear to him now as they had been then. A terrible, mind-rending scream of terror and then, before the final darkness....

Hobbes had never consciously recalled the symbol painted on the door of the lorry's cab and yet, somehow, it had remained ingrained in the deepest recesses of his memory. Great God almighty... the triangle... *the same bloody blue triangle!*

The ghosts began to swirl away into the mists as he became aware that Karen was there, still speaking to him. "Mr Hobbes, if you need time to think it over, I'll understand."

Hobbes looked past her, his eyes prickling with tears, to the framed photograph on his desk. The faces of a woman still young and a little girl just five years old. Their heads close together, both smiled lovingly into the room. In the same instant, Hobbes pictured to himself the nightmare image of a broken ship foundering in the freezing, lonely waters of the Antarctic and the quick, ready grin of Alan Tregenza.

"Call me Barrie," he whispered thickly. "Alan always did. That is, if we're to work as a team."

"You'll do it?" Karen could hardly believe it.

Beyond all hope, he thought. *A second chance. This time...*

"This time," he said, determination edging his words, "we'll tighten the screws until the pips squeak."

Chapter 3

Antique Gold

⤛ 10 ⤜

3 January 2015
Whitehall,
London, UK

Leaden skies over London threatened snow as the dark grey Jaguar XJ-S swung into the underground car park off a quiet Whitehall street. The driver, its only occupant, was pleased to note that the stonework of the vast Victorian building above the car park had been sandblasted clean of its accumulated grime. Now it seemed to gleam against the ominous blanket of dark cloud that loomed over the city.

Stopping at the lowered and, he knew, reinforced barrier arm, he showed his identity pass to the discreetly armed guard and, as the barrier raised, drove through to a half-empty parking area and selected a space close to the lift doors.

An inch over six feet and built like an athlete, Commander Donall McEwan Lindsay RN was now thirty-eight years old. His brown eyes were, through professional habit, watchful and his thick dark hair was worn a little longer than naval regulation length, a concession to the specialist nature of his work. Lindsay had graduated from Dartmouth Royal Naval College back in 1997 and entered straight into the Submarine Service. In 2002, during the invasion of Iraq, Lindsay had played a part in a covert mission landed from *HMS Seawolf* which, as circumstances dictated, called for him to participate to a degree that was somewhat above the call of duty and well beyond his training. The episode remained within classified archives, but the fact that Lindsay had performed so well and with such clear thought in an unaccustomed role brought him an immediate approach from the Department of Royal Naval Intelligence. For three years he resisted persuasion, preferring to serve in "Her Majesty's Sardines", until finally a personal approach from the Department's head, Admiral James Garvie, changed his career for good.

Lindsay entered the lift, nodded a greeting to the ever-present attendant and noted, for the thousandth time, the barely discernable bulge under the left armpit of the man's jacket. He stepped out on the building's fifth floor and into a secretarial concourse, where a man ten years older than himself broke off a conversation with a typist, came over and shook Lindsay's hand warmly. Like Lindsay, Michael Rochester, the Department's Chief of Staff, was a serving officer, with the rank of Captain.

"You're looking fit, Don," he greeted, appraising Lindsay's lean appearance and putting it down to the gruelling Special Forces training schedule that Naval Intelligence field operatives were required to attend at regular intervals. "I imagine they've put you through it a bit at Hereford."

"Never really got the chance to find out," Lindsay's voice held just the trace of a Highland accent. "I'd only been there forty-eight hours before getting the recall signal. It was still long enough to find out that their new combat instructor's got a mean streak. I have the bruises to prove it." He gave Rochester a grim smile. "On the other hand, so has he. What made it worse was that I had to go and miss Hogmanay." He cocked an eye towards the ceiling. "So, what's the urgency on the sixth floor that forces me away from such wonderful hospitality?"

"You may as well go on up and find out for yourself. Everyone got here early, so they'll be ready for you."

"Everyone?" Lindsay had expected the usual one-to-one briefing from his chief.

"Exalted company, my boy. It seems you're the chosen one of the gods. The boss has a senior Treasury bod with him and the Minister of Defence himself."

"Sir Henry Williamson? It must be quite a matter if he's here." Lindsay glanced down at his own dark, well-cut suit. "You make it sound more like a dress uniform job. Whatever, I'd better get myself up there. Maybe I'll see you for a drink later, Mike."

Rochester shot him an ironic glance. "If you get the chance."

Lindsay took the stairs and entered a small reception office. Its single occupant, a pleasant faced redhead, gave him a warm smile and pressed the button on her old-fashioned desktop intercom.

"Commander Lindsay's here, sir."

"Very good," the intercom speaker rasped. "Wheel him in, would you, Maureen."

Lindsay rolled his eyes. "'Wheel him in.' God, how I hate that expression."

"If you'd have done your full stint at Hereford," Maureen Strangways said mischievously, "we might be wheeling you in in a literal sense."

"Don't you start. I may yet recommend the entire secretarial staff to be sent for a week or so at the same friendly holiday camp with the very same smiling redcoats. See how you like it," he shot back as he knocked on the oak-panelled door.

He entered the room to meet the familiar gun-barrel gaze of his department's director, Admiral James Garvie.

"Sit down, Commander. I believe you know Sir Henry Williamson." Lindsay returned the elderly minister's nod of greeting while Garvie introduced the slight, mousy-haired man on Williamson's left. "This is Neville Franklin, a senior official at the Treasury."

The little man half-rose from his seat and offered his hand. Lindsay took it and was mildly surprised by the firm strength of Franklin's handshake. The man gave the outward appearance of a Treasury stereotype, a numbers nerd, physically lacking but mentally buzzing with figures and statistics. The sort of man who stuck to precise movements, precise routines and precise suits. The strength of Franklin's handshake rather put the lie to this, but Lindsay wasn't to know that the little man spent much of his spare time tackling severe-grade rock faces in Snowdonia and on the sea cliffs of Cornwall. Lindsay sat back, switching his gaze to the strong lines of his chief's face.

"I'll come straight to the point, Commander." Garvie's gaze was matched by his habit of shooting words out like bullets. "The matter in hand centres on the recent attacks upon shipping in the North Atlantic. You're doubtless aware of these incidents." The admiral didn't wait for confirmation. "The Minister of Defence and the Prime Minister have authorized an investigation and Sir Henry has specifically asked that the task be assigned to you. Something to do with your record in recent years. Minister?"

Sir Henry Williamson looked at Lindsay over half-moon spectacles set halfway down his narrow nose. "If you'll bear with me, Commander, I'll briefly run through the list of incidents thus far," he said, fishing a sheet of A4 paper out of his briefcase. "You'll find the same information in the file on the desk in front of you. Feel free to make any notes or ask any questions that may arise.

"Now, it would appear that there were events prior to the more recent ones in the Northern Atlantic. Between March and June last year, a number of curious sightings were reported along a more-or-less westward course between Tasmania and Cape Town. These may or may not be linked with what happened thereafter.

"On the 8th of June, during a confrontation with Greenpeace activists off St Helena, a Japanese whale-catcher—the *Izu-shoto*—suffered severe and sudden damage to her steering gear. The Greenpeace people were not responsible for this and, in fact, shot some rather indistinct video footage showing a massive disturbance in the water and what are purported to be two simultaneous spouts of water reaching more than a hundred feet high. I might add that the whaler's rudder was completely torn off during this episode.

"The next few months were fairly uneventful, apart from an isolated and rather similar attack upon a Norwegian whaler south of the Cape Verde Islands on the 29th of June. Then, in September, the attacks resumed in earnest, extending to freight vessels as well as whaling ships. The area of operation was the North Atlantic."

Williamson paused to adjust his spectacles. "On the 15th of September, the bulk carrier *Daniel Gainsborough* was disabled and, on the 26th, the freighter *Marco* was similarly damaged. Two whalers were attacked on the 13th of October and another on the 24th. The French freighter *Abbeville* suffered an attack on the night of the 5th of November and then, a week later, a Norwegian whaling vessel, the *Christiansen*, was rammed a hundred miles south of the Faeroes. On December the 6th, it was the turn of another bulk carrier, the *Lady Jane Grey* and, on the 16th, yet another bulk carrier, the *Margarita Sanchez*. A fourth bulk carrier, the *Dogger Bank*, was the latest victim just two days before Christmas.

"In most cases, the assailant was neither seen nor identified and, thankfully, none of these attacks have resulted in any loss of life. In fact, I believe that the only human casualty thus far has been a seaman on the *Izushoto*, who suffered two cracked ribs after the impact threw him across the engine room."

At this point, Admiral Garvie took over the briefing. "Three common factors can be noted, Commander. Since September, these incidents have been confined to an area of the North Atlantic west of a line drawn between Cape Clear and Finisterre and running out into the Atlantic for roughly a thousand miles. The northern and southern limits have been the latitudes of the Faeroes and the Azores.

"The second common denominator is the fact that no one has yet had a clear view of the assailant and, therefore, we still have no idea who or what is responsible.

" Thirdly, the method of attack. There would seem to be a deliberate intention to disable these vessels, not to sink them. In every case so far, the damage has been confined to the rudder and screws."

"In other words, sir, extremely selective and precise," Lindsay offered. "For me, that rules out collisions with wild life. I've seen the usual tabloid hysteria and, to be honest, I can't buy the giant whale theory. To begin with, cetaceans rarely, if ever, launch deliberate attacks on ships and even if one did, it would have to possess a skull of solid granite to take the rudders off bulk carriers. The animal would certainly kill itself in the attempt.

"What intrigues me," Lindsay held up a page from the file, "is this report from the *Abbeville* night attack. According to her captain, a bright light suddenly appeared in the water a mile or so away. This was stationary for a while, then moved at quite a rate. At one point, or so it says here, while the ship itself was doing seventeen knots, the light actually circled it at a speed described as 'incredible'. Then it went out and the impact occurred.

"Natural phosphorescence does occur at sea but it is never bright. Nor does it move, at any speed. Whales don't tend to be phosphorescent unless they've swum through the stuff. Taken at face value, this report can't be easily explained. However, given the apparent nature of this light, and the precision of these attacks, I can only assume a human hand behind it."

"I believe that Sir Henry's list can be added to," Garvie said. "The early reports the minister mentioned were filed by small time fishermen, coastal natives and so on. The sort of people whose word is all too easily dismissed by officialdom. It's this recent publicity that has caused them to re-examine their files and, over the last few weeks, I have received a thoroughly absorbing list of incidents.

"Chronologically, it runs like this. On the 9th of March last year, a whale of unnatural size was sighted south of Tasmania then, on the morning of the 26th, what was thought to be a similarly huge whale sank a boatload of pirates in the Sunda Straits. Krakatau, to be precise. This pirate vessel was in the act of launching an armed raid on a civilian yacht and, in this case, the sinking resulted in the deaths of ten Malaysian pirates.

"The next sightings are reminiscent of the *Abbeville* affair. On the Indian coast, the inhabitants of a small fishing village near Calcutta got excited about a large moving light in the water. That was on the 28th of April. A similar light was observed off the Somali coast on the 10th of May and then, just two days before the incident between Greenpeace and the Japanese whale-catcher south of St Helena, another sighting of an impossibly large whale was reported off the Cape of Good Hope.

"All these sightings and incidents, if one can stretch to assuming that they involve a single object, follow a definite path from perhaps the southern Pacific, into the Indian Ocean, then around the Cape into the South Atlantic and, finally, onto our doorstep where it seems to have set up shop on a more permanent basis.

"Now, the Tasmania sighting came just fifteen days after the Deep Watch vessel *Aurora* was lost with all hands in the northern Ross Sea, to the south of that position. The director of Deep Watch, Sir Robert Maynard, seems convinced that our mystery assailant was responsible for the loss of his ship and one has to take that possibility into serious account."

Garvie looked up from his papers. "Gentlemen, I accept that the Atlantic incidents have resulted in no loss of life and only one minor injury. Nevertheless, the *Aurora* and Krakatau episodes serve to suggest that this thing may indeed be a killer." He glanced at Lindsay. "You have a point to make, Commander?"

"I was just thinking, sir, that one category of targets has been whaling vessels. As I understand it, the *Aurora* was on an anti-whaling mission. What would be the motive for sinking her?"

"Sir Robert provided a possible answer to that," Williamson said. "The *Aurora* was a converted Hull trawler. At night, or in poor visibility, her lines may have been mistaken for those of a whale-catcher. Why she was sunk instead of being merely disabled like the others is a riddle we can't answer, unless it was an attempt to cripple her that went wrong."

"Do we have any leads at all?" Lindsay asked.

Garvie leaned forward. "As a matter of fact, we do. During the most recent incident, the US frigate *Appalachian* went to the *Dogger Bank's* aid and encountered a highly unusual vessel in the vicinity. The Americans have supplied us with the few details that emerged from the encounter, and you'll be briefed on them later, Commander. For now, I want to bring in Mr Franklin. He has a problem that might seem very different. I'll leave you to consider whether it's related or not."

The Treasury man opened a briefcase and used both hands to draw out a heavy, cloth-wrapped bundle. He laid it carefully on the desktop before unwrapping it to reveal a gleaming bar of solid gold. The little man blinked and cleared his throat delicately.

"A recent development has been giving rise to considerable concern among the world's treasuries, particularly the United States Federal Gold Reserve which does tend to be the first to fret about this sort of thing.

"Over the last ten months a number of these bars have appeared in circulation, or have been seized by the authorities. Most of them emanated from black market sources. In all, fourteen have turned up in various parts of the world and the worry is that someone may be out to flood the market. Commander, would you please examine the bar."

Lindsay picked it up, appreciative of its considerable weight.

"That is what we call a Good Delivery Bar," Franklin told him. "It weighs ten point five kilograms or, in plain old English, twenty-three point five pounds Troy weight. It is remarkably pure. To be acceptable, these bars must conform to a minimum fineness of 995 parts per thousand. This bar has a fineness of 998."

"What sort of value am I holding here?" Lindsay asked him.

"In round terms and at current rates, about one hundred thousand pounds Sterling."

Lindsay laid the heavy bar in his lap. "Exactly where did these turn up and when?"

Franklin donned a pair of reading glasses and consulted a typed sheet. "The first two appeared in Melbourne at the end of March last year, two more in Singapore during April and a further two in Calcutta at the end of the same month. Then, on the 11th of May, there was a most curious incident.

"Staff at the International Red Cross headquarters in Mogadishu found they'd been broken into during the night. Nothing had been taken, nothing damaged apart from a deadlock. Instead, the director found two of these gold bars on his desk with a note that simply said: *For the children of Somalia*. The note was signed with a simple initial *N*.

"On the 4th of June, in Cape Town, the South African police succeeded in breaking a major operation in illicit gold and diamond trading. They recovered three of these bars that had been sold privately to the dealer three days previously. The vendor was followed to the dockland area where he disappeared.

"Another gold bar turned up in Rio at the end of June, a further one in Dublin during October and the last one in Cardiff only three weeks ago."

Lindsay was noting the information with quick strokes of a pen. "What makes you think that each of these bars is connected?" he said. "I understood that gold was untraceable."

Franklin gave him a thin smile. "Would you turn the bar over, Commander."

Lindsay complied as the Treasury man continued. "Throughout history, it has been the practice for such bars to be stamped by the originator. As you can see, these are no exception."

Lindsay examined the bar and the curious stamp impressed into its face. "Good God," he exclaimed. "It's an antique. Spanish, three hundred years old."

Franklin nodded. "Exactly, and all fourteen bars bear the very same stamp, that of Philip V of Spain and each dated 1702. Now, in 1868, a quantity of these bars turned up in Crete during the Candiote Insurrection. No one knows how they got there but no others have ever been recorded in circulation. Having said that, others certainly exist. Hundreds, if not thousands, of them. You see, Commander, I know the provenance and history of this gold and, if you'll bear with me, I think you might find it an absorbing story…."

Lindsay had to admit to himself that, for a second time, he had misjudged the little man. Far from listening to the narrative of a financial dullard, he found himself hanging onto the Treasury man's every word.

"You missed your vocation, Mr Franklin," he remarked. "You'd have made one hell of a history teacher."

Franklin positively beamed. "Considered it once," he admitted. "I took a First Class Honours degree in history at Balliol. I decided against a career in education after comparing its salaries to those of civil service."

Lindsay inclined his head sympathetically. "So teaching's loss is the Treasury's gain. You're certain that no one is known to have recovered this gold from its resting place?"

"Not as far as anyone knows and, after all, to do so would be a major undertaking. The 19th century appearance of it in Crete, and these present finds are complete mysteries. There have been many schemes planned for recovering the gold. The Spanish government itself has considered it on more than one occasion but nothing ever came of it. Until now, it's been assumed that the gold is still there."

"Thank you, Mr Franklin," Garvie said. "Any observations, Commander?"

"I can see what it is you're driving at, sir. These sightings and incidents at sea, and the appearances of this gold share very similar dates and locations. I might almost say too similar. Put quite simply, your antique gold and our ship-crippling whale seem to be travelling hand-in-hand around the world."

11

Fleet Street
London, UK

Unlike most of its competitors, the offices of *The Sentinel* newspaper had remained in Fleet Street, expanding into adjoining premises vacated by its rivals. Founded in 1832, this newspaper was one of the few to remain fiercely independent of political bias or affiliation, a tradition appreciated by a high proportion of the news-reading public who set a great deal of store by *The Sentinel's* honest, factual and in-depth method of reporting. It was also the newspaper that had once, for an eight-year period, been graced by the investigative reports of Barrington Hobbes.

In spite of the increased space and introduction of new technology, there was still much around him that was familiar to Hobbes, not least the frosted glass door through which he and Karen Marshall were being guided by the editor's secretary. The only difference here was that the legendary name of Alexander Porteous, *The Sentinel's* editor throughout Hobbes's years with the paper, had been replaced with that of Anthony Saunders.

The genuine nature of Saunders's smile of pleasure was unmistakable as he rose from his chair. A tall, big-shouldered man with a shock of sandy hair, he rounded his desk to grasp and pump Hobbes's hand vigorously.

"Barrie, by all that's wonderful! You look good. My God, has it really been ten years?"

"Long enough for you to rise from staff hack to editor," Hobbes grinned back. "You've done well for yourself, Tony."

"I can't complain, but Alex Porteous is a tough act to follow."

Hobbes introduced Karen to him. "Karen's a freelance reporter down in the Westcountry," he said. "But, more to the point, she was engaged to Alan Tregenza, the mate on the *Aurora*."

"The Deep Watch ship? The one lost in the Antarctic last February?"

"The very one," Hobbes said. "Look, Tony, we've turned up something that relates to the loss of the *Aurora*. We also believe that there's some link with this current wave of attacks on shipping out in the Atlantic."

Saunders gave Hobbes a long look before returning to his chair and inviting them both to be seated. "Are you trying to tell me that, after ten years of exile in darkest Cornwall, we're about to witness the comeback of Barrington Hobbes?" He laughed out loud. "Are the ungodly again about to sleep less soundly in their beds? Why, Barrie? What's persuaded you to poke your head over the battlements again?"

"Tregenza wasn't only Karen's fiancé," Hobbes told him. "He was also a very good friend of mine. You might recall that my home town, Falmouth, was the *Aurora's* home port, so, through Alan, I also knew her skipper, Seán McKenna. Tony, it's been the best part of a year since she was lost. Her sinking was never explained and it's high time that it was."

"I appreciate that, Barrie." Saunders switched his gaze to Karen. "I don't mean to be insensitive, Miss Marshall, but the story's run its course. It's worn out. Lack of evidence just turned the story into trivia and wild speculation. There's nowhere else for it to go."

"I don't agree," Hobbes said firmly. "Not one iota. Some evidence *has* come to light, enough to convince me that someone's mounted a clandestine operation on the wreck. You know me, Tony—that I take nothing lightly, that I grasp at tree trunks, not straws. What I'm telling you is real and there's also enough to suggest some kind of link between the *Aurora*, these incidents in the Atlantic and with my own past."

Saunders looked at each of them in turn. "All right, Barrie, I'll accept that from you but both of you have a personal involvement in this. Ask yourself if that's a good thing. Heaven knows, the loss of a loved one or a good friend is bad enough but will it hinder you from giving an objective view?"

"It'll give us all the incentive we need," Hobbes answered. "It's my belief that only this sort of personal involvement is going to crack the story open. It's going to be dangerous country, Tony, and I'll tell you why quite bluntly. Whoever's at the bottom of this ended my career and, effectively my life, until now. These are the same people who killed my wife and child." He fixed the editor with a gaze of such intensity that Saunders almost shrank back. "Would you call that incentive enough?"

The editor rose from his chair and turned to stare blankly from the window at the roofscape of London. Behind him, Karen made a move to speak but Hobbes halted her with a gesture that clearly asked her to give the man time to think.

Eventually, Saunders returned to his seat. "Barrie, you were a legend. No investigative hack of your time or since could hold a candle to you. You had a solid reputation for integrity, honest reporting and a resolve that no one could ever match. A man like you doesn't change his basic character, not even when his own world caves in.

"Neither *The Sentinel* nor any other newspaper has come anywhere near to unravelling any of these cases—the *Aurora*, what's happening at sea right now, or what happened to you ten years ago. Now you come to me, claiming that you have a key to unlocking all three." He drew a deep breath. "All right, Barrie, I'll go for it. But are you sure you're physically fit enough?"

"I'm not quite the man I was," Hobbes admitted. "The legs don't function as well as they once did but I can assure you that my brain's intact. Now, Karen here is young, fit and a promising journalist, too, so—for once—I go for teamwork. Karen's legwork, my experience."

Saunders threw up his hands in a gesture of defeat. "Okay, Barrie, I've heard enough. If you, of all people, say you have a lead on these mysteries, then who am I to dispute it? If I missed an opportunity like this, the owners would have my guts. Even ten years on, your name will double this paper's circulation overnight.

"If you both agree to work exclusively for *The Sentinel* on a freelance basis, I'm willing to offer all the finances and facilities you need. However, there is a complication.

"I already have a staff reporter assigned to the shipping incidents and I'm going to want him on your team. His name's Ian Neale, you may have seen his work. He's been with us for four years and I'll warn you that he's young, ambitious and just a bit brash. That aside, he's got real promise and I think he can go far, especially if he has someone like you to learn from. For you to accept him onto your team is my one and only condition."

"If Neale's as brash as you say," Hobbes said, "is he going to be willing to work with us?"

"He'll do as he's told," Saunders said firmly. "If he kicks against it, then he's a bigger bloody fool than I've taken him for. Don't worry, even if he doesn't like it, he'll do it." The editor leant back in his chair and let out a laugh.

"My God, the return of Barrington Hobbes. It's the biggest thing since the return of Sherlock Holmes! I can almost see my competitors quaking in their Savile Row suits!"

12

Whitehall
London, UK

The panelled door of Admiral Garvie's office closed behind Neville Franklin as the Treasury man was ushered out behind the Minister of Defence. Garvie waited for a moment before turning his gaze back to Lindsay.

"You latched onto that pretty quickly, Commander," he said. "There is, as you say, an undeniable correlation between these sightings and incidents at sea, their dates and locations, and Franklin's gold. Any thoughts about what that connection could be?"

"Too early to tell, sir. At the moment, I'm more interested in the motive behind these current attacks. I could understand the whaling targets if the reason's an environmental one, but that wouldn't explain the assaults on merchantmen or, if Sir Robert Maynard is right in his concerns, the sinking of the *Aurora*, an environmental vessel. We need to know more. You mentioned an intelligence brief from the *Appalachian*. How much light does that shed on it?"

"A little but not enough to go on," Garvie told him. "For what it's worth, the *Appalachian* went to the aid of the latest victim, a bulk carrier, and had an unexpected run-in with what appeared to be an unidentifiable submarine. She challenged her, got no response and, with NATO's blessing, loosed off a reduced charge torpedo.

"The sub pulled off some neat—if unusual—evasive manoeuvres and actually succeeded in fooling the torpedo into homing in on its own originator. Only some first class gunnery by the *Appalachian's* crew prevented her from sustaining severe—not to say embarrassing—damage.

"This submarine's performance data takes quite a bit of swallowing." The admiral tossed a thin dossier across the desk. "It's all in this report by Admiral Walter Greene who was aboard the *Appalachian* when this happened. Take your time, Commander."

Lindsay took a few moments to scan the document and let out a low whistle. "This can't be right, sir. Forty-five knots? A last reported depth of five thousand feet? I can't accept it, the submarine that's capable of either has yet to be built."

"Those were my thoughts, too," Garvie agreed. "But I know Walter Greene. He's a very shrewd and accurate observer."

"He says here that the sub had no conning tower but possibly a pair of small deck structures that may or may not be retractable. It's unheard of. If anyone had developed a new design of sub, it could never have slipped through the intelligence net." He studied the document again. "I might have missed any assessment of how she's powered."

"It is there and it's equally curious," Garvie told him. "She's not nuclear. The *Appalachian's* sensors detected none of the characteristics that give away a nuclear powered engine. In fact, she's extremely quiet which will pose a considerable problem if we ever hope to locate her."

Lindsay's brows drew together. "That only leaves conventional power. A diesel-electric job. I know of no such engine that can come anywhere near to producing the speed and acceleration rates given here. And another thing, sir. If the *Appalachian* fired on her, why didn't she fire back? Greene says here that she never even flooded her tubes."

"No one else can figure that out, either," Garvie agreed. "In fact, in none of these attacks have torpedoes been used. In every case, the damage seems to have been caused by ramming."

Lindsay's expression turned to one of complete incredulity. "Ramming? I'm sorry, admiral, but I can't accept that. Not for a minute. For any submarine, that's suicidal. One ramming of a steel ship would cave her nose right in and send her straight to the bottom. For any craft to clatter as many ships as this one is supposed to have done just isn't possible. There has to be another explanation."

"Another riddle for you to solve, Commander," Garvie said. "It's your job to get to the bottom of these incidents, effective immediately. Any thoughts on what your first move might be?"

"I'll need to find out more about the damaged vessels," Lindsay answered. "See if I can find any common factor that would explain the motive behind it. According to Admiral Greene, the *Dogger Bank* was towed into Lisbon but the previous victim, the *Margarita Sanchez*, is presently in dry dock at Falmouth. She might be worth an inspection."

The admiral placed the palms of his hands on the desk and leaned forward in his chair. "Very well, Commander, carry on. Contact the Chief of Staff for anything you might need and, if you do come up with anything at Falmouth, use the secure line from the intelligence office at Culdrose. We'll let our man there know you're about."

The admiral's eyes bored into Lindsay's. "Keep in mind that this department is under considerable pressure, political and commercial, to get this issue wrapped up quickly and efficiently. I wish you good hunting, Commander."

13

4 January 2015
Whitefriars Street
London, UK

The convivial surroundings of the King William IV Inn and the golden pint of Worthington bitter in front of him did little to suppress Ian Neale's ill-concealed hostility. Karen felt distinctly uncomfortable in his company but silently marvelled at the patience of Barrington Hobbes who seemed content to sit back and let the man sound off.

"It's under protest," Neale was saying, "and you should know that right from the outset. Personally, I haven't a clue what Tony Saunders thinks he's playing at, letting two complete strangers muscle in on my story and insisting that I work with them. I prefer to work alone. I get results that way, which he knows perfectly well. Damn it all, I'm a staff reporter. I don't see why I should have to put up with impositions like this.

"Look at you," he glared at Hobbes. "You're yesterday's man. Brilliant in your time, I'll grant you, but your time was ten years ago, not now. You can't turn back the clock just like that."

Hobbes gazed benignly at the angry journalist and calmly supped his Guinness. Neale was barely thirty, a short, squarely built man with fair hair that flopped over his temples and a short goatee beard that looked completely out of place on him. His green eyes blazed as he kept on at the older man.

"These incidents at sea have been my preserve ever since they began and that's precisely how I want it to continue. You have no right to come barging in like this, no right at all." He checked back a little, glancing at Karen. "Of course, Miss Marshall, I realize that your fiancé was lost on the *Aurora* and it's not my intention to upset you by decrying your right to get at the truth. But look at it from my point of view. I've been a staff reporter on *The Sentinel* for four years now and I've been on these sea stories ever since the *Aurora* was lost.

"Suddenly I'm asked—no, *told*—to team up with a freelance provincial hack who's been tucked away in the sticks reporting village fêtes, and a man who's been retired from the game for a decade. It insults my professionalism that my own editor sees fit to let you just come in and poach on my ground."

Hobbes spoke quietly as Karen inwardly seethed at Neale's cutting and tactless remarks. "Ian, I've seen your material. Its quality should give no one any reason to doubt your professional competence and, before you say it, I patronize no man. Tony Saunders is well aware of your abilities and if you have any doubt in his belief in you, you should put it out of your head right now. You are an accomplished reporter but reporting is exactly that, the art of providing informative accounts of particular events. You do that better than most, in my opinion, but this subject needs more. It needs investigative journalism. Now, how much of that have you done?"

"Not much, to be honest, but enough to know that all the damaged merchant ships were attacked on their outward journeys," Neale said. "In each case, they left a British or European port. Beyond that, there is little else that's significant. The ships in question are owned by a variety of companies and most of them sail under flags of convenience. That's hardly unusual these days.

"I've even checked their cargo manifests and there's nothing that stands out as remarkable. As for whoever or whatever is carrying out the attacks, no one has seen anything like enough to draw any real conclusions. Nobody's yet claimed responsibility and, to make life even more difficult, we're now getting typical sea stories. Funny lights zipping about in the water, that sort of garbage."

"What about the *Aurora's* sinking?" Hobbes asked him. "Have you turned anything up on that?"

"Nothing," Neale said. "Except that Sir Robert Maynard's been making the Prime Minister's life intolerable with his repeated demands for a full investigation. Christ, he even wants the wreck found and brought up. There just isn't anything further to know about the *Aurora*, and I doubt that even you could do any better."

"Well, that's just the point," Hobbes said mildly. "We have turned something up and I can tell you right now that Maynard's too late."

Neale blinked at him. At Hobbes's nod, Karen produced the hunter watch and handed it to Neale.

"Who's Holman George?" the journalist said after examining the watch.

"Alan Tregenza's maternal grandfather," Hobbes told him. "Alan regarded it as a lucky mascot. He never went anywhere without it, including his sea voyages."

Neale's mouth opened as he realized the implications of what Hobbes was saying.

"Unbeknown to you or me or, it seems, anyone else, the wreck of the *Aurora* had already been found," Hobbes went on. "Someone has mounted, financed and equipped an operation to reach the wreck. Not only that, they've gone to extraordinary lengths to keep the whole thing secret. Why it's secret, how the hell it was achieved and by whom are the questions we need to answer."

Neale was silent for a moment, knocked out of his stride by the revelation. When he spoke again, all trace of his annoyance has vanished.

"There's something else," he said. "Another puzzle. Since the *Aurora* went down, there have been all sorts of weird sightings and incidents at sea, along a path that goes halfway round the world. Now, what I'm about to tell you was leaked out to me by a source in Westminster. You never heard it from me and I'd be grateful if you never heard it at all, if you understand me.

Noting the nods of agreement, he went on. "Gold ingots have been turning up in ports along the same route and on dates that broadly parallel the individual sightings. These ingots are identical and each is a museum piece. Every single bar has a stamp dated 1702 and bearing the arms of King Philip V of Spain. No one seems to have a clue where they came from."

"Good grief." It was Hobbes's turn to register surprise. "Yet more bloody mysteries."

"Well, if it's mysteries you like," Neale said. "Here's another one for you." He held out Alan Tregenza's hunter watch. "While we've been talking, I've been fiddling with the winder on this. Maybe you can explain why, if this watch has been two miles down in the Ross Sea for months on end, it's still working."

14

Falmouth
Cornwall, UK

A low winter sun cast a yellowish light over the glittering waters of Falmouth harbour and a keen breeze rattled the halyards of the hundreds of yachts at their moorings, or drawn up on shore for the winter.

Don Lindsay leant his back against the Jaguar XJ-S, having parked high up on Castle Drive. This was a vantage point where the road, pavement and a lower viewing terrace stood on top of a sheer rock face above the docks. In summer, this stretch of road would be full of cars and people, but on a cold January afternoon it was totally deserted.

Directly below him, the *Margarita Sanchez* lay in the Queen Elizabeth dry dock, the largest of the four dry docks within the facility. He studied her through the viewfinder of his long-lensed camera, unaware that he was in precisely the same spot from which Barrington Hobbes had taken his photographs two weeks earlier.

The dockyard workforce had succeeded in detaching the bulk carrier's massive rudder which now lay discarded on the dockside. Lindsay was astonished by the amount of damage that had been inflicted on it. The rudder had been almost bent in half, crumpled by what could only have been a stupendous impact, the nature and cause of which he could not even begin to imagine.

He clicked off a series of photographs and turned his attention to the cargo that was in the process of being moved to an outside jetty. He let the camera dangle from the strap around his neck as he reached into the open car window for his copy of the local newspaper, the *Falmouth Packet*, unconcerned by the green Vauxhall Nova drawing up behind the Jaguar.

He flicked through the paper in search of the column that gave the week's shipping movements.

He quickly found what he was looking for. Repair works to the *Margarita Sanchez* would, according to the columnist, take several more weeks to complete. Her cargo was to be transferred to another bulk carrier, the *Noordzee Marquess*, due to dock on the coming morning. Lindsay tossed the paper back into the car, took another series of photographs and turned to leave.

A man stepped from the Nova and sauntered towards him. Lindsay nodded a polite greeting that was pointedly ignored. The man merely gestured at his camera.

"We don't welcome the paparazzi," he said gruffly. The fingers of an extended hand made a beckoning motion. "I'll have the camera, friend, and please don't try to make this difficult."

Lindsay's eyes narrowed imperceptibly, weighing him up. The man was not over-tall but big, built like a front row forward. His bulk would suggest to some that he was running to fat but Lindsay guessed that, in fact, he was running to a good deal of muscle. The white of the man's scalp showed through the close-cropped greying hair. Heavy facial features, particularly the shapeless nose and old scar tissue around the eyebrows, testified to him being no stranger to roughhouses. The voice, though, was educated and Lindsay's well-honed senses told him that this man was both dangerous and clever.

"And what gives you that sort of authority," he challenged. "Whose interests do you represent? And is this official or non-official?"

"None of your damn business," came the snapped answer. "I warned you not to make this difficult. Now, give." He took a step forward that was countered by Lindsay's immediate backward step that maintained the space between them.

"And if I choose to be difficult?" Lindsay enquired mildly.

"Then I'll take it from you." The big man made a sudden lunge, grabbing for the camera. Lindsay sidestepped, moving fast, and swung his left hand to connect with a vicious backhanded slap to the face. The other reeled back, gasping and half-blinded as his eyes watered. His jacket swung open and Lindsay glimpsed the automatic in his waistband in the instant his assailant's right hand made a move for it.

Again Lindsay moved swiftly, knocking the gun hand to one side with a powerful, tensed right forearm and smashing the heel of his left hand into the man's sternum. He felt something crack but it seemed to have little effect. The gun hand swung back. Lindsay ducked low into a crouch, flinging up his left arm to deflect it as the man loosed off a shot which passed narrowly over his shoulder. Lindsay stiffened the fingers of his right hand and came up from the crouch like a rocket, ramming the rigid fingers under the arch of the ribs with tremendous force.

His attacker stopped in his tracks, the gun dropping onto the tarmac from nerveless fingers. The man emitted a strangled gurgle, his eyes rolling up as his heart ruptured under the force of Lindsay's lethal blow.

The naval man caught the body under the arms before it collapsed into the road and glanced about. There was no one else in sight and, with any luck, the single shot could well have been interpreted as a car backfire by anyone who might have heard it.

He dragged the body to the Vauxhall and, with some difficulty, manoeuvred the body into the driver's seat, using the safety belt to keep it upright. He adjusted the headrest to support the lolling head. Quickly, he fetched the newspaper from his own car, spread it open against the Nova's steering wheel, pressed home the locking button on the inside of the car door and closed it.

Lindsay picked up the gun and pocketed it before surveying his handiwork. To any passer-by, the car's occupant would seem alive, well and engrossed in reading the local news. The death might not be discovered for several hours and it would take an autopsy to establish the cause of death.

Perturbed by the fact that it had happened at all, Lindsay composed himself, went back to the Jaguar and dialled a number from his cellphone. He spoke quickly and concisely, using standard code phrases that would be undecipherable by any eavesdropper, then drove away, heading for the Royal Naval Air Station at Culdrose, ten miles away.

15

Cheapside
London, UK

The décor of the City Wine Bar was expensive but, to Karen Marshall's way of thinking, bland and devoid of any real character. She shook her head at the prices charged for two dry white wines—at home in Cornwall she could have bought an extra glass for the same money and still have collected change.

The attractive brunette at her table wore an expression of delight as Karen brought the drinks back. "How long is it since we last got together?" Anne Collinson said. "Three years? Four?"

"Five," Karen smiled back. "When I look back, our university days were definitely the best by a long way. I miss those times."

"So do I, except for having to live on the breadline, never getting a real break and starting life with a student loan debt to pay back."

"You haven't done so badly since then." Karen exaggerated her visual appraisal of the other woman's Versace suit.

Anne Collinson laughed, revealing white, even teeth that could have graced a toothpaste advert. "Lloyd's of London might have had its problems over the last ten years or so," she said, "but it's a good job to have and they pay well." She leant forward. "Thank God we kept in touch. I was beginning to feel that we'd never meet up again. What on earth brings you to London anyway? I thought you had a pathological loathing of cities."

"I do." Karen pulled a face. "Too hemmed in, too crowded, too impersonal. Cities like this are far too claustrophobic for a country lass like me. You can't beat the wide-open spaces, the moors and the cliffs. Places where you can breathe. I can't abide being anywhere where you can't see a natural horizon."

Anne, who'd been brought up on a Lincolnshire farm, smiled ruefully. "I know you're right. Cities are unnatural places. I often used to get away up onto Lincoln Edge. When I got the job here, I found it so hard to adapt to city life." She paused, briefly drinking in the nostalgia. "So, Karen, what really brings you here?"

Karen glanced down at her wine glass. "To try and get at the truth of how Alan died. And why he died."

Anne's face fell. "Oh, God, Karen. I'm so sorry about that and even sorrier I couldn't get down for the memorial service. I remember meeting Alan and thinking how lucky you were to have found such a nice genuine man."

"It was an empty service," Karen said quietly, still gazing at the wine glass. "It seemed so meaningless with no one knowing what really happened, and the fact that he was never found and brought home." The tears were close as she added, "There's no grave to visit, nothing but memories to show that he even existed."

She took a deep breath and fought off the tears. "Anne, I need your help. Being a registrar at Lloyd's, you're the right person in exactly the right place."

"If there's anything I can do to help, I will." Anne reached forward and took Karen's hand, sensing her distress. "Just tell me what you need."

Relieved, Karen nodded her thanks, produced a sheet of notepaper and handed it across. "That's the date of the *Aurora's* sinking and her last known position. Is there any way you can find out which were the nearest ships to her at the time?"

Anne examined the noted figures and pursed her lips. "Not the easiest task, but not impossible," she said. "I'll certainly give it a try. Is there anything else?"

"Well, yes, if you can fit it in. These merchant ships that have been attacked out in the Atlantic—is there anything you can find out about them? Owners, ports of departure and destination, anything at all."

"That should be easier," Anne told her. "What about the whalers that were similarly damaged?"

Karen shook her head. "Just the merchant ships for now. I need to know if they have anything in common."

"To find a reason why they're being attacked?" Anne sat back, examining Karen's determined expression. "The North Atlantic's a long way from the Antarctic, Karen. You think these incidents are connected with the *Aurora*, don't you?"

"Yes, I do, but don't ask me what that link might be. At least, not yet." She smiled appreciatively. You know, Anne, there's one thing about you that hasn't altered since our university days. You still don't miss much."

16

Royal Naval Air Station, Culdrose
Helston
Cornwall, UK

The Royal Naval Air Station at Culdrose is seldom referred to by its proper title, *HMS Seahawk*. Europe's largest military helicopter base, it specializes in coastal patrol and air-sea rescue. The closest naval base to the Western Approaches, its complex includes a naval intelligence office although budgetary cuts have reduced its staff to one officer and a single secretary.

The one intelligence officer, Lieutenant-Commander Charles "Baggy" Oxford, sat in the officer's wardroom bemoaning his lot to Don Lindsay and the station's commanding officer, Commodore Roderick Browning.

"Whitehall has no earthly idea of the workload," he lamented. "Signal after signal from ships, aircraft and subs. Not only our own, NATO's as well. The bloody politicians just cannot get away from the misapprehension that, since the Berlin Wall went down, all's well with the world apart from a few raggle-taggle terrorists. They honestly believe that there's no real need for intelligence at all, but what that lot would know about intelligence isn't worth the telling.

"Even the Minister, old Henry Williamson—a Navy man, God bless him—listens less and less to what the Admiralty tell him.

"All sorts of threats exist out there, both real and potential. The world's full of bloody madmen and, what's more, the Russians, the Americans, the French, not to mention ourselves, have been selling them weapons, warships and technology they should never be allowed to have. It's the same old story… money means far more than common sense and it's always some poor unconnected bastard that cops the consequences."

"You're preaching to the converted, Baggy," Commodore Browning laughed. "I know the truth of what you're saying only too well and, from what I hear of his exploits, so does Commander Lindsay here."

"True enough," Lindsay agreed. "Take this latest panic, these disabled merchantmen out in the Atlantic. Who do you think's having a go at these ships and how are they doing it?"

"Beats me," Browning shrugged. "I can't find the logic in it, whichever way I look. It seems to be a new form of terrorism but what are the motives? To panic the stock markets, perhaps? What about the demands? Have there been any? Has anyone claimed responsibility?"

"The only answers I can give are don't know and no," Lindsay admitted. "But there is more to this than meets the eye. One of the recent victims, a ship called the *Margarita Sanchez*, is currently laid up in Falmouth. Someone was most anxious that she shouldn't be photographed. Very insistent, in fact."

Oxford glanced meaningfully across at Lindsay. "Ah, yes. I sent in a cleansing team the moment you called in. Very efficient lads. There'll be no trace."

Browning didn't miss the meaning of that. "Good grief, Commander. You haven't bumped someone off already? You haven't been on the job more than five minutes."

"At the point of a loaded gun held by someone ready to use it, I wasn't given a lot of choice." Lindsay broke off as a rating approached, bearing a sealed package.

"From the printing room, sir," the rating said, handing the package to Oxford and beating a retreat.

Oxford handed it over to Lindsay. "Your photos, Don."

Before he could open it, Browning got up and shook his hand. "Time for me to leave," he said. "This is none of my business, so I'll leave you cloak-and-dagger merchants to get on with it."

Lindsay consulted his watch as Browning left. "That was quick work," he said appreciatively, opening the flat package and drawing out the twelve-inch by eight colour prints. He examined each of them in turn, passing them on to Oxford who whistled at the damage to the bulk carrier's rudder.

"I see they're shifting the cargo," he said, as the second print was handed to him.

Lindsay nodded. "It's being transferred to a ship called the *Noordzee Marquess*," he said. "She's due to dock in about six hours and scheduled to sail for Rio the day after tomorrow."

Oxford was peering intently at two prints of the cargo-moving operation brought into close view by the camera's long lens. What had caught his interest was an aggressive-looking figure, standing slightly apart from the workers. In one picture he was pointing, the other showed him gesticulating angrily. He was a thick-set, hard-faced individual with short-cropped fair hair. As far as could be told from the photograph, the man appeared to be in his middle to late fifties. Oxford brought him to Lindsay's attention.

"This character here," he said. "Seems to be running the show. I'm bloody certain I should know him. What do you think?"

Lindsay held the photograph closer to the light, noting the distant tugs on his memory. "You know, I think you may be right, Baggy. I do know him but I'm damned if I can tag a name to him. Why don't we upload these to head office and get them to run a trace?"

"Fair enough," Oxford said. "Finish your drink and we'll go and wake them up."

Oxford's telephone rang less than hour later. Safe in the knowledge that it was a secure, encrypted line, he listened for a moment and passed the receiver over to Lindsay. "The Chief of Staff," he told him.

Rochester's rich voice came over strongly. "You've caused one hell of a stir here, Don," he said. "We've put a name to your man and all hell's breaking loose."

"So who is he?" Lindsay asked.

There was a short pause. "Hans-Dieter Wolf," Rochester said heavily. "Remember him? The Linden Wolf? The former *Stasi* interrogator who maimed or killed dozens of internees, even though only in his mid-twenties. When the Berlin Wall came down, he did a bunk and hasn't been seen since."

"Hell, Mike, he's wanted by every security service in the west."

"Not surprisingly, he doesn't tend to operate under that name these days," Rochester said. "We've managed to do a snap trace now that we have this merchant navy connection. Crew lists show him as Jürgen Krabbe. It seems that he was acting bo'sun on the *Margarita Sanchez* and is being transferred to do the same job on another bulk carrier called the *Noordzee Marquess*."

"Onto which the *Margarita's* cargo is to be transferred," Lindsay pointed out. "She's due into Falmouth in a few hours."

"Yes, we know. Interesting, don't you think? Both cargo and bo'sun on immediate transfer to a ship of a different line. Strikes me as unusual to say the least. Don, I think you're going to have to take a closer look at that cargo, and him. How do you fancy a little sea trip?"

"On the *Noordzee Marquess*? With Wolf as bo'sun? Jesus, Mike, I'd rather sail with Bloody Morgan."

"I'm afraid the admiral insists, Don. Listen, we're putting a few things together for you—papers, union cards, all the usual trappings of an undercover ID. We'll do the routine fiddle to get your name on the crew list. I'll be flying down with everything to brief you at oh-nine hundred tomorrow.

"Oh, and one other thing," Rochester could barely conceal the laughter in his voice. "The admiral asks me to inform you that you've been cashiered. From Commander down to deck-hand!"

17

5 January 2015
London, UK

"Of course I'm bloody furious!" Ian Neale sounded off into the telephone. "These shipping incidents were my story, and mine alone."

"And the gold?" said the voice on the other end of the line. "I trust you're not thinking of making that public just yet."

"No, I'm keeping that in reserve," Neale said defensively. "In any case, I need to interview some of the foreign police and treasury people involved in turning it up."

"I should damn well hope you were," the voice said sharply. "If you made that public too soon, our own Treasury would start an immediate investigation into the leak and that could make my own position difficult. Might it not be simpler for you to stop ranting and tell me what your real problem is?"

"Tony bloody Saunders has forced me to share the exclusive on the shipping attacks with a nobody girl from the boondocks and a has-been out of ancient journalistic history, that's what the problem is," Neale retorted.

"Has-been?"

"You'll recall the name," Neale told him. "Hobbes. Barrington Hobbes. Someone's dug him up from somewhere. He reckons he has a lead on the *Aurora* sinking and on these current bouts of piracy so, of course, Saunders falls for it and welcomes him back into *The Sentinel's* embrace. At my expense," he added bitterly.

Neale heard the sudden intake of breath on the other end of the line. "Hobbes? Damn it, Ian, the man might be ancient history to you, but he's clever and bloody dangerous. This could cause a major problem. I specifically asked you to take on the piracy story so that I could be kept fully informed. There's more at stake here than you know. Where is he now?"

"I've no idea. He said something about seeing some naval historian but didn't give a name. Hobbes is a secretive bastard. Keeps his cards close to his chest."

There was a pause and a heavy sigh. "Ian, play along with him for now, but watch his every move. Inform me every step of the way. In the meantime, there are other people who need to be apprised of this development."

"Such as who?" Neale demanded.

"Don't push your luck, Ian, these are dangerous waters. Just play along and report anything of significance to me. Don't delve into my side of things, not if you're wise. Look, I've given you all sorts of tips from inside Westminster and they've done much to further your career. Do this for me and I'll see you don't regret it."

Neale expelled a sigh of exasperation. "Very well, I'll do as you ask. I'll be in touch."

At the other end of the line, a suddenly very anxious Secretary of State replaced the handset and steeled himself to pass on the bad news.

"Good lord, Barrie, you don't want much from me, do you?" Dr Melvyn Hunter waved his tumbler of Woodford Reserve Kentucky whiskey at Barrington Hobbes. The paunchy maritime historian was in his late fifties, with wild salt-and-pepper hair and full beard. He wore an old plain blue sweatshirt and black cord trousers and his sockless feet were tucked into tartan slippers. A hole in the right slipper exposed the tip of a big toe. "You expect me to work out how these ships are being disabled and who's doing it? You must think I'm a bloody miracle worker."

Hunter and the journalist sat in armchairs they had freed from piles of books, documents and charts. The naval historian's Knightsbridge flat consisted largely of books that lined every square inch of wall and carpet, as far as Hobbes could tell. In one corner of the room stood a desk equally covered in papers and journals except for a Macintosh computer and even that supported yet another pile of books.

"Should be an easy enough task for you," Hobbes said lightly. "Nothing happens in any ocean of the world that Mel Hunter doesn't know about, hasn't studied, analysed, recorded and filed."

"Like, for example, the fact that another whaler was rammed last night or, to be precise, at three this morning, our time?" Hunter replied tacitly.

That caught Hobbes unawares. "What? Tony Saunders mentioned nothing of that sort to me in this morning when I saw him about hiring a car in *The Sentinel's* name."

"Well, he wouldn't, would he?" Hunter said. "Seeing that he doesn't know about it. Quite simply, Barrie, the Admiralty has decided that these incidents are to be kept under wraps. It has something to do with the fact that an American warship had a highly embarrassing run-in with these bright buccaneers just before Christmas. As a result, NATO's developed the heebie-jeebies about our nautical enigma. I'm not sure of the exact reason but the whisper is that there's something about this oceanic mystery that has the NATO High Command frightened witless."

Hobbes narrowed his eyes. "None of that got into the papers, either," he said flatly.

"No, well, it wouldn't. Sometimes the Admiralty can shut things up remarkably well. Even so, I should be able to ferret out a little more information. What I can tell you—strictly off the record—is that they have a man on the case. A good one, too, by all accounts."

Hobbes settled back in the armchair and sipped his whiskey. "Proves my point then, doesn't it? In maritime matters, the Great White Hunter knows all, sees all. So, how about my request?"

"For old times' sake, Barrie, I'll give it a try—and because I can't resist it. I'll call you if and when I turn anything up." The historian walked across the book-laden floor as Hobbes heaved himself out of the armchair and enveloped him in a rib-cracking bear hug.

"I can't tell you how good it is to see you back in circulation, Barrie. If what you tell me is right, if these are the same people who nearly did for you ten years ago, then you're skating on bloody thin ice.

"By your own admission, you're driving for the first time since you took that header off the M5. Remember who you're up against and, for Heaven's sake, keep your wits about you."

Chapter 4

Pyramus

⤛ 18 ⤜

6 January 2015
Hotel du Soleil
Paris, France

Within the luxury surroundings of a sealed conference room, the Chairman of the organization known as the Pyramus Group scanned his assembly of directors. There were twelve present, with five more conveying their apologies due to more publicly visible commitments.

It was normal for these secretive gatherings to have no written agenda, nor would there be any transcribed minutes. Instead, and only the Chairman himself knew of this, a single recording on a compact disc would, later that night, be dispatched as usual to the vaults of a Geneva bank.

The Chairman turned to address the fleshy, balding American who, in public life, was a major industrialist and Republican Congressman. "Harvey, as project manager of the Antarctic facility, your progress report would be most welcome."

Harvey Walterson remained seated, as was the custom at meetings of the Pyramus Group. "Indeed, Mr Chairman, I'm pleased to report that the development works are currently running ten weeks ahead of schedule and that storage has already commenced in the facility's completed sections.

"In the interests of refreshing everyone's memory, the facility is located within a small mountain on the Antarctic coast. Its upper levels were developed by enlarging and adapting existing natural cavern formations within the body of the mountain itself and took just over two years to complete.

"Already, and on a temporary basis, upwards of one hundred fifty nuclear warheads from decommissioned French and Russian weapons are in storage within these levels. Eventually, they will be transferred to the lowest levels, along with medium and high level nuclear wastes. When complete, those levels will be at a depth of one thousand feet, or three hundred metres, below sea level.

"The transfer of those decommissioned weapons into our care has been successfully carried out under the utmost secrecy. Their disposal has been a perennial nightmare to the nations concerned and I can assure this meeting that no one who is not directly involved is even aware that the transactions have taken place.

"Also in storage on the completed levels are more than ten thousand obsolete conventional warheads, from well over a dozen nations worldwide.

"The payments made by those countries to the Pyramus Group have, in every case, been concealed by effective budget juggling in accordance with the formula devised by our French colleague, Dr Thierry Lefèvre, whose mathematical genius has benefitted this organization on several occasions." He waved a hand at the bespectacled Frenchman who sat unmoved by the polite handclaps of appreciation. The Chairman nodded his own acknowledgement of Lefèvre's contributions before asking Walterson to continue.

"The upper levels," the American reported, "are also beginning to take storage of several toxic chemical wastes from more than twenty industrialized nations and it is estimated that our current, risky practice of dumping these materials at sea will be obsolete in approximately six months from now. Furthermore, our current method of shipment by surface vessels will also become obsolete three years from now. Designs for a submarine cargo vessel, displacing some 37,000 tons and which will replace much of our surface fleet, are at an advanced stage. Negotiations for its construction are already in progress and she will be nuclear powered.

"With regard to the stored weapons, both nuclear and conventional, it was decided three meetings ago that, although our main intention is to provide disposal facilities, the Pyramus Group will not be averse to any application to purchase. I should therefore inform the meeting that approaches have been made to our representatives by two countries, one in Central America, the other in the Middle East. All directors will be kept fully informed of developments in this potentially very lucrative sideline.

"To return to the Antarctic facility, its lower levels are under construction as we speak. These are reached by way of a spiral shaft with an incline shallow enough to allow fully laden transporters to be driven up and down. Submarine Levels One and Two, at 170 and 340 feet below sea level, are now complete, and work on Level Three, at a depth of 500 feet, is two-thirds finished. The spiral shaft has now been sunk to what will be Level Four, at 750 feet. Level Five will be close to a thousand feet down. No major geological problems have been encountered."

The Chairman placed his elegant hands on the table before him and leant forward slightly. "This is excellent news," he said. "Excellent. You will please inform all those involved in the construction that they will receive a substantial bonus for their efforts. I am most impressed, Harvey. Have you a revised estimate of the completion date?"

"Necessarily approximate," Walterson said carefully. "But, barring any unforeseen major problem, my estimate now stands at three and one half years from now."

"A good twelve months sooner than originally envisaged," the Chairman said approvingly. "And what of its defence system? Isao," he addressed a stony faced Japanese, "that is your department."

Isao Mifune, better known as the Minister of Defence in his own country's government, gave a respectful bow. "The defences for the facility"—he had trouble with the word—"are complete and operational. There are eight personnel permanently on the site, housed in excellent and most comfortable conditions. These, on a rota basis, monitor a radar installation around the clock.

"Three 75-millimetre guns cover the seaward approach, in addition to which we have surface-to-air and surface-to-surface missile installations, all concealed within the topography of the mountain. We have also acquired a most impressive mobile surface-to-surface missile launcher, carrying a battery of twelve missiles. This is a tracked vehicle, essentially a larger version of the Sno-Cat, and can be sent out onto the ice to augment the existing armament, or cover any landward threat. Our ammunition stores are well-stocked."

"I am aware that your government has been most generous in this respect," the Chairman said. "I should be grateful if you would convey my thanks to those concerned. I also understand that they have agreed to contact the Pyramus Group with the disposal of their surplus plutonium stocks. Potentially, a highly profitable development."

"The agreement," Mifune said gravely, "was not entirely unanimous. Environment Minister Mitsura, a notorious liberal, spoke most strongly against the proposal and voted accordingly."

A dry smile touched the corners of the Chairman's lips. "Might I presume this to be the same unfortunate Mitsura who, ten days ago, took pilgrimage to the peak of Fuji-san and gave himself to the gods of fire?"

Mifune bowed his head in assent.

"And tell me, Isao, did he cast himself into the crater of his own volition, or by way of a helping hand?"

The Japanese director was visibly shaken. "You knew that?"

The Chairman gave him an easy smile. "I have my sources of information, as I'm sure you're aware, Isao. No matter, it was well done. There was a considerable risk that he might reveal all he knew and he was therefore a very real threat to this organization. Alas for Mitsura-san."

He turned back to Walterson. "Harvey, are there any problems with access to the storage facility?"

"None. The site's selection was partly influenced by the existence of a warm- water current that creates a permanently open channel through the pack ice, even in winter. It is suspected that a large subterranean river, originating from some volcanic hotspot somewhere inland, issues from the coastline adjoining the complex.

"Deliveries continue to run smoothly." Walterson looked at the faces around the table. "For those of you not familiar with the operation, the wastes, construction equipment and provisions are supplied by our own cargo vessels. These have strengthened double hulls designed specifically for polar conditions. On arrival, their cargoes are off-loaded onto a submersible barge—another highly successful design by our Japanese colleagues—which then enters the facility through an entrance excavated forty feet below mean sea level.

"The dock is located entirely within the mountain. It is designed to cope with any possible or sudden sea-level rise of up to fifty feet and can be sealed off from the rest of the complex by watertight doors in case of any abnormal event such as, say, a tsunami."

"Thank you again, Harvey." The Chairman gazed at the occupants of the room. "Gentlemen, I think we must all be agreed that these reports represent a very remarkable success. I thank each and every one of you for your efforts. We have all risked a very great deal in order to create an essential service to the industrial and military world, however unlawful that same world might consider it to be.

"That risk is compensated by the considerable profits this enterprise attracts, and will continue to attract. Our current assets and profits stand at a combined sum of close to two hundred billion US dollars. We, the directors of the Pyramus Group, are also the sole beneficiaries and each of us is worth several millions. Our work force alone enjoys undeclared salaries several times greater than it would receive elsewhere and that alone ensures loyalty and silence."

He paused to collect his thoughts on what he had now to reveal. When he resumed, the assembled directors noted the added strength in his voice.

"Until now, our operations have remained undetected and there has been little in the way of threat. Any potential danger has been swiftly dealt with, as in the case of the unfortunate Mr Mitsura.

"It is now necessary to report that a trio of new problems have arisen. These could be extremely damaging and must be taken seriously by every one of us. Two of these problems emanate from the United Kingdom and I am in no doubt that they must be met both firmly and… ah, finally." His tone left no doubt as to his meaning.

"The first of these is the resurrection of an old ghost. Some of you will recall that, ten years ago, in the early years of the Pyramus Group, the British journalist Barrington Hobbes came uncomfortably close to uncovering our entire venture. The appropriate action was taken and it was unfortunate that, although his family did not survive, Hobbes himself cheated death. However, he was left in a condition, both physical and mental, that ended his career and effectiveness.

"Hobbes has now resurfaced with two assistants, their initial aim being to probe the sinking of the Deep Watch vessel *Aurora* last February. Their enquiries have already touched upon our operations and this situation cannot be allowed to continue. It would be unwise to underestimate Hobbes, whose former epithet—the Sherlock Holmes of Fleet Street—was well merited. Make no mistake, this man is a very real danger. We may have succeeded in silencing him for ten years but it is my considered opinion that he must be permanently dealt with. Are all in agreement?"

The Chairman's eyes registered the unanimous nods of assent.

"Then it is settled," he said. "The *Aurora* incident was unavoidable. Her position coincided with the northward course of our vessel, the *Emperor*. It was essential that no questions be asked as to why a freight ship should be steaming north from Antarctic waters, for reasons that should be obvious to all of you. Captain Schiller carried out his orders efficiently and it was particularly fortunate that the remoteness of the spot, and the extreme depth of water in which the *Aurora* lies, have discouraged any possibility of a serious investigation.

"Hobbes claims to have some tenuous lead on the *Aurora* incident and, already, one of his assistants has made approaches to Lloyd's Registry and Insurance. They are unlikely to gain much from there but we cannot afford to take chances. Orders for his elimination will be issued tonight and without him, the assistants will be helpless.

"The second problem and, indeed, the third, concern the recent spate of attacks on our vessels in the northern Atlantic. Unsurprisingly, the British government has assigned an officer from their Department of Naval Intelligence to the case. On the face of it, this is good news. However, our United Kingdom representative," he indicated the senior government minister sitting two places away to his left, "brings the disturbing news that this officer is currently aboard our own vessel, the *Noordzee Marquess*, in the guise of a deckhand."

The buzz of concern that erupted round the table was quelled by a small movement of the Chairman's hand.

"There is no reason," he told them, "to believe that he has discovered any link between the ship and our operations, or that such operations even exist. His presence aboard is, however, inopportune. The *Noordzee Marquess* is scheduled to carry out disposals of chemical wastes in mid-Atlantic, having taken on the cargo originally carried by the *Margarita Sanchez*. Happily, that cargo was not closely inspected during her lay-up in Falmouth. We cannot risk bringing it into the ship's port of destination and, therefore, the disposal operation will go ahead. Captain Greer has been informed of the situation and will carry out his orders.

"By sheer good fortune," he added, "my chief enforcer, Jürgen Krabbe, was assigned to oversee the disposal of the waste, in the role of ship's bo'sun. He, too, has been made aware of this naval agent's presence on board."

The Portuguese director, Lisbon lawyer João Valdera, spoke up, his face betraying concern and distaste. "Mr Chairman, we are all fully aware of who Herr Krabbe is and, more to the point, who and what he was. Is it truly in the interests of the Pyramus Group to continue employing such a man?"

The Chairman's response was one of carefully controlled patience. Valdera was a highly valued member of the Pyramus Group whose views merited respect.

"Very much in our interests, João. Although money is extremely adept at encouraging loyalty and discretion from our employees, it does not necessarily provide a guarantee. Fear is the most effective silencer and Krabbe provides that commodity most efficiently.

"Of course, we are all aware of his record, his true identity and the fact that he remains on the wanted list of several western nations. In turn, we provide him with sanctuary and this ensures his own loyalty, an arrangement that works remarkably well. One of Krabbe's team will be instructed to dispose of Barrington Hobbes and Krabbe himself will deal with this naval agent in a fashion that will appear to be purely accidental.

"To press forward," the Chairman continued, "the third threat is potentially the most dangerous of the three. Whoever is attacking our ships has, without any doubt, some knowledge of our operations. The only freight ships that have been set upon have been our own. This is no mere coincidence. Both the *Margarita Sanchez* and the *Dogger Bank* were attacked as they were commencing to offload their drums of waste. This implies that each of the ships was shadowed. It also implies that the link between them has been discovered and that is something I find extremely disturbing."

"Perhaps," said the Brazilian, Edson Enriques, "we should allow this intelligence man to continue his assignment in the hope that he may succeed in putting an end to these pirates."

"You forget, Edson. This agent is aboard our ship, a ship laden with canisters of dioxins and trichloroethylene which do not appear on the cargo manifest and which we are about to dispose of illegally. We have already received payment for this service and must, therefore, carry it out. He cannot fail to witness it. The man is a professional with an outstanding record and could very well put an end to us.

"The attacker, on the other hand, is a wholly unknown quantity. It remains unidentified but is most likely a submarine of some sort. It appears and disappears. Her engines are quiet and difficult to detect. We cannot yet ascertain exactly how she succeeds in disabling our ships but it is done swiftly and accurately.

"Her motives would appear to be environmental. Her only targets have been whaling vessels and our waste disposal ships. I believe this to be a weakness we can exploit."

The Chairman's gaze fell upon the British government minister. "You, my friend, carry considerable influence among your cabinet colleagues. When this meeting is concluded, you and I must discuss the demise of our underwater adversaries."

19

17 January 2015
Knightsbridge
London, UK

The streets of Knightsbridge were quiet under a grey drizzle as Barrington Hobbes parked the hired car in the private rear courtyard of the stylish Victorian building that housed Dr Melvyn Hunter's expensive third floor flat. He announced his arrival at the street door intercom and the security lock clicked to let him in.

The man who answered his knock was dishevelled, tired and unshaven. Hobbes raised an eyebrow at the marine historian's appearance.

"Been burning the candle at both ends?" he remarked lightly, casting another glance at Hunter's red-eyed look and into a room crammed with even more books than before.

"And you can take the entire blame for it," the historian responded, ushering him inside. "I'll have you know that I've been working bloody hard on your behalf, day and night, and my throat is suddenly dry." He looked expectantly at Hobbes and added hoarsely, "If you get my drift."

Hobbes produced the anticipated bottles of Woodford, placing them on what little available space he could find on Hunter's desk. Beaming happily, the historian fetched a pair of heavy tumblers and a jug of water.

"Now that the evening has suddenly become civilized," he said, pouring out two generous measures and handing one to Hobbes, "we can settle down and make a start. What do you know about the Indian Mutiny of 1857?"

Hobbes blinked at the unexpected question. "Only that it happened. Indian soldiers rose up in revolt against their Imperial masters and came second. Might I ask what the hell it has to do with my line of enquiry?"

Hunter fixed him with a triumphant glare. "Everything, my boy. Everything." He gestured at a book-cluttered armchair. "Chuck those off, drag the chair over to the desk and park your arse. You and I are in for a long evening and, I'll warn you now, there are things to tell you that you'll find rather hard to accept.

"You may as well know that in the last forty-eight hours, I've kissed the Minister of Defence's ample backside, dug into classified Admiralty archives, spent a bloody fortune on both phone and e-mail to the States and had damn-all sleep into the bargain. So, I'd appreciate a tolerant ear.

"You are most definitely onto something, Barrie. Believe your uncle Melvyn, it'll shake you rigid."

The journalist cleared the armchair, pushed it over to Hunter's desk and sat down. "I can't wait. Just one thing before you start, how did you get access to classified files?"

"Blatant nepotism," Hunter grinned. "Being the Minister of Defence's favourite nephew does have its uses. In any case—and you've don't have to know more than this—HM Government owes me a few favours. Once I'd convinced Sir Henry that I wasn't about to screw the security of the nation and that the documents in question dated back to the eighteen-hundreds, the necessary strings were duly pulled."

"Good old Uncle Henry," Hobbes commented sourly.

Hunter wagged a long finger at him. "I'm well aware of your opinion of politicians, not that I can entirely blame you, but Henry's not a bad old bugger. Anyway, as I said, the government owed me."

"So what did you come up with?"

"Patience, my boy." Hunter took a sizeable swig of his Woodford. "You need to hear this from the beginning. I want you to bear with a history lesson about nineteenth century India. Why will become clear later." He settled deeper into his seat.

"There is—or at any rate, there used to be—a small but rich mountain state of India known as Bundelkhand. It's since been absorbed into Madhya Pradesh. Now, I'm talking about the early nineteenth century when India was under the British heel. Bundelkhand's ruling rajah was well regarded by his people. A wily old bird, he knew that, to have any chance of successfully opposing the British occupation, his successor would need to compete on at least an equal intellectual footing.

"He had just the one son, the Prince Dakkar who, even in childhood, showed exceptional promise. In 1823, his father sent the boy to be educated in Europe at the finest seats of learning. No expense spared. The boy's education lasted for twenty years, studying in Stockholm, Paris, Vienna—he even spent a couple of years in America.

"The Rajah's estimate of the boy's potential was, if anything, understated. The lad was a genius who could absorb knowledge like a sponge. As he grew older, so he started to specialize. Art collection was one particular field. He spent a king's ransom purchasing original works of the Masters, not just paintings but books and musical manuscripts. Science was another speciality. He studied chemistry, physics, biology, astronomy, hydrostatics—you name it, he was brilliant at it. Strangely, for the future ruler of a landlocked state, he developed a keen interest in naval architecture, admiring people like Robert Fulton."

"I'm familiar with Fulton," Hobbes broke in. "American engineer who developed the world's first commercial steamship and the first steam-powered warship. Died in 1815 or thereabouts." He smiled at Hunter's obvious surprise. "You can't be born and raised in a seaport without gaining some knowledge of ships and the sea," he said.

"I'm impressed," Hunter said approvingly. "But you left out his best known invention."

"Best known, perhaps, but hardly all that important or successful, was it?" Hobbes said. "I'm aware that he developed a primitive form of submarine but it came to nothing. As I recall, he expanded on the principles used by Bushnell in his *Turtle* and came up with a far better design but, even then, Fulton's craft could only carry three men. It had no engine, no practical depth or range capabilities, and could only stay submerged for a couple of hours at most."

"But it was a start," Hunter said. "Nearly paid off for him, too. The US military weren't too interested in the idea, so Fulton tried to flog it to Napoleon. He set up a demo to prove its destructive power, succeeded in attaching a mine to an old hulk and blowing it out of the water. Napoleon was horrified, or so he made out. He called the very idea dishonourable whilst actually dreaming up a way to steal it. Fulton only found out in the nick of time and got out of France in a hurry.

"He then gave the idea one last try with the British—in revenge against Boney, I guess—but they weren't interested, either. Wasn't gentlemanly, you know—what? Simply wasn't cricket. Fulton gave up after that and concentrated his efforts on developing steam-powered surface vessels.

"We've gone way off-track here, Barrie. Let's get back to our academic prince, shall we?" Hunter drained his glass and refilled it.

"By the time he was twenty," the historian resumed, "it was clear that Dakkar was well on his way to becoming a scientific and intellectual giant, an accomplished statesman and everything else his father had dreamt of. He still remained a chip off the old block and resented Britain's occupation of India as deeply as his father did. That was in the blood. Dakkar was a nephew of a legendary Indian hero, Tipu Sahib, Sultan of Mysore, who had died fighting against British forces in 1799 at the Battle of Seringapatam. Dakkar was working towards the day when he could instigate the overthrow of the occupation and rule a free people. That remained his dream and his single driving ambition. Already, he'd attracted a dozen or more able followers, many of them Europeans who resented Britain's imperial activities and who would have followed Dakkar to the gates of Hell.

"When he was thirty, Dakkar and his band of companions returned to settle in Bundelkhand. He married an Indian noblewoman who shared his views. The couple adored each other and the two sons they produced. Then, in 1857, came the Indian Mutiny, the great Sepoy revolt."

The word jogged Hobbes's ample memory. "Sepoys, Indian soldiers in the employ of the British East India Company," he said.

"The real power in India," Hunter added. "Founded in 1600 to control the trade in East Indian spices. By the mid nineteenth century it had become a political power in its own right and ran most of the occupation's administrative offices.

"Thirty thousand Sepoys took part in the intial revolt, egged on by regional rulers and princes. It began at a place called Meerut and escalated into a bloody Anglo-Indian war. Once the rebels had captured and repossessed Delhi, just about every town and province of northern India joined in.

"Our Prince Dakkar was drawn right into it. He helped to finance and plan the rebellion and even fought in the front lines. It's said that he was wounded ten times in as many engagements but just kept coming back. The rebels were banking heavily on external aid, particularly from Russia, but it never materialized. If it had done, Britain could have kissed goodbye to her interests in India."

"So what happened?" Hobbes asked.

"Britain reacted heavily, sending in huge reinforcements under Field Marshal Sir Colin Campbell, later Baron Clyde. One of the hardest bastards ever to command a British army. With typical ruthlessness, he quelled the revolt and recaptured Delhi. By May 1858, less than a year after the revolt had started, Campbell had regained control of India and begun rounding up and executing the ringleaders.

"Dakkar went to ground and Campbell put a massive price on his head. Even then, the British couldn't find a single soul willing to sell him out, so they put his family under close arrest. They were tortured barbarically, even the children, poor little sods, but they gave up not a word of information. The chances were that they probably had no idea where Dakkar was holed up. In the end, each member of Dakkar's family—parents, wife and children—was put to death."

"Dear God!" Hobbes was horrified. "British soldiers did that? I don't believe it."

Hunter shrugged his shoulders. "Why ever not? Curious lot, we Brits. We so love to kid the world and ourselves that, as a nation, we're purer than the driven snow. The great champions of civilization, freedom and decency. Forever on the side of the angels and at the right hand of God. Don't you ever bloody believe it.

"Just consider the number of countries we've invaded, subjugated and humiliated. How many cultures have we destroyed, just to satisfy the lust of a few for superiority and profit? The cold truth is that when it comes to war crimes and atrocities, we're right up there alongside Attila, Pol Pot, Hitler, Amin, Hussein and Milosevic.

"Who do you think invented the concentration camp? Nazi Germany? Not a chance, my friend. They got the idea from us. We beat them to it by half a century, during the Boer War.

"That's historical fact, Barrie, nicely edited from the sanitized crap they teach our kids. Perpetuating the lie. Don't you ever talk to me about British fair play and integrity. Those animals never existed."

Hobbes sat back, astonished by the vehemence of Hunter's tirade. "Message received and understood," he said. "Take a deep breath and tell me what happened to Dakkar, not that I've the slightest idea where this is going."

"Got clean away," Hunter said, after another pull on his Woodford. "But his world lay in ruins. His own country was barred to him, his family lay dead and his future was utterly destroyed. Somehow, he got away with the bulk of his fortune and his entire art collection which had, in any case, been stored in Europe. His followers and members of his palace retinue went with him, no one knew where. It was rumoured that Dakkar had previously purchased an island somewhere but the evidence was far too vague for the British authorities to go on. To all intents and purposes, he simply vanished from the face of the globe."

"A sad end to a promising life," Hobbes commented. "I still don't see what any of it has to do with my enquiries."

"I haven't finished yet," Hunter said patiently. "Let's jump forward in time some twenty years or so to when five American balloonists got caught up in a hurricane and blown halfway around the world. They were wrecked on an uncharted, uninhabited island in the southern Pacific.

"Led by a US Army engineer, a Captain Cyrus Harding, they were stranded there and forced to live off their own ingenuity for four years. Ingenuity was the word in their particular case. They started off with nothing but the clothes on their backs and yet they ended up taming the island, building bridges, roads and even a working telegraph. But they couldn't manage everything."

Melvyn Hunter leant back and steepled his fingers. "To cut a long story short, it became clear that they were receiving help from another quarter, from someone who had no wish to reveal himself. They searched the entire island but found not a trace of anyone.

"It was three and a half years after their arrival when the island's volcano started to erupt and only then did this mysterious guardian angel decide to make himself known to them. They followed instructions sent through their own telegraph and found him in a flooded cave system under the island. They'd come to expect some kind of superman but what they actually found was a seventy-year old man, totally alone and on the point of death.

"He told them his life history, identifying himself as Prince Dakkar, a name he hadn't used since fleeing India all those years before. All his former companions were dead and he himself had been on the island for several years, having gone there to die. The arrival on the island of the Americans had initially alarmed him but he had watched them closely and realized that these were men with whom he could make some sort of peace with that human society he'd rejected for years. He died only twenty-four hours later.

"The volcano blew the island off the map a few months later but the Americans somehow survived. Thanks to measures that Dakkar had taken before his death, they were rescued by a British civilian vessel.

"Cyrus Harding's descendants still live on a large estate in Iowa that he and his fellow castaways bought with part of a fortune in pearls and diamonds given to them by Dakkar. That," he added, "is why I've been in contact with the States—to locate Harding's great-great grandson for verification of the story."

Hobbes regarded the historian through eyes narrowed in thought. "There's something about that part of your story," he said, "that rings a faint bell. I've heard something like it before, but I'm damned if I can remember where."

Hunter's eyes gleamed as he broke into Hobbes's memory search. "Well, Barrie, try this for size. When Harding and his men met with Dakkar in the cave under the island, they found that his dwelling place was something wholly unique… to them, mind-blowing. Something they'd never dreamed of, the like of which would not be seen again for many a decade and certainly not in their own lifetimes."

The historian leaned forward as if to underline his words.

"A submarine," he said. "An advanced, electric-powered, ocean-going submarine."

"We've got something!" Karen Marshall was jubilant as she rushed into Ian Neale's office at *The Sentinel* building. "Anne Collinson at Lloyd's came up with the goods."

"Such as?" Neale looked up wearily from his computer screen.

Karen flopped onto a chair. "On the night the *Aurora* vanished, by far the nearest vessel to her was a cargo ship called the *Emperor*. The records show that, at one stage, she was only a few hundred miles away and might have been even closer."

"Vague," Neale shrugged. "Far too vague. A few hundred miles might as well be a few thousand. It doesn't put her in anything like the same waters. What about the whalers the *Aurora* was chasing? Where were they?"

"Much further east than had been reported at the time," she answered, "and sailing eastward, well away from the *Aurora* which wouldn't have got anywhere near them."

"So why get so excited about the *Emperor*?"

Karen could hardly contain herself. "According to Anne, the records show that she left Sydney harbour with a cargo of construction equipment. Excavators, drilling gear, that sort of thing. She was bound for Valparaiso and wasn't due to dock anywhere else en route. The trip took six days longer than it should have done. The captain, a man called Schiller, reported that he'd experienced engine failure east of New Zealand and drifted south into the Antarctic Convergence before they could complete repairs."

"Things like that happen at sea," Neale said. "Look, Karen, as far as journalism goes, you're inexperienced. You can't point a finger at a ship that might not have been within five hundred miles of the *Aurora* just because she broke down. You're going to need far more than that instead of clutching at straws."

"Is that what you think?" she shot back. "Then try this for size. What they unloaded from the *Emperor* in Valparaiso wasn't construction equipment. It was a full cargo of roadstone."

Neale sat up. "That has to be some kind of clerical error."

"I don't think so," she said. "It was exactly what the people who took delivery were expecting. The Sydney harbour authorities remain adamant that construction gear was loaded aboard at their end. What's more, when she docked in Valparaiso, the *Emperor* had extensive bow damage. Captain Schiller's report made out that she'd hit a small iceberg when drifting in the Antarctic Convergence fog but that report was filed in Chile, not at the time it allegedly happened."

"Interesting," Neale conceded. "But is it enough?"

"Let's try a reconstruction," Karen said. "Just suppose that something's being built down in Antarctica. Something that needs to be kept secret. The *Emperor* takes construction equipment there, offloads, and takes on stone that's been excavated from the site. Now, on the way out, she detects a ship that might see and report her presence but the secret has to be kept at all costs. Questions must not be asked. So, the *Emperor* runs down and sinks the *Aurora*, then arrives at her destination six days late and with a crumpled bow."

Neale shook his head. "Fantasy. Sheer fantasy. You don't have a shred of real evidence to support a wild tale like that. If we printed any such thing, we'd be flayed alive and rightly so."

Karen resisted an urge to throw a punch at a man who seemed intent on putting her down at every opportunity. "All right then, smartarse," she said through gritted teeth. "I'll give you the rest, then you can tell me what you've managed to come up with so far.

"Let's take these other ships that have been set upon out in the Atlantic. Just the merchant ships. Put the whalers aside for now. On the face of it, all those vessels are owned by a variety of companies. Anne dug deep and came up with the fact that those same companies act as a front to a single parent company, a concern called the Pyramus Group."

"All of them?"

"All of them," she replied flatly. "Now we have a common denominator."

Neale stared at her, waking up to the fact that this upstart freelance reporter from the sticks, as he saw her, had gathered more facts in the last few days than he had managed in weeks. His dreams of the exclusive story began to evaporate around his ears.

"Anne can't produce any further details of this parent company," Karen went on. "All computer reference to it is encrypted."

"Is it, by God?" Neale exclaimed.

"That's not all," Karen persisted, enjoying herself. "The *Emperor* herself is a Pyramus ship."

Neale knew when to concede defeat. "We'd better get this to Hobbes," he said heavily. "Where is he, by the way?"

"Knightsbridge. He has an old friend there who might be useful. A Dr Melvyn Hunter."

"The naval history man?"

"That's him," she said.

Neale reached for the telephone. "I'll get us a cab."

"Before you do," Karen said, eager to get one last punch in, "there's another fact you ought to hear. Anne says that insurance details show the *Emperor* to be built like a battleship, double-hulled with heavily reinforced bows."

"Why would that be, if she's a common or garden cargo ship?" Neale asked.

She gave him a triumphant smile. "Because she started life as an Antarctic supply vessel!"

"Impossible," Barrington Hobbes protested. "I can't buy that, Melvyn. It's sheer science fiction. No submarine worthy of the name existed until well into the twentieth century."

"Certain of that, are you?" Hunter turned the screen of his Apple computer into Hobbes's field of vision and switched it on. "Barrie, I've fed in all the details of our mystery craft that I can glean." He waved a CD-Rom and placed it in the carrier. "This disc contains a database of the design specifications of every submarine known to man. It even has those of the old Eastern Bloc and China, and goes back as far as Bushnell's *Turtle* and the nineteenth century French experiment *Le Plongeur*.

"I can tell you right now that our sub's details fail to match with any known design, civil or military, and that includes deep water submersibles such as *Trieste* or *Deep Scout*."

"So, basically, you came to a dead end," Hobbes said wearily.

"Not quite," Hunter said. "It simply meant that I had to cast my net a little wider. I got to thinking about these current incidents and recalled that, back in the 1860s, there were a series of strange events and sightings that weren't too dissimilar.

"In July 1866, the steamer *Governor Higginson* saw what was thought to be a reef a few miles off the east coast of Australia, except that it shot a pair of apparent geysers a hundred feet or so into the air and sank beneath the surface. Another steamer, the *Columbus*, saw exactly the same thing three days later, but two thousand miles away. Just over a fortnight later, and this time in the Atlantic, two more ships, the *Helvetia* and the *Shannon*, saw a whale of immense size, far bigger than any previously reported.

"After that, and over a period of time, there were many more reported sightings, none of them verifiable. Then, off Newfoundland on the 5th of March 1867, a passenger ship, the *Moravian*, had part of her keel broken off by something she had evidently passed over. It wasn't a rock for the simple reason that the waters there are two and a half miles deep. Fortunately, this damage wasn't serious but all that was seen was a strong eddy in the water.

"There was a more serious incident just over a month later, three hundred miles west of Cape Clear when something hit the Cunard paddle steamer *Scotia* on her port side and holed her. Fortunately, she'd been constructed with several watertight bulkheads that allowed her crew to isolate the leak. When she limped into Liverpool, her iron plates had a triangular hole six feet across punched through them by something that had immediately drawn itself back out again.

"That really got me thinking. There was something else I had to match against the specifications I have. I'll admit that it seemed like a desperate flight of fancy but, guess what, Barrie. There she was."

Hunter scrabbled about on his desktop, located a scrap of paper covered with hasty scrawls and waved it meaningfully.

"Right, these are the details we do have of our pirate ship, such as they are. Length, 220 to 250 feet. Hull shape, double-ended tapered cylinder with sharply pointed bow." Hunter was feeding each item into the computer as he spoke. "Estimated displacement, 1,500 to 2,000 tons. Large single screw, four-bladed. Maximum observed speed, forty-five knots and maximum observed depth, five thousand feet.

"All this comes from US Navy and Admiralty sources, Barrie. Don't ask how I got hold of it, but you can take it as reliable. Now, those last two items are pretty staggering and you can now understand why it is that the NATO naval chiefs are running around like headless chickens. Up to now, the only operational subs that could come anywhere near either of those capabilities were the titanium-hulled *Alfa* class nuclear attack boats the Soviets used to have, and even they couldn't match this. Barrie, in anyone's language, this craft is dynamite."

Hunter went back to his notes as Hobbes sat stunned by the information. "Ballast pumps capable of ejecting twin spouts of water to a height of a hundred feet," he continued, "and that's colossal power. Her configuration's highly unorthodox, too. When surfaced, her deck is only an estimated three feet above the waterline. No conning tower, sail, fairwater, fin or whatever you want to call it—just a pair of small, low deck structures. These are sometimes visible, sometimes not, which suggests they're retractable. If so, they're unique. There's a single pair of hydroplanes set halfway along her hull, again, unique." The historian continued to tap in the data as he spoke.

"A large, bright phosphorescence observed at night, presumably some sort of floodlight or searchlight," Hunter recited. "Very quiet engine noise. No coolant circulation was heard and, therefore, not nuclear powered but her sound signature is quite unlike any conventional diesel-electric engine."

"Curiouser and curiouser," Hobbes remarked.

"Lastly," Hunter said, "and most remarkably, she's built with the strength to carry out repeated rammings without sustaining appreciable damage. I'll admit that's an assumption, but there's simply no other way that she can carry out these attacks with the consistent accuracy shown. I'll remind you that, in every single case, it's the steering gear that's been targetted and hit.

"This vessel is more than special. The Admiralty, NATO and the Pentagon have combed intelligence records for any slightest hint that such a vessel has been built in the recent past. So far, they've come up with nothing and, in fact, there's nothing for them to find. In here," Hunter patted the top of the computer, "is the reason why. I've tried this more than once, but the same answer comes up every time, rejecting all others.

"Just watch, and prepare yourself for one hell of a shock."

Hunter tapped the command key. The screen flashed up a "Searching" message and took just twelve seconds to display its conclusion.

Barrington Hobbes could only stare it, his mouth open in sheer disbelief.

20

North Atlantic Ocean
500 miles east of Cape Clear

Seaman Derek Lynn stared out into the night from the cargo deck of the *Noordzee Marquess* and his blood ran cold.

He had been at least partially prepared for this but not even that could prevent a slack-jawed astonishment and, underneath, a peculiar, crawling tinge of apprehension stemming from a fear of the unknown that lies dormant within every person. He could tell that the same blend of feelings coursed through the entire ship's complement as they crowded the rail. He could almost smell the fear in some of them.

Half a mile from the vessel's port side, the ocean was ablaze with light, a huge oval of searingly white incandescence, its centre almost too bright for the eyes to bear. It seemed as motionless as the *Noordzee Marquess* herself, her engines having been stopped for a reason that Lynn could not as yet fathom.

"What in God's name can cause that?" one voice said, close by. Lynn himself could not even begin to guess. He had seen oceanic phosphorescence before but nothing that remotely matched this. The natural phenomena were always dim, ghostly glows, never such a blindingly bright light. It seemed to him that its source did not lie on the surface, but a few fathoms beneath it.

A louder voice interrupted his thoughts. Above him, the ship's captain had moved out on the open wing of the bridge to shout down at the crew.

"Stand away from the rail, there. We've all seen it, now get to work. I want the derrick over Number Two hold in action and the hold emptied in thirty minutes. Now we're clear of the continental shelf, I want that crap over the side in double-quick time." His voice softened. "After all, boys, every one of us will be getting a handsome bonus for it."

The knowing laughter from some members of the crew caught in their throats, turning to gasps of surprise and fear.

Without warning, the unearthly light in the water had moved, darting forward with astonishing speed. The men were back at the rail, their orders forgotten. Lynn could scarcely believe his eyes as the brilliant oval patch did an entire circuit of the ship at a tremendous rate, leaving a glowing, turbulent track behind it. He heard the captain swear out loud.

The light returned to its original position and stopped. Then, with a surge that numbed the senses, it turned sharply, aiming straight for the side of the *Noordzee Marquess*. Cries of alarm rang out as men leapt back from the rail, bracing for a collision that never came.

To Lynn's utter surprise, the light went out, abruptly, as though it had been switched off. Then, as suddenly as it had vanished, it reappeared on the starboard side of the ship and again took up a stationary position half a mile away.

Derek Lynn had been expecting something strange, but nothing remotely like this. In spite of himself, his skin crawled with apprehension. He fought to suppress the primitive instincts of fear that rose within him. *The Flying Dutchman*, the Jack Harry's Lights of Cornish pilots—these supernatural things did not, could not, exist. Or, an inner voice said as a renewed thrill of fear coursed through him, could it be that they did?

21

Knightsbridge
London, UK

Suddenly, Barrington Hobbes was angry. "Is this some sort of bloody joke?" He glared at Melvyn Hunter, infuriated by the historian's patient expression and by the damn fool message on the computer screen. "And just when am I supposed to publish this… this story of the fucking century? April the bloody first?"

Hunter's voice remained as calm as his expression. "Believe me, Barrie, this is no joke. This doesn't even faintly amuse me but, by God, I'm bloody excited. Take a good, hard look at me, will you. I got these bloodshot eyes slaving away for forty-eight solid hours on your behalf. I was looking for facts, not dreaming up practical jokes." He sighed heavily. "I thought you knew me better than that."

Hobbes felt his anger subside a little as the historian waved a hand at the computer.

"How do you think I felt when this answer came up the first time?" Hunter said. "Or the second, third and fourth times? Believe you me, I was just as annoyed by the sheer damned absurdity of it—and then I remembered something.

"Preposterous or not, it had to be double-checked, which meant me digging through those old naval archives and making long calls to the USA. What I found backs this answer to the hilt, and there's no getting away from it.

"Like it or not, Barrie, the answer on that screen is the only one that fits. It is not fiction. It's fact. It's as real as the chair you're sitting on."

Still incredulous, Hobbes looked again at the screen, just to check that he had not imagined the solution it had given. The words remained exactly the same:

IDENTIFICATION:	*The* Nautilus*: private non-military submarine*
LENGTH:	*70 metres/229.7 feet*
BEAM:	*8 metres/26.25 feet*
DRAUGHT:	*7 metres/23.0 feet*
DISPLACEMENT (*submerged*)*:*	*1507 tonnes/1658 tons*
PROPULSION:	*Electro-magnetic induction engines*
SCREW:	*Single, four-bladed, diameter 5.8 metres/19 feet*
ARMAMENT:	*None, but equipped with reinforced ram*
COMPLEMENT:	*approx. 20*
MAX. SPEED:	*50 knots submerged*
CONSTRUCTION DATE:	*1865*
DESIGNER/BUILDER:	*Prince Dakkar of Bundelkhand, India* (*alias Captain Nemo*)

Nautilus *believed destroyed by volcanic eruption of "Lincoln Island", southern Pacific Ocean, March 1884, following death from natural causes of*

Dakkar/Nemo. (*Refs. Verne, Jules:* Vingt Mille Lieues sous les Mers; L'Île Mysterieuse)

22

North Atlantic Ocean
The Noordzee Marquess

The bulk carrier's deck was bathed in the glare of its own floodlights as the cover of Number Two hold was removed. Anonymous among the working gang, Derek Lynn gazed down at the stacked drums inside the cavernous space.

They were the very same canisters that had been stacked on the dockside at Falmouth. Each bore the same label, a simple, underlined blue triangle motif. A peculiar smell wafted out of the hold in spite of the tight sealing of each drum. Lynn observed that the men working inside the hold wore industrial face-masks and his own nostrils tightened against the odour. He instinctively knew what the drums contained.

Electric motors whined thinly as the derrick above him began to swing round. Lynn moved back, feeling the ship's rail hard against his spine. Like many of those around him, his eyes kept flicking out to sea. The uncanny patch of light was still there, motionless, half a mile away. Again, he felt that thrill of nameless fear.

"Why do you slack, Englishman?" It was an accented voice, heavy with sarcasm. Lynn turned to look into the unpleasant features of Krabbe, the German bo'sun. "There's work to be done. Either you break sweat or I break some bones. It's up to you. Now, get to it!" The thick lips leered before Krabbe moved away to harangue and threaten some other unfortunate deckhand.

The electric motors altered tone. Lynn watched as the hoisting straps were lowered into the hold where men waited to guide them around the first pallets of the stinking cargo.

Out of the night came a piercing, throaty whistle, a drawn-out sound like water or steam being forced out at high pressure. Pale-faced, each member of the *Noordzee Marquess's* crew turned back to the rail, staring fearfully at the brilliant static light in the water. The crane motors stopped. A series of long, husky pants could be clearly heard in the night air.

"I don't like this," said the man next to Lynn, his Lancashire accent strong. "Not one fucking bit. Whatever that is out there is alive... and, by the sound of it, bloody big."

A massive hand, its back coated with fair hair, grasped the seaman's shoulder, hauling him round with little apparent effort. The back of the other hand slashed viciously across the crewman's face. He crashed backwards to the deck where he lay, half-stunned, against the rail. A thin trickle of blood dribbled from one corner of his mouth.

Lynn felt a heat blast of rage surge through him. He took an angry step forward, halting as he found himself facing the bo'sun's pale eyes and the gleam of a gutting knife.

"So," the German sneered. "You English are all alike. A strange light, a queer noise and you stand there babbling like frightened children. Anything to avoid hard work. Jürgen Krabbe does not fear the dark but you will learn to fear him. I have told you once. I will not tell you again. When I say work, you work, *ja*?"

"How big are you without the knife, Krabbe?" Lynn said dangerously. The German's face twisted in sudden rage and Lynn instinctively dropped into the sort of fighting stance that an ordinary seaman would not be expected to adopt, not unless he had undergone a great deal of unarmed combat training. That fact was not lost on Krabbe, whose eyes narrowed to a pale slit of suspicion.

"Bo'sun, what's going on down there? Why are the men not working?" the captain's voice cracked down from the bridge. Krabbe palmed the knife, relaxed and slid it away out of sight. He gave Lynn a hard, cold stare before roaring, "Get to work, you idle bastards!" He added, threateningly quiet, "You are trouble, mister. I smelt it the moment you came aboard. I will not forget this, I promise you that."

Lynn's response, "I'll be waiting," was cut into by another, fearful, shout.

"It's moving! It's turning again!"

Krabbe gave Lynn the benefit of his best and most malignant sneer of contempt, then moved away from the rush of men to the rail. Lynn turned in time to see the bright oval of light begin to move in towards the ship, gathering speed as it came and leaving a ghostly trail of phosphorescence in its wake. He clearly heard the rush of water as the thing speared its way towards the *Noordzee Marquess*. Behind that sound was another, a peculiar high-pitched whine, a sound that seemed to ooze power then, for the first time, Lynn's eyes, screwed against the dazzle, glimpsed the long, dark shape at the blazing heart of the light, and the shining vee of its huge bow-wave.

God almighty—this time it means to hit us!

Almost at once, an impact astern gave the ship a tremendous jolt. Two huge columns of water jetted high into the air with unbelievable force, crashing down and cascading heavily over the decks. Men tumbled and rolled under the force of it. In the same instant, the whole huge vessel lurched, loosening Lynn's grip on the rail and sending him staggering back. The framework of the loading derrick groaned and sagged as a supporting leg sheared. Something struck Lynn a sickening blow to the back of the head and, through the burst of pain, he heard a low, guttural laugh.

Then, as the ship rolled back, a rough hand planted itself between his shoulder blades and shoved hugely. Helpless, Lynn pitched forward, the strength of the push and the roll of the ship sending him clean over the rail and down into the cold, inky blackness of the North Atlantic.

23

Knightsbridge
London, UK

Barrington Hobbes drew a deep breath, refilled his glass and blinked across the desk at Melvyn Hunter.

"Do you mean to tell me," he said, "that the *Nautilus* actually existed outside Verne's imagination? That she's still sailing the seven seas—or under them—a hundred and fifty years later, like some underwater *Flying Dutchman*? Is that what you really expect the newsreading public to swallow?"

"Something like that, yes." Hunter tossed a sheaf of paper across to the journalist. "Try disputing the evidence of the Harding family. That little lot was faxed over from the States only an hour before I called you. It's a copy of Cyrus Harding's journal or, at least, the part relevant to our enquiries. I can assure you that it's one hundred per cent genuine."

Hobbes took a few minutes to leaf through the bundle. There was one page that he examined twice. This was Harding's narrative of Nemo's deathbed account of his own life. The journalist gave a low whistle.

"Now I understand the reason for the history lecture. I wonder why Dakkar renamed himself?"

"The Latin word *nemo* means 'no one'. In classical mythology, Odysseus identified himself as such to confuse Polyphemus, the Cyclops. It's an apt enough name to reflect Dakkar's self-imposed alienation from human society."

Hunter leaned forward onto his elbows. "Those Admiralty archives I managed to see contained further evidence that corroborates the existence of the *Nautilus*. In Verne's book, Nemo was said to have rammed and sunk two unidentified warships. The first incident was in the eastern Indian Ocean on the 18th of January 1868. The second took place in the Western Approaches on the 3rd of June in the same year.

"You'll see from Harding's account that Nemo identified these ships as British and, at that time, both the locations given by Verne were exclusively patrolled by the Royal Navy. Nemo still considered himself at war with Britain, which was hardly surprising, given the subjugation of his country, the loss of his kingdom and the execution of his family.

"Those dusty old archive documents, still classified after all this time, confirm that in those very locations and on those same dates, *HMS Warlord* and *HMS Severn* were inexplicably lost with all hands. Now," Hunter said firmly, "how much more convincing are you going to need?"

Hobbes swirled the whiskey around in his glass, his mind reeling under the onslaught of evidence. "It's incredible," he finally said. "We're talking about two of Jules Verne's classic works of fiction. Now you tell me that they're weren't fiction at all."

"In essence, not." Hunter wore a far-away look. "It seems that Verne got the first story from Professor Pierre Aronnax, assuming that was his real name. I'll want to delve into that in due course. Aronnax was one of three men cast on board the *Nautilus* in 1867. Verne probably wove his tale around the facts he was given, adding just enough fantasy to make the whole thing look like a literary invention—the South Pole discovery, attaining impossible depths and, in the first book at least, concealing the nationality of the warships sunk by Nemo.

"Now here's another oddity. Did you know that, until recently, all the English language editions of *Twenty Thousand Leagues* omitted nearly a quarter of Verne's original and contained deliberate alterations? Much of that was Victorian political censorship intended to conceal the less than honourable part that Britain played in Nemo's life and times. The same censorship was applied to the final chapters of *The Mysterious Island*. By way of example, in the English version, the dying Nemo, in defending his right to have sunk the second ship, says: 'It was an enemy ship.' The French original reads: 'It was an English ship.'

"The English versions make no reference to the execution of his family, nor do they detail the portraits of freedom fighters on the wall of Nemo's cabin—probably because one of them was the Irishman Daniel O'Connell.

"Verne also played games with dates, deliberately confusing them to disguise the fact behind his fiction. He had Harding and his companions become escapees from an American civil war prison camp, but that war ended in 1865, the same year in which the *Nautilus* was actually launched. And yet Verne has the dying Nemo, only three and a half years later, stating that he had lived aboard the submarine for thirty years and that the time Aronnax was aboard—and, remember, that was 1867-68—had been sixteen years before.

"In fact, as we now know from Harding's own evidence, Nemo actually spent eighteen years on the *Nautilus*. The records say that Verne published *The Mysterious Island* in 1874, just four years after the first book, but he couldn't have. Harding's journal clearly dates Nemo's death in 1883. It's my belief that the book wasn't published until the late 1880s and that the publication date records were falsified in order to maintain the illusion that both books were fiction.

"In the original versions, Verne called Harding 'Smith'. Only in the later editions, after the real Harding's own death, was his true name restored. None of these are chance errors. Verne was a well-educated, highly intelligent man, a trained lawyer with a very precise mind. He knew exactly what he was doing. His publisher, Pierre-Jules Hetzel, made some changes to the original drafts because he feared political repercussions, and could very well have re-dated the publication of the second book."

"You put a fair argument," Hobbes conceded. "I find it hard to understand how Nemo managed to build the *Nautilus* without giving himself away. You can't keep a revolutionary idea like that secret for long."

"Ah, but he did hide it. You have to give him credit for being the genius that he was. When he and his friends fled from India, they scattered all over the globe, each with a particular mission. Under their different and probably assumed names, they each ordered pre-designed components from engineering firms in different countries. Firms like Cail and Company, and Creusot in France, Scotts of Glasgow, Lairds of Liverpool, Penn and Company here in London, Krupp in Prussia and Hart Brothers in New York. None of them had the slightest idea what their orders were meant for, or that each was contributing to a single project.

"All the parts were shipped to the Pacific island owned by Dakkar where he and his twenty companions built the submarine to his own design. Most of them were specialists in one or another scientific or engineering field. The vessel was a hundred years ahead of its time, as were the ideas these men turned into reality. For example, they took Bunsen's and Ruhmkorff's principles of electric power storage and developed them to an amazing degree. Nemo himself redesigned the Rouquayrol-Denayrouze regulator and demand valves to come up with the first true aqua-lung almost a century ahead of Gagnan or Cousteau. Sheer, unbridled genius.

"They launched the *Nautilus* in 1865 and destroyed every trace of their activities on the island before vanishing under the sea. Dakkar, now calling himself Captain Nemo, named his craft in honour of Robert Fulton's early submarine attempt. Incidentally, it's from the Greek word *nautilos*, meaning 'sailor' or 'navigator'."

Hunter paused for a moment to light one of the poisonous cigars for which he was notorious. He drew in deeply, exhaled strongly and examined the patterns of smoke as they curled up towards the ceiling.

"It's worth putting Nemo into proper perspective," he said, still gazing at the wreaths of smoke. "He only seems to be remembered for sinking ships as though he were some sort of mad scientist. The modern films portray him that way when, in reality, he only sent two ships to the bottom in eighteen years. Just two isolated acts of revenge.

"What really seems to have fired him was the desire to withdraw from so-called civilization in a quest for freedom. He achieved that and a lot more besides. He didn't waste those years at sea. He was in a unique position to study the oceans in depth, if you'll excuse the bad pun. If Verne is right, there'll be records on that boat that could triple our knowledge of oceanography.

"Whatever else he may have done, Nemo did not sink ships indiscriminately. When the American frigate *Abraham Lincoln* hunted him in the belief that the *Nautilus* was some kind of sea monster, Nemo was content to simply rip her rudder away, even though he was under intense fire. Later, he expressed his regret to Aronnax that he'd been forced to disable one of the US's finest fighting ships."

Hobbes sat up suddenly. "He took her rudder off? Mel, that's precisely the same tactic she's using now, if it really is her. Surely Nemo can't have made a comeback from the grave. He'd be what? Getting on for two hundred years old?"

Hunter laughed. "No, he's long gone, more's the pity. We have Cyrus Harding's testimony to that. Whatever else, his scientific talents weren't *that* good!" He resumed his assessment of Nemo's character. "The man was a mass of conflicting emotions," he said. "Grief, hatred, desires for peace and independence, love for the sea and, strangely enough, for his fellow human beings, the conquered and oppressed peoples of the world.

"He discovered fabulously rich shipwreck sites, stripping them of every last gold or silver piece. Among them were the Spanish ships scuttled in Vigo Bay, on Spain's west coast, in 1702 after being trapped there by a British fleet. He rifled the wrecks to amass a fortune of billions. When he told Aronnax that he could pay off the national debt of France without even missing it, it was no idle boast. Verne recorded that he donated several million to aid the oppressed. An entire chest of gold ingots was delivered by Nemo to the Candiotes of Crete to aid their uprising against the Turkish occupation."

"Ingots?" Hobbes wore a strange expression, remembering the information given to him by Ian Neale. "Spanish ingots dated 1702?"

"What about them?"

"You've only gone and solved a second riddle. Ian Neale picked up a Treasury leak that, over the past seven or eight months, antique gold ingots have been turning up in seaports across the world, on the same track and similar dates to what may be sightings of the sub. The international treasuries are as worried as hell that someone may be out to flood the market but what if there's another motive? Could they have been sold simply to provide someone with cash in international currencies?"

"You say these were antique ingots?" Hunter said.

"Every one of them," Hobbes responded. "Each ingot is stamped with the arms of Spain's King Philip the Fifth, and the date 1702."

Hunter gaped at him. "Bloody hell, Barrie. The Vigo Bay ingots—they can't possibly be anything else. This clinches it. The boat we're looking for *has* to be the *Nautilus*—there's no other feasible or possible explanation. There were probably dozens of ingots still on board when Nemo died."

"Well, let's say it's so," Hobbes said. "How come she's reappeared after all these years? Why hasn't she dissolved into a heap of rust or, better still, how come she wasn't destroyed when Lincoln Island blew up? Mel, what happened to her after Nemo's death? Could Harding and his men have used her to get away from the island?"

Hunter shook his head. "That wasn't possible. During the time that Nemo was there, seismic forces constricted the mouth of the cave in which he'd harboured the *Nautilus*, effectively sealing her inside. Nemo was as trapped on that island as Harding was.

"He would have preferred to be interred beside his former crew in their undersea cemetery somewhere south of Java. That wasn't possible, so he instructed Harding to seal his body inside the *Nautilus*, which was then to be submerged into the depths of the cavern lake. It's clear from his journal that Harding carried out those instructions to the letter."

"And then the island blew itself off the map," Hobbes finished. "The *Nautilus* should have gone with it, so how come she's still sailing the world's oceans doing to whalers and merchants ships what Nemo did to the *Abraham Lincoln*?"

Hunter spread his hands. "Who knows, Barrie? The force of the eruption could have blown her out of her tomb. If the water had acted as a cushion against the blast, it's possible she might have been ejected relatively unscathed. Not likely, but just about feasible. Let's also assume that the jolt, the sudden heat or some other factor, caused her tanks to blow, bringing her to the surface." Hunter turned back to the computer, tapped instructions into its keyboard and waited for it to complete its search. "It so happens that I've been pondering that question as well," he said as an image flashed up. "Take a look."

A colour map of the southern Pacific had appeared on screen. Hobbes leaned forward to study it.

"Now," Hunter said enthusiastically. "Both Verne and Harding gave Lincoln Island's position at 150 degrees 30 minutes west, 34 degrees 57 minutes south." He tapped in the coordinates. "That puts it here."

A tiny white circle, centred on a location some 1,500 miles east of New Zealand's North Island, appeared on the map.

"The cave in which the *Nautilus* lay," Hunter explained, "faced west and was on the west side of the volcano itself. It stands to reason that the blast would have blown her out in a westerly direction. Cyrus Harding recorded that the final eruption took place on the 9th of March 1884, at 2 a.m. local time so, if we punch that information in, we can ascertain the normal surface currents and prevailing winds for that time of year." Again, Hunter's fingers played a tattoo on the keys. "Now we'll set a small cross to represent the *Nautilus*, drifting at the complete mercy of wind, tide and current, and speed up the passage of time. Now, Barrie, watch what happens."

Hobbes shuffled forward in his seat, getting closer to the screen as the historian expertly keyed in his instructions. A tiny white cross began to move across the map, leaving a line trail behind it, sometimes on a curving course, sometimes a straighter one. At one point, it eddied quite dramatically but the direction of drift took it ever southwards, deep into polar waters. Hobbes watched, fascinated. At last, the cross and extending line came to a halt on the ice-bound coast of the Antarctic continent, on the eastern side of the Ross Sea near Cape Colbeck.

Melvyn Hunter beamed triumphantly at the journalist. "The Sulzberger Ice Shelf," he announced. "That, my boy, is where she's been all these years, caught fast in the pack ice. It would also explain why she hasn't corroded away. Nothing rusts down there, the extreme cold halts the process. How she got free of the ice, I can't explain for sure, but I'd guess it has something to do with global warming and increased rate of polar melt in recent years."

"But that area's been pretty thoroughly explored," Hobbes pointed out. "Surely someone would have spotted her?"

"Not necessarily. Have you ever seen compressed pack ice? Utter chaos. People could have passed within yards of her and not seen her, especially under layers of snow and ice." The historian sat back, clasping his hands behind his head.

Hobbes drained his Woodford and poured himself another. "This is staggering, Mel. You achieved all this in forty-eight hours? I'd never have believed it from what little information I could give you. You've sold me on it, however fantastic the answer is. My God, and I blew up at you. My humble apologies, Mel. My conduct was totally unjustified."

Hunter dismissed the apology with a shrug as the journalist shook his head in amazement.

"If I could only track her down," Hobbes muttered. "Hell, it *would* be the story of the century. Imagine it, if I could prove that an advanced submarine, a hundred and fifty years old and supposedly a fictional creation, is still operating and apparently at her full potential. It would be a public sensation.

"Can you imagine how strong she must be to survive a volcanic disaster, a century in the ice and be able to take the rudders off giant-sized steel ships without sinking herself? No modern sub can even compare with her..."

Hobbes broke off short, staring at the computer screen with renewed disbelief. "Melvyn, where was the first sighting of her and when?"

"Early March last year, south of Tasmania. Why do you ask?"

Hobbes continued staring at the screen. "March... Tasmania. My God," he whispered. "*My God!* Is it possible?"

To his great surprise, Hunter saw a huge smile of absolute delight spread across the journalist's round face. "Barrie? What are you on to?"

Hobbes could scarcely believe the thought that had struck him like a bolt from the blue. "Her crew, Mel... her new crew. God help me, I know who they are."

"What?" Hunter's look was one of sheer scepticism. "You're joking. How the hell can you have worked that out?"

Hobbes looked him straight in the eye, his face animated.

"It just dawned on me," he said.

24

North Atlantic Ocean

Deep in the North Atlantic's dark, icy coldness, there lay a measureless world of peace. In a state of semi-consciousness, the body of Derek Lynn gently twisted downwards towards its heart.

His mind could no longer distinguish whether he was in the process of drowning or already dead. It could not sense his body's automatic resistance, seeking to retain what little air remained in its lungs and to keep the enveloping waters from entering them. He felt only a deep serenity and the strengthening hug from the ever-increasing pressure of the ocean depths.

And yet, somewhere in the swirling mists of his mind, there lay an acknowledgment, an acceptance, of his inevitable end. He felt no fear, no regret, not even sadness. He was leaving nothing behind. There was no wife, no family, to grieve over him, not any more. There only remained a readiness to surrender, a gentle willingness to embrace death, a belief that it was only a deep sleep without dreams, without end.

Perhaps it had already come. Numb from the intense cold of the water he could no longer feel, he had no way of knowing. Strands of unreality surrounded him.

Music… the muffled, distant strains of a pipe organ. Johann Sebastian Bach… *Jesu, Joy of Man's Desiring*. Inwardly, he felt a glow of pleasure. He had always loved the timeless strength and emotion of Bach's compositions.

Light… as his helpless body spiralled downwards, his unfocussed eyes took in the wonderful brightness that seemed to be all around him, a glorious radiance from which a figure rose with slow and graceful movements to take him gently into its embrace.

Lynn's sluggish processes of thought pieced together the realization that he might well be required to account for himself, his life, his deeds and misdeeds. His name would be called. Before his thought processes closed down at last to make way for a serene void, he remembered that his name was not Derek Lynn.

25

Knightsbridge
London, UK

Ian Neale paid the cab driver as Karen Marshall climbed the flight of tiled steps to the door of the Victorian block containing Melvyn Hunter's flat. The panelled door was closed and secured. To one side were four nameplates with buttons over an intercom speaker. Karen pressed the button beside Hunter's name and waited for a reply.

"Dr Hunter, it's Karen Marshall," she said. "Is Barrie Hobbes with you?"

"He is indeed." There was a pause. Muffled voices could be tinnily heard on the speaker. "He's on his way down."

Hobbes appeared at the door moments later. "I wasn't expecting you two," he said.

"I know," Karen responded, "but we thought you'd want to hear the latest. We might have a breakthrough."

"*You* have a breakthrough." Hobbes said. "I'd better hear it."

"Anne Collinson rang from Lloyd's just after you left. She was doing a run-down on the merchant ships that were attacked. At first glance, they appear to belong to different companies, most of them flying flags of convenience."

"That much we already know," Hobbes reminded her.

"Yes, but there's more. The companies concerned are Gainsborough Marine of Liverpool, the Figueroa Shipping Company based in Valencia, Spain, Waveways of Bristol and Mer du Nord whose offices are in Le Havre.

"On the face of it, there's no apparent connection between them. Then Anne discovered that the cargo of the *Margarita Sanchez*, a Figueroa ship, was being transferred to the *Noordzee Marquess*, a ship belonging to the Noordzee Line of Rotterdam. The name Noordzee is a direct Dutch translation of Mer du Nord.

"Anne thought it a bit odd that a cargo assigned to one company should be transferred without apparent negotiation to a ship owned by another, so she dug a little deeper. All of a sudden, or so she said, chasing down the records seemed like wading through mud, as though everything had been made deliberately difficult, but she kept at it."

"Go on," Hobbes said.

She took a deep breath. "Every one of those companies acts as a front to a single parent company known as the Pyramus Group. That was as far as she could get. No address, no phone, fax or e-mail number. Nothing. It's so well wrapped up that it's all but invisible. Anne then tried to get more information on the Lloyd's client database, only to find that access is restricted."

Hobbes raised an eyebrow. "Is it, now?"

"Anne doesn't have the authorization. She could only come up with one other detail."

"Which is?"

"Photographic records on the insurance files show that each of the ships which are ultimately Pyramus owned share a single distinguishing feature, irrespective of which company name they parade under," Karen said. "It's small and unobtrusive, virtually unnoticeable but on the forepeak of every ship is a little plaque with an embossed symbol."

Hobbes knew. Instinctively, he knew. "A blue underlined triangle," he said breathlessly.

She beamed triumphantly. "You win the giant teddy bear."

What an evening! Hobbes drew a deep breath. "Karen, can you get back to Miss Collinson? See if she can find out who does have access to those files. Dr Hunter will let you use his phone, I'm sure. And we need to contact Company House in the morning. We have to start putting names to these people."

He turned to Neale. "Ian, do you drive?" As he nodded, Hobbes dug the car keys out of his pocket and tossed them over. "Get back to *The Sentinel*. Pull out any and every reference to this Pyramus Group that you can find. Any mention at all, no matter how brief." He jerked a thumb to his left. "I've a hire car in the courtyard at the back, the blue Ford Mondeo. We'll take a cab back to the hotel." He grinned sheepishly. "In any case, I've had a few too many Woodfords to get behind a wheel."

"Okay," Neale said. "And what will you be doing in the meantime?" Still that flash of professional hostility.

Hobbes knew better than to rise to the bait. "To be honest with you, Ian, I'm not altogether sure. There may be something to follow up on the nautical side of things and I think Mel Hunter may be onto something. Bring the car to our hotel in the morning, nine o'clock, and the three of us will pool what we have."

"Fair enough. I'll see you then." Neale turned and walked away.

"That man's attitude infuriates me," Karen said, watching Neale vanish around the corner to the courtyard. "How do you stay so calm with him?"

"Practice," Hobbes said. "He's not the first to have his professional nose put out of joint and I don't altogether blame him. He might be resentful but at least he's cooperating."

"Was that true?" Karen said. "Is Dr Hunter onto something?"

"It's a long story," Hobbes said. "And takes a bit of—"

The blast was deafening. A thunderclap that lanced the eardrums and stunned the senses. All around them, windows shattered in a hail of flying glass as Hobbes and Karen instinctively crouched in self-protective huddles. On the three-storey building across the street, a huge section of stucco render cracked off and fell into the street in a billowing cloud of dust. Slates were torn from roofs, a deadly, razor-edged cannonade that zipped across the street, embedding themselves in walls, doors and car bodies.

Hobbes felt a searing blast of hot air as he glanced up. A vast rolling cloud, tinged with flame, burst out of the side street and rolled over the rooftop above him, dimming the orange glow of the sodium streetlights. Slowly, he rose to his feet, helping Karen to do the same, and gingerly picked slivers of glass from the fabric of his jacket. It was a miracle that neither of them had suffered any injury worse than a painful throbbing of the ears.

By now, people were venturing out of the buildings, among them Melvyn Hunter, his face as ashen and shocked as the rest. The eerie silence following the explosion was broken by a babble of voices raised in speculation as to whether it had been a terrorist bomb or a gas blast.

Hobbes sensed that it had been no gas explosion. A feeling of dread began to engulf him He cast a look of horror at Hunter and Karen and took off around the corner as fast as his bulk and limping gait would allow.

Of the Ford Mondeo, little remained that was recognisable except for a twisted registration plate in the roadway, widely scattered heaps of scorched, distorted metal and smouldering rubber. The stench was appalling. Flame blossomed from a misshapen pile of material and licked at a blackened, horribly mutilated huddle lying in a spreading pool of crimson.

Hobbes gagged, flinging a hand to his retching mouth and turning quickly to block the view from Karen, who had followed quickly behind him. It was a futile gesture. The carnage could not be so easily concealed. White-faced and on the edge of hysteria, she could nothing except repeat, "Oh, God… Oh, God…" over and over.

The shock in Melvyn Hunter's face was plain but, outwardly at least, he remained the calmest of the three. Hobbes turned to him in horror.

"It was meant for me, Mel," he said hoarsely. "*It was meant for me!*"

Chapter 5

Mobilis in Mobili

↞ 26 ↠

8 January 2015
St James's Street
London, UK

Unusually for a weekday lunchtime, the only people occupying the lounge of Wyatt's Club were Sir Henry Williamson, Gerald Calloway and Sir Robert Maynard. The mood and expression of each man was sombre. The patient Burridge served them drinks on a silver tray and withdrew.

"Dead?" Maynard was incredulous. "Is this certain?"

The Minister of Defence's face said it all. "No doubt about it. Admiral Garvie received the signal himself, first thing this morning. Commander Lindsay's had it. The Prime Minister's shaken rigid by the news."

"But how could it happen?" Calloway pressed. "Lindsay was reputed to be the best operative in the service."

Williamson's features hardened. "Not just reputed to be, Gerald. He was. As you know, we placed Lindsay aboard a ship called the *Noordzee Marquess*, posing as a deckhand. All I'm able to tell you about his assignment was that we received intelligence that this ship was a likely target, and so it proved. She was attacked last night, just like the others. Lindsay was standing by the rail when the ship was rammed. Most of the crewmen overbalanced when the impact heeled the ship over. Lindsay was pitched clean over the side.

"In common with the other vessels, the *Noordzee Marquess* suffered crippling damage to her steering gear, and that ruled out a proper search. Boats were lowered and searchlights trained on the water in the hope of finding him but not a trace of him was seen." Williamson sighed heavily. "January in the North Atlantic, gentlemen. Lindsay could not have survived the cold for more than a few minutes."

Maynard offered the elderly Minister a cigar. "I'm so sorry, Henry. I know you held the man in the highest esteem. You had all your hopes pinned on him."

"Bob, it was I who requested him for this assignment. It was I who sent him to his death and I must take full responsibility for it."

"Nonsense, man. It was a hazard that Lindsay faced in every assignment. He knew that as well as anyone. The responsibility lies solely with those who attacked the ship. There can be no doubt now. Whoever these people are, they're killers. They have to be stopped before they kill again, whatever the cost.

"We can only assume that these were the people who killed ten men at Krakatau last year. All right, the men who died were pirates who probably got what they deserved, but also remember that an American warship was almost sunk by these terrorists only a couple of weeks ago. They evidently have no compunction about killing when it suits them and it remains my firm belief that they also sank my *Aurora* last February, taking ten more lives. That makes a possible death toll of twenty-one."

"Twenty-two," Calloway said. "It now looks as if they have land-based support right here in London. If you hadn't heard, a car bomb went off in Knightsbridge last night. The police haven't yet released any firm details but I have it on good authority that the intended target was the journalist Barrington Hobbes. Remember him? Probably the best investigative hack the Press ever saw until his car crash ten years ago.

"It appears that Hobbes has made a comeback to look into the loss of the *Aurora* and is partnered by a woman journalist who was engaged to the *Aurora's* mate. Like you, Bob, he's apparently established a link between the loss of your boat and the current attacks, and that's alarmed somebody. That same somebody put a bomb under his hired car but, instead of killing Hobbes, it got Ian Neale, *The Sentinel's* staff reporter. Killed him outright. All hell's been let loose and Hobbes has apparently disappeared and got the hell out of London, wise chap."

Maynard was grey with shock. "Dear God, Gerald, this is dreadful. It can't be allowed to go on. These people have to be stopped."

"I quite agree," Calloway responded. "We need concerted action. Whoever they may be, they need to be hunted down and brought to trial or, if all else fails, eliminated as terrorists deserve. If the whole story comes out, the public will demand it as well as the shipping companies and Lloyd's."

Williamson sucked on his cigar. "Since the *Appalachian* incident, NATO High Command has become involved. The PM and I had a long chat with CINCLANT* at NATO HQ in Brussels this morning. He's open to the idea of coordinating naval action in accordance with any workable scheme that can be drawn up. Heaven knows, that's difficult enough against an identifiable enemy. One that's unknown, operating in the open ocean and using a quiet submarine that can outrun and outdive any military sub in service, is a bloody tall order in anyone's book. To find her in the expanse of the North Atlantic makes finding a needle in a haystack look like a five-minute task. We have no idea where she'll strike next. There are good brains at work on this but, to be honest, any brainwaves will be gratefully received."

"What's needed here," Calloway said thoughtfully, "is a Trojan Horse, some sort of nicely weighted trap. A situation and place of our own choosing. If you like, make the mountain come to Mahomet."

"Easier said than done," Maynard observed.

"But not impossible. Look, we've been concentrating our concern on the damage to merchant shipping but a number of whalers have also been attacked, yes?" Maynard nodded agreement as Calloway began to warm to the idea blossoming in his mind. "Would you happen to know where Greenpeace and Deep Watch vessels are operating right now? Specifically, are any of them in the North Atlantic?"

Maynard took a long sip of his drink, sat back and searched his memory. "I don't believe so, Gerald. My remaining ships are both in the Pacific. Sea Shepherd's lurking somewhere off Japan, waiting for plutonium carriers. Greenpeace also has ships in the Pacific and the Indian Ocean, plus one in Rio for the international debate on the rain forest issue. To my knowledge, none of us have vessels in the North Atlantic but I can get my staff to verify that."

* Commander-in-Chief, Atlantic Fleet.

The Trade and Industry Minister's face was a picture of satisfaction. "If you can confirm it, Bob, it would be just perfect. We wouldn't want them drawn in."

"Good grief, Gerald," Williamson broke in. "Do you mean to say that you've dreamed up some sort of plan?"

"I do believe I have. It would need to clear couple of obstacles, though."

"Such as?"

"Well, first of all, we need the blessing of the Prime Minister and NATO and, secondly, the cooperation of the Director-General of the BBC."

27

North Atlantic Ocean

Don Lindsay's return to consciousness met with a nagging ache behind the eyes and a racking dryness of the throat aggravated by what tasted like a cocktail of brine and bilge oil. He also had a sore head. This combination of unpleasant feelings brought the shocked realization that, somehow, he had not found eternal oblivion in a watery grave. Instead, he found himself lying under a warm blanket in a small, metal-walled room lit by a half-globe of frosted glass set into the ceiling. Lindsay frowned. Was it a ceiling or a deck-head?

His nostrils wrinkled to the familiar, welcome tang of hot coffee and he looked around for the source. A metal tray holding the pot, a mug and a covered plate sat on a table in the centre of the room.

As Lindsay sat up, he realized that, under the blanket, he was naked. There was no sign of his own clothing but a set of unfamiliar garments was neatly folded over one of the stools ranged around the table. He eased himself off the cot onto a fibre-matted floor and picked up the clothes, feeling the warmth of a strong, silky material he could not identify. He put them on, noting that the trousers and high-necked shirt were a passably good fit. There were also long socks of a similar material and supple, calf-length boots of what might have been sealskin.

The aroma of coffee was irresistible. Lindsay poured himself a mugful of the hot, black liquid and took a welcome mouthful whilst examining the pot, the tray and its contents. Their severe Victorian style was somehow unreal and seemed more in keeping with a country house than a ship.

Assuming that he was on a ship. There should have been familiar, identifiable signs and sounds—engines, activities of the crew, the sea washing against the hull, movements of pitching and rolling. Lindsay could only detect a still silence .

He looked about the room. The walls—bulkheads?—were of rivetted sheet metal plates, painted white, like those found on ships throughout the world but the silence and lack of any perceptible motion did not add up. Was this place on land or sea?

The strong, life-restoring coffee purged the awful taste from his mouth. Lindsay decided that solving mysteries could wait until he had eaten. Removing the plate cover revealed fried eggs, toast and sausages. Like the coffee, the food was hot and could only have been brought moments before he had come round. He sat down to enjoy the most welcome meal he could remember.

The cutlery was as unusual in design as the tray and the coffee pot. Each piece was inscribed with a curious device, a flamboyant capital N and a three-word script that his still unfocussed eyes could not quite decipher. It seemed to be in Latin.

A cut of toast and egg halted halfway to his mouth as a door unexpectedly opened on the far side of the room. A man stepped inside. Of medium height, he was sturdily built with a shock of black hair, a full, piratical beard and dark, watchful eyes. He appeared to be unarmed but Lindsay mentally summed him up as a potentially dangerous combination, an intelligent bruiser.

The man's voice was deep and pleasant, the words delivered with a quiet strength. Lindsay placed the accent as British, West Country, but could not pin it closer.

"Good morning. I'm pleased to see you've recovered. How's the breakfast?"

"Good," Lindsay said. "Very good. My compliments to the chef."

The bearded man smiled widely. "The chef is delighted to hear it. I figured you might wake up with an appetite. Go ahead, eat up while it's hot. There's plenty more if you want it."

He continued talking as Lindsay resumed his meal. "You may well be wondering how it is you're warm, well and fed instead of decorating the bottom of the North Atlantic. The fact is that we just couldn't bear to see a good man go to waste, so we pulled you out."

"Very humanitarian of you," Lindsay said, sourly. "I suppose it makes a change from crippling innocent ships."

The bearded man shrugged off the sarcasm. "I really wouldn't know. We've never touched an innocent ship, just the guilty ones. That includes the *Noordzee Marquess* but, then, you may have seen enough to have worked that out for yourself. In any case, all we've ever done is to render them useless." He cast his eyes down to the floor. "There was one exception, and none of us is proud of it. We sank a Malay pirate boat in the Sunda Strait last year. She was attacking a helpless yacht and her crew would have murdered innocent people if we hadn't intervened. There wasn't time to consider alternatives, so we sank her."

"And killed ten men into the bargain," Lindsay said sharply.

The stranger sat down suddenly, his mouth open in what seemed to be genuine shock. Lindsay knew it was no act as he noted the man's sudden pallor.

"Oh, no..." He seemed lost for words. "For the love of God, keep that between you and me. Don't let the others know... it would destroy them. They've been through enough already." His words tailed off. Obviously agitated, the bearded man stood up and began to pace the room.

Lindsay silently observed the man's discomfort until, after two or three minutes, he seemed to pull himself together and sat down again on the opposite stool.

"I was going to ask you not to think of us as terrorists or murderers, Commander Lindsay. But now..."

Lindsay stiffened at the unexpected use of his name. A piece of egg slid off his fork and landed on his plate with a soft *plop*. The other man gave him a taut smile.

"Commander Donall McEwan Lindsay, Royal Navy," he elaborated. "Or to be more precise, Royal Naval Intelligence. Your renown somewhat precedes you. I suppose we should be honoured to merit the attentions of such an accomplished man. I should add that we did take the liberty of removing your ankle holster and gun. We really couldn't have you running around armed to the teeth. Speaking of which, Commander, would you be kind enough to return your knife to the breakfast tray? You really have no need for it. I give you my word on that."

Lindsay gave way to a rueful smile as he removed the knife from his waistband, laid it on his plate and pushed the tray away from him. "You're an observant bastard, I'll grant you that much." he commented.

The man looked hurt by that. "Bastard, am I? Now what sort of bastard willingly prevents a man from keeping a date with Davy Jones? Not the sort of bastard that tipped him in the oggin in the first place. I don't have to make any guesses about that, do I? The Commander Lindsays of this world don't go falling off ships—not without unwelcome help.

"For what it's worth, I'll tell you what I make of it and you can judge for yourself how near I am to the mark.

" You were placed aboard the *Noordzee Marquess*, posing as an ordinary seaman, in a bid to track us down. By either luck or judgement, probably the latter, you picked a ship that was carrying rather more than her cargo manifest would indicate. Then, someone sold you out. Probably a signal was sent to warn the captain that he had an undercover naval agent aboard and that he had to be dealt with before he saw too much. It would be best to make it look like a tragic accident.

"So, just as they're about to break international law and dump a load of nastiness over the side, we show up. And our attack gives them the perfect excuse to deep-six the pride of naval intelligence.

"By now, you will be posted as 'missing, presumed dead'. Unfortunately, your demise will be squarely blamed on us. In officialdom's eyes, the mysterious ship-cripplers will also be the murderers of Commander Lindsay. We will not be forgiven. The hunt for us will really be on now."

Lindsay folded his arms and looked the man straight in the eye. "In that case, what's stopping you from finishing the job?"

The bearded man was taken by surprise. "Now, why the hell should we go to the trouble of fishing you out of the Atlantic if we had the slightest intention of dumping you straight back in it? On that argument, it would have been far easier to have just left you to drown.

"Look, crimes are being committed on the high seas, but not by us. Let's get that clear. The same people who tried to kill you also tried to murder us, and the bare truth of it is that we're literally in the same boat. We need your help and you're going to be needing ours."

Lindsay took a deep breath. "I'll require a lot more than that if I'm going to even start believing you. For now, I want answers to three basic questions. Firstly, just who the hell are you people and, as I carried no identification, how come you know so much about me? Lastly, where are we? On a vessel or somewhere on land? I don't feel any of the movements I'd associate with a ship."

"Fair questions, all three," the other said. "As to the last one, you'll have to take my word that you're still at sea. You'll have the others answered within the hour, but not in here. This is a cheerless little room, don't you think? We'd feel better regarding you as a guest rather than a prisoner so, if you're up to walking about, you might like to follow me to more comfortable surroundings." He gave Lindsay a wry look. "I've a feeling you'll have a thousand more questions before we're through."

He had not been kidding, Lindsay reflected as he was conducted for'ard. If this was indeed a vessel, then he'd seen nothing remotely like it. A passage outside the cabin led into a well deck from which an open metal stair led upward to a half-landing and beyond.

"The boat has an upper deck," his host explained. "The after section contains accommodation and storage; for'ard leads to more storage and equipment space, access to the ship's boat, and the wheelhouse."

Lindsay frowned a little at that. In spite of all he had heard and seen, that last statement ruled out a submarine for the simple reason that submarines do not have wheelhouses. Nor do they have tenders.

"On this deck," the bearded man went on, "the way aft passes further accommodation, bathrooms, the galley and a diving chamber—always a useful thing to have—on the way to the engine room."

A watertight door in the forward bulkhead of the stair well led into a totally unexpected room sixteen feet square. A massive table of polished oak and antique style was bolted to the centre of the mat-covered deck. High oak dressers, inlaid with ivory, stood against the side walls and exquisite, gilt-framed paintings stared back at Lindsay.

A second watertight door on the far side led into another room of similar size but rather higher. This one was surrounded by packed bookcases and shelves reaching to the luminous ceiling. Elegant, leather-backed seats were fitted beneath the shelves, each with a pull-out arm or book rest. This room also had a central table, piled with magazines and papers yellow with age. Lindsay idly picked one up as he passed and stared at the date on its cover.

March 1865.

He replaced it and gazed at the serried ranks of books, every one of which seemed to be of antiquarian value if their rich leather bindings were anything to go by.

"Twelve thousand volumes," his guide remarked. "Or so I'm led to believe. I'm not up to counting them all."

Lindsay shook his head in disbelief. "It must have cost a fortune to fit this vessel out," he said.

"I'll say it did. A king's ransom, not that we can claim any credit for it."

The naval agent caught the expression of wry amusement on the man's face. "What's the big joke?" he demanded suspiciously.

"No joke, Commander. You're just reminding me of how I felt when I first saw all this. Believe me, until you've seen the next room, you've seen nothing."

Lindsay later admitted that his face must have been a picture when his host opened the next watertight door. The fact that there were several people in the room was virtually lost on him as his first sight of the room itself rocked him back on his heels.

Thirty-three feet long and more than twenty wide, this saloon measured fifteen feet from richly carpetted floor to a luminous ceiling decorated in ornate gilt arabesques. Where the walls did not drip with luxurious tapestries, they were covered with paintings. Lindsay, himself a lover of art, was astonished to recognize the authentic styles of Holbein, Titian, da Vinci and Raphael, even though the paintings themselves were totally unfamiliar.

"Every one of them an authentic Old Master," the bearded man told him. "In total, they're probably worth billions."

"That puts a new slant on the case," Lindsay said coldly. "I had no idea you were involved with art theft. Isn't simple piracy enough for you?"

To his surprise, his guide laughed out loud. "No, Commander, I don't think that really suits us. If you were to look into official records, I think you'd find that these pieces have been listed as 'lost' or 'missing' for decades. The truth of the matter is that they've been here all the time."

Lindsay was in no mood for riddles and decided to drop the issue for the moment. Instead, he let his eyes inspect the remainder of the room. Its corners held exquisite statuettes of marble and bronze on fluted pedestals and against the after bulkhead, beside the door he had entered by, stood a beautiful miniature pipe organ, complete with a full set of stops, foot pedals and dual manuals.

The centrepiece of the room was a vast oyster shell a good six feet across which had been adapted into an electrically operated fountain, the playing water being lit by tiny spotlights to produce an almost magical effect. Around this were a series of glazed display cases containing shells, corals and pearls. An ornate pediment raised above these and the fountain bore the same capital letter N and the three word Latin motto he had seen on his breakfast ware. This time he could read it without difficulty:

MOBILIS IN MOBILE

N

The bearded man noticed Lindsay's interest. "You can translate that in various ways," he said. "'Moving within movement', 'Changing with change' or perhaps 'Free in a free world'. Personally, I prefer the first translation."

The seating in the room was magnificent, gently curving, richly upholstered couches and divans. Of the five people present, three were women; a blonde who had given him a brief wave and a dazzling smile; a brunette who had merely glanced up from the pages of a book and a pretty, dark-haired girl who seemed to be little more than a teenager.

She had looked openly frightened of Lindsay but had now resumed sketching a man's portrait from a large sepia-tint photograph taking pride of place on the forward bulkhead above an array of dials and instruments. The picture attracted his curiosity. It was of a neatly bearded man in his late forties or early fifties, with dark hair greying at the temples and falling to the shoulders. The face was handsome with a proud expression bordering on the haughty. The nose was straight and finely chiselled, and the dark, large-lidded eyes were widely spaced and almost hypnotically powerful.

Beneath the portrait, on either side of a small table, two men were playing chess. One was a tall, long-limbed Scandinavian type with hair so blond it was almost white. In complete contrast, his opponent was a powerfully built Afro-Caribbean whose face plucked faint chords of familiarity within Lindsay's memory. The contrast between the two men was heightened by the fact that the pale Scandinavian was playing the black chessmen while his ebony opponent played the white.

Lindsay's curiosity was cut short as, without apparent warning, the room lights dimmed. There was a sliding sound as panels drew back and brilliant light burst into the room through what seemed to be widening splits in the walls on either side. He tensed, taking an involuntary step back before moving to the revealed oblong window on the port side and staring out in sheer disbelief.

28

Extract from The Sentinel *newspaper,*
KNIGHTSBRIDGE BOMB OUTRAGE
Sentinel *Reporter Killed*

TERRORISM struck at the heart of London last night when a massive bomb exploded in a private courtyard in Knightsbridge, killing one person and causing extensive damage to property over a wide area.

For the editor and staff of this newspaper, the extent of the outrage is compounded by the death of its sole victim, The Sentinel's *staff reporter Ian Neale. It can be revealed that the bomb had been placed under a Ford Mondeo hired by* The Sentinel's *former investigative journalist, the legendary Barrington Hobbes, who appears to have been the intended victim.*

Hobbes, forced into retirement in 2005 following an attempt on his life which killed his wife and daughter and left him with severe injuries, was effecting a comeback specifically to probe the mysteries surrounding last year's sinking of the Deep Watch ship Aurora, *and the current wave of attacks upon shipping in the North Atlantic. Neale was partnering Hobbes and freelance journalist Karen Marshall, both of whom escaped the blast without injury.*

No one has yet claimed responsibility for this atrocity which has robbed this newspaper of a young and highly talented reporter. Ian Neale, 30, was single and his 68 year-old mother, resident in Buckinghamshire, is currently under sedation and being looked after by friends.

The whereabouts of Barrington Hobbes is not currently known but he is understood to have left London....

A deeply troubled Tony Saunders reflected upon his editorial as he trudged through the London drizzle. God in Heaven, he thought, it's only been five days since Hobbes turned up in my office. Could he have come so close to the truth in this short time? There was nothing else that could have explained the bombing. Saunders himself knew little more than that but, as he knew from the past, Hobbes always operated with his cards held close to his chest.

The editor found an empty call box that had not been wrecked by some mindless moron and, using his Phonecard, dialled the number he'd been given. He glanced at his watch, noting that he was only a minute late for the prearranged call.

The voice at the other end was unmistakably Hobbes.

"Where the hell are you?" Saunders said. "Why all this running around call boxes when there's a perfectly good phone on my desk and another in my pocket?"

"To make sure no one's listening in," Hobbes said tersely. "Call it paranoia if you will, but to have checked under the car would have paranoic. No one did and Ian's dead."

Saunders closed his eyes and was silent for a few seconds. "The police want to talk to you," he said eventually.

"Sure, they do," Hobbes growled. "They'll do nothing to find the killers. It'll be just like ten years ago, Tony. When the word comes down from on high to back off, they'll do just that. Oh, they'll go through the motions, make it look good and then, when people start to forget, the case file ends up on a basement shelf.

"The police won't find the bastards that killed Ian, Tony, but I will. You can count on it. I'm aware that he resented me—he didn't exactly conceal it—but when I was a brash young hack, I'd have resented any invasion of my territory as well."

"That's a charitable sentiment, Barrie. However, to repeat my first question, where are you?"

"Bristol, waiting for a flight to Lisbon. Karen's with me. I had a long chat with Melvyn Hunter earlier today. He has a contact out there who might be able to get us closer to these Pyramus people. In the meantime, Tony, I'd be grateful if you'd keep the police off my back and, for Heaven's sake, keep them away from Hunter. Whatever you do, keep his name well out of it. I'll speak to you when we get back."

Saunders sighed. "All right, Barrie, I'll profess ignorance about Dr Hunter and your whereabouts. Good luck in Lisbon."

The line went dead. Saunders stared at the humming receiver, worry creasing his forehead.

29

North Atlantic Ocean

Dumbstruck, Don Lindsay looked out through double panes of thick glass into a beautiful turquoise world. Misted by distance, shapes moved; giants whose outlines were dimmed by the density of the water until they moved closer in. Lindsay expelled his breath as they came into clear view.

Diffused rays of sunshine filtering down into the depths dappled the backs of the huge creatures as they swam alongside in tranquil, effortless motions. His awed gaze took in their vastness, bodies fifty feet or more in length, the huge blunt heads and narrow underslung jaws studded with cone-shaped teeth. With it came the realization that he was, in truth, aboard a submarine, the like of which he had never before seen or even imagined.

"Impressive, aren't they?" The bearded man was standing at his shoulder. "*Physeter catadon*, the Sperm whale. They can grow up to sixty feet and weigh anything from thirty-two to forty-five tons. Their life expectancy is similar to our own, seventy years or so if left alone. They're capable of diving to incredible depths, two miles or more, where they chase after their greatest foe—after man, that is—the giant squid, *Architeuthis dux*. You'll see quite a few of these whales, mostly the bulls, with scarred sides. Battle scars. The squid's suckers contain some nasty hooks that can do a fair bit of damage. The squid's beak can inflict even worse injuries."

He pointed at the nearest whale. "Take a look at that bottom jaw. It holds a couple of dozen six-inch teeth that fit into sockets in the upper jaw. The top jaw has teeth as well but, for some reason, they never erupt through the gum. The Sperm whale also has a single blowhole on the left side of its head, so that its blow is lopsided and angles forward. You can easily identify them on the surface because of that.

"Look there, Commander. And over there. Females with calves. Now, that's a rare sight but, then, precious few people have ever been able to view Sperm whales like this. It's pretty humbling to think that there swims the biggest brain that's ever existed on Earth. It often makes me feel like a mere mortal standing on Olympus in the company of the gods."

"As I recall," Lindsay said, "the gods of Olympus were an unpredictable lot who could dish out some pretty severe retribution when the mood took them. There's a big bull there that could smash us to atoms without even thinking about it. Don't they get protective of their females and calves?"

"Sure they do, but we needn't worry. They know that we're no threat to them. After all, they came to us. Probably out of curiosity. If we do get too close, they'll warn us off with a gunshot."

"Gunshot?"

"They can belt out a powerful sonar burst which originates in that massive forehead. They use it to stun their prey and there's no mistaking it when it whangs off the hull. It sounds exactly like a gunshot, too. If you were unlucky enough to be out there in a wetsuit, and they aimed one at you, it would scramble your insides like a grenade going off beside you. It's not on our recommended list."

Lindsay watched apprehensively as the huge bull he had pointed out swam closer, gliding to a position not twenty feet from the window. He saw the great eye calmly watching, evaluating and appraising them with an intelligence that was almost frightening.

The bearded man seemed unconcerned. "Sometimes," he said, "I wonder just which of us is studying the other." The great whale fixed him with its gaze as though it had heard and understood him, then serenely banked away to lead the rest of the herd away into the distance and out of sight.

"Show's over," he said, turning to Lindsay. Again, that wry amusement in the eyes. "Let me take you aft, Commander. You might find that engine rooms can be good places for getting answers to questions."

✦

Not for the first time, Lindsay found himself astonished by what he could see. More than sixty feet long, the vessel's engine room was unlike any he'd ever set eyes on. For a start, it was clean. Spotless. Expanded metal catwalks on two levels ran down both sides of the long, tapering space, the entire centre being occupied by machinery that gleamed as if new. This resembled a series of long, sheathed and conjoined drums of varying diameters, the largest being a good fourteen feet across.

All that he could hear was a low continuous hum. Lindsay stretched out a tentative hand to touch the surface of the nearest component, expecting extreme heat. It surprised him to find that it was no more than comfortably warm.

The curving sides of the engine room were, for a length of thirty feet, lined out with bank upon bank of what he supposed were batteries, although their form and design were totally unfamiliar. The entrance through which he'd been brought was, in effect, a short corridor between two massive sets of machinery filling both forward corners of the room. His guide waved a languid hand at them.

"Pumps and water distillation units," he explained. "The pumps are pretty damn powerful as you may have noticed when we shot water from the ballast tanks over the *Noordzee Marquess*. We do that for the sake of effect in the hope that it puts the fear of God into the bastards. The boat's heating system is here as well. We pipe hot water around her, keeping a constant internal temperature of twenty-one degrees Celsius."

For Lindsay, the engine room's most remarkable feature was its quietness, his companion's unraised voice being clearly audible over the hum of the engines that were undoubtedly generating enormous power. He said as much.

"Everything by electricity," he was told. "Our engineer could explain it better but, in basic terms, what you're looking at is a massive electro-induction motor with pretty revolutionary transmission and clutch systems. What you can hear right now is the level of noise created by turns for fifteen knots. She's a little bit noisier at fifty."

Lindsay swung round. "At *what* speed?"

"Fifty knots. That's her maximum." The bearded man raised an eyebrow. "I see you have some difficulty in believing that, Commander."

"No submarine is capable of that sort of speed. The old Soviet *Alfas* could do forty at a push but they were nuclear powered and bloody noisy with it. It's just not possible for an induction motor to drive a boat this size at fifty."

"This one can. You'll just have to take my word for it."

Lindsay went silent for a moment, trying to digest the facts he'd been given. "What's the smell?" he said eventually, noticing a faint, peculiar odour in the room.

His guide indicated the banks of batteries. "A slight drawback to this system," he confessed. "These are sodium-mercury batteries which produce and store a hell of a lot of power. The induction coils are a totally unique design, making these the most efficient and powerful batteries you'll find anywhere. In fact, batteries isn't really an adequate term for them. They're far better described as fuel cells.

"In this system, it's only the sodium that depletes and that is the only fuel we use. Of course, mercury's a risky substance but these cells are well sealed and we don't get exposed to it. Unfortunately, the reaction process produces this smell but I gather it's harmless. It used to be a lot worse. The boat had to be vented to the atmosphere every twenty-four hours before the previous owner found a way to vent off the excess gas to the sea."

"So where do you get your sodium?"

"From the sea. Over thirty per cent of the sea's mineral content is sodium. All we have to do is extract it, which is a simple enough process. Running a boat like this, Commander, is not only efficient, it's also easy and ridiculously cheap." A light appeared in the man's eyes. "I can tell what you're thinking, my friend. A system like this could revolutionize the Royal Navy. Its ships could be run at a fraction of the present cost and make defence budget cuts a thing of the past." He shook his head. "I'm sorry, you'll have to put that notion out of your mind. Neither the Royal Navy nor anyone else will get the chance to share this technology, cheap, clean and eco-friendly as it is, although there's nothing to stop you from floating the idea at them. They'll have to develop it for themselves. No, the secrets of this system will remain strictly aboard this vessel."

"Why? What's your reason for not sharing it? You could be millionaires overnight."

"We neither need nor want the money. The secret isn't ours to give and, in any case, we owe a debt. You could say that we're honour bound not to share this boat's secrets with anyone, least of all the British. You'll have to be content with that for now."

There was a movement halfway down the length of the room that caught Lindsay's eye at that moment. A gnome-like figure emerged from beneath the engine, scuttled across to a bank of dials, blinked at them owlishly, then scuttled back out of sight. Lindsay took half a step forward. Who the hell did the little man's mannerisms remind him of?

The gnome reappeared, mopped his brow with an oily rag, leaving a thin smear across his high forehead, and approached, grinning widely.

"A wee bit different from *HMS Seawolf*, don't ye think, Commander? A fair few years have gone by since we served together on that old scow."

Lindsay's blood ran cold. "God almighty… McLeish? Robbie McLeish? But you—"

"Died on the *Aurora*? Aye, man, I'm dead. So's everyone else on this boat, including you by all accounts."

Lindsay's breath caught in his gullet. "The *Aurora*!" he gasped. "By all that's holy, you're her crew! But how…?"

"I said you'd get answers," the bearded man broke in. "I could have provided them myself but I thought you'd accept them better from someone you knew. Now we've got that over with, my name's Alan Tregenza. I'm the mate on this boat, the same position I held on the *Aurora*.

"Can I suggest we go back to the saloon, Commander. You look as though you need a drink. The skipper, Seán McKenna, will be down to say his piece to you while I relieve him at the helm. He'll tell you all you need to know, and that includes a nasty little tale of cold-blooded murder."

To Lindsay, Seán McKenna's open smile and firm handshake were disconcertingly engaging. He accepted a generous measure of vintage port from the Irish captain but declined the offer of a cigar. McKenna lit one for himself, noticeably enjoying the first draw on it.

"Ship's stock," he said. "Made from a nicotine-rich seaweed and a very fine smoke it is too. Welcome aboard, Commander."

"I'm grateful to you for pulling me out of the Atlantic," Lindsay responded. He gestured at his surroundings. "This vessel, I've seen nothing like her. How did you get hold of her? Come to that, how did you and your people survive when the *Aurora* went down?"

"By way of a series of miracles," the tall Irishman said. "Which answers both questions. No, you won't have seen anything like this boat. She's totally unique and a miracle in herself. What would you say if I told you she was built in 1865?"

"A word like 'balls' springs to mind." Lindsay looked askance at the captain. "In those days, they were only experimenting with the idea of submarines, producing primitive contraptions that tended to sink rather more often than they were intended to. Some used manual pedal power, although there was one French effort that was powered by compressed air. The tanks took up most of her available space."

"*Le Plongeur*," McKenna named the French experiment. "Historical records would tend to agree with you, Commander. In 1865, an ocean-going submarine like this one would have been considered an utter pipedream. Totally impossible—so impossible that, when she first sailed, the sea-lanes were full of reports of a monster on the loose. She could not exist, but exist she did. By the grace of God and the skill of her builder, she survived all the intervening years to be on hand to save our lives, and yours, too. Please, sit down, Commander. This is a story you should hear."

McKenna's grey eyes grew misty as he recounted the events of the night on which the *Aurora* had been sunk, the callous, deliberate ramming that had torn her in half, sending Colin May and Paul Calvert, trapped in the sheered-off bow, to their deaths.

"The stern section," he spoke so quietly that Lindsay had to lean forward to catch his words, "stayed afloat just long enough for those of us who'd survived to get into exposure suits, grab a few essentials and scramble off in the two inflatables we had aboard. We had no chance to send out a distress signal. Our radio had been smashed to hell in the collision.

"So, no radio and precious little food and water. We lashed the two Zephyrs together and drifted in the hope we'd be spotted. We hadn't the chance to collect the outboard engines to either of the boats, so we were down to just two sets of oars. Even in exposure suits, the cold was crippling and we had to huddle together for warmth.

"Towards the end of the second day we saw a search plane way off on the northern horizon. We had no flares to attract his attention—the Zephyrs were operational craft rather than lifeboats, so they weren't equipped with any. I guess the plane just didn't see us. He was miles away, the light was fading… we just didn't see him again."

McKenna paused to pour them both another glass of port. "By dawn on the third day, we were in poor shape. We were taking turns to row, just to work up some warmth. Then Rob spotted a ball of mist a couple of miles away and we knew what it meant—ice and, therefore, fresh water. A touch of hope if nothing else. Two of us grabbed the oars and pulled towards it.

"As we got close, we could make out the shape of the berg through the mist. It seemed to be old, rotten pack ice rather than one calved from a glacier, but it had a strange shape. It had a slumped look, evidently melting by degrees, but its northern end had what looked like a sharp cone lying over on its side. That got us wondering. It was darker and looked so much more solid and stable than the rest of the berg.

"When we rowed around the end of the berg," he continued, "we could see that the cone was just one end of an object lying on the ice. At first, we couldn't identify it—just a long black cigar shape with pointed ends, its belly encased in the ice and canted over slightly towards us. We could see what looked like a flat deck on top with a low, round-windowed piece of superstructure at either end. In the middle of the deck was an empty recess, shaped like a boat. The handrail around the deck was a little bent and the whole thing was lightly covered in frost. It was the strangest thing—it gave you the distinct feeling there were ghosts."

Lindsay smiled at this emergence of Celtic other-worldliness but said nothing as Rob McLeish took up the tale.

"To my mind, its shape suggested a submarine, not that it looked like any that I'd ever clapped eyes on and I've seen a fair few. As well you know, Commander, I served aboard Her Majesty's sardines for twenty years.

"This vessel was like no submarine of anyone's navy, past or present. There was no conning tower but, as Seán said, just these two wee deckhouses with round ports like those you'd find on deep-water submersibles. The bow wasnae rounded like most modern subs, nor was it raked like the old models. Instead, it tapered down to a solid point. I could only identify her a submarine due to her general shape, the rudder and screw and the hydroplanes set in an unusual position, halfway along her hull."

McKenna resumed the narrative. "We moored to the berg and melted some ice for drinking water. We had a couple of handlines and managed to hook a few fish for at least a half-decent meal. Alan then pointed out that, as the berg was drifting north and would eventually touch upon shipping lanes, we'd be better off staying with it, particularly as it was a source of fresh water. As I saw it, that was fine as long as the berg lasted.

"The sub—by then we were assuming it was a submarine—looked to be pretty sound. There wasn't a trace of rust anywhere on her. There was no visible evidence of her being holed and, to be honest, we didn't think she was very old. Stress fractures were already appearing in the ice and it was obvious to me that it wasn't going to bear her weight for much longer.

"We decided to board her and see if she was in any way serviceable. Even if she couldn't motor she looked as if she should at least float. If we could get inside, we stood an even chance of sheltering from the outside elements and surviving.

"We thought it safest if only two of us went exploring, so Alan and I got aboard with flashlights. We found a deck hatch and, although it took the combined strength of the two of us to free it up and get it open, we got inside. It was pitch dark and felt twice as cold as it was outside. You can imagine how we reacted when we opened the doors to the dining room, the library and, especially, this room. That's when we found the body."

Lindsay sat up. "Body?"

"Lying over there." McKenna indicated an empty divan in the opposite corner of the room. "The corpse of an elderly man. His head was propped up on pillows, although the blankets that must originally have covered him lay in a heap on the floor. The body was strapped in place and amazingly well preserved, doubtless due to the intense cold and the airtight sealing of the room.

"I can still see his face, the closed eyes, high forehead, straight nose. Aristocratic features. White beard, long white hair down over his shoulders. Everything pointed to a natural, peaceful death. His arms were crossed on his chest and there were a number of signs that he'd been looked after at the last, that he hadn't died a lonely death. The arrangement of the pillows, the strapping in of the body—a dying man couldn't have done those things for himself. You'll notice, Commander, that we never use that divan, out of respect, you could say.

"There was something about it all that struck a deep chord of memory with me, but there was no time left to dwell on it. We had to get everyone aboard and damned quick.

"We both felt the boat move and knew that the ice was going to give way under her at any moment. We only just got the others aboard in time. Before we knew it, we were free of the ice. The whole thing gave one hell of a lurch. We managed to get one of the Zephyrs on deck, but lost the other. The ice just crumbled away beneath her and, by God, she floated.

"Robbie and Ross here," McKenna indicated the Afro-Canadian and Lindsay at last recognized the features of Ross Jourdan, the former heavyweight boxer, "made a beeline for the engine room where they started to work their own brand of miracles. They worked at it non-stop for forty-eight hours and, suddenly, we had light, heat and even fresh water. Better still, we had working engines.

"By this time, we'd worked out who the dead man was. We confirmed it when we found the ship's log and other books including a complete technical manual for the boat. From these, we ascertained that his preferred burial place was at a spot in the Java Sea, so we placed him in a crate we found in a storeroom aft and packed it with ice for the journey."

"Not the most pleasant of tasks," Lindsay said.

McKenna smiled. "Not as bad as all that," he said. "My uncle was an undertaker and, when I was a kid, the only way to earn pocket money was to help him at his work. I soon got used to it.

"To identify the body was also to identify the boat. None of us could even start to believe what boat she was but, having found her manuals, we could sail and maintain her. We couldn't then get much more than fifty per cent power out of her, but it was enough. We found trawl nets in a store on the upper deck and got them over the side to catch our next meal. There's a well-equipped galley just for'ard of the engine room, with electric ovens fitted with platinum hobs. Within hours, we were warm, safe and feasting like lords.

"By then, we'd made our decision. Even though our friends and families believed we were dead, to all intents and purposes we had to stay that way. We'd seen details of the ship that ran down the *Aurora* and could testify to those. I don't think the owners of that ship would have been pleased to hear of our survival and none of us believe that the presence of that ship in those waters was something the owners would want publicized. If they'd tried to kill us once, they'd do so again or, if our survival was broadcast, our families would then be at risk in order to keep us quiet. Those are the sort of bastards we're dealing with. What we stumbled across is part of a big operation, we're certain of that, and the merchant ships we've hit are all part of it.

"This boat not only saved our lives but has given us the perfect chance to hunt these people down and to stay anonymous until such time as we have enough to nail them with." This thought seemed to disturb McKenna. There were lines of strain in his face before he continued.

"It took a hell of a lot of nerve to try the boat submerged and there we thanked God for Rob who'd forgotten nothing from his navy days. He taught us all everything he knew. Most of us have the grasp of it now and the truth is, she's easier to handle than I would have dreamed possible.

The Irishman's eyes ranged about the incredible room they were gathered in and gave Lindsay a lop-sided smile. "I really wasn't joking when I claimed she was 150 years old, Commander. The dead man we found and later buried was her designer, her builder and her captain. He lived on board for eighteen years and, in that time, amassed more knowledge about the world's oceans than the rest of mankind has gathered since the day he died." He drew Lindsay's attention to the sepia-tint portrait on the forward bulkhead. "That's him, Commander Lindsay. Our benefactor."

"Who was he?" Lindsay asked.

McKenna picked up a book from the table at his side. "You'll find much of it in here," he said. "Aboard this boat, that book is required reading. The real man was once the crown prince of an Indian province. He was Prince Dakkar of Bundelkhand, not a name that many people know. On the other hand, there are very few people who haven't heard the name he adopted when he built this vessel."

He handed the book to Lindsay, who glanced at its cover.

Jules Verne: Twenty Thousand Leagues under the Seas.

Startled, Lindsay looked up at the portrait.

"I see that you comprehend, Commander," McKenna said. "You are aboard the *Nautilus*. The original and only *Nautilus*. Read the book. Compare its descriptions to what you see about you.

"And, yes, you are looking at a genuine photograph of Captain Nemo."

30

9 January 2015
Lisbon, Portugal

"Burglary," José Marcelo Torres said quietly, "is something I do not ordinarily approve of."

Karen Marshall accepted a glass of rosé wine from the small, elderly man and studied his avuncular features as he passed another to Barrington Hobbes. The retired Portuguese vice-admiral, splendidly attired in white slacks, open-toed sandals and a bottle-green smoking jacket, looked troubled as he settled in his seat on the open balcony. It was comfortably mild and calm, warm enough for them to sit out in the open. Torres stroked his trim, pointed white beard and gazed out over the broad estuary of the Tagus, its waters sparking in the January sun.

"I have spoken with Dr Hunter several times during the past thirty-six hours," Torres went on in his excellent, almost Oxford-standard English, "and have done some homework in response to what he had to say. What you are trying to investigate is a grave matter, I might even say dangerous, but I hardly have to tell that to either of you. This Pyramus organization is, indeed, unusually difficult to track down but, as I have told Dr Hunter, there is one possible opening.

"In the past five years, three breaches of maritime law were committed by ships that, according to the information gleaned by your Miss Collinson, are Pyramus owned. On each occasion, the owners—who, incidentally, were not in court—were represented by one of Lisbon's most able lawyers, Senhor João Valdera, who defended the actions with his usual competence. If, as seems likely, Valdera is the organization's legal representative, he might well hold records that could shed light upon the Pyramus group.

"Any such record will not be held on computer, simply because Senhor Valdera is well known to have an intense dislike of them, preferring to conduct and record his business in the old-fashioned way. The only way to gain access to those records—"

"Will be to break into his office," Hobbes finished.

Torres turned back to his view of the Tagus, which was dominated by the vast spans of the 25 de Abril suspension bridge. "Indeed," he murmured. "But, while I may not approve of such tactics, they must be weighed against the greater crime of the murder which took your young colleague's life. Not to mention that of your wife and child, Mr Hobbes, or, Miss Marshall, your fiancé."

Hobbes spread his hands. "I've never broken into anywhere in my life," he said. "I wouldn't know where to start, or how to by-pass the alarm systems that Valdera's bound to have."

Torres wore a strange little half smile as he swung slowly back to him. "Mr Hobbes, let me first tell you that there have been certain suspicions about Senhor Valdera for some considerable time.

"Fifteen years ago, he was a small time lawyer operating from a dingy back street office. Then, and virtually overnight, he was a wealthy man, with a passion for fast cars and even faster women. He acquired prestigious offices on the Avenida de Liberdade. This sudden wealth was, it seems, perfectly legitimate. Valdera had become a specialist in maritime law, with international shipping companies employing his services.

"The view of government and police officials was that something smelt rather badly about Valdera but there was nothing tangible to accuse him of. Now, through your own researches, we find that these same shipping companies are subsidiaries of a single parent body. An organization that no one can apparently penetrate.

Hobbes nodded in agreement. "And the bad smell becomes a positive stink."

"Precisely that." Torres inspected his watch. "Melvyn Hunter has been a good friend for many years and I trust his word implicitly. He and I have discussed this matter in some detail and, last night, I took the liberty of having a quiet word with two of our most senior army chiefs. They have unofficially approved the suggestion I put to them and, in turn, spoke to the man I had in mind. I am pleased to tell you that he has agreed to carry out what is termed a black operation on Senhor Valdera's offices but you must understand that such operations can never be officially sanctioned.

"Captain Félix Saldanha is a serving commando officer and I can tell you, in the strictest confidence, that he rather specializes in black operations that have, from time to time, been required by our government. He is fluent in several languages, including your own, and is extremely adept at what he does." Torres consulted his watch a second time. "I asked Captain Saldanha to be here at four o'clock and," he smiled as the door chimes sounded, "he has a habit of always being punctual."

Saldanha was a good-looking man in his early thirties, under six feet in height but strongly built. Super-fit was the term that Hobbes mentally used. After introductions, Saldanha lost no time in getting down to details.

"One of you," he said to Hobbes and Karen, "will have to accompany me because only you will recognize what you're looking for. I am afraid that it cannot be you, Mr Hobbes. I have noticed that you walk with a pronounced limp and—I mean no offence—you are carrying far too much weight. If things should go at all wrong, and we attract the attention of the *Guarda Nacional Republicana*—the police—we will need to move fast. Remember that what we shall be doing has no official approval and is, therefore, illegal. Miss Marshall, on the other hand, is young and looks to be fit."

He noticed the colour drain from Karen's face and his features creased into a smile. "You will be just fine if you do exactly as I ask, Miss Marshall, but I must stress the importance of you doing so. Every instruction that I give must be acted on immediately. Should we find ourselves in trouble, there will be no time for questions. Is that understood?"

She nodded in spite of the qualms in her stomach. "When do you suggest we do this, captain?"

"Félix," he said firmly. "Tomorrow night at one o'clock in the morning. There will be many people about. The Lisbon nightlife is busy and a good circulation of people in the street will help to conceal any sound we may make. This will also be useful should we need to hide ourselves in a crowd."

"What about Valdera's alarm systems?" Hobbes said.

"Hopefully taken care of," Saldanha replied. "After I was approached by my chief last night, I went to have a look at the target site. Valdera uses an electronic code lock that also activates the night alarm system. When the door is locked, the alarm is automatically set. Unlocking it, using the correct code number, disengages the alarm.

"Before leaving the concourse outside his office, I was able to place a miniature high-resolution camera in a suitable position. Playback of Valdera entering and leaving his office should give us the push-button code. It's simple enough, at least in theory."

31

North Atlantic Ocean

"This is the BBC World Service News.

"Condemnation has poured in from environmental pressure groups as Norwegian fishermen prepare to unilaterally breach the worldwide embargo on whaling. Reports that a large whaling fleet is assembling at the port of Narvik and intending to sail in two days time have been greeted with dismay and disbelief by Greenpeace and similar bodies, none of which is believed to currently have ships in the area.

"Calls for naval enforcement against the actions of the whaling fleet have so far received a cool response from the Norwegian government which has yet to issue an official statement.

"A spokesperson for Greenpeace said today that, if the fleet sails as planned, the group will launch an immediate worldwide campaign to encourage the boycotting of all Norwegian goods…"

"Damn it all, that changes everything." McKenna was grim-faced as he turned away from the radio.

Lindsay narrowed his eyes. "Meaning what exactly?"

"I was debating with myself what I should do with you," McKenna said. "One side of me is saying I should put you ashore, while the other's keen to keep you aboard. From my point of view, you pose a risk either way. Ashore, you could broadcast who we are and, by doing so, put our families in jeopardy. Here, though, a man of your particular talents could easily find a way to sabotage the boat or manoeuvre us into a corner too tight to get out of. You understand my dilemma?

"It's a problem that'll now have to wait. We'll not be going into British waters for several days, Commander. You heard the report. Neither Greenpeace nor anyone else has ships anywhere within reach of Narvik. No current government has the will or the backbone to enforce international law so, if this obscenity is to be stopped, it's down to us."

"By what means? By attacking the whaling fleet?"

"If necessary, yes. We will only be defending the law. Norway was a signatory to the whaling embargo, which makes it legally binding on them. And don't give me any lectures about not taking the law into our own hands, because if no one else bothers to enforce that law, someone has to."

"And that justifies vigilante action?"

"Yes, when nobody else is willing to act, it bloody well does. I'll remind you that it was only such vigilante action by Greenpeace, ourselves and the other groups that forced this embargo in the first place. It forced nuclear disarmament. People-power exerted without bloodshed can work, and has worked, miracles. It wasn't politicians that brought down the Berlin Wall, Commander. It was ordinary people, united in a determination to bring freedom.

"This is what we devoted our lives to, both now and when we sailed on the *Aurora*. In your own way, you're little different. You put every effort into your profession just as we do with ours. So cut us some slack, Commander. Don't make me have to keep you under lock and key."

Lindsay's eyes went cold.

"Let's not even go into that," McKenna said hurriedly. "Look, when we get to Narvik, we'll put out a radio warning that any whaling ship that sails will be disabled. Then it will be their choice and their risk. Now, are you prepared to accept that?"

"For now, McKenna, I'll reserve judgement," Lindsay said. "Perhaps I should see at first hand how you do operate. I will agree to let you get to

Narvik without interference from me but, if any action of yours puts as much as a single life at risk, I'll spread you and your boat all over the Norwegian Sea. Now, do we have an understanding?"

McKenna gave him a wry smile. "I call that fair enough."

Lindsay relaxed. "We must be sixteen hundred miles from Narvik. I'm interested in seeing just how this boat intends to get there in forty-eight hours."

"Never underestimate the *Nautilus*, Commander. Just sit back and enjoy the ride."

32

10 January 2015
Lisbon, Portugal

Tense with the fear of being caught red-handed, Karen Marshall had to admit to the comparitive simplicity of gaining entry to João Valdera's suite of offices. Félix Saldanha had recovered his camera earlier that evening and, as he had hoped, it had clearly recorded the security code that the lawyer had punched into the electronic lock. The same code had worked for them and they were both inside. She just hoped that no one would notice that the little red light, indicating a live alarm, had been extinguished.

Saldanha moved silently in the darkness of the office, using only a shielded flashlight the size of a fountain pen. A simple skeleton key was enough to unlock the row of filing cabinets. At his signal, Karen went through them, her gloved fingers sliding the drawers open as quietly as she could. With her nerves on edge, every smallest sound seemed like a thunderclap. She could see nothing under *Pyramus* or under the names of the any of its known vessels.

The drawers were slid shut and relocked as Saldanha checked the walls of the room. "Karen, look for a safe," he said softly into her ear. "If this Pyramus Group is as secretive as you say, any details are likely to be kept in a safe."

She guided his arm and the flashlight around to the right. "There," she whispered. "The wall behind his desk. Floor level."

Saldanha nodded, noted the make of the safe and flashed a smile as he fished a medical stethoscope from his pocket. "A common make," he said. "Not difficult. I should have this open in ten minutes."

The nine minutes it actually took him seemed like an eternity to Karen, to whom every sound was the arrival of the police. "Where did you learn to do that?" she hissed.

"Standard training for the sort of regiment I belong to," he grinned. His gloved hand reached into the open safe and drew out a folder. "Now what have we here?"

Karen took a look at the contents as Saldanha directed the torchlight onto the pages. "My God, Félix, this is it. Let me get the camera out."

"Simpler to use Valdera's photo-copier," he said. "Right over there by the window. There are plenty of people out in the street making enough noise to cover the sound. Just be sure to keep the lid down to mask the light."

She got to work quickly, Saldanha keeping a discreet eye on the street outside. The machine had copied a good three-quarters of the material when Saldanha decided to take a second look inside the safe for any compartment or document he might have missed. The tiniest of red lights stared back at him and he froze momentarily.

"Karen," he hissed urgently. "Leave it there. Take what you have and follow me out. The safe has its own independent alarm, probably connected straight to the *Guarda*, and we've tripped it. Quickly, we'll have company at any moment."

She felt a surge of panic as she heard footfalls in the passage outside. "Oh, my God, Félix, they're here already!"

"Ante-room," he said. "It has a fire escape into a side alley. Take the copies and let's move!" She silently blessed the thoroughness of the commando's reconnaissance, stuffed the damning documents into her shoulder bag, and followed him at the run.

Their feet had no sooner touched the cobbles in the alley than a uniformed figure leant out of the third floor window they had only just left. Shouts followed Saldanha and Karen as they fled down the alley. Fifty yards behind them, more figures in uniform turned into the alley from the main street.

"Alto! Alto!"

As the commando's fleeing figure veered into a second, darker alley, a shot rang out, the bullet striking the wall above Karen's head and whining away into the night. She froze like a cornered rabbit.

"Félix!" she cried out.

Saldanha seemed to materialize from nowhere, crouching low at the run. "Karen, move it!" He grabbed her arm with astonishing strength, pulling her away and around the corner. Booted footsteps pounded heavily behind them.

Karen's heart almost failed her. "Félix, it's a dead end! We're trapped!"

The *Nautilus*

Chapter 6

Maelstrom

⸺ 33 ⸺

11 January 2015
Vestfjorden, Norway

It was McKenna's decision to take the *Nautilus* up the Vestfjorden on the surface and in full view. He figured that, after the *Appalachian* incident, there was no further point in disguising the fact that the threat to the whalers was a submarine and that any sighting of the long menacing black shape cutting its way northwards might be deterrent enough to prevent the whaling fleet from sailing. It would be a brave or insane whaling captain who would take his boat to sea knowing what was lying in wait out there. He toyed with the idea of putting out a radio warning but put the thought aside after passing a trawler and making sure of steering close enough to be seen. Frantically pointing figures at the trawler's rail was all he needed to know that warnings over the radio would be sent by Norwegians themselves and taken seriously.

At this moment, McKenna was more concerned about the trio of shapes dead ahead that had only just shown up on the radar that was the weakest link on the rejuvenated boat, for the reason that its scanner could not be mounted at any appreciable height. For practical reasons, Jourdan had been restricted to purchasing a Garmin GMR 41 slimline radome, which could be mounted on the wheelhouse roof, the highest part of the surfaced boat at only seven feet above the waterline. Mounted on the mast of a yacht, this would have a range of 34 nautical miles but at such a low height, this range was reduced to little more than the visible horizon and was subject to confusion from wave-clutter.

It was his summons over the intercom, just minutes later, that had Alan Tregenza clambering into the cramped wheelhouse of the *Nautilus*, taking the routine care to secure the watertight hatches behind him.

"Problem, Seán?" he said.

McKenna gestured out through the forward view port. The wheelhouse's slanting sides were fitted with four circular ports, one to each side and fitted with laminated lens-shaped glazing a foot thick. The side and aft ports were eighteen inches in diameter, the forward one half as big again. The wheelhouse itself, half-sunk into the vessel's hull, was less than seven feet square and, like the main hull, was double-skinned with an immensely strong cellular construction.

The helmsman sat in a newly fitted leather bucket seat with headrest and restraint straps. In front of him, the wheel itself was a perfect miniature of an old-fashioned ship's wheel, of dark oak with polished brass fittings, but barely larger than the steering wheel of a family saloon car.

Everything lay within easy reach. On the helmsman's left was the telegraph to the engine room alongside independent engine room controls, while the diving plane and ballast tank controls were on his right. The trim bubbles were suspended above him. The sloping surface of the narrow console panel held the gyro compass and only a dozen or so instruments and dials, most of them original fittings. Much more recently, Ross Jourdan had found room to squeeze in a modern on-board intercom, ship-to-ship radio and and underwater ULF telephone.

Jourdan and McLeish had also fitted compact radar, sonar and Sat-Nav receivers in slim new housings at the rear of the wheelhouse along with a second seat that cramped the space even further. These, like the rest of the ship's instruments, had been duplicated below in what had once been Nemo's own cabin.

"You tell me," McKenna said. "Looks like a reception committee."

Tregenza peered over his shoulder and out into the grey light of early morning. A stiff south-easterly chopped the waters of the Vestfjorden into short, white-capped waves. Spray whipped across the low-lying deck of the *Nautilus* and ran down the glass of the starboard view port as she headed north-eastward up the wide channel.

Away to port, the dark, mountainous humps of the Lofoten Islands marched away into the distance, their heads embedded in cloud. Squinting, Tregenza could just make out a trio of light grey shapes on the water, perhaps four miles ahead. McKenna passed him a set of binoculars.

"Naval vessels of some kind," the mate said. "Not large, probably fishery protection ships. How far out are we from Narvik?"

"A hundred miles at least, but it wouldn't do for us to get too close. The fjord gets a mite cramped up there. The whalers will have to come this way and I figure it best to stooge around here, or maybe a little further up where there's still enough room for us to manoeuvre. Let them come to us."

"Well, let's not get any closer to those three. We lie low in the water so, if we can only just make them out, the chances are that they haven't spotted us yet, especially as we're bow on to them. Unless they've tagged us on radar. They could be there to persuade the whalers not to sail, except that they're facing the wrong way. Has it occurred to you that they may be an advance guard waiting for Greenpeace to show or, for that matter, us?"

"Point taken, Alan. We were seen by a local trawler thirty minutes ago but these guys could never have got here from Narvik in that short time. I agree, we'll keep our distance. We don't want to give them any excuse to use us for target practice."

Tregenza turned to leave, glancing out of the after port as he turned. "I think you might have neglected to check astern," he said tonelessly.

McKenna twisted round in his seat. "What is it?"

"Seán, get someone to bring Lindsay up here and tell them to make it quick."

Just a couple of minutes later, Don Lindsay was looking around the wheelhouse with great interest after being guided up through the hatch. Three people in its confined space scarcely left any room to move.

"Well," he said. "This is different. A submarine that lets you see where you're going. What's in the deck housing behind us?"

"Searchlight," Tregenza told him. "Similar to a lighthouse where the light source is contained and intensified by a series of prismatic lenses. It's mounted on gimbals and capable of penetrating the water for a healthy distance around us."

Lindsay was suitably impressed. "Which explains the mysterious moving light in the water," he said.

"Exactly. The wheelhouse, searchlight housing and deck rail can all be hydraulically retracted into the hull. Reinforced deckplates then slide over the openings for additional protection."

"Under those circumstances, how do you get to see where you're going?"

Tregenza pointed forward. "Recessed ports, one either side of the deck forepeak, coincide with the forward wheelhouse port when fully retracted. They look a little like torpedo tubes but, of course, they're not. Visibility isn't perfect, but just about adequate."

McKenna interrupted brusquely. "We didn't bring you up here for a guided tour, Commander. We need your recognition skills." He handed over his binoculars. "Take a look dead ahead and tell me what you see."

"Corvettes, probably Norwegian," Lindsay said after studying the lines of the three vessels to the north. "Armed, of course."

"Much as we thought," McKenna said. "Now, take a look astern."

Lindsay took a long look and whistled. "Now there we have serious trouble. At around five miles range we have four warships, line abreast, nicely spaced apart and heading on the same bearing as ourselves. I can't be a hundred per cent certain but I'd suggest a French C70 guided missile destroyer, two British frigates—an Amazon class and a Type 23—and a Dutch Tromp Class destroyer. That last one's a definite from the massive radar dome aloft of the bridge. Very distinctive. They'll all have us on their radar scopes. By going in on the surface, McKenna, you've unzipped our fly." He handed the binoculars back and gave the Irish captain a wry smile. "Not to put too fine a point on it I'd say that, as far as you're concerned, the Vestfjorden's doing a pretty good impression of Shit Creek. You're well boxed in and I'd suggest you've been very nicely set up."

"Set up is right," McKenna said bitterly. "Bloody BBC. A lie, a deliberately concocted lie which was intended to lure us up here. What's the betting there are no whalers at Narvik and never damn well were? A well-laid trap and we've sailed straight into it."

Lindsay leant nonchalantly against the bulkhead. "Ships from four navies. A NATO operation and believe me, McKenna, NATO has more than enough clout to manipulate the BBC. You have to admit, it's clever. They've chosen the perfect killing ground."

"I do wish you wouldn't use words like that," McKenna murmured ruefully.

Ignoring the comment, Lindsay rubbed it in even further. "Norway to the east, the Lofoten Islands to the west and the seaway blockaded fore and aft. At least one of the vessels astern of us will have the Mark 60 torpedo. The *Nautilus* might have brought us sixteen hundred miles in forty-eight hours, but she can't outrun one of those like she did the *Appalachian's* Mark 46. Which reminds me to ask why you hung about after hitting the *Dogger Bank*?"

"A problem with the retraction hydraulics," Tregenza confessed. "We couldn't raise the wheelhouse until Rob fixed it, and that had to be done on the surface. Since then, he's given the gear a thorough overhaul and, with luck, it shouldn't happen again."

A light flashed on the console in front of McKenna, who slipped on a pair of headphones and listened. "A courtesy call from one of the British ships," he announced calmly. "I'll put it on speaker."

"... *HMS Challenge*, Royal Navy, acting under NATO orders. Richard Priest commanding. Please respond. Over." The clipped tones of a public school education.

"In your situation, I'd advise a response," Lindsay said.

McKenna sighed deeply. "I suppose you're right. What do you think, Alan?"

"Can't do any harm," Tregenza said.

McKenna picked up the handset. "*HMS Challenge, HMS Challenge*, this is the private environmental protection submarine *Nautilus*," he transmitted, using a jocular tone. "Good morning, Captain Priest. What can I do for you? Over."

"Lieutenant-Commander Priest, actually, *Nautilus*. Have I the pleasure of speaking to Captain Nemo?" There was no mistaking the sardonic tone.

McKenna grinned delightedly in spite of the situation. "You have no idea how close to the truth you are, Commander Priest," he responded with obvious relish.

"Very droll, *Nautilus*," came the laconic reply. "You are required to heave-to, stop your engines and prepare to be boarded. Your vessel and crew are under arrest. Do you understand? Over."

"I don't appear to be in breach of any law that I'm aware of, *Challenge*," McKenna drilled back. "What is the reason for your request?"

"I should have thought that a string of disabled ships was reason enough, *Nautilus*. Nor is this a request. Are you prepared to accede to my orders?"

"Are you sure you're chasing the right people, *Challenge*? Oh, I don't deny incapacitating certain vessels that were breaching international maritime law by unlawfully disposing of toxic substances. Why have you not targetted them? Have any of those ships been inspected and arrested? If not, why not?

"I won't stoop to denying my actions. Why should I? Sea Shepherd's been ramming Japanese plutonium carriers for years but no one sends a naval flotilla after them, do they? No, it's my vessel, isn't it, Commander Priest? Your governments have realized her rather remarkable performance capabilities and someone wants to lay their greedy hands on her. Am I right?"

"That is not my concern, *Nautilus*. I will ask you just once more. Do you intend to obey my instructions?"

Play for time, McKenna thought. "*Challenge*, while I have no wish to hand my vessel over to anyone, you will appreciate that this is a civilian vessel where, unlike a military vessel, a measure of democracy applies. Will you allow me time to consult my crew and assess their wishes?"

"Very well, *Nautilus*, you have your moment." The tone of the voice strongly implied the unspoken thought of: *You cheeky bugger*. "I will allow you fifteen minutes only. If, after that time, you decide to defy my orders, or fail to respond further, I will have no choice but to open fire on you. Do I make myself clear?"

"Perfectly clear, thank you, *Challenge*. *Nautilus*, out." McKenna turned to Tregenza. "Ideas needed, Alan, and fast."

Lindsay broke in. "Let's just look at the situation here—"

"Spare us the lecture, Commander. We can see how bad it is."

"Hear me out, McKenna. On the face of it, there's no way out. On the other hand, maybe there is."

"By giving ourselves up, I suppose? You listen to me, two of our friends lie dead at the bottom of the Ross Sea and we were intended to join them. Now, you tell me how we root out their killers from the confines of a cell? Always assuming, of course, that we didn't meet with an unfortunate accident before we ever got to that cell.

"And another thing. Strange as this might sound to your ears, we owe a deep debt to a man who's been dead for more than a hundred years. This vessel, *his* vessel, saved our lives. She saved yours as well, Commander, in case you'd forgotten. Do you think we're about to allow his *Nautilus* to fall into the hands of the very forces that subjugated Nemo's country and murdered his family? To let them dissect her and gain from his genius?

"Not a hope, Commander. To hell with the people behind Priest's orders—the politicians and the profiteers, and, how bloody often the two are the same. They're the only people on earth who oppose and obstruct what we, Greenpeace and the other environmental groups do. What about the ordinary people, millions of them, who support us to the hilt? This is their planet, too. They're just as sick of what the profiteers are doing to it, all in the name of laying their grubby hands on as much money as they can during their own short, worthless, greedy bloody lifetimes. They don't give a flying fuck what sort of world their own children and grandchildren will inherit, but the rest of the world does give a damn. If there's any way out of this trap, we have a duty to take it and not betray them by surrendering."

Lindsay gazed at the animated Irishman. "Have you quite finished, McKenna? I'm not about to suggest any such thing. There is a way out if only you'd shut up and listen."

McKenna's eyes narrowed with suspicion. "Now why would you do that for us?"

"My specific orders," Lindsay said patiently, "were to get to the bottom of the shipping incidents. So far, I've found out who's responsible and why, but as far as I'm concerned, that's a long way from the root of the matter. I take your point that you can achieve nothing from the inside of a cell. It's in my interests to keep you from being apprehended which, as you rightly say, would only serve to keep the real villains of the piece concealed. It would appear that, from here on in, your mission and mine are one and the same.

"I can suggest an escape route—one which ought to shake off the cavalry. If we're mad enough to take it, we'll be going where they dare not. Are either of you gentlemen familiar with these waters?"

"Can't say that I am," McKenna said. "How about you, Alan?"

The Cornishman shook his head.

"What I'm going to suggest is, at best, a bloody rough ride," Lindsay told them. "At worse, it could be the end of us. Does the name Moskenestraumen mean anything to you?"

"Not to me," McKenna answered. "Sounds like a Teutonic opera."

Lindsay indicated the soaring hump of cloud-capped land to the west. "That's Lofotodden, the southern tip of the island of Moskenesoy. A five-mile gap separates that from a small island called Mosken, then there's a series of islets and shoal waters until the island of Vaeroy that are too full of hazards to even consider navigating through. That leaves us the gap between Mosken and Moskenesoy. The Moskenestraumen.

"Because of the underwater topography, we are even further restricted to the northern three miles between Lofotodden and two little islets called Kjeldholm and Hogsholm. As we enter—if we enter—we'll have to watch for a submerged ledge known as the Herjeskallen that we have to leave on our port side. That usually creates a lot of white water, even in calm conditions, so it shouldn't prove too difficult to avoid it.

"The three mile gap that remains is free from concealed hazards but, between tides, it's a hazard in itself. In fact, it can be the worst stretch of water anywhere in the world. Personally, I've never clapped eyes on the place, let alone been through it, but the *Nautilus* has, way back in 1868, according to Nemo's log. This sub came through then and, with luck, she might just survive it again. No one in his right mind would even try this, but we can also be pretty damn sure that no sane man would dare follow us.

"If you're willing to take the chance, McKenna, you'd better decide fast. However, if you agree to it, it will be with me at the helm for the simple reason that I do know at least something about this place. It's only fair to tell you, though, that the Moskenestraumen has more than one name.

"It's better known as the Maelstrom."

SEÁN McKenna stared at Tregenza with an expression born from sheer horror.

"He's mad," he stated blankly. "The Maelstrom? Jesus, if it's anything like the descriptions given by Verne and Edgar Allan Poe, we're dead men if we even consider trying it."

"Poe and Verne both over-dramatized it," Lindsay said. "Just remember that this boat survived. This is where Aronnax and his two companions, Conseil and Land, finally got away from the *Nautilus* in her tender—and lived to tell the tale.

"The Maelstrom doesn't take the form that those writers describe, but it can still be deadly. In reality, it's a massive reversing tide race, navigable only at high and low water slacks. In full spate, the difference in sea level at either end of the channel can be anything from three to ten feet, so the current barrels through at a hell of a rate. Anything between seven and twenty knots depending on conditions. It's at its worst when there's a strong wind against the current, especially at spring tides. Under those circumstances, it can form whirlpools over fifty yards across and create waves up to forty feet high. Both can destroy small vessels outright, or drive larger ones onto the rocks. Over the years, the Maelstrom has taken a lot of lives."

"Oh, wonderful," McKenna groaned. "Welcome to your worst-case scenario, Commander. We have a rising spring tide and a strong sou'easter blowing straight in its teeth."

"In which case, we'll get one hell of a battering," Lindsay shrugged. "It's your decision, McKenna. The choice is that, arrest or getting blown out of the water. Dickie Priest was never noted for his patience."

"It's madness. Sheer bloody insanity." McKenna swapped glances with Tregenza. "But he's right, Alan, and I wish to hell he wasn't. It's the only choice open to us." The mate looked grim but nodded his agreement.

McKenna paused for half a minute. "All right, Commander, the helm's yours. God knows why I'm doing this, but Rob tells me you're experienced with submarines from the days when you and he served together."

"A long time ago," Lindsay said, "and with vastly different submarines. What I have in mind is this. I intend to take a long turn to starboard, away from the Maelstrom. That will give me the chance to at least get the feel of her and create the illusion that we're turning back towards the NATO ships. I'll keep her on the surface and take her nice and steady to keep the deception going for as long as I can. I'll continue the turn through two-seventy degrees, until we're directly facing the passage, then give her every ounce of power she has, aim straight through the middle and hope to hell she holds together. Any problems with that?"

"There's a question," McKenna said. "Alan, let everyone below know what they're in for. Get them to brace themselves as best they can. Better still, get them to strap themselves into their bunks and that includes Rob. Prise him out of that engine room even if you have to brain him and carry him. Secure anything that's loose. I'm staying up here in case the Commander needs a hand."

"Or an eye kept on him," Lindsay said wryly. "All right, gentlemen. Let's take a look at her trim, shall we?"

From the bridge of *HMS Challenge*, Lieutenant Commander Richard Priest studied the long, low shape of the *Nautilus* through powerful Zeiss binoculars. "What do you make of her, Peter?" he said to his First Lieutenant.

"Never seen the like of her, sir. Unique design, to say the least." He peered intently through his own glasses. "She's taking a turn to starboard. Could be making back towards us. She doesn't appear to be in any great hurry."

Priest frowned. "I wonder who they are? Did you notice that her captain avoided identifying himself?"

"Yes, sir, I did. His accent was southern Irish, maybe the west coast of Ireland. Funny comment he made, though."

"Which comment in particular?"

"After your remark about Captain Nemo. He said, 'You have no idea how close to the truth you are'. What do you think he meant by that?"

"God knows, Number One. What bothers me is this environmental protection claim. Are they part of a known organization, or a one-off? If

Greenpeace, Deep Watch or one of those had got hold of a submarine, we'd have heard about it. Especially one as peculiar as this. She's hardly likely to be a second-hand acquisition. We'd have known about her before. That only leaves private construction. Now, who the hell could build a vessel like that in secret, let alone afford her? The whole thing makes me bloody uneasy."

"Wait a minute, sir." The First Lieutenant had his glasses up again. "She's not coming out of her turn. She's port side on to us, taking a north-westerly course. And putting on speed." He gave a low whistle. "Bloody fair rate of acceleration, too."

"North-west?" Priest took another look at the *Nautilus*, now throwing up a huge bow-wave and leaving a dazzling wake curving behind her. "Surely to God they can't be *that* bloody mad?"

"Sir?"

"The Maelstrom's in full spate and they're intending to run it! Get him on the radio, Number One. Get him now!"

Don Lindsay shot a glance over his shoulder at McKenna, now firmly strapped into the second seat. "*Challenge* on the blower. Do you want to respond, or shall I?"

"You do it, Commander. I'll stay strapped in here, all nice and safe."

"As you wish. *Challenge*, this is the *Nautilus*. What is your message? Over."

There was a brief pause. Lindsay correctly assumed that the different voice, with its faint Scottish tinge, had them wondering.

"*Nautilus*, you are standing into danger. I repeat—you are standing into danger. Do you have the slightest idea what you're attempting? Turn away, *Nautilus*. Turn away!"

Above the mounting whine of the engine and the rush of water surging past the submarine's hull, Lindsay's ears detected the express train roar of a shell passing overhead. Away to starboard, the surface of the sea fountained. He shrugged.

"Routine warning shot across our bows," he told McKenna. "Don't fret, he hasn't turned serious just yet. If he does, we have the advantage of lying so low in the water that he has precious little to aim at. Just as long as he doesn't decide to start loosing off torpedoes."

"*Nautilus!*" the radio barked once more. "Turn away now or I will open fire. Great God, man, are you demented? You're committing suicide!"

Lindsay's mind raced. *Every second is vital. What can I say to make Priest hesitate? Surprise him. Make the bugger think.* He allowed himself a grin before responding.

"You always were a hard-nosed bastard, Dickie," he said easily. "Why worry? This boat ran the same passage once before and came through. There's no reason why she can't do it again and, more to the point, old son, go where you can't."

I hope, he added to himself.

The pause gave the *Nautilus* another cable length's grace between her and the warships.

"*Nautilus*, do I know you?" Lindsay knew better than to answer that. Priest continued, his voice tinged with what might have been grudging respect. "You are either brave men or bloody lunatics. Good luck, whoever you are. You'll forgive me if I don't offer escort facilities."

"Far rather you didn't, *Challenge*. Give my love to Veronica. *Nautilus*, out."

"That should keep him wondering," Lindsay said over his shoulder. "It must be four or five years since I last ran into Richard Priest and his very lovely wife. He gave in pretty easily, which makes me think he only has orders to arrest us, not destroy us. Now all we need worry about is the job in hand." He glanced at the instrument panel. "Thirty-five knots and she handles beautifully."

The intercom buzzed as Tregenza came through. "All secure below. I even managed to get Rob out of the engine room. The engines are under your direct control from the wheelhouse."

"Thank you, Mr Tregenza." Lindsay spoke to McKenna. "We'll go to full speed the moment we feel the resistance of the current. Keep your fingers crossed, clutch your shamrock or whatever you do, McKenna. From this moment on, we're committed. Take a look."

McKenna swivelled his seat to face forward and peered through the forward view port over Lindsay's shoulder. Even after all these months, he still marvelled at the design of the *Nautilus* which ensured that, even at high speed, the water thrown up by the forepeak of the deck casing, shaped like the ram bow of a 1890s warship, was dispatched well to either side, leaving an unobstructed view forward.

The gunmetal water was already streaked with lines of foam even though the gap lay a good four miles ahead. To the north rose the black, thousand-foot cliffs of the Helsegga at the tip of Moskenesoy. Around its head, clouds of seabirds wheeled and screamed at the flying spray far below them. On the opposite side of the channel, small islets lay between the *Nautilus* and the barren, triple peaked island of Mosken with smaller, foam-footed crags between it and the larger, misty shape of Vaeroy.

The minutes seemed to fly by. Two cables to port, white water leapt wildly over the hidden reef of Herjeskallen as Lindsay aimed the bow of the *Nautilus* precisely at the mid-point of the channel.

McKenna went pale and checked his safety straps. A hoarse whisper of "Holy Mary, Mother of God," burst through from residual memories of his Catholic childhood. In all his long experience he had never seen such a sea as the one facing him now. Already an eerie confused moan was rising, audible even through the plates of the double hull. Ahead, the sea was lashed into an impossible fury. The *Nautilus*, all 230 feet of her length and 1660 tons of weight, gave a sudden lurch fore-and-aft as the force of the tide race hit her.

"That was just by way of introduction," Lindsay said. "Another reason to thank Nemo for his design—just imagine how that would have felt in a modern blunt-nosed sub." He reached for the intercom. "All hands, brace and brace hard! We're in for the mother of all batterings. Believe me, this will be hell on earth."

"Just get us through in one piece, Commander," Tregenza's voice responded.

At the very same moment, the vessel took an almighty bound forward as Lindsay transferred the full power of her engines to the screw, hurling the spindle-shaped hull into the raging force of the Maelstrom's current.

To McKenna's way of thinking, the fires of hell had turned to water and ascended to the surface of the sea. Massive waves, raggedly creamed, converged on each other, deflected by the coasts and shoals on either side of the channel. As they met, they merged, rearing into tremendous, green, sharp-sided pyramids, spray whipping from their crests. There was no hope of predicting when and where the next would suddenly spring up. The *Nautilus* gave a huge lurch to port, rolling onto her side as a monstrous peak of water erupted beneath her. Lindsay wrestled with the wheel as McKenna clutched the sides of his seat, wincing as the leather straps bit into the left side of his body.

"What depth do we have here?" he shouted above the demented roar of the waters outside.

"Hard to say. The channel's depth varies from ten to thirty fathoms, with up to two hundred at either end. Don't even think about us going under this. It'll be just as bad all the way to the bottom and God only knows what's down there. If whirlpools form here, there'll be ridges and shelves of rock helping to create them. We wouldn't know until we smashed head-on into them. Believe me, McKenna, we have to stay on top."

The *Nautilus* rolled back onto her keel. McKenna shot a look through the side ports, catching his breath as he glimpsed a huge gyre of spiralling water less than a cable away from the port side. Further away were others, smaller but still too awesome to be classed as mere eddies.

He braced as a sudden wall of gleaming water threw the vessel's bow high into the air. Her sharp spur, streaming water, gleamed briefly as she crashed over the top of the giant wave, hitting the surface with a shuddering jar. Half-winded, McKenna shrugged off the heavy impact. Instead, he stared, slack-jawed, over Lindsay's shoulder at the wild sea ahead.

"God save us all!" he whispered.

Too shocked to say anything, Lindsay tightened his grip on the helm.

The whirlpool lying in wait was immense, a dizzy spiral at least a hundred and fifty feet in diameter, its edge marked by a hurtling belt of foam. Again, the *Nautilus* was tossed high on an unexpected peak of water, giving both men an unwanted but irresistible view of the whirlpool's interior. There was no visible funnel, the current was far too swift for that, just a whirling confusion of raging foam but both men knew that beneath the surface would be a steeply angled, spinning vortex twisting all the way to the bottom like an undersea tornado.

Their own crazy speed faltered as the vessel's stern was thrown bodily above water, the great blades of the screw spinning in thin air. The bow slewed drunkenly to one side, plunging below the explosive surface of a sea gone mad. The interior of the wheelhouse went dark. Outside the view ports, a solid mass of greenish-white bubbles boiled like the depths of a witch's cauldron. God, McKenna thought, how much more can the old girl take?

"It's drawing us in!" Lindsay shouted. "If we don't get her back on the surface, we've had it!"

McKenna unclipped his safety straps and clambered out of his seat, staggering like a drunk as the *Nautilus* heaved under his feet. A deafening roar, the voice of the Maelstrom, filled the wheelhouse before a sickening jolt threw the Irishman off his feet. He threw out a hand, grabbing the back of the helmsman's chair to save himself. He yelped as a sharp pain speared through his wrist.

"What the hell are you trying to do?" Lindsay bellowed at him through the whirlpool's appalling howl. McKenna gritted his teeth as he hauled himself, grunting with pain and reaching for the levers on Lindsay's right.

"Got to get the diving planes up," he gasped. "Ten degrees should do it. Give her full left rudder, Commander, and pray like hell. If we don't get her away, the force of this gyre will slam us straight into the bottom."

Lindsay obeyed without question. He heaved the wheel hard over as the incredible pull of the whirlpool tugged savagely at the vessel. Her hull groaned under the opposing stresses then, wonderfully, her screw found solid water to bite on. The *Nautilus* bounded forward, her nose angling up. Daylight broke through the streaming ports.

McKenna kept the diving planes up in an effort to prevent the vessel from being drawn under a second time. "Keep that rudder hard over," he rasped out.

Once again, their speed faltered as the propellor was thrown back above the raging waves and just as suddenly bit again on firm water. The *Nautilus* again shot forward, rolling horribly as she edged away from the immense vortex at ninety degrees from her original course. Her nose now pointed south-westward towards the island of Mosken.

Lindsay shook the sweat from his eyes. "We got away, by God! I swore it had us. I could almost see the old guy with the scythe."

McKenna nodded breathlessly. "You and me both, Commander. I don't believe I want to see this place again as long as I live."

"It's not over yet, although I think we've seen the worst of it. We've still a couple of miles of rough stuff. When's high water?"

"Not for another hour and a half, by my reckoning. Why do you ask?"

"The warships'll be able to get through at the slack, so the sooner we're out of here, the better. Strap yourself in again."

Lindsay turned the wheel slowly, easing the vessel back onto a westerly course. A Royal Navy Lynx helicopter passed low ahead of their bow, close enough for him to see the pilot's salute. He placed his own hand palm-first against the forward port in response, then concentrated on getting the *Nautilus* out of this maritime inferno. The old submarine stoically endured a further ten minutes of the Maelstrom's weakening violence before the waters ahead ceased to be a raging carpet of white.

Above her, the Lynx pilot shook his head in admiration as the *Nautilus* cut back her speed, heading out into a moderate Atlantic swell, before slipping beneath the waves to the peace and safety of two hundred fathoms of water.

Lindsay unstrapped himself, swivelled his seat to face the Irish captain and extended his hand. "Twice through the Maelstrom," he said, wonderingly. "Nemo left you a bloody fine boat, Seán. She may be a hundred and fifty years old but, by Christ, she's a wonderful boat!"

McKenna smiled at the use of his first name, looked at the offered hand and took it. The handshake was brief, but it spoke volumes.

34

Westminster
London, UK

Sir Henry Williamson regarded his Cabinet colleagues gloomily. "The news," he said, "takes some believing. This rogue submarine has actually got away from the trap laid for her off the Norwegian coast. She utterly outwitted the NATO vessels and, frankly, the way she did it is incredible."

"The fact remains, Sir Henry, that the plan failed," Gerald Calloway said grimly. "Was it incompetence?"

"Hardly, Gerald, and I do appreciate that it was your idea in the first place. The NATO and Norwegian warships had her dead to rights but, as you know, NATO High Command would not agree to her being destroyed. They want a complete vessel so that the secrets of her performance can be fully inspected."

"So what happened?"

"I don't know if anyone here is familiar with the Maelstrom. It's a passage between two of the Lofoten Islands and probably the worst stretch of sea anywhere in the world. Five miles of barrelling currents and whirlpools that would frighten the Devil himself. In full spate, it's not only hell on earth, but a death trap. No sane person would ever contemplate trying to get through it.

"This submarine, which apparently goes by the name *Nautilus*, did just that and succeeded in powering her way through. But only by the skin of her teeth. One of the NATO choppers observed her progress and reported that it made horrific viewing. According to his report, she took a hell of a beating and, at one point, came within an inch of foundering. The sheer insanity of her crew's action amply demonstrates just how desperate they are.

"The warships could not follow until slack tide some time later, by which time this *Nautilus* was through and had gone deep. God alone knows where she is now.

"There was one curious report, though. In a radio exchange with *HMS Challenge*, the submarine's captain claimed that his boat had run the Maelstrom once before. If that's true, the man must be certifiable."

"So we're back to square one," the Prime Minister commented. "Leaving the merchant fleet in continued jeopardy. We already know what the knock-on effects of that are on the economy. I also have to add that the Norwegian government stuck its neck out on this operation, as did the BBC. They are going to be highly embarrassed by this failure.

"The reports of a whaling fleet gathering at Narvik have turned world opinion against Norway's government, which is desperately trying to undo the damage by claiming they have persuaded the whalers not to sail. Eventually, the fact that there was never any whaling fleet in the first place is going to leak out and double the embarrassment. Nevertheless, I have called a complete press blackout.

"The Norwegian Prime Minister is, to put it plainly, furious. He's now calling for a full-scale NATO resolve to seek out and destroy this submarine. At this stage, I do not want a hunt on that sort of scale but, if this *Nautilus* attacks another ship, this Government will have no choice left but to support that demand, whether or not the Admiralty and NATO want her secrets."

"I should add, Prime Minister," Sir Henry said, "that Lieutenant Commander Priest, commanding this operation, is blameless. His orders were solely to arrest this boat and not to open fire unless attacked. Even so, NATO High Command is as furious as the Norwegian government and looks very much like backing their call. In my view, the situation has been allowed to go too far in any case. I firmly believe that a seek-and-destroy operation will be proposed and approved within a matter of days, if not hours."

35

12 January 2015
Hotel Metropole
Paris, France

"Where the hell are you now?" Tony Saunders's voice came strongly over the line.

"France," Barrington Hobbes answered vaguely. "I'm having to run the risk of someone listening in to this call, Tony. There's really no time to make safer arrangements."

"Understood. How was Lisbon?"

"We opened a few doors," Hobbes said.

"So I heard."

"Come again?"

"Come off it, Barrie," Saunders said patiently. "The Portuguese police are going through the city room by room for two people who broke into a lawyer's office, one of whom was a British woman heard to be addressed as 'Karen'. All at a time when you two just happened to be in town."

Hobbes chuckled. "She got away by the skin of her teeth, too. Luckily this commando chap we were lent had done his homework and got her out of a dead-end alley through the sewers. I've never smelt anything as bad as those two when they got back. It was worth it though. The lawyer's involved in Pyramus up to his ears and the photocopies we got make interesting reading."

"Good work, both of you. But why France?"

"It never pays to be predictable," Hobbes said. "Now we're a good deal closer to the truth, the death of Ian Neale will only be the start of it. They'll come after us the moment they get the chance."

"There's hell to pay over Ian," Saunders told him. "The explosive used, by the way, was Semtex."

"Untraceable," Hobbes observed.

"The police still want to talk to you."

Hobbes snorted down the phone. "Sure they do. They're falling over themselves to solve this murder just like they were ten years ago. As I told you before, Tony, the case will simply be allowed to fizzle out and gather dust likewise. The people behind it are simply too damned influential."

"Look, Barrie, you'll have to tell them something."

"I'll tell 'em nothing. Tony, if they come to you again, just tell them I'm out of the country on a story. Let them make do with that."

"Fair enough," the editor said after a thoughtful pause. "I won't press you now on what you have so far, but bear in mind that *The Sentinel's* investing a great deal of money in you. After Ian's death, the proprietors are as nervy as hell. I need to assure them of positive progress."

"You can certainly do that," Hobbes said firmly. "What we took in Lisbon is dramatic stuff. It's progress, but still not nearly enough."

"All right, Barrie, I'll keep the owners sweet. Oh, by the way, a fax came in for you this evening, from somewhere in Scotland. Can't make head nor tail of it myself. I'll read it out if you've a pen handy."

"Right here as always, Tony. Fire away."

"It's short, sweet and signed with the single initial N. It reads: *Deep Down 14.01.1530.* That's all of it. Does it make any sense to you, Barrie? Barrie?"

In Paris, Hobbes had gone white. His hands shook as he scanned the single line again and again. Saunders heard a muffled exclamation issue from the receiver.

"Tony, we're on the move again. We need to get to Cornwall. I'll be in touch. Believe me, this story just turned into a bloody sensation."

None the wiser, Saunders heard the line go dead and replaced his receiver, unaware that, in an adjoining building, a recorder also registered the end of the call and switched itself off.

⤛ 36 ⤜

14 January 2015
St Just
Cornwall, UK

The clifftop landscape was wild beyond description. Scarred heather-clad slopes topped sheer faces of dark rock plunging three hundred feet to a restless sea seamed with foam. Here and there, broken ruins reared up from the wilderness like the remains of a lost city. Some were the tapered remnants of round stone chimneys, others were four-square granite edifices that had once housed steaming beam engines. Low ring walls encircled the gaping black mouths of vertical shafts hundreds of feet deep. In one place, a modern but abandoned shafthead framework of bare steel rose starkly above reddened mounds of shattered stone.

In summer, many people come to gaze at the spectacular remains of Botallack Mine and, in particular, the pair of roofless spray-drenched engine houses which perched on ledges at the foot of the beetling cliff. But this was January. Hobbes and Karen Marshall were the only people in sight.

"Isn't it time you explained this?" Karen said to a strangely preoccupied Hobbes. "Why drag us down to this god-forsaken place? Is this somehow connected with that *Deep Down* message you received?"

"R.M.Ballantyne," Hobbes said. "He's the connection. The same chap who wrote *The Coral Island*. He also wrote a book about this place, when it was still a booming mine, and called it *Deep Down*. It's one of my favourite books and the person who sent the message was well aware of the fact."

"There can't be many people who'd know that," she said. "Are we here for some kind of meeting?"

Hobbes avoided the answer. "Let's go on a little further," he said. "This isn't the right place to find what we're looking for. We'll try the Wheal Cock section of the mine. It's even more isolated than this is, there's a more sheltered sea approach and the cliffs are carved out into deep zawns. That's a far more likely place."

Starting to lose patience, Karen swung in front of Hobbes and stood in his way. "Barrie, just what *are* we looking for? A far more likely place for what?"

There was a strange gleam in his eye that she did not fail to notice. "The end of the rainbow," he said. "The pot of gold. Tell me, Karen, where would you hide a submarine? Especially if you needed to take quick runs ashore?"

"A sub?" She caught her breath. "You mean the one that's been attacking the Pyramus ships? My God, here?"

"If I'm not completely on the wrong track, she's somewhere here. Maybe right under our feet. There are places where the mine workings were stoped out into huge caverns, sometimes so close to the cliff that the sea has broken through since the mine was abandoned a century or so ago. Someone who knew his ground could conceivably hide a boat in a place like that, especially if it's relatively sheltered."

Karen looked confused. "There's a lot you've not been telling me, Barrie. Why? I'm just as much a part of this as you are."

"Yes," Hobbes stared blankly into space. "And to be honest, I've been holding out on you ever since the night Ian was killed. The truth is that I learned a damn sight more that night with Mel Hunter than simply the fact that a submarine calling herself *Nautilus* was carrying out the attacks. I didn't dare tell you any more in case I was badly wrong. Now, I know for certain I wasn't wrong. The *Deep Down* message was enough to make the difference.

"Let's find ourselves a place where we can get out of the wind and take the weight off our feet. Then I'll tell you the rest of it."

He picked out a more or less comfortable seat on a rock covered with grey lichen in an area that held less in the way of ruined structures. Here, the rocky clifftop overlooked a small bay on the northern side of which was a square topped natural arch under which the sea ran whitely. Closer to hand, the metamorphosed rock was black and plunged down into deep, sunless chasms, Hobbes's 'zawns', running well back into the cliff itself. Karen waited for Hobbes to explain himself.

"Back in the 1870s," he began, "a French author called Jules Verne wrote a world classic featuring a revolutionary electric-powered submarine. The *Nautilus*."

"*Twenty Thousand Leagues under the Seas*," she broke in. "Everyone's heard of that and most have probably read it or seen the film. So, the submarine we're looking for is named after it."

"It's rather better than that. You see, Karen, only parts of what Verne wrote were actually fictional. Until now, no one has realized that he was relating a more-or-less true story. We're not after any boat named for Verne's submarine. We're looking for the original.

"Both the *Nautilus* and her creator, the man who called himself Captain Nemo, were real. Both were believed destroyed by a volcanic disaster in the southern Pacific back in 1884 but it seems that the *Nautilus* survived. Nemo himself had died a few months before the eruption, but his boat drifted south into the Antarctic pack ice where she was held fast for over a hundred years, perfectly preserved by the sub-zero cold. The increased rate of global warming and polar melt in recent years must have released her, since when she's been sailing around the world with a brand new crew."

"A new crew?" she echoed.

"Hear me out, Karen. They've worked their way around the world and funded all their needs by selling gold ingots that were already on board—ingots from a Spanish treasure fleet scuttled in Vigo Bay in 1702 and picked off the sea-bed by Nemo. Since her reappearance, she's been attacking whaling ships and merchant vessels that I reckon have been illegally dumping toxic waste materials into the sea."

"The photos delivered to me at the *Gazette*," Karen said. "The ones showing leaking drums on the sea floor."

"Exactly. Unfortunately, the *Nautilus* is a total enigma and she's now a hunted ship. When I spoke to Mel Hunter on the phone from Exeter Airport this morning, he told me a tale he'd heard through his usual high-level sources, and one that's been kept out of the papers.

"At about the time you and I were clearing out of Lisbon, the *Nautilus* got herself lured into a well laid trap off the coast of Norway. She found herself sandwiched between NATO warships and Norwegian gunboats. She escaped by pulling just about the craziest stunt any ship could possibly attempt. She ran the Maelstrom and somehow got through the most dangerous stretch of water in the world. She did the very same thing when Nemo commanded her only, this time, she made utter fools of modern, hi-tech warships. She will not be easily forgiven for that. Old she may be, but she's fast, deep diving and highly manoeuvrable, so much so that she's putting the fear of God into the naval chiefs."

"Deep diving enough to have gone down to the wreck of the *Aurora*?" Karen said. "Could she have salvaged Alan's watch?"

"She didn't have to." Hobbes held up a hand before she could break in again. "Her crew are best equipped to answer that question."

Her eyes narrowed. "You know who they are, don't you? Who, Barrie? Tell me."

He wore a peculiar expression as his gaze shifted to stare seawards over her shoulder. "The dead," he said.

Karen gave him a horrified look, before turning to follow his gaze. Her blood froze.

A man stood on the cliff edge, silhouetted against a silver sea by the low sun of a January afternoon. The figure stepped forward. Karen stiffened, unable to suppress a gasp of deep shock. The stocky build… the way he moved… *this can't be happening… it isn't true…*

"Karen." The man's voice was close to breaking.

"Alan… ALAN!" In a half-second she had launched herself into the arms of a man she had believed dead for almost a year.

Eventually, her tear-streaked face turned back to Hobbes. "You bastard, Barrie. You knew. You *knew*!"

Hobbes shuffled uncomfortably. "I guessed, Karen. That was all. I couldn't build up your own hopes on the strength of a mere guess. If I'd turned out to be wrong, it would have torn you apart. I couldn't risk that."

Tregenza extended a hand to the journalist, who took it gratefully. "Barrie, my eternal thanks for all you've done. Thank God you understood my message."

"And the *Nautilus*? She is Nemo's boat, isn't she?"

Tregenza was visibly shaken by the questions. "How the hell could you possibly know…?" He laughed suddenly. "Of course, I was forgetting who I'm talking to. The magic journalist. It's good to see you've lost none of your touch, Barrie.

"The *Nautilus* is right beneath us as we speak, in a cave where the sea broke through to the old Wheal Cock workings. There's another way in through the shallow adit halfway down the cliff.

"You should see her, Barrie. The finest boat ever built. She's everything Jules Verne said she was."

"Who else is on board?" Hobbes said.

"All the old crew except for Paul Calvert and Colin May." Tregenza's face darkened. "They went down with the *Aurora*. The rest of us were lucky." He went quiet for a moment. "It was a deliberate sinking. A planned act of murder. We didn't dare let the world know we'd survived. We'd apparently seen too much and, to protect ourselves, and those we love, we needed to stay dead.

"Finding the *Nautilus* gave us the means to survive and to track down the murderers. It was more a case of the *Nautilus* finding us, daft as that may sound but, if it hadn't happened, we'd have died of exposure within days. We couldn't operate openly for fear of being recognized and that's what made us decide to give the two of you enough to get moving on our behalf. To do so, and not let on where it was coming from, is probably the hardest thing I've ever had to do.

"Since then, we've acquired a new crew member, at least, for a while. A Royal Navy intelligence man, who was assigned to track us down. He's supposed to be dead, too, at the hands of the same bastards who sank the *Aurora*."

"So why reveal yourselves now?" Hobbes asked him.

"We heard on the radio about the car bomb that was meant for you. That's how I knew you were back with *The Sentinel*. They won't give up, Barrie. They'll try again until they succeed. We can't risk your lives a moment longer. It's time the pair of you disappeared as well, so we drew you here to get you aboard with the rest of us."

Tregenza glanced up sharply at the high snarl of motorcycles somewhere on the coastal track nearby.

"Boys on trials bikes," Hobbes said. "They've become a bloody nuisance on the cliff path in recent years. Look, Alan, what progress can I make if I'm to be shut up on your boat? I have to follow things up right here on dry land." He pulled a package from inside his coat. "This is what Karen and I have so far. Much of it came from a lawyer's office in Lisbon, a man closely involved with the people who sank your ship. Details of the organization responsible for that, as well as this toxic waste scam. The same people who killed my wife and child ten years ago."

"Jesus," Tregenza whispered. "Barrie, you're going to have to get together with our navy spy."

"Not if I'm about to have the Official Secrets Act draped around my neck," Hobbes retorted. "This needs to be public knowledge, not something to be squirreled away in a government archive."

"I agree with you," Tregenza said, "but I don't think he's in any mood to put a gag on you. Talk to him, Barrie. Work with him. Let him nail these bastards to a wall, then you and Karen can tell it to the whole damn world."

Holding onto Tregenza as if afraid to let go of a dream, Karen pleaded with Hobbes. "Alan's right, Barrie. It's not as if we have any options left..."

The clifftop atmosphere suddenly shattered as two bright-liveried trials bikes shot high into the air from a low ridge a stone's throw away, landing heavily and sliding to a dramatic stop in a shower of stones and dust. The single rider of the first bike, and the pair sharing the second, all wearing sporty leathers, flipped open the tinted visors of their helmets. Their free hands moved rapidly.

Tregenza was the first to register the automatic pistols and reacted like lightning. Even before the first flashes of gunfire, he threw Karen behind the greenstone outcrop like an old sack, grabbed Hobbes by his collar and dragged him back as he threw himself on top of Karen to shield her from the bullets. Hobbes's heavy body landed across his own, knocking the breath out of both himself and the woman beneath him.

The three gunmen were off their bikes, walking slowly towards the rock. Tregenza, able to see them through a narrow fissure, glanced desperately around for a way out but he knew there was none. They were finished.

From somewhere to his right came a peculiar sound he could only liken to a husky, suppressed cough. The nearest gunman froze as if suddenly stricken with paralysis, then toppled slowly onto his face. His limbs twitched strangely and then he was still. There was no apparent sign of either wound or blood.

The remaining gunmen swung to face the new threat as a second cough sounded. Through the crack in the rock, Tregenza saw a second man fall, again with an unnatural stiffness and spasmodic jerks of the limbs. Pinned down as he was by Hobbes's weight, he could not see who or what had come to their aid. He could only see the third man, now in a crouch, whirling and heading back to his motor cycle at a dead run, zigzagging as he went.

A third cough had no obvious effect. The gunman hurled his stocky body onto the machine's saddle, kicked the bike into life and roared off across the barren heath towards the coastal track, bending low over the handlebars.

Tregenza felt something warm and sticky on his neck as he heaved the bulk of Barrington Hobbes off his back. At the same time, Don Lindsay stepped into view, examining the strangely shaped gun he held, a short rifle with a cylindrical stock sheathed in black rubber.

"Accurate enough," he remarked, "but a limited range. A pity, I should have taken out all three of them."

"Don, help me," Tregenza rapped out. "Hobbes is hurt."

"I'm all right, though, thanks for asking," Karen said, sliding out from under Tregenza's body. Then she saw the blood. "Oh, God, no…"

The bullet had penetrated the centre of the journalist's chest, horribly close to the heart. Tregenza could instantly see that it was a critical wound. "Don, we need to get him to a hospital, and bloody quick."

Amazingly, Hobbes's eyes flickered open, filled with pain. He groped for Tregenza's hand, gripping it tightly. "No, Alan. No time… it's too far. They'll be back… not safe to wait. Get me on the *Nautilus*."

"Christ, no, Barrie. You need professional help."

"Don't argue with me, Alan. I'm finished."

Tregenza glanced up as Lindsay laid a hand on his shoulder. "The man's right, Alan. Stay with him. I'll get a stretcher party up here."

"Jesus, Don, we can't move him. Not in his condition."

"Do as he says, Alan." Hobbes's voice was a wheeze of pain. "I've had it. Don't risk yourselves any further."

Lindsay handed the curious gun to Tregenza. "Take this, just in case. I don't think our friend will be back for another try, not on his own." Seeing Karen's querulous look, he explained. "One of Nemo's underwater hunting guns. Compressed air fires lead-coated glass pellets filled with a lethal charge. They electrocute on impact. Hold on here, I'll be back as fast as I can."

The man-made cave, set halfway down the cliff and reached by a precarious path, was small and forbiddingly dark. The stretcher-bearers, Ross Jourdan and Lindsay, could not avoid the occasional jolt from stumbles on the uneven rock floor, but Hobbes bore them stoically, grinding his teeth against flame-jets of agony.

The passage sloped downwards, curving for fifty paces between walls reddened with oxydized tin. Then, in near-total darkness, their movement echoed in the vastness of a huge unseen cavern. Lindsay called a halt, warning Karen not to move.

"Lights!" he shouted.

The brilliance of the light that snapped on made Karen flinch and stagger back against the only wall the passage now had. Its right side dropped sheer into an immense cavern, its walls dappled by the reflections of the intense white light on the surface of the dark water fifty feet below.

Hobbes stirred on the stretcher. "Let me see," he gasped. "Let me see her." Lindsay and Jourdan gently lowered the stretcher to the hard rock floor so that Hobbes could turn his head and see what Karen Marshall was already staring at wordlessly. The source of the light, the sleek, dark shape of the *Nautilus*, lay on the surface of a narrow lake in water so clear that even the submerged parts of her 230-foot length, from the needle-sharp prow to her four-bladed screw, were clearly visible. The deep breath that he drew rattled dangerously in Hobbes's chest.

"Magnificent," he whispered. "So beautiful..."

"And ours, Barrie," Tregenza said softly. "She saved our lives in the Antarctic and now she's passed to us, the first to sail her since Nemo died."

"For Christ's sake, let's get him aboard," Lindsay said sharply as the journalist's face contorted with pain. "He can't take much more. At least we have morphine and a doctor on the boat."

They would never know if it was the morphine administered by the ship's doctor, Carla Schumann, or simply the ebbing away of life that smoothed the pain from the face of Barrington Hobbes. Heavily bandaged and lying on a divan, his eyes calmly explored the fabulous contents of the submarine's saloon.

Karen Marshall, silent, held the dying man's hand as the rest of the crew sat helplessly by. Lindsay was among them, he and Jourdan having returned from what the naval agent termed a 'mopping-up operation' to conceal the bodies of the two gunmen he had killed.

Hobbes sought him out among the strained faces. "Commander." His voice was extremely weak now. "I give you my word… these are good people."

"I've learned that much already," Lindsay assured him. "Rest easy. My job's to find the cause of the shipping attacks. Their actions have been the effect, not the cause. You know that international crime lies at the bottom of this and, from now on, this crew's quest is the same as mine. They have nothing to fear from me."

Seán McKenna moved into Hobbes's field of vision. "I'll vouch for that, Barrie. The Commander here saved our skins in the Lofoten Islands when it would have been far easier for him to have turned us in."

"I hear you, Seán," Hobbes whispered. "Commander, listen to everything that Karen has to tell you. Read the documents we brought back from Lisbon." He smiled weakly. "I'm sorry, I won't be able to discuss them with you myself."

Lindsay nodded, unable to find words.

What happened then was strange to the point of eerieness. Hobbes's head turned slightly, fixing his eyes on a point somewhere beyond Alan Tregenza's shoulder. There was a look of awed surprise on the dying journalist's face. He tried to raise his head but his strength was gone except for the vestige that found its way to his voice.

"Captain—" Hobbes said. The word had an edge of urgency. McKenna, sitting away from the direction in which Hobbes was staring, frowned in puzzlement. He could not help following the journalist's gaze but it was towards an empty corner of the room and an unoccupied couch on which a dead man had once lain for more than a hundred years. It was disturbing, scary. The intent gaze at no one and nothing, the weak lift of a hand and the desperate quality of a dying man's plea.

"Guide them, Captain. Help them..."

There was a brief silence. Hobbes gave a sudden wide smile, a beam of contentment. Then his eyes glazed over and he slumped back onto the pillow.

37

15 January 2015
Falmouth Bay
Cornwall, UK

At a depth of fifteen fathoms, the *Nautilus* rested on a seabed of sand in the centre of Falmouth Bay, south of Hobbes's home town. Night had fallen and the submarine's searchlight, dimmed to a third of its full intensity to avoid detection from the surface, was all that lit the scene.

The diving chamber door in the vessel's port flank, just forward of her engine room, lay open. From the short ladder that led downward from it, a trio of divers moved across the flat bottom, two of them gently manoeuvring a long, bulky object, the body of Barrington Hobbes.

Tregenza and Karen Marshall had insisted on attending to the dead man and, with the help of McKenna, had sewn his body into a flag of the *Nautilus*, the black banner bearing a capital N embroidered in gold. It was a repeat of the burial of Nemo himself during March of the previous year when the vessel's new crew had located the cemetery of their 19th century predecessors, on the floor of the Java Sea off Cocos Island, and reunited the legendary captain with his original crewmen.

The rest of the modern crew watched in silence from the port panel in the submarine's saloon as the divers, Tregenza, Lindsay and Deanne Fischer, dug a shallow grave to receive the body and, after a reverent pause, backfilled it and raised a small cairn at its head.

Half an hour later, the entire complement of the *Nautilus* had gathered in the saloon, sombre and withdrawn from the death and burial of

Barrington Hobbes. Every one of them had now experienced violent death at close quarters and it showed in their faces.

"Well, what now?" Tregenza's question broke the heavy silence. "We've lost our bolt-hole. The killer that got away will be able to lead the ungodly straight to it."

"Alan's right," Lindsay said. "The mine's no use to you now and I'm only sorry that the man in question got away. Of all the villains I've encountered, he has to be the most dangerous of the lot."

"You knew him?" a surprised McKenna asked.

"On the *Noordzee Marquess*, he called himself Jürgen Krabbe," Lindsay told him. "A bo'sun straight from the days of the *Bounty*. He was the bastard who dispatched me over the side when the *Nautilus* struck the ship. His real name is Hans-Dieter Wolf. He's been a man on the run ever since the Berlin Wall came down. In those days he was an interrogator for the East German secret police, the *Stasi*, and was solely responsible for the torture and deaths of God knows how many men, women and even children. Somehow, he's in with these Pyramus people who evidently find his particular talents useful. They must have air-lifted him off the ship to prevent him from being detained."

"My God," Jourdan swore. "The whole damn world's after us, from NATO warships to mass-murderers. I'm open to suggestions as to where we go from here."

Lindsay got up and poured himself a drink. "I have one, Ross," he said. "We could try to force some of these people into the open. Hobbes and Karen here did a vital job of work in Lisbon and, thanks to them, we can now identify at least some of the Pyramus directors. They're internationally far-flung and highly influential. Among them are some very interesting names. Eight of them hold senior positions in their respective governments. Others are extremely powerful industrialists. That, by the way, includes the nuclear and arms industries. There's a Chairman, the man at the very top but, as yet, we have no name for him. It's my guess that he's heavily shielded, in which case it'll take a miracle to winkle him out."

He paused for a moment to collect his thoughts. "As you all know only too well," he continued, "the disposal of nuclear and other toxic wastes is a global headache for all concerned. That will include the disposal of decommissioned nuclear arms and obsolete conventional weapons.

Everyone wants to get rid of the filthy stuff but no one wants to touch it. It's regulated to the eyeballs and, for years, the door's been open for some enterprising villain to make a killing in that field. That, in my view, is what Pyramus is about.

"We're pretty limited in what we can do, but we can try to draw out and, if possible, isolate one of those top men. For that to happen, though, I'm going to have to come back from the dead. It's a tough decision for all of you but I propose that you drop me ashore.

"Official eyes still view you people as unidentified maritime terrorists. I, on the other hand, am an experienced naval intelligence officer and, hopefully, above suspicion. The question for you is, how much trust are you ready to put in me?"

Seán McKenna turned away, walking slowly to the open port panel and gazing out at the cairn of stones marking the grave of Barrington Hobbes.

"Tell me what you want, Commander," he said finally.

"I want you to risk running the *Nautilus* up the Channel and dropping me off as close to London as you dare, or as the depth of water allows," Lindsay said. He gave a taut smile. "One other thing. Some back-up might not go amiss."

Chapter 7

The Hostage

38

17 January 2015
Whitehall
London, UK

Accompanied by the solid figure of his chief, Admiral James Garvie, and in full naval uniform, Don Lindsay gazed detachedly around the richly oak-panelled conference room at the Ministry of Defence and at the faces of the people who stood by the chairs surrounding the big rosewood table.

Sir Henry Williamson, Minister of Defence, was the only one he had met in person. The others he only knew from newspaper photographs or television interviews. The Trade and Industry Secretary, Gerald Calloway, had a way of looking down his nose at people, a trait that many found intensely irritating. Squarely built and a youthful forty-one, he was nonetheless tipped by many pundits as the 'young pretender' poised to replace a beleaguered Prime Minister.

Home Secretary Malcolm Gallaher, fiftyish and bespectacled, was known to tend towards pomposity. Often lampooned for it by the popular press, this fault made him increasingly unpopular among the nations' electorate and by a fair few on his own backbenches. It was these two, Calloway and Gallaher, that Lindsay knew would be the hardest to deal with.

Foreign Secretary Nicholas Parnell-Whyte, silver-haired and kind-faced, had, like Williamson, a long pedigree of top-level ministerial experience. He was a fair man and well respected for it. Christopher Knowles, the Shipping Minister and, at thirty-six, the youngest of the gathering, could be obstinate. Lindsay appreciated that he'd been first in the firing line of the CBI, the shipowners and Lloyd's as a result of the war of attrition being waged by the crew of the *Nautilus,* which was now lying low on the bottom of the Channel off the Kent coast.

The sole woman in the room was Treasury Minister Gillian Allardyce. In Lindsay's opinion, press and television cameramen consistently failed to do justice to her devastating good looks. His smile of greeting was, however, answered only by a frosty nod of her immaculately groomed head.

A panelled door opened at the far end of the room. Accompanied by his personal secretary, the Prime Minister entered, invited all present to take their seats and poured himself a mineral water. He was taller than Lindsay had envisaged and his features clearly betrayed the strains of office. The Premier carefully positioned his glasses further down his nose in a well-practised move and looked down the length of the table over the top of them.

"Commander Lindsay," he opened. "I appreciate that, in your profession, debriefings are normally only carried out in the presence of the Director of Naval Intelligence and his Chief of Staff. This meeting is therefore highly unusual but you will acknowledge that your mission is also rather singular and has a direct bearing on each of our departments. I have decided, in this instance, that your report should be heard directly by the Ministers concerned.

"I should congratulate you on a most remarkable return from the dead. Worthy of Lazarus, one might say."

Lindsay smiled briefly. "Thank you, sir, but even Lazarus required a helping hand."

"Quite. Well, shall we get down to it? Admiral Garvie's telephone call to my office was necessarily brief and, as this meeting was convened at short notice, I shall come straight to the point. Am I to understand, Commander, that in a remarkably short space of time, you have solved the mystery of these attacks upon merchant shipping?"

"That is correct, sir, but only up to a point. I can confirm that ramming operations have indeed been carried out by a submarine, as suggested by the *USS Appalachian* among others. In each case, the attacks were precisely measured in order to disable the ship's rudder and propellers and to cause no damage other than that."

"Forgive me for interrupting," Sir Henry Williamson glanced at the Prime Minister who nodded leave for him to continue. "The ships concerned have, I understand, been hit with considerable force. Throughout my own fairly lengthy naval experience, I have found submarines to be somewhat fragile creatures. They are simply not built to ram without sustaining severe, if not fatal, damage to themselves. I fail to comprehend why this is not the case here—and we are talking of not just a single ramming, but several."

"Sir Henry," Lindsay countered. "The submarine concerned carries no armaments of her own. She is not a military vessel. However, she is built like a battleship and to a specification unparalleled in submarine construction. She has a double hull, each one of which is over two inches thick. Between them is a unique cellular system of braces and cross-braces giving her immense strength.

"Modern submarines have a rounded bow, older ones a raked bow like a conventional boat. This vessel is very different. Her bow tapers to a fine point, finishing in a sharp, solid spur. When engaged in ramming procedures, her design distributes the shock evenly throughout her entire length but, even so, the first ten feet of her bow section amounts to little more than a massive shock absorber. This makes her entirely capable of repeated ramming operations."

Williamson's brows shot up. "Good grief! Then, as you say, Commander, this vessel is unique. What about the reports we have regarding her speed? Are they accurate?"

"Well, sir, I can confirm that she has a top speed of fifty knots submerged and, to add one superlative to another, in the past she has attained the remarkable depth of twelve thousand feet. There isn't a military submarine in the world, past or present, that can match either capability. Yes, sir, she is unique."

"Uniquely dangerous, too. How is she powered? Nuclear?"

"No, Sir Henry, electric."

Williamson stared at Lindsay. "Commander, I have considerable experience of diesel-electric submarines. Not one of them is capable of more than thirty knots and then at a push. Is this some revolutionary new design?"

"Revolutionary, yes, but not new. In fact, I'm confident that this vessel has been around for some considerable time." Lindsay leant back in his chair. "She has no diesel generators. Her motors are essentially electromagnetic induction engines powered by sodium-mercury fuel cells. In fact, the only fuel she requires is sodium. As you will know, Sir Henry, that element comprises more than thirty per cent of the mineral content of seawater. In other words, her running costs are virtually nil, and the power she carries is enormous.

"Her dimensions are similar to those of our Upholder Class conventional submarines. She's lighter; fifteen hundred metric tonnes as opposed to the Upholder's twenty-three hundred. That would be accounted for by the fact that her engines are less bulky, she carries no armaments and was designed for a much smaller complement."

"In other words, Commander," Gerald Calloway interjected, "a perfect machine for oceanic terrorism which is presumably still on the loose. Now, I understand that you were actually on board this craft. Is that true?"

"Perfectly true, Minister. I was aboard the *Nautilus*, as she is called, for a period of nine days."

"Nine days." Calloway gave his ministerial colleagues the benefit of his best point-scoring expression. "More than enough time, I would have thought, for an experienced operative to have eliminated, neutralized or apprehended the terrorists on board." Calloway set his jaw. "Or even to have put the vessel out of action. I'm sure we would all like to hear your reasons for failing to do any of these things, and for leaving these people free to continue their murderous activities. Need I remind you that your orders were to hunt these people down and put a stop to them?"

Lindsay fought to keep his rising anger from betraying itself in his face and voice. "No, sir, those were not my orders. As Admiral Garvie will doubtless confirm, my assignment was to investigate the cause of the attacks. So far, I have ascertained who is carrying them out and why. The facts are such that, in my judgement, this is still a long way from the root of the matter. My mission is, therefore, incomplete. I must remind you that, whilst engaged on field operations, it is my judgement and mine alone that counts, not uninformed opinion such as that I've just heard."

He ignored the sudden intake of Garvie's breath in reaction to his verbal stamp on a Minister of the Crown. "You use the word 'murderous',

Minister," Lindsay continued. "With the sole exception of her sinking a Malaysian pirate vessel that was on the point of slaughtering the crew of an innocent yacht, I do not recall that the recent actions of the *Nautilus* have cost as much a single life. On the contrary, she has been responsible for saving the lives of the people on that yacht, two Greenpeace activists in the South Atlantic last June, and my own life when I was heaved over the side of the *Noordzee Marquess*."

"There was, as you say, that pirate ship," the Prime Minister said quietly. "Commander, the director of Deep Watch, Sir Robert Maynard, is convinced that this submarine is connected with the loss of his vessel *Aurora* and her entire crew in southern polar waters last February. Can you shed any light upon that?"

Lindsay guarded his response. "Like Sir Robert, I do not believe that the sinking of the *Aurora* was any accident. Nor do I believe that the *Nautilus* was directly involved. It is worth noting that her activities have been broadly in line with those of environmental groups such as Deep Watch and Greenpeace. She has consistently targetted whaling and commercial vessels operating outside international law. Granted that Greenpeace and Deep Watch tend to use passive methods such as harassment, demonstrations, lobbying and so on. Others, like Sea Shepherd, take a more direct course of action, and the *Nautilus* is no different.

"As you know, sir, I was placed aboard the *Noordzee Marquess* in the guise of an ordinary deckhand. At the very moment that she was attacked by this submarine, that ship had commenced the unlawful mid-ocean dumping of canisters containing what I believe to have been dioxins. There were a great many of these canisters on board, none of which were entered in the cargo manifest. I don't doubt that, once she was towed into port, they were spirited away onto another ship, just as these very canisters had originally been part of the *Margarita Sanchez's* cargo, a transfer that was carried out in Falmouth."

"I hear what you say," Knowles, the Shipping Minster, broke in. "But where's your proof? We require much more substantive evidence than a mere verbal report."

Lindsay ignored the question and the whispered advice from his chief to take care. "There is further evidence," he said firmly, "that each of the shipping companies involved in this illegal operation are themselves fronting an obscure parent company known as the Pyramus Group.

"An interesting point here is that when Sir Robert Maynard's *Aurora* was sunk, the nearest known vessel to her position was the *Emperor*, a Pyramus-owned ship that curiously left Auckland with a cargo of construction equipment but arrived at her destination, Valparaiso, several days late, carrying a full load of stone and suffering from a badly damaged bow."

"The discrepancies in the cargo descriptions could be nothing more than a clerical error," said Gillian Allardyce. "It still doesn't constitute hard evidence, Commander."

Lindsay ploughed on. "The Pyramus Group employs some highly questionable people. For example, the man in charge of transferring the *Margarita Sanchez's* cargo to the *Noordzee Marquess* also turned up as the *Marquess's* bo'sun. This man, a German named Jürgen Krabbe, is a particularly unpleasant piece of work. His current name is not his real one. Several countries have him on their records and wanted lists as Hans-Dieter Wolf, the former chief interrogator of the old East German secret police, the *Staatsicherheitdienst*—the *Stasi*.

"When the Berlin Wall came down, Wolf was among the first to make a run for it, having tortured to death dozens of political detainees, including women and children. East German people used to shake in their shoes at the mere mention of the Linden Wolf, as they called him.

"He is one of the bloodiest criminals alive and, incidentally, it was he who attempted to kill me by shoving me over the side when the *Nautilus* struck the *Noordzee Marquess*. Any organization that employs and shields such a man must itself be placed under grave suspicion and, from that fact alone, you will appreciate that my investigations are far from complete."

"Again, Commander," said Calloway. "This meeting requires proof, not mere words."

This time Garvie spoke up. "With every respect, Minister, Wolf is most certainly listed as wanted by every intelligence service in the West. My department has in fact positively identified Wolf from photographs taken at Falmouth by Commander Lindsay, who is perfectly correct in what he says."

Lindsay gave his chief a grateful glance as Calloway inclined his head with a degree of deference that seemed to border on the sarcastic. "Indeed,

Admiral, I accept your point," Calloway said. "However, and returning to the subject of murder, are you aware, Commander, that the base of this *Nautilus* in Cornwall was located and penetrated by members of the Special Boat Service only yesterday? I think Sir Henry can confirm this."

"Indeed," Williamson responded. "I regret to report that the submarine itself was absent but the bodies of two men were found within the disused mine workings. Strangely, there were no outward signs of how they died, except that each had a small red mark on his skin. I was informed this morning that an autopsy concluded that both died of massive trauma consistent with the effects of electrocution."

"Were you aware of this, Commander?" Calloway pressed.

"Perfectly aware," Lindsay said, unperturbed, "owing to the fact that it was me who killed them."

Ignoring the gasps that erupted around the table, he carried on. "The *Nautilus* has a collection of ingenious air-guns that fire lethally charged electrical pellets. They were actually designed for underwater hunting but they're also pretty efficient at eliminating paid assassins on dry land.

"Three men followed the journalists Barrington Hobbes and Karen Marshall from Exeter Airport to a meeting they had arranged with the crew of the *Nautilus*. There, they attempted to murder both of them. I took two of the killers out, the third unfortunately got away. That man was Wolf himself."

"My God." Gillian Allardyce had paled considerably. "How can you sit there and blandly tell us that you've killed two men?"

"Three during the course of this assignment," Lindsay calmly told her. "There was also a man who pulled a gun on me in Falmouth when I was observing the handling of the *Margarita Sanchez's* cargo. He had every intention of using it. I took the appropriate action."

The Prime Minister interceded, speaking softly in an attempt to defuse the rising tension in the room. "Perhaps it is time that you identified the submarine's crew members, Commander. I take it that you do have names for them?"

"Yes, sir, I do. However, as I said earlier, I cannot consider my assignment to be anywhere near concluded. It would be wholly unwise for any professional operative to prematurely divulge information that might jeopardize the success of his mission. Respectfully, sir, and for that reason, I must decline to answer."

For a second time, Admiral Garvie drew in his breath as the Premier frowned deeply, adding, "You fear a leak from this room?"

Lindsay steeled himself. "Sir, I must fully consider that very possibility."

Calloway gave out a sound midway between a snort and a gasp. "You have the temerity to suggest that Cabinet Ministers, or even the Prime Minister himself, would leak such information?"

"It wouldn't be the first time," Lindsay shot back, tiring of the man's arrogance. He didn't like the smug smile that crept into the Minister's face.

"Well, for your information, Commander Lindsay, it is your conduct that I call into question." Calloway glared triumphantly at him before turning to the Minister of Defence. "Perhaps it's time we heard the tape, Sir Henry."

With a resigned sigh, Williamson opened his briefcase and drew out a small cassette player. He glanced at the Prime Minister. "This tape recording was handed to me by Lieutenant-Commander Richard Priest, the commanding officer of *HMS Challenge*. It contains an exchange between himself and this *Nautilus* off the Norwegian coast a week ago during the NATO operation that intended to entrap the submarine. With your permission?"

The Prime Minister nodded assent. Inwardly, Lindsay groaned. He should have known that Priest would record the radio conversation. Blast the bloody man! The damning tape hissed and came to life:

—Nautilus, *turn away now or I will open fire. Great God, man, are you demented? You're committing suicide!*

—*You always were a hard-nosed bastard, Dickie. Why worry? This boat ran the same passage once before and came through. There's no reason why she can't do it again and, more to the point, old son, go where you can't.*

—Nautilus, *do I know you? You are either brave men or bloody lunatics. Good luck, whoever you are. You'll forgive me if I don't offer escort facilities.*

—*Far rather you didn't,* Challenge. *Give my love to Veronica.* Nautilus, *out.*

Calloway's expression hardened. "That was your voice, wasn't it, Commander? You were neither prisoner nor guest on that submarine. At that precise moment, you were in command of her… willingly collaborating with the very people you were sent to stop. Do you deny it? Don't look at your chief for guidance, answer me now!"

Lindsay glowered at him. "Of course I don't bloody well deny it. Now ask me why? Ask me why I refuse to divulge their identities. No? Well, I'll give you the answers.

"Vested interests are what it boils down to. Like any other company, the Pyramus Group is headed by a number of directors. Their identities, like the company's operations, are jealously guarded but I can tell you that they're of various nationalities. Each is a major industrialist or a senior politician. At their head is a Chairman, an extremely powerful man whose name is more heavily protected than Fort Knox.

"These people are responsible for the loss of the *Aurora*, for the murders, ten years ago, of Barrington Hobbes's wife and child, for the murder of the journalist Ian Neale and, just three days ago, for the murder of Barrington Hobbes himself."

Lindsay scanned the shocked faces. "Yes, you wouldn't have been aware of that, would you?" he said. "Wolf and his cronies gunned him down before I could intervene. Hobbes died of his wounds aboard the *Nautilus* and was buried on the sea-bed off his home town of Falmouth.

"The curious thing is that, apart from those of us who got away on the *Nautilus*, the only other person who could have known, or suspected, that she was holed up in those old mine workings was Hans-Dieter Wolf. Yet, within forty-eight hours, the SBS mounts an assault on the very same mine workings. So, which Pyramus director in high office—which one of you—did Wolf report to?"

The silence that followed was profound. Sir Henry Williamson had gone as pale as a ghost. The pencil that Calloway had been rolling between his fingers snapped, the broken ends dropping onto the polished tabletop. The Prime Minister looked as though he had been slapped.

Seething with white-hot hostility, Calloway rose from his chair. "I think we've heard quite enough." His voice was dangerously icy. "Prime Minister, I must formally request a five-minute recess."

The Premier agreed with a single, quietly spoken word, then stood to address Garvie. "Admiral, would you please be kind enough to accompany your officer into the reception room. You will be called when we are ready to reconvene."

Admiral James Garvie stood by the window of the reception room, gazing down into Horseguards Court. Lindsay knew from the hunch of his shoulders that a broadside was imminent.

"Bloody hell, Commander," Garvie said suddenly, turning from the window. "What do you think you're playing at? We came here to brief the PM and several of his most senior ministers and you end up accusing them of murder and God knows what else besides! Just what in hell do you think you're doing?"

"I stand by what I said, sir," he said stubbornly.

Garvie stared at him. "Yes," he said eventually, "I can see that you do. Well, Commander, God only knows what'll happen now. I seriously doubt that any of them have been spoken to like that for years. I only hope you can back up your claims."

"I will if I get the chance, sir. Somehow, I think that one person in that room will move heaven and earth to see that I don't."

"Which one?"

Lindsay paused, then shook his head. "I'm sorry, Admiral. Without concrete proof, words will achieve nothing. They were right about that, at least."

"Have it your own way, Lindsay, but you'd better get that proof."

"As I said, sir, *if* I get the chance. If they insist on my resignation, they can have it and welcome. It'll make no difference. I'll finish this job whether I'm still a member of the service or no."

"Resignation? Good God, man, has it come to that? Surely they wouldn't dare? An officer with your record..."

"A record that will count for nothing here. How about your own, sir? Over forty years exemplary service. Decorations galore. So how come Richard Priest's tape was withheld from you? As head of Naval Intelligence, you should have been the first to hear that tape but you never even knew it existed, did you? I saw your expression in there.

"No, sir. It was kept back from you as a nice surprise to add emphasis to the case being built against me. Anything to help ensure that I'm removed from this mission."

Garvie turned back to the window. "I only hope you know what you're doing. That was more than a hornet's nest you stirred up in there. If it's any help, my personal trust in you remains. I can't, and won't, dismiss a service record like yours lightly. Just don't let me down. On the other hand, what happens now is at ministerial level and any decision they make cannot be countermanded by me."

"I appreciate that, sir. And, yes, your trust in me does help. Greatly."

The door opened. The admiral gave Lindsay a long, hard stare.

"Well, we'll soon know, Commander. Time to face the music."

The faces around the table were no less hostile than before. Lindsay glanced at the Foreign Secretary and at Gillian Allardyce. Their stony expressions gave him precious little comfort. The Prime Minister sighed audibly, took off his glasses and laid them carefully on the table in front of him. This was a familiar gesture, habitually made whenever he was about to utter some grave pronouncement.

"Commander Lindsay," he said wearily. "Things have been said in this room that you would perhaps wish to reflect upon and reconsider. I have little alternative but to advise you that, should you prove unwilling to retract certain remarks, the consequences may be grave. Do I make myself clear?"

"Perfectly clear, sir." There was a resolute quality about Lindsay's voice and body language that caused discomfort to more than one person in the room. "I need no time to reconsider. The statements that I have made are founded upon solid investigation and, in due course, the evidence you require will be forthcoming. I have spoken to Admiral Garvie and confirmed to him that I stand by my report. I regret nothing of what I have said and nothing of my actions during my assignment thus far. If, however, this meeting requires my resignation—"

The Premier halted him by raising a hand. "Your resignation is not an issue, Commander. However, you have uttered accusations against Her Majesty's Government that you are not prepared to substantiate. This is conduct that cannot, under any circumstances, be tolerated. I therefore regret that, at this point, I must hand over to my Secretary of State for Defence. Sir Henry?"

Williamson rose heavily to his feet, clearly not relishing the task. "Admiral Garvie, it has been concluded that, after the evidence we have heard today, there is no other course open to us but to order an official Inquiry into your officer's conduct. That Inquiry will decide whether a case is to be brought before a Court Martial.

"You will, therefore, comply with my instructions. Commander Donall McEwan Lindsay is, from this moment, to be placed under close arrest until such time that the Inquiry I have referred to is convened."

Behind Lindsay, the door opened. He looked round. Two military policemen, each with holstered sidearms, stood there at textbook attention. Lindsay turned to a devastated Garvie.

"Well, sir, it seems they lost no time. Whatever happens now, don't lose that trust in me."

He looked at the military policemen. "Gentlemen," he said, "shall we go?"

It was all over remarkably quickly. The flanking escorts, each keeping a hand close to the exposed butts of their sidearms, marched Lindsay along the corridor and down the wide stairway leading to the foyer of the building.

"Which hell-hole will it be then, lads?" Lindsay said cheerily. "Colchester?"

The reply was abrupt. "Keep your eyes ahead and your mouth shut. Once inside the vehicle, handcuffs will be applied. Any attempt to escape will receive one clear warning to halt, which if disobeyed, will result in the opening of fire. Is that clearly understood?"

Lindsay paused on the step, turning slowly to the man and peering under the slashed peak of his cap. "Do tell me, sergeant," he said. "Do you order breakfast from your wife in that fashion?"

A hand moved onto the grip of the holstered gun, a small movement that wasn't lost on Lindsay.

"Move your fucking self… sir."

Lindsay shrugged and sauntered on. "The poor woman," he murmured then, determined to keep the needle applied, turned to his colleague and loudly asked him how recently the sergeant had learned to stand erect.

People in the street had noticed the arrival of armed military police and formed a small, jostling group outside in the hope of seeing some action.

"Move aside!" came the expected order. Some of the gathering group moved back, seeing the hands on holsters. One big black man seemed too mesmerized by the incident to hear the command.

"I said, move aside!" The hand came off the gun to shove the man away. Like lightning, it was grabbed, pulling the sergeant on to the huge ebony fist that exploded in his face. The sergeant rocketed back, unconscious, onto the steps. In the same instant, a stocky, bearded man launched into the second escort, using an expert and totally illegal short-arm rugby tackle that snapped the man's head back. He tottered and a straight left from Lindsay finished the job.

He paused only to snatch the prostrate man's gun from its holster and fling it deep inside the building. The black assailant repeated the action with the sergeant's gun. Within another half-second, all three had disappeared into the growing crowd.

From a second floor window, Admiral James Garvie, the only man in the room to have witnessed the incident, suppressed a smile, gathered up his briefcase and walked away.

39

Wychwood Grange
Sussex, UK

For once in his life, Gerald Hugh Calloway MP, Secretary of State for Trade and Industry, was a worried man. His head hunched into his shoulders as he gazed, unfocused, through the drawing room window at a bright gibbous moon rising over the silhouetted trees of the parkland surrounding the house.

Wychwood Grange, for two hundred years the Calloway family seat, was a rambling structure erected in the Regency period on the site of a Tudor mansion. During the Victorian and Edwardian periods, it had been added to at various times and in various ways to produce startling oddities of design that fascinated architectural scholars such as Nikolaus Pevsner. The house sat in its own extensive park set in a hollow of the rolling

Sussex Downs, the product of a family fortune enhanced by vast profits gleaned by the builder of the house, Oliver Calloway, from Jamaican sugar plantations worked by African slaves.

Gerald Calloway cared nothing for the moral questions that hung over the family wealth that had been added to by successive generations through shrewd investments and business ventures. The Minister himself was a multi-millionaire by way of inheritance and industrial interests.

He had good reason to be anxious. Since its inception, the Pyramus Group of which he was part and its illicit purpose of disposing of the world's glut of dangerous chemical and nuclear wastes, had operated without let, hindrance or detection. True, there were certain governments who knew of its existence but, from their point of view, the desirability of getting rid of their untouchable waste products far outweighed the organization's unlawful procedures. Now, out of the blue, a considerable threat had materialized.

It was true to say that the elimination of the journalists Hobbes and Neale had removed a sizeable chunk of the danger. Calloway was particularly grateful to have heard the news about Hobbes who, ten years earlier, had come so close to blowing the whole operation. Without him, the third journalist, Karen Marshall, was of little consequence, as far as he was concerned. She was a small-time hack from the provinces and way out of her league without the guile and expertise of Hobbes to guide her. In any case, and to all intents and purposes, she had vanished from the face of the globe, although Calloway had few doubts as to her whereabouts.

What really disturbed the Minister was the escape of the naval agent, Lindsay. He had an outstanding service record showing a startlingly high percentage of successful assignments. The majority of these had been solo efforts, which more than indicated that the man was exceptionally resourceful. Already, within weeks of being assigned to the case, he had become aware of the existence and activities of the Pyramus Group, identified their man Krabbe as the fugitive Hans-Dieter Wolf, and killed three of Wolf's henchmen. In addition, and this was Calloway's biggest worry, it appeared that Lindsay had acquired some knowledge of the Pyramus heirarchy.

Calloway had done his level best to set Lindsay up and get him removed from the case and from circulation but there was nothing he could have done to prevent the escape. That, he was certain, had been aided by members of this rogue submarine's crew. He had no idea where the man was now, or what his plans might be: a lack of knowledge that spelled danger. It was time, Calloway decided, to bring the Chairman up to date with events.

He drew the heavy curtains, noting with grim satisfaction the dim raincoated figure passing outside the window with scarcely a glance at the Minister. This was one of the three security personnel, attached to Special Branch, that were assigned to all Cabinet Ministers. Calloway stopped to listen, making sure that none of the house staff were about. He didn't need to worry about marital interruptions. Gerald Calloway had never married, although he kept a string of mistresses, none of whom had the slightest inkling that he had others in tow. Somehow, he had managed to keep their existence away from the attentions of the media. He was a man who lived life to the full, had the means to do so, and was used to getting what he wanted.

He made his way to his private study and crossed the darkened room to a heavy Victorian cabinet behind his big oak desk. This he unlocked and opened. An internally fitted light was all he needed to operate the Motorola satellite telephone that was built into the cabinet. This gave him a direct line to the Chairman of the Pyramus Group and was equipped with a scrambling device that ensured that any deliberate or accidental interception would only gain access to a meaningless garble being automatically coded and decoded by the devices at each end of the line. It also served to disguise voices by distortion.

The Chairman responded almost immediately and listened to Calloway's account of the day's events with quiet patience. He spoke only when the Minister's report was complete.

"This is disturbing news, Gerald." The voice on the small speaker was calm and unruffled. "What mechanisms are in place for tracking Lindsay down?"

"An intensive search was mounted several hours ago," Calloway told him. "All ports and airports were put on immediate alert but I don't believe he'll turn up at any of them. His escape was aided by two men that I'm convinced belong to this renegade submarine and my guess is that he's back aboard her. I presume she's in the English Channel or the North Sea, but where she may be hiding is anybody's guess."

"More's the pity," came the response. "Unfortunately, it's the easiest thing in the world to hide a submarine. One simply fills the ballast tanks, stops engines and sits her on the bottom."

"You're quite right, of course," Calloway agreed. "But she can't do that indefinitely. The Minister of Defence has already ordered a search of the Channel, North Sea and Western Approaches by ships and anti-submarine helicopters using both passive and active sonar arrays as well as magnetic sensors. If she is lying on the bottom, we'd be very fortunate to detect her but there's a greater chance of doing so if she's on the move. Even then, it's reported that her engines are unusually quiet and don't produce enough of a heat signature to be easily picked up by infra-red satellite scans. Having said that, the navy also reports that she's apt to cavitate when running at shallow depths."

"Cavitate?"

"The way Sir Henry explains it is that, at speed, the movement of the screw causes air bubbles to form between its blades. When they burst, it creates noise, often quite considerable noise, easily picked up by passive sonar. Experienced operators can even tell from the noise how many blades a particular propeller has. This *Nautilus*, for example, has a large diameter four-bladed screw with broad blades."

"I see. And has this submarine crew given any indication of their intent?"

"Very little. Lindsay's report was guarded. He knows the identity of her crew but refused to divulge any details even when ordered to do so by the PM. There is no doubt that they know of the Pyramus Group and our operations in general but there's no hint that they're aware of our southern project."

"That's a blessing at least," the Chairman commented. "Is the Marshall woman known to be aboard?"

"Without a doubt. She hasn't been seen since Krabbe killed Hobbes on the cliffs down in Cornwall and he is certain she didn't return overland. That leaves just one possibility."

"With Lindsay also aboard, it would seem that all our eggs are in one basket," the Chairman mused. "Still, it is most gratifying to learn of Hobbes's demise. He was by far the biggest threat to us."

"With all respect," Calloway said carefully, "we shouldn't underestimate this submarine or her crew. Her recent record suggests to me that the navy's on a bloody expensive wild goose chase."

"I hear what you say, Gerald. I agree that there's no room for any further error. Lindsay and Marshall apart, we still have no idea who these people are and precious little about the vessel itself. What concerns me is how much they actually know. For example, how much did they learn after breaking into João Valdera's office in Lisbon before the Portuguese police got there?

"Which reminds me, Gerald. Valdera will not be attending any future Pyramus meetings. I regret to inform you that he died in a tragic car accident last night. João always did have too much love for fast cars. He will be sadly missed."

Sans brake fluid, *sans* life. Calloway kept the thought to himself.

"I feel it prudent," the Chairman continued, "to send Krabbe down to the southern facility to head up its security. It is entirely possible that the submarine crew might now be aware of its existence from material in Valdera's office and attempt to locate it. I need Krabbe to carry out one further task for me in London and then he will leave."

Calloway smiled grimly to himself, wondering if Krabbe had been in Lisbon on the previous evening. "We can't afford not to exercise due caution," he agreed. "In fact, Mr Chairman, might it not be the right time to make the additions to the *Emperor* that we discussed last month?"

"A useful notion," the Chairman commented. "She is currently in Yokohama having extra reinforcement added to her bow. An afterthought to the repairs that were necessary after she sank the Deep Watch ship last year. I'll contact our Japanese colleagues and get that extra equipment installed immediately.

"In the meantime, Gerald, use every ounce of your political influence to convince the Prime Minister that it's essential to get NATO searches for the submarine stepped up. For as long as this *Nautilus* remains on the loose, she's a danger to us. Keep me fully informed."

The line went dead. Calloway switched the systems off and locked the cabinet.

"A most enlightening conversation," a voice said unexpectedly. "I wouldn't have missed it for the world."

Calloway froze as the room lights came on, revealing two figures standing at the far end of the room, a towering black man and a white one. His heart sank as he recognized the European.

"Lindsay—how the hell…?"

"Did we get in here?" Lindsay finished the sentence. "Not difficult. Your Special Branch guards are competent enough but they're too predictable and somewhat lacking in subtlety. Those always were their weaknesses. They haven't been harmed. Just sleeping soundly. The guy patrolling outside your windows is our own man. And your alarm system is hardly the best I've ever dealt with."

Calloway went pale. "Damn your bloody nerve, man. How long have you been here?"

"Long enough to have heard your entire discussion and confirmation of who sank the Deep Watch boat. We were already aware of your involvement. Your name cropped up in a Lisbon lawyer's records. Correction, a late Lisbon lawyer. You Pyramus people really don't put too much value on human life, do you?"

Calloway moved slowly to his desk and sat arrogantly in his leather-backed chair as Ross Jourdan padded down the room. "I see," he said, ignoring the Canadian's considerable presence towering over him. "And how much more have you learned?"

"Not enough, evidently," Lindsay said. "We'd love to hear more about this southern facility."

"Would you, now?" Calloway's right hand, shielded from Jourdan's view by his own body, eased open a desk drawer, reaching inside for the automatic pistol he always kept there. The Canadian's sharp hearing must have detected some slight sound and he reacted like lightning. The politician cried out in fright and pain as a boot slammed the drawer shut on his fingers. A massively strong hand grasped Calloway's collar, hauling him out of the chair while Jourdan's free hand opened the drawer, drew out the gun and tossed it down the room to Lindsay.

The agent examined the 9-millimetre Browning automatic and checked the full twenty-round magazine. "Shame on you, Minister," he said. "Fancy a man of your standing keeping toys like this. You do realize that privately owned handguns like this are outlawed? Service issue, too. I wonder how you came by it?" He pocketed the gun and looked up at a choking, red-faced Calloway and the man who held him fast.

"Don't asphyxiate the poor sod, Ross," Lindsay said languidly. Jourdan dropped the half-strangled minister into his chair, none too gently, and hauled the chair away from the desk.

"Guns," Lindsay lectured, "are dangerous and highly anti-social. When people like you have them handy, it forces people like us to take similar measures. Show him, Ross."

Jourdan moved back into the Minister's view. Calloway's streaming eyes took in the curious weapon that the big man produced from under his coat, a short rifle with a strangely cylindrical stock and, as it swung to bear on him, a sinisterly large bore.

"If fired," Lindsay told him, "your Browning would make a hell of a noise, whereas the weapon pointing at you now wouldn't be heard beyond the walls of this room.

"Technically speaking, it is not a firearm and therefore, under present legislation, quite legal. It's well over a hundred years old but extremely effective at short range. In effect, it's a powerful air-gun firing pellets that contain a lethal electrical charge. A nice, clean kill every time. No blood and brains all over the carpet, just a tiny red burn on the skin. As you heard me say earlier today, it's a tried and proven weapon."

"My God," Calloway whispered, remembering the details of how Krabbe's men had died in Cornwall.

"I'd have got Krabbe himself if only the gun had a greater range."

"But you didn't get him, did you, Lindsay? A fact you'll come to regret."

"Not from what I just heard," Lindsay replied. "It seems he'll be busy elsewhere."

Calloway stared blankly at him. "What do you intend to do?"

Lindsay leaned nonchalantly against the door jamb. "I couldn't help but notice this afternoon," he said, "just how pale you looked. You spend far too much time in the city, cooped up in offices and government chambers. So, we've come to offer you a holiday. A nice little sea-trip, at our expense."

"Kidnapping is a serious offence," Calloway sneered. "Abducting a Government minister might even be considered an act of treason, for which you'd get life. You'll never get away with it."

"That remains to be seen. Bear in mind, Minister, that it will be tomorrow before anyone realizes you've gone missing. Your security men certainly won't be awake before then. Ross?"

A huge hand clamped onto Calloway's shoulder. A pungent smell invaded the Minister's nostrils seconds before the moist pad was placed firmly over his nose and mouth. He panicked, struggling futilely to escape the strength of Jourdan's grip. The old-fashioned chloroform-impregnated pad worked quickly. Calloway's eyes rolled up in their sockets and the Canadian found himself supporting a dead weight as the minister blacked out. The big man dropped the pad into the waste paper basket under Calloway's desk and hoisted the unconscious man onto his shoulder with consummate ease.

40

18 January 2015
Downing Street
London, UK

The normally imperturbable Prime Minister was in a towering rage.

"Never!" He brought a clenched fist crashing down on his desk. "Never in the history of the British Parliament has anyone dared to abduct a Cabinet Minister." His furious eyes glared in turn at Sir Henry Williamson and Admiral Garvie.

"Great God in Heaven," he raged on. "Not even our greatest enemies ever attempted such a thing. If the press get as much as a whiff of this there'll be all hell to pay. They already suspect something's up from the activity down at Wychwood Grange. Our disinformation machine's working on overdrive but, sooner or later, the truth will out and I'll be facing some highly embarrassing questions."

"Can we be sure who's responsible?" Garvie asked.

The Prime Minister angrily thrust a sheet of paper at him. "I scarcely think there's any room for doubt, Admiral."

Garvie examined the sheet. It was headed with a device based around an ornate capital letter N and the Latin motto: *Mobilis in Mobili.* The letter simply read:

Sir,

Gerald Calloway MP, Secretary of State for Trade and Industry, regrets that he is unable to discharge his ministerial and other duties for the foreseeable future, having embarked on a sea voyage which, it is to be hoped, will prove beneficial.

Any further correspondence will be addressed directly to Admiral James Garvie at the Naval Intelligence department of the Admiralty.

The crew of the Nautilus

Expressionless, Garvie passed the letter to the Minister of Defence. "How in Heaven's name did they get to Calloway?" the admiral said. "Surely there were security officers assigned to him?"

"It was professionally planned," the Premier said tersely, "and professionally carried out. It's patently obvious to me that your man was behind it. It would have needed someone of his proven ability and experience.

"There were three Special Branch officers assigned to protect the Minister, all highly trained men. They were each rendered unconscious, apparently by the use of chloroform."

Williamson looked up from the letter. "What on earth would they want with Gerald?" he said. "This letter contains nothing in the way of threats, terms or demands. I don't understand their motives."

"Doubtless we'll find out in the fullness of time. Lindsay hinted that a member of my Cabinet was mixed up with these Pyramus people. He evidently suspects Gerald Calloway, although I can't for the life of me see why." The Prime Minister sighed deeply.

"Gentlemen, this episode has got completely out of hand. Already we know of five deaths, three of them at the hands of Commander Lindsay by his own admission.

"The *Nautilus* remains at large, having somehow secured the services of an experienced naval intelligence officer. We have a string of damaged ships and now this… this outrage!

"It has got to stop. My Government will not submit to terrorists and in that description, Admiral, I must include your officer. Henry, you will seek the agreement of NATO High Command to escalate the hunt for the *Nautilus*. I want her apprehended in short time or, if all else fails, destroyed.

"Even at the expense of Gerald Calloway's life."

41

19 January 2015
Victoria Wharf
London, UK

Anne Collinson pushed the door of her flat shut with the sole of a foot and put her bags of shopping down on the floor. She went through to the kitchen, taking only the carrier that held frozen food, stacked it away in the freezer and filled the kettle.

Back in the living room, she kicked off her shoes and flopped onto the sofa, staring out through the balcony windows that overlooked Victoria Wharf to where the darkness of a winter evening cloaked the waters of the Thames. The reflections of light in the water held her eyes as her mind whirled.

A frown of puzzlement and anxiety was furrowing her brow. Determined to help Karen Marshall track down her fiancé's killers, she had tried every which way to break through a barrier of computer security the like of which she'd never seen at Lloyd's. Anne had lost count of the number of times that the words ACCESS DENIED had emblazoned themselves on the screen of her desk terminal. She had put in hours of covert effort and all that had emerged was the name of the Pyramus Group. Lloyd's Insurance and even Company House files had proved equally frustrating.

She had even tried to discover just who did have access to those heavily protected areas but, again, without the slightest success.

Now, Anne Collinson was worried. As she had learned from Karen, Pyramus was big, powerful and, as the terrible death of Ian Neale had rammed home, ruthlessly nasty. By now, it was more than likely that someone within its network had twigged her attempts to breach its defences. Eventually, someone would be asking some hard questions and she needed time to compose sufficiently convincing answers.

Even if she had succeeded in getting any further, how was she now supposed to get that information to Karen? No one had seen or heard of her and Barrington Hobbes since the bomb blast that had killed Neale. Her queries to *The Sentinel* had only met with guarded answers. Karen was out of town. Beyond that, no details were going to be offered.

The door intercom buzzed, startling her out of her thoughts. She pressed its button and spoke. The male voice that responded was that of a stranger and heavily accented, not unusual in modern London.

"Miss Collinson? Miss Anne Collinson? Abel Klein, Lloyd's Security. I regret invading your private time but I'm afraid I need to ask you some questions."

Anne's stomach plummetted into her stockinged feet. She fought desperately against rising waves of panic, a sudden knot in her insides and an urge to be sick.

"You'd better come up," she said. Try as she might, she could do nothing to keep the quaver of fear from her voice.

Oh, God, she thought. *What am I going to tell him? If I tell the truth, or if he realizes that I've been passing information to journalists, I'm finished at Lloyd's. I won't even get a job on a supermarket till after this. Christ, they might even bring criminal charges. Think, girl, think. Klein will be here at any moment. How can I stall him?*

A measured knock at the door shook her into gear. Anne swallowed hard and slipped the security chain into place. She opened the door and peered through the three-inch gap allowed by the chain. The visitor looked every inch the security type, late-fifties, medium height and thick set with muscular shoulders. He was smartly dressed in a grey suit with blue shirt and grey silk tie.

"Miss Collinson? Abel Klein. May I come in?"

She studied the heavy face and cropped fair hair. The thick-lipped mouth formed a comforting smile that was not reflected in the uncomfortably pale, unwinking blue eyes. Somehow, she managed to compose herself.

Do you have any identification?" she asked calmly.

"Identification? Yes, of course. One moment." Klein's hand went to the inside pocket of his jacket. He produced no identity card, just a dull black automatic pistol, made ugly by the squat silencer fitted onto the barrel.

Anne Collinson had scarcely registered the gun before the bullet precisely pierced her left eye, fragmenting inside her skull and blowing half her cranium across the room.

The man called Abel Klein had other names. Once he had been Hans-Dieter Wolf and now he mostly used the name Jürgen Krabbe. With the calm, unhurried movements of the professional killer, he pocketed the gun and pulled the door of Anne Collinson's flat shut before exiting the building unnoticed.

42

20 January 2015
North Atlantic Ocean
200 miles SE of the Azores

SEÁN McKenna turned away from the starboard view port as a tight-lipped Lindsay entered the saloon. The Irishman raised an amused eyebrow at the naval man's pale features and tense posture.

"If you'll take a piece of advice, Commander," he commented. "You might think about loosening up a little. I take it that Mr Calloway's being a tad difficult?"

Lindsay's glance flashed dangerously. "Try 'bloody impossible'. He's admitting nothing and laying on the superiority with a trowel. Arrogant, supercilious little turd."

McKenna glanced down. "Your hand's bleeding." He added reproachfully, "You wouldn't be exercising brutality on our honoured guest, would you? I thought that was Herr Wolf's department."

In spite of his simmering anger, Lindsay gave a dry grin. "Don't I wish. I might have loosened the bastard's tongue a little." He examined a couple of skinned knuckles. "I locked him back in and took it out on the bulkhead."

McKenna tutted. "Unwise. Sheet metal doesn't tend to give too easily, but I can't say I don't sympathize. Calloway does have that effect upon us lesser mortals."

"Tell me about it, Seán."

The captain laughed. "Never mind, Commander. I have the very thing to take your mind off it. I was about to drag you away from Calloway in any case."

There was a curious light in McKenna's eyes. "We've reached a rather interesting part of the ocean and I'm sure you wouldn't want to miss it. Come on over and take a look."

The instruments mounted on the forward bulkhead told Lindsay that the *Nautilus* was travelling at a mere five knots on a south-easterly course at a depth of 1,400 feet. From the starboard window, he could see that she was gliding just forty feet above the featureless ooze of the ocean floor which, although floodlit by the submarine's searchlight, was nonetheless strangely tinted by a rosy glow.

"Five knots?" he queried. "Why so sedate?"

The Irishman pointed upwards. "NATO ships and aircraft are still looking for us, even as far out as here. So, the name of the game is slow and dead quiet, just as it was getting out of the Channel and the Western Approaches. At this speed, they'll never hear us, not that they're likely to get to us at this sort of depth. It also gives us time to enjoy a decent view."

"As we're so safe in your hands," Lindsay said, "just what are we supposed to be seeing?"

McKenna spoke softly. "Patience, Commander, we're almost there."

As he spoke, the sea floor dropped away beneath them, a vertical wall into a trench some fifty feet deep. The lights of the *Nautilus* barely reached its rubble-strewn foot as she slowed to a mere three knots.

The far side of the trench came into view. Lindsay thought he glimpsed hints of straight jointing in a wall of rock that seemed far too smooth and regular to be any natural formation. His eyebrows drew together in question as he noted the wall curving gently to their left before fading into the rose-tinted murk beyond the range of the vessel's lights.

The ocean floor was again close under the submarine's keel as she cruised over the inner wall of the curious trench, its level surface coated with grey ooze. Here and there, what looked like geometrical shapes showed through. Lindsay had no time to ponder them as, for a second time, a vertical wall fell away beneath them. It was exactly as before, a wide curving trench of similar width and depth to the first and, again, hints of vertical and horizontal jointing to its walls. He glanced quizzically at McKenna.

"There's one more of these to come," the Irishman said, somewhat enigmatically.

The third curving trench, of the same dimensions as the first two, was coming into view. The unexplained glow outside intensified for a moment, allowing a better view of the rubble at the bottom that seemed to consist solely of squared blocks of stone lying in confused heaps. The inner wall of this trench, unlike the others, rose considerably higher than the outer one. The *Nautilus* rose to clear it, then turned to follow its rim.

Lindsay pressed closer to the window. Now, there was no doubt at all in his mind. This wall, and surely the others that he had seen, was entirely artificial, built up in courses of huge, square-cut basalt blocks. Its upper edge was ragged, large sections of masonry having, at some time, fallen away to the bottom of the trench. It was evident that the visible part of the wall formed an arc of a perfect circle that might be half a mile across, the outer trenches perhaps forming concentric circles around it.

The *Nautilus* again changed direction to traverse the raised but flattened-off centre of the innermost circle. Areas where faint rectangular patterns protruded through the grey silt came into range of the light. Lindsay felt a chill spreading up the length of his spine as he turned to stare at McKenna.

"Just as Plato described it," the Irishman commented, almost casually. "And exactly where he said it was. Not Santorini, not Bimini, Heligoland, the Great Sole Bank or anywhere else. Nor is it a myth."

Lindsay was almost lost for words. "Are you telling me that this is the ruin of Atlantis? It isn't possible… and yet this is clearly man-made. Dear God… people have dreamed of this. How on earth did you find it?" He couldn't turn his eyes from the enigmatic rectangular shapes on the ocean floor only feet away.

"Simply by following directions," McKenna said. "You see, Don, we didn't find it. Nemo did. He put it on his charts and even carried out a preliminary survey. If we ever get the chance, we'll come back here and finish what he started. We'll put together a full photographic mosaic and then, perhaps, we'll share it with the world's archaeologists.

"What you see here is the central citadel with the foundations of what Plato said were the royal palace and the temple of Poseidon and Cleito. As you saw just now, it's surrounded by three concentric circular canals. Amazing pieces of engineering. Plato described them as being crossed by bridges and connected by tunnels, both high and wide enough for a trireme to pass through. There's nothing left of the bridges except pier foundations and most of the tunnels have collapsed but we have seen one that looks to be more or less intact.

"The outer canal was linked to the sea by a straight waterway and the whole system was surrounded by a walled city. Most of that outer wall can still be traced."

"Just where are we?" Lindsay asked.

"As near as we can determine, this is a spur of the Mid-Atlantic Ridge south-east of the Azores."

"I thought that core samples had proved that the Ridge had never been above water," Lindsay countered.

That surprised McKenna. "I'm impressed, Commander. You've obviously done some reading on the subject.

"You're right of course, but that may only have been true of those parts of the Ridge where the core samples were taken. Back in 1975, scientists at the University of Miami showed that around eleven and a half thousand years ago, meltwater from the ice-sheets then covering the USA and other northern land masses raised world-wide sea levels by a considerable amount, possibly covering this area. Now that date broadly agrees with Solon's estimate for the submergence of Atlantis, not to mention evidence of other drowned structures researched by Graham Hancock."

"The Biblical flood, perhaps?" Lindsay offered.

"Quite likely. This area's also pretty unstable, a region of intense tectonic and volcanic activity. A physical slump may have occurred as well. One of those volcanoes is the cause of this glow outside. It's been active a long while, certainly when Nemo was here, and it's only two or three miles away. Nemo didn't give it a name as far as we can tell so we decided to call it Mount Poseidon. That seemed pretty apt to us."

"Hell of a place to build a city," Lindsay said. "Right under an active volcano."

McKenna shrugged. "We do it all the time. Take Naples, directly under Vesuvius. Or San Francisco, built on one of the planet's most unstable tectonic fault zones. The human race might be clever but it's never been as intelligent as it likes to believe. Where disasters happen and are bound to recur—Naples and San Francisco being prime examples—what do we do? Rebuild in exactly the same location."

Lindsay smiled at McKenna's argument. "A detailed survey of Atlantis would be an incredible project," he said. "If, as you say, you ever get the chance. It strikes me that you won't unless we can prise some decent information out of Calloway."

"I've been thinking about that," McKenna said. "You've tried everything bar the rack and the thumbscrews so maybe we ought to adopt another approach."

"Such as?"

McKenna's smile twitched mischievously. "How about we scare it out of him?"

On the surface, the *Nautilus* rolled in a sluggish swell under greying skies. Seán McKenna clambered onto the wheelhouse roof to scan the horizon. There was no sign of either aircraft or shipping.

That Nemo had not envisaged the need for the boat to be equipped with a periscope was no great disadvantage as far as McKenna was concerned. Just to bring the wheelhouse itself above the surface could give him an equally good all-round view and there were powerful Zeiss binoculars to give him any magnification he might need.

He climbed back onto the deck, which rose about three feet from the waterline, and ran a lazy eye over the hull's slightly overlapping plates which were both welded and flush-rivetted. Thc wheelhouse, already partially sunk into the body of the craft, rose about four feet from the forward part of her deck, its inclined sides punctuated by the round, convex view ports. In the mid-part of the deck, the tender, its own interior sheathed and protected by sliding metal deck plates, protruded to about knee height. The open hatch lay between the boat and the lantern casing. This was rather smaller than the wheelhouse, although of similar design.

McKenna cast another eye around an empty horizon and walked to the hatch. "Bring him up," he said.

He leaned nonchalantly against the lantern housing as a struggling Calloway was hauled on deck by the massive figure of Ross Jourdan. As solidly built as the politician was, he was helpless in the grip of the former heavyweight boxer.

Calloway glanced at the empty ocean around them. "What is this, McKenna?" The demand was meant to be belligerent but a tremor of uncertainty took the edge off his words.

"Commander Lindsay's been asking questions, Minister," McKenna said quietly, "and we'd all like the answers you're refusing to give."

The minister twisted vainly in Jourdan's grasp. "Lindsay is nothing but a criminal," he spat, "as are you all, each and every one of you."

"Is that a fact, now?" McKenna said, his voice calm. "You would even brand Madeleine Duvall a criminal, would you? That innocent little lass, Minister, is barely twenty years of age. What did she ever do to deserve the attempt by you and your cronies to put her, and the rest of us, on the bottom of the Ross Sea?"

"Why don't you go and fuck yourself?" Calloway sneered.

The Irishman winced. "Oh, the language on the man! Am I to take that, Minister, as your last word on the matter?"

"You'll get nothing from me, McKenna. Neither you nor Lindsay."

McKenna gave a curt nod. Calloway felt cold metal on his right wrist and the snap of a lock as Jourdan shackled him to the deck rail. "What the hell do you think you're playing at?" Calloway shouted, suddenly fearful.

"You're no use to us, Mr Calloway," McKenna said. "On this boat, you're nothing more than dangerous deadweight. If it's an answer to your question you want, then I'm playing at submerging this boat and forgetting that you ever existed."

He walked slowly to the deck hatch and began to follow Jourdan below.

"Goodbye, Mr Calloway," he said before pulling the hatch cover down. "I can't honestly say it's been a pleasure to know you."

McKenna climbed into the wheelhouse. At his word, Alan Tregenza handed the helm over to him and took station by the after view port to watch the wild-eyed and thoroughly terrified politician struggling vainly with the shackles that held him.

"Are you serious about this, Seán?" There was concern edging Tregenza's words. "This isn't like you at all. I agree that Calloway's an asshole but is this quite the civilized thing to do?"

"'I am not what you would call a civilized man,'" McKenna intoned. "'I have finished with society for reasons which seem good to me and I no longer obey its laws.'"

"What?" Tregenza was taken aback.

McKenna turned his head, a strange smile playing at the corners of his mouth. "A quote from Captain Nemo. I must admit that I'm beginning to empathize with his views."

Tregenza blinked and looked back as the sea swept over the sinking deck, driving Calloway back against the rail. For an instant he saw the politician straining to keep his head above water then, after a swirl of bubbles, saw him thrashing desperately beneath the surface. McKenna began to move the *Nautilus* forward, a motion that hauled Calloway's body above and away from the rail, the chain of the shackles taut as the man was dragged along.

"Throttle down, Seán," Tregenza said urgently. "For Christ's sake, you'll tear his fucking arm off."

McKenna said nothing but sat hunched over the wheel. Worried, Tregenza looked at the hunter watch he had now regained. Twenty seconds had passed since the submerging boat had dragged Calloway under the waves. Now it was thirty. Tregenza moved quickly to McKenna's shoulder.

"Seán, we don't want him dead. Bring us up before he drowns." McKenna ignored him. "Seán, for Christ's sake!"

Tregenza leant forward, trying to prise the captain's grip from the controls. An age seemed to pass before the Cornishman's strength began to tell. McKenna's grip loosened and the mate moved fast, cutting the forward speed and hitting the ballast tank vent controls. The submarine rose, breaking the surface. A quick glance took in a motionless body on the streaming deckplates.

Then, McKenna turned to look at him. Tregenza stepped back on seeing an expression so strange that the Irish skipper no longer looked like the man he'd known for so long. His eyes were glazed and his face wore a deathly pallor. He stared at Tregenza as though he was a complete stranger then, unexpectedly, the grey eyes rolled upwards and he slumped unconscious in his seat.

The *Nautilus* hung motionless at a depth of six hundred feet, some fifty miles west of Madeira. In her sumptuous saloon, Seán McKenna sat on a divan, his body slumped forward, head held in unsteady hands. Carla Schumann and Deanne Fischer hovered close by, trying to press a hot drink on the bemused skipper. Madeleine Duvall, her eyes wide with anxiety, sat beside him with an arm around the Irishman's shoulder.

"Seán?" McKenna raised his head slowly as Tregenza approached. "You okay, skip? How do you feel?"

McKenna looked blankly at him for a moment, his own thoughts gradually unclouding. A degree of colour had returned to his face, the glazed look of the eyes had gone and, to Tregenza's relief, there was no sign of the facial expression that had disturbed him so utterly.

"Feel?" The captain sounded like a man emerging from a deep sleep. "I'm not sure how I feel. It's weird… like something inside me has upped and left."

"So what the hell happened up there?"

Carla Schumann, the ship's doctor, broke in. "I think he had a blackout, Alan. The most likely cause is stress and, God knows, Seán's had more of that than anyone has a right to expect."

"I won't argue with my doctor." McKenna gave a slight shrug of his shoulders. "To me, it felt like I was being crowded out of my own mind, almost like someone else had taken over. And before you say it, I'm thinking clearly enough now. I don't remember much else until I heard you shouting at someone. You sounded as if you were miles away."

"I was bellowing right in your ear," Tregenza told him. "You had me scared out of my own wits. You had such a grip on the controls that it took everything I had to prise your hands off them. At the same time, you didn't actually do anything to stop me. Your eyes were glassy and then, as I was taking the boat up, you blacked right out."

"Taking her up?" McKenna was genuinely puzzled.

"Calloway, Seán. We'd shackled him to the deck-rail, remember? It was an even bet which would happen first, that he'd drown or his arm would tear off at the shoulder."

The captain was shocked to the core. "Christ, Calloway… I'd forgotten all about him."

"Lucky for him that I hadn't. We only just got to him in time. As it was, we had to pump half the Atlantic out of him. I've never seen a man so bloody terrified." Tregenza started to chuckle. "We even had to get him a fresh set of trousers and underwear and ditch his old ones. You don't get much more frightened than that. Don Lindsay's delighted… he can't get the bastard to stop talking now."

"That was an inspired idea of yours, Seán," Lindsay said as he walked into the room. "Even if you did come close to overdoing it."

"It was no idea of mine," McKenna muttered.

"Of course it was your idea. It was you who suggested scaring Calloway into talking by chaining him on deck and sinking the boat under him."

"Perhaps I did, but it still wasn't my idea. I wouldn't have gone that far by choice but it seemed to me that the thought had been, well, planted in my mind. I could do nothing to resist it."

"Planted?" Lindsay stopped as he caught sight of the look in McKenna's eyes. "God, man, you're serious about this."

"Of course I'm bloody serious. I'll tell you now that I'm getting a distinct feeling we're not alone aboard this vessel. There's been something strange about her ever since we first came on board.

"Tell me this, Commander… who the hell was Hobbes speaking to before he died? His words weren't directed at any of us. He was staring right at that divan over there in the corner, like he could see someone we couldn't. The very divan that Nemo's body was lying on when we found this boat."

"Dying people see strange things," Lindsay offered. "Sometimes they see long-dead relatives and friends. It was probably nothing more than the product of a mind seeking solace before death. We'll never really know. Psychoanalysts would have one explanation, parapsychologists another." He paused for a moment, taking in what McKenna had said. "Oh, come on Seán, you can't be seriously suggesting that Nemo's still here?"

"Explain this to me," McKenna said patiently. "When we were set upon burying Nemo's body with those of his old crewmen, I knew exactly where to look. And I mean, exactly. Sure, the place is marked on his charts but a small cemetery's a bloody hard thing to find on a big ocean floor. I took us straight to the exact spot and I still can't account for it."

"Nemo's journal," Tregenza suddenly said. Everyone turned to stare at his expression of disbelief in a face drained of colour and watched as he walked, tight-lipped, to the door of what had once been Nemo's cabin, set in the canted corner of the room on the port side of the forward bulkhead. He went inside and came back with a bulky leatherbound volume.

"For the benefit of the uninitiated," he said, "this book is Nemo's own journal. So far, I've read about two-thirds of it. It contains his complete life story, his undersea discoveries and technical information about all aspects of this boat. For some reason, he wrote it in several languages.

"The autobiographical section has something that might just have a bearing on what's happening here. It's a terrible thing for anyone read, but I think it's time you all heard it."

"What does it say, Alan?" Karen asked softly. "Read it out."

"Yeah, read it, man," Jourdan agreed.

Tregenza searched for the page, found it and sat down. "The entry has a date in the margin," he said. "May the tenth, 1858."

"The end of the Indian Mutiny," McKenna said. "Nemo was one of the rebel warleaders."

Tregenza nodded. "Spot on, Seán. This is what happened after the Mutiny had been suppressed by the British and when Nemo was on the run." He began to read aloud:

"This was the day on which my life was destined to change forever. Alone, weaponless, hunted like a wild animal, I crouched in a high recess of the mountainside, a concealed vantage point from which I could gain a clear view into the British-held fortress. With the aid of my telescope, I took full stock of the tall, impregnable walls surrounding the courtyard, the heavy, barred gates and a guard that had been doubled in strength. I cursed my forefathers for having built a fortress so strong.

"It was evident to me that the enemy had acted in anticipation of a rescue attempt. Equally evident was the fact that any such attempt would have been doomed to failure and death unless one had an army of thousands.

"The sun rose over distant forested peaks into a cloudless sky. In the stillness of the air, I could clearly hear the calls of command. The beating of a military drum seemed no less loud than that of my own fearful heart.

"My hand so trembled that I was forced to rest the glass against an outcropping of rock to still the movement that jarred my vision. It was at this moment that I saw the procession issue from a square solid building at the rear of the courtyard; the drummers at its head, then the red-coated riflemen ranked on either side of five pathetic prisoners whose torn clothing, once so white and dazzlingly fine, now ragged and filthy, contrasted so vividly with the immaculate dress uniforms of the soldiers.

"Never had I felt so helpless, so utterly powerless. I could not look away. The glass was sufficiently powerful to bring faces into clear view as the prisoners were placed in line, their backs to the great wall. My father, white-haired and proud, remained a Rajah to the last, despite his rags and the grime that coated him. He stood firmly erect, holding his head high in silent defiance of his fate and his oppressors. His left arm clasped the shoulders of my mother, my poor mother, now so old and bewildered. Age had shrivelled her once astute mind, a cruel blow and yet, at this moment, so merciful. I am certain that she had no comprehension of what was happening to her.

"Then my wife, my beautiful Jameena, each arm tightly encircling the wide-eyed children. My heart tore in two and yet swelled with pride as she, like my father, took up a dignified and defiant stance. At such a distance, she could not have seen me but, for one heart-rending instance, her eyes looked up at the mountain on which I lay hidden and seemed to gaze for a last time into my own. To my dying day, I will swear that the movement of her lips formed my name.

"A British sergeant stepped forward, bearing strips of cloth for blindfolds, but was called back into line by his commander. They were to be refused even the smallest of mercies. The chattering drums ceased abruptly. The commands rang out. I saw the crisply drilled movements of the riflemen and then the gouts of gunsmoke bursting from the barrels in perfect unison.

"My father fell to his knees and toppled slowly over onto his face. My mother, torn from his embrace, pitched backwards into the dust at the foot of the wall. My beloved wife, my Jameena, lay perfectly still, face down, while my precious sons, young Tipu and little Tantia, had fallen in such a way that their outflung arms lay across their mother's body in a final embrace, their very lives spreading and soaking away into the dust. Then I heard the brief, loud crackle of the rifleshots that had taken them from me forever.

"I know that I cried out. The echo of it remained long after those of the gunshots had faded. Tears ran hot upon my cheeks, streaming into my beard, but I wiped my eyes clear for one last gaze through the glass.

"My cry of anguish had been heard. Surprised faces turned and were raised to the mountain. I sought the one face I burned to see, and found it. The commanding officer. He who had ordered the torture and murder of those I loved more than life itself. I saw his baleful eyes, the taut smile of triumph that curled his lips as he heard, and knew, the cry from the mountain.

"I knew him. I had faced him at Banda and would have killed him on that field had not the press of battle forced us apart. In that moment of my greatest grief, I cursed him. I cursed him in the name of the Christian god, the gods of the Hindus, the Brahmins and the Buddhists, and in all the myriad names of the Creator. I cursed him and all his seed that they should, throughout each successive generation until the extinction of his line, be men devoid of honour, without virtue, without redemption.

"I cursed Colonel Hugh Melville Calloway and all his seed forever."

The room was in total silence as Tregenza stopped reading and lay the book down. Deanne Fischer's eyes were moist. Others in the room were frozen with the horror of what they had just heard.

"Oh, God." Carla Schumann's voice was the first to break the spell. "I've never heard anything so terrible. The poor man… to see his own family being put to death."

"Calloway?" said Jourdan.

"It would explain a lot," McKenna said. "Our man's middle name is Hugh. He could well be a direct descendant. What price rational explanations now?"

"Are you trying to say that Nemo's still here?" Chris Janssen broke in. "On board this boat? How can he be? We buried him alongside his crew months ago."

"Only his body, Chris," Maddy Duvall said, her young face streaked with tears. "You can only bury a body, not the soul."

"Makes sense to me, Maddy," Jourdan agreed. "The *Nautilus* was his creation, his home—his whole existence, dammit—for eighteen years. He said himself that he loved her as if she were his own child. Do you think a little thing like death could really part him from her? As far as I'm concerned, it was no accident that we found this boat. Hell, we didn't find her. She found us. There's nothing in this world that's ever going to convince me otherwise."

Lindsay ran a hand through his hair. "I was brought up to respect realities, Ross," he said. "All I'm willing to say right now is that, if the guy in that journal does turn out to be Gerald Calloway's ancestor, then my logic's in for a heavy beating. For now, I prefer to keep an open mind on the subject." He turned back to Tregenza. "Alan. You said that you've read most of the journal. What was Nemo's story after that?"

"His companions were also hiding out in the mountains," Tregenza said. "Most of them were Europeans but a few were also Indian, his own family retainers in fact. He rounded them up and they fled the country.

"Most of his wealth was banked in Europe. He recovered it all, including all his art treasures, and then—in France, I believe—they formed their plans.

"Nemo had actually dreamed up the concept of the *Nautilus* a few years earlier when he saw the idea of a submarine monitor as a key to liberating India. He realized that, in his day, the strength of any occupying power was heavily dependant upon their sea power and sea-borne supplies. The defeat of such a navy by an undetectable and highly revolutionary craft, as a submarine would have been at that time, would have left the Imperial power in India isolated and vulnerable.

"The Indian Mutiny blew up before he could develop the idea. Now that he had no country, no family and a huge price on his head, Nemo saw his submarine concept in an entirely different light. As the means to a freedom he was denied on land. The next few years were spent in designing her down to the last rivet and then, after obtaining all the materials and components, they put the *Nautilus* together on a Pacific atoll he'd purchased some years earlier. As you know, they launched her in 1865 and, from that moment, he abandoned the name of Prince Dakkar and renamed himself Nemo, the Latin word for 'no one'

"His companions, now his crew, were mostly highly educated and talented men. Engineers, scientists in any number of fields. With Nemo the mastermind, there was nothing their combined talents couldn't achieve." He looked around him meaningfully. "We can judge the results for ourselves."

Lindsay contemplated this in silence. He poured himself a stiff measure of Scotch, downed it in one, then got up and left the room.

Wrapped in a blanket and with one wrist handcuffed to the iron bedframe, Gerald Calloway looked anything but a Cabinet Minister. His features remained pallid after his recent brush with death but his eyes filled with hatred as Lindsay unlocked the door and entered the cabin.

"I'll see you in hell for this," Calloway hissed at him. "Treason still carries a life sentence and, in your case, Commander, I'll see that it's carried out to the letter. I'll see you rot."

Lindsay ignored the tirade. "Tell me, Minister," he said quietly. "Was a Colonel Hugh Melville Calloway a forebear of yours by any strange chance?"

"What did you say?" Calloway's surprise turned the question into more of a yelp.

"You heard me. Was he?"

Calloway threw back his head in a gesture of conceited pride. "51st Lancers. My direct ancestor, yes. A hero in India. A great military hero."

Lindsay drew a hand across his brow and shook his head sadly. "No, Minister, I don't believe so. From what I've heard, he was a butcher. A coward. A murderous, first degree bastard and a war criminal no better than Goebbels, Pol Pot and Milosevic."

"That's a lie! A filthy, contemptible lie! Just what the hell do you mean by it?"

Lindsay gave him an almost pitying look. "What I mean, Minister, that I've just discovered how bloody fortunate you are to be alive."

43

21st January 2015
The Canary Islands

The strange sounds that roused Donall Lindsay from his slumbers were not what he would expect to hear in mid-ocean. He hitched himself up onto one elbow, cocking his head to listen and checked the luminous dial of his Seiko diver's watch. It was 0655 hours Greenwich Mean Time.

He heard it a second time, the slow rasp of something solid scraping along the hull. Lindsay placed the tips of his fingers against the bulkhead, feeling faint vibrations with leisurely rhythms suggesting that the vessel's engines were at dead slow.

He hauled himself from the bunk, switched on the cabin light and dressed himself. A soft breath of cool air from the vent above the door heightened his curiosity. Again he touched the bulkhead, this time feeling no vibration at all. The engines had stopped and the cool air from the vent obviously meant that the vessel was lying on the surface. Lindsay could not understand why there was not the slightest hint of her rolling in a mid-Atlantic swell.

He left the cabin and made for the central stairwell, reaching it just as McKenna was stepping through the watertight door on the half-landing above him, evidently on his way back from the wheelhouse. The Irishman secured the door and glanced down.

"Good morning, Commander. How did you sleep?"

"Like a baby. I'd have slept on longer but for those sounds. Like something scraping along the hull. Did we foul anything?"

McKenna, looking none the worse for his experience of the previous day, was apologetic. "Poor helmsmanship, I'm afraid. My fault, Commander. The passage is a tad tight for those not accustomed to it."

"What passage?"

"Come up on deck and see for yourself."

Lindsay climbed the steps, taking them two at a time, and followed the skipper up through the open hatches and onto the submarine's deck. To his utter surprise, it was totally dark.

"What the hell?" he said. "But this isn't the middle of the night." His words reverberated strangely, like echoes in some vast cathedral.

"Oh-seven-hundred GMT, according to the ship's chronometer," came McKenna's voice. "Take a look directly overhead."

Using the searchlight housing for support, Lindsay craned his neck and caught sight of a faint gleam far above him, a small indistinct patch of grey only barely lighter than the profound blackness around him.

"It's not quite dawn," McKenna said. "It'll get lighter soon. In the meantime, I'll get Ross to turn the searchlight on. I'd shield my eyes if I were you, Commander."

The Irishman's footfalls on the metal deckplates were eerily magnified as he made his way forward to the wheelhouse. Lindsay heard him rap a rhythmic tattoo on one of its glass ports. As he protected his eyes, a sudden brilliance scorched between his fingers, causing him to flinch. He allowed himself a moment to adjust to the glare but was still totally unprepared for what he saw.

The *Nautilus* was floating on a still lake of black water three hundred yards across. All around her, immense walls of columnar basalt rose vertically for five hundred feet before leaning inward like a colossal inverted funnel. The apex of the cavern, three hundred feet higher still, was a circular opening where Lindsay guessed he'd seen that faint patch of light.

"I don't believe this," he said after a second or two of astonished silence. "What is this place?"

"Have you never been inside a volcano, Commander?" The Irishman smiled broadly. "Sail with Captain McKenna, my friend, and anything might be possible."

"I'm beginning to believe that. Sailing with you is like voyaging with bloody Sinbad. If this is a volcano, I hope to hell it's a dead one."

"So do I. Volcanoes are fickle creatures but this one's been quiet for four or five centuries at least."

"Are you sure of that?"

"Reasonably. This was one of Nemo's hideaways, commander. We've been here before. After limping halfway around the world, this is where we stopped to refit and overhaul the *Nautilus*."

Lindsay recalled the unexplained hiatus in the submarine's activities between June and September the previous year as McKenna carried on.

"Everything that Nemo had left behind him was still here. Workshops, stores, furnaces, spares, even a replacement tender. He'd already got through two of those. Aronnax and his companions escaped in the first one, and the second boat was rowed away by the castaways on Lincoln Island after Nemo's death.

"We purchased some of the modern extras locally. There are some wonderful chandlers hereabouts who supplied us with the radio, sonar and SatNav equipment."

"And just where is 'hereabouts'?"

"The Canary Islands. The Spaniards who colonized them in the fourteenth century called this island La Roque del Fuego, the Fire Rock, so presumably it was still active then. Lanzarote's just a leisurely boat trip away.

"We were here for a couple of months last summer. Peak holiday time, ideal for mingling with the crowds. Some days we worked on refitting and repairing the *Nautilus*, some we actually spent lazing on the beaches, making our purchases and doing some homework. By that I mean using the local cyber cafés to track down the Pyramus symbol that Alan saw on the bow of the ship that rammed the *Aurora*. We managed to identify several ships that carried the same symbol. We then bought our own computer and used that to find out their sailing dates, ports of departure and destination and so on.

"We used the Zephyr to cruise around the islands after we'd painted out the *Aurora's* name on its sides. We even had the barefaced cheek to replace it with *Nautilus*. After all, who'd ever expect it to refer to the Jules Verne boat? We just looked like typical tourists, enjoying ourselves as best we could and causing no one to start asking awkward questions.

"It might sound idyllic but, believe me, Don, it was bloody difficult. For the first time in months, we were on land, among people. For some of the crew, the hardest thing to endure was to resist the temptation to contact their families. Not so hard for Robbie and me, we have no families but can you imagine the sheer heartache that someone like young Maddy Duvall had to go through? Or Alan, with a fiancée at home thinking him dead?

"It was only later when we realized how vital she and Barrington Hobbes were to us. Hobbes was a friend of Alan's and we needed someone of his abilities to do the on-shore investigations. Even then, we had to be bloody careful not to let on who we were. All we could do was give them enough to whet their appetites and hope they would follow them up. It only took a couple of crafty phone calls to find out they'd swallowed the hook and that Hobbes had been taken on by his old newspaper."

McKenna lowered his voice. "Madeleine doesn't know it yet but she'll be seeing her parents soon enough. That's something you and I need to discuss later, Commander. Her father runs a computer firm in Marseille and we're going to need someone of his own particular expertise to help fill in the blanks.

"And don't look like that. I'm fully aware that going into the Med is one hell of a risk. You're going to tell me it's a dead-end trap. Trust me, Commander, it's less of a risk than you think."

McKenna turned away and gestured widely at the huge cavern around them. "Magnificent, isn't it? Verne exaggerated its size but not its sheer splendour. What architect could ever design something so impressive? Nature has much to teach us, if only we'd learn."

"I can't argue with that," Lindsay said. "But why should Nemo have needed a haven at all? I thought he was self-sufficient?"

McKenna sat down on the submarine's boat that was three-quarters embedded in the ship's hull. "When this volcano was born," he explained, "it thrust its way up through the sea floor and vast beds of coal that were laid down millions of years ago when this part of the Atlantic was above water. Somehow, Nemo discovered this. He and his men dug into those seams, brought the coal to surface and used it to fire the furnaces he used in the process of extracting sodium from sea salt. The smoke from the furnaces escaped through the volcano's crater. The natives on the other islands—this one's far too small and rocky to have been inhabited—would have assumed that it was still simmering.

"Luckily, we don't need to do any of that. Nemo left huge stockpiles of sodium here, enough to power the *Nautilus* for years. All we need to do is ship it aboard as and when we need it, and restock the fuel cells. Of course, Nemo also needed workshops in case the boat had to undergo repairs and you have to agree that a place like this is as secure as you can get."

"How did we get in here?" Lindsay asked.

"It would seem that during its last eruption, the volcano vented out through its flank," McKenna said. "That pipe is now thirty feet below sea level. As you heard, it's a tight squeeze, but navigable enough if you know what you're doing."

Overlooked by the works of Titian, Leonardo da Vinci and Rubens, Don Lindsay relaxed in the saloon of the *Nautilus*, musing over the character traits he could deduce from the photographic portrait of Captain Nemo on the forward bulkhead.

Rob McLeish and Chris Janssen were deeply engrossed in a game of chess while Ross Jourdan, wearing a stained tee-shirt, played softly on the organ that stood against the after bulkhead.

McKenna, sitting between Carla Schumann and Maddy Duvall, chuckled at the opinions that Lindsay and Deanne Fischer were putting forward. "The only sure way to get inside that man's head," he said, "would be to read his journal. I've only read parts of it—I was concentrating more on his technical notes—but Alan says it's quite an eye-opener. He's read far more of it than I have. It's in Nemo's old cabin, on the desk, if you want to look it up."

The after door of the saloon opened. Tregenza himself ambled in, ruffled Karen Marshall's hair and kissed her softly on the forehead.

"How's our guest?" McKenna asked him.

"Don't even ask," the mate scowled. "I don't believe the bloody man. He seems to have forgotten how much we broke him down yesterday. He's back to the old arrogant Calloway, claiming we'll never prove anything against him. That he'll deny everything we forced out of him. The bugger even threw his breakfast at Ross."

"Well, let the bastard go hungry then. Once we've taken a stock of sodium on board, he'll find himself a little less cocky."

"Why?" Lindsay said suspiciously. "What have you got in mind for him this time, keelhauling?"

"Nothing so dramatic." McKenna shot him a conspiratorial grin. "Just a little old fashioned maritime justice."

Gerald Calloway glowered at the three men who stood inside the door of his cell-like cabin. "Just what do you want now?" he demanded.

"Well," Lindsay replied lightly, "there are still a few things you haven't given us. Like the name of the top man of Pyramus, for instance."

"You can rot in hell, Lindsay."

"I had a notion you'd be saying something like that," the naval man shrugged dismissively. "Never mind, we'll get it all eventually, with or without your cooperation."

"You'll get nothing more from me," Calloway snarled. "No matter what you do. I'll not make the same mistake a second time. I've come to realize that you can't kill me. Not one of you has the balls to kill me. And even if you did, you'll lose all hope of more information."

"We don't need it," Lindsay said. "Not from you." He glanced at Jourdan. "Over to you, Ross."

"Get your contemptible ass on deck, *Mister* Calloway." Jourdan's voice rumbled ominously like an impending storm.

"So that you can half-drown me again? I think not," Calloway said. Jourdan raised a huge right fist and took half a step forward.

"It really wouldn't be wise to argue," Lindsay advised. "That same fist got Ross within an ace of the WBO World Heavyweight championship a few years ago. You might even remember that. You wouldn't enjoy being on the receiving end and I, for one, wouldn't dream of stopping him. God knows, you've given him reason enough to use it already." He glanced meaningfully at the splattered eggstains on Jourdan's broad chest.

Lindsay's words sent Calloway's mind back some five years. He remembered the televized title bout. No one who had seen it would ever be likely to forget it. The fight had been a titanic contest, one of the finest ever staged. For round after punishing round, there had been next to nothing in it then, in the closing minute of the final round, Ross Jourdan had unleashed an almighty right cross that sent the defending champion crashing to the canvas.

An ordinary man would never have got up from that punch in a month of Sundays but the champion was no ordinary man. He had staggered back to his feet on the count of nine, seconds before the final bell.

Despite the knockdown, a split points decision went the champion's way. He went on to fight three more successful defences of the title but Jourdan, his right eye severely damaged during the course of the fight, never fought again. A year later, after successful operations to repair a detached retina, he picked up on his earlier electrical career and joined Deep Watch, an organization he had always deeply admired and generously donated to during the course of a lucrative boxing career.

Remembering that, Calloway finally recognized the wisdom of obedience and allowed himself to be led out of the cabin and up on deck.

The *Nautilus* had now been brought alongside a rib of rock that jutted into the underground lake like a natural jetty. Aghast at his bizarre surroundings, Calloway struggled wildly as Jourdan manhandled him ashore.

"What are you going to do with me?" The minister's natural arrogance had deserted him and his voice held a shrill note of sheer dread.

"In days of yore," McKenna explained, like a patient schoolmaster, "it was the custom for ship's captains to maroon on-board criminals on deserted islands. As captain of the *Nautilus*, it is my intention to exercise that same right. You can take some comfort, Minister, in the fact that you'll be the first person in history to be marooned *inside* a desert island."

"You are far too much of a liability for us to risk keeping you aboard. One slack moment on our part could mean you having an opportunity to sabotage the boat. It's not a risk I'm prepared to take.

"Here, you can do us no harm, nor is there any way for you to escape. No one lives on this island or anywhere near it so you can shout and holler all you want. Chris Bonington in his prime couldn't have made the climb to the crater and no man's lungs have the capacity to attempt the swim. The passage into this place is thirty feet down and a quarter-mile long."

"You can't do this," Calloway pleaded hoarsely, horrified at the prospect.

"I can and I will," McKenna said coldly. "You'll have food and water enough for three months in the crates the crew's bringing ashore. The variety's somewhat limited, no gourmet specialities here. There are also a few Ruhmkorff lamps that should last you for about the same period of time, if you're prudent. Some extra clothing, a sleeping bag and a blanket or two.

"You should be thankful, Mr Calloway. Ross was all for lashing you to a boulder and dropping you in the lake. Can you imagine how deep that must be? A flooded volcanic vent?

"You had better hope and pray that your partners in crime, or NATO for that matter, don't find a way of sinking us en route because we're the only hope you have for ever getting out of here. No one else even suspects that this place exists so, if we don't make it, neither do you. There's no harm in telling you that we're off to find your facility in the Antarctic. Once we've found it, we intend to expose it to the world and shut it down. Permanently."

"You don't stand a chance," Calloway said.

"Then neither do you. How long can you stand your own company? For as long it takes you to run out of food and water? On the other hand, solitude isn't such a bad thing. They say it's good for the penitent soul. In fact, I recall you saying as much at your own Party Conference a year or two back when you called for a greater use of solitary confinement in prisons. This experience should get you used to the cell that awaits you after we get back, and after your eloquence of yesterday."

Calloway suddenly looked more confident. "You'll need a damn sight more than hearsay evidence to get me convicted, McKenna."

"Oh, I don't know. A DVD recording should be sufficient." McKenna threw up his hands theatrically. "Oh, did I not tell you, now? How very remiss of me. You should have taken a close peek at the ventilation grille over your cabin door, Minister. We stuck a camcorder in there and your little speech was captured in full sound and glorious technicolour. Commander Lindsay can't wait for us to pull in at the nearest post-box."

As Calloway stared speechlessly at McKenna's smug expression, Lindsay brushed past, lugging a box to stack with the others already ashore. No one saw as he pulled a gun—Calloway's own Browning automatic—from his waistband and empty all but one of its bullets from the magazine. No one saw as he pushed the gun deep down among the containers in the box or as he turned away to drop the extracted bullets into the lake.

"That the last one?" McKenna asked as Lindsay returned.

"That's the lot, Seán."

"We've got all the fuel we need, so we'll bid you farewell, Minister."

McKenna looked around the vast chamber of rock. "You know," he said conversationally as Jourdan pushed Calloway down among the boxes, "there's no such thing as a dead volcano. They have this terrible habit of making you think they're extinct, and then bursting back into life without the slightest warning."

He followed Jourdan and Lindsay back onto the deck of the *Nautilus* and started below. A sudden distraught scream of terror shrieked out as McKenna reached up to close the deck hatch.

"You can't leave me here! For the love of God, man!"

McKenna stuck his head out of the half-closed hatch as the *Nautilus* backed slowly away from the natural jetty. "Love?" he said, tonelessly. "God? I doubt you understand the meaning of either word, Calloway. Maybe this will give you time to reflect upon them both." He slammed the hatch down and secured it for sea.

From the submarine's cramped wheelhouse, McKenna and Lindsay coldly watched as the vessel moved out towards the centre of the lake. The rays of her searchlight reflected from Calloway's staring eyes as the demented politician hopelessly twisted and turned on the rock jetty, falling to his knees as the *Nautilus* began to sink beneath the black water. His fists pounded uselessly at the rock and his screaming mouth opened and closed.

The water closed over the wheelhouse ports, blotting him from their sight.

Chapter 8

The Net

44

22 January 2015
Whitehall
London, UK

Admiral James Garvie wearily took possession of the files brought to him by his secretary and stacked them neatly on the corner of his desk.

"Thank you, Maureen. One last thing before you go home." He paused, closing his eyes and passing a tired hand across his brow. "Would you bring me Commander Lindsay's service file."

A flicker of expression gave away her concern, not only for the missing agent but also for a boss she looked upon as very much a father figure. "Of course, admiral." She took a hesitant step forward. "Sir? Are you all right?"

"What?" The elderly admiral's shoulders slumped. "Oh, just a touch of tiredness, Maureen. I fear that my age is beginning to tell. It won't be long before the buggers put me out to grass and, if my faith in Commander Lindsay proves to be misplaced, it'll happen a damn sight sooner. When heads begin to roll, it's pretty certain that mine will be the first." He broke off as the desk intercom buzzed. "Garvie."

"Chief of Staff, sir. A signal from Gibraltar has just come in. I think you should see it."

"In my office, if you'll be so good, Chief. Maureen, forget Lindsay's file for now. If this signal is what I suspect it to be, I might need you here to take notes. If it turns out to be a late do, I'll have someone run you home."

The Chief of Staff, Captain Mike Rochester, knocked and entered at Garvie's call. He sat opposite the admiral and handed him a sheet of paper. "Admiral, our friend the *Nautilus* has entered the Med."

"Good God almighty!" Garvie sat up. "Then she's trapped herself. If NATO blockades the Straits, we've got her. I don't understand why they've done it, Chief. Surely they know that it's madness to get trapped in there. Can we be absolutely sure that Lindsay's aboard? I can't see him agreeing to this sort of venture, not for a moment."

"He almost certainly is on the sub, sir. Whatever they're up to, she slipped through the Straits less than an hour ago. It took a combination of SOSUS sensors and the side-scan sonar they've been testing for the last three weeks to pick her up. She apparently waited for a suitably noisy old steamer to enter the Straits and craftily went in with her, just underneath her keel. We can thank providence for the side-scan tests, sir. SOSUS alone would never have got her under those circumstances." The SOSUS system that Rochester spoke of was utilized in chains of passive hydrophone sensors and data relay cables laid on the sea floor of strategic waters around the Atlantic, the Straits of Gibraltar being just one of a number of such sites.

"NATO's responded quickly," Rochester added. "Gibraltar's already blockaded by two hunter-killer subs, one French, the other ours, and they have surface back-up from a Spanish frigate. Between them, they've set up an active-sonar net and, basically, there's no way out there for this so-called *Nautilus*.

"The Egyptians have agreed to keep a full alert on the Suez Canal, not that I think for a minute they'd be stupid enough to attempt the Canal. We've even got the Turks keeping a close eye on the Bosphorus. Within the Med, American, British and French ships are already coordinating a search.

"In short, sir, I'd say the *Nautilus* is finished."

"If Lindsay's aboard, I wouldn't be too sure of that, Chief." Garvie sat back for a moment, contemplating the world map that that covered one wall of his office. "Why in the world has she gone into the Mediterranean? From our point of view, it's an act of sheer lunacy but, up to now, this submarine's done nothing without a reason. Now what, I wonder, could that reason possibly be?"

"I haven't an earthly, sir, but to be honest—and whether Don Lindsay's aboard or not—I wouldn't give a tuppenny cuss for her chances."

45

24 January 2015
Marseille, France

The sad eyes of a broken man stared down from the window of his hilltop villa at the lights of Marseille. It was a sight that used to gladden his heart but now those lights seemed to have dimmed. For Marcel Duvall, all light had gone from his life.

He glanced at his wife who sat at her needlepoint with blank eyes. It was all she ever did these days and her work was more automatic than considered. In eleven months she had scarcely uttered a word. The doctors were still insisting upon keeping her under sedation, even this long after the tragedy, and Duvall feared for her sanity.

He himself had somehow battled on with his life but, with all his enthusiasm gone, his lack of motivation meant that he had increasingly left the day-to-day running of the Duvall Computer Company to his managers. It was now almost a week since he had been anywhere near the offices and he was grateful that his managers were both competent and understanding.

Duvall switched his gaze to the south where night cloaked the sea with darkness. He thought, as he often did, of the only child of his twenty-five year marriage, of Madeleine who, for almost a year, had lain in a deep, icy, unmarked tomb at the bottom of the world. As ever, tears pricked at his eyes and he turned away to ensure that Hélène did not see them. Duvall sensed that, if ever he were to give vent to the grief bottled away inside him, it would send her over the edge into madness.

The sound of the door chimes interrupted his morose train of thought. Duvall was almost grateful. He glanced at Hélène, who showed no sign of having heard them, and went to the door himself. It was late, well past ten and an unusual time for callers. Duvall took the precautions of turning on the porch light and slipping the door's security chain into place.

Two men in dark coats stood under the light, both of them tall. One was dark-haired, the other fair. Both were complete strangers.

"Monsieur Duvall?" the dark-haired man said. Duvall inspected them both through the narrow gap of the restricted door opening and detected the hint of an accent that was not French.

"I am Duvall," he replied in English. "It is very late. How may I help you?"

"Forgive me, monsieur, but this is a delicate matter. It concerns your daughter, Madeleine."

Duvall's eyes turned icy. "My daughter, monsieur, is dead."

"What if I told you otherwise?" the dark man said. "That she's alive and well?"

Duvall felt an uncontrollable surge of anger. He unhooked the chain, flung the door wide and stepped forward to confront the stranger. "How dare you, monsieur!" he hissed. "How can you be so cold-blooded as to play such a sick, cruel joke? Just who the devil are you?"

The man's calm gaze never left the Frenchman's face. "My name is Commander Donall Lindsay. I am an intelligence officer attached to the Royal Navy. My companion here is Seán McKenna, lately captain of the Deep Watch vessel *Aurora*, on which your daughter served."

"So you persist with these callous lies. Why, Mister Lindsay, why? What do you hope to gain from this? Captain McKenna died eleven months ago, along with the most precious thing in our lives, our only child. You will leave now, both of you. If you do not, I will call the gendarmarie."

Behind the two strangers, a slight figure moved into the loom of the porch light. A tearful voice said, "*Papa! C'est moi, Madeleine.*"

Duvall stumbled backwards. *"Non! C'est impossible!"* Then, as Madeleine Duvall rushed into her father's arms, "*Hélène! Hélène! Viens ici! Maintenant! C'est Madeleine! Sacre Dieu, c'est Madeleine!*"

A white-faced Hélène Duvall appeared in the hallway and let out a scream as she ran to embrace her daughter. Lindsay and McKenna stepped away as the reunion erupted in tears and shrieks of sheer joy. Marcel Duvall called them back.

"*Messieurs*, I do not know how this has been possible. How can I thank you for this… this miracle?" His tears were flowing without shame or embarrassment. The discomfort was McKenna's.

"Perhaps by accepting my deepest apology," he said.

"I do not understand," Duvall responded.

McKenna's feet shifted nervously. "We've kept the fact of Madeleine's survival secret from you all these months. The same applies to the families of all the *Aurora's* crew. None of them know that we survived the sinking and there are two, in Britain, who will eventually have to be told that their sons did not survive. We have put you all through hell. To keep this from you has been the most difficult thing we have ever done, but, believe me, it was essential that we did so, and we'd like the chance to explain why."

Duvall sensed the man's sincerity. Lindsay took advantage of the momentary silence to interrupt. "Monsieur Duvall, we need your help. Your computer expertise, and most of all, any experience you may have of computer hacking." He drew a small package from a pocket of his jacket and smiled grimly. "At some stage, I'd also like to find a post office."

The Frenchman waved them into the house. "Then you must tell me everything and you must leave nothing out. Only when I know the true reasons for your actions will I decide whether to accept your apology and provide the help you require." He looked at his wife and daughter locked together in a tearful embrace. Beneath the tears he saw a radiance in Hélène's face that he had not seen for months.

As he turned off the porch light and began to close the door, Duvall glanced up at the night sky. For the first time in all those months, he saw the stars. The light had come back to his life.

Perhaps, he thought, *it will not be so terrible a thing to allow these men a chance to explain. They have given me back my daughter… and they have given me back my wife.*

Shocked by the details of the story that had been related to him, and equally staggered by the secret of the *Nautilus*, Duvall took longer than he would normally have expected to hack into the files being requested by Lindsay and McKenna. By half past one in the morning,

Lindsay had a sheaf of printed hard copies to study. Some of the information would, he knew, be unhelpful but, on the other hand, there was much that had already left him breathless.

By now, McKenna was dozing lightly in a chair. Duvall was still hard at it with Lindsay beside him studying the screen intently.

"Hold it there," he said suddenly. Duvall scrolled the text back slightly for Lindsay to read. "Well, I'll be damned," Lindsay said softly, then reached out to shake McKenna from his slumber. "Seán, I think you'd better see this."

The Irishman was awake in an instant, staring at the screen as Lindsay pointed out the damning piece of information. His face went grey and he looked as if every last breath had been knocked out of his body. Lindsay asked for a final print out.

Lindsay took advantage of the print run to turn back to McKenna.

"So just what is your game plan, Seán?" he said. 'You're dead set upon returning to Antarctica, but what are your intentions once we get there?"

McKenna's eyes were thoughtful. "First, we need to get a fix on the exact location of the Pyramus site," he said carefully. "The reverse course of the *Emperor* on the night she sank the *Aurora* gives us a datum to start from. Once we find it, the *Nautilus* can get us in close. Even if they have a sensory array, she's the quietest thing in the ocean at low speed, but we'll catch all hell if we are detected—under the ice is not the best place to get caught and I haven't underestimated the danger, believe me. If we're lucky, though, we'll get the chance to find out everything we can about the place, then shout every last detail to whoever might just take it seriously.

"We might even find an easy way in," he added. "In which case, having a man of your profession aboard..."

"You can put that thought right out of your mind," Lindsay broke in. "Whatever else I might be, Seán, I'm no James Bond. My coat buttons don't have concealed thermo-nuclear devices. I don't even have any weapons, apart from the gun you squirreled away somewhere, and a fat lot of good that would be. The same goes for the boat's hunting guns. Not against the numbers and firepower they have down there, if Calloway's to be believed."

Laughing, McKenna raised a placatory hand. "Hold on there, Commander. I did somehow think you'd take a dim view of that idea. So, I moved up to Plan B."

"Which is?"

"Let me put it this way. Who's going to listen to us? You've seen the list of Pyramus directors. Industrialists, financiers and even government ministers, from all sorts of nations, including the United States, Japan, France and Britain. Those countries are in it up to their necks. We'll get no help from them—hell, three of them have their navies hunting us down right now.

"So, which nations with half-decent defence forces have no involvement with Pyramus and are rather closer to the action than the rest?"

"Australia and New Zealand." Lindsay gave the Irishman an admiring stare. "I've underestimated you, Seán."

"And you can't tell me that a Naval Intelligence man of your experience doesn't have contacts in their services."

"Right again," Lindsay conceded. "One question, though. How do we get the word out? The *Nautilus* has no satellite link."

"True," McKenna grinned. "So, we need someone who does. Leave that part to me, Commander." He brandished a single page print-out. "Thanks to our host, I know exactly who will be where in that part of the world, and at least one of them will have precisely the comms equipment we need."

"You have everything you want?" Duvall asked, as the print run came to an end.

Lindsay nodded. "I believe so. Monsieur Duvall, if anyone detects that their files have been broken into, can they trace it to you?"

Duvall smiled. "Not immediately. I use a particularly elaborate encryption. It is not foolproof, of course. No computer security is, as you have seen for yourself. It will take them a considerable time to track down the hacker but, eventually, they will have me. But what about yourselves? What will you do now?"

"Follow it through," Lindsay said. "We have little choice and, from now on, life will get a sight more dangerous. Believe me, monsieur, the whole world's out to kill us off and the Pyramus people will try to eliminate anyone they find to be connected with us. That, as we explained, is why McKenna's people had to keep their survival secret. My advice to you is to get yourself and your family out of Marseille today, preferably tonight. Is there anywhere you can go that will be hard to trace?"

"I have a cousin, a mountaineer, who is currently on a Himalayan climb. He owns an isolated property in the Swiss Alps. He left his keys and his car with me. Only my wife and I are aware of this. We shall go there and I shall use his car. There is nothing else in this house that would link that place with me."

Lindsay gave him a look of approval. "That seems good enough, but you must go quickly. If you have to leave a message, say that you have gone to the Pyrenees for a while—anywhere but where you are actually going."

"I will do that, and we will leave tonight. Monsieur, what do you intend for Madeleine?"

"We didn't bring her back only to break up the happy home again," McKenna said. "Take her with you, but make certain that no one knows she's alive. She'll be far safer with you than with us. The bald truth is that we may not live through this. The Commander's right, the whole damned world is after us. NATO is bound to know that we're in the Mediterranean and they'll have the Straits of Gibraltar heavily blockaded by now."

Duvall was shocked. "Then you're trapped. You'll never get out."

McKenna's slow smile mystified him. "I think, Monsieur Duvall, that you underestimate the *Nautilus*. We're banking on NATO doing likewise."

"But with Gibraltar blockaded?"

"Who needs Gibraltar? Look, we'd better go if we're to get away while it's still dark. Say goodbye to Madeleine and your wife for us. It's best we leave them alone."

Duvall shook hands warmly with them both. "God go with you all," he said. "Commander Lindsay, your package. I will see that it is promptly posted."

46

27 January 2015
Whitehall
London, UK

It was a perplexed Sir Robert Maynard who was ushered into the office of the Director of Naval Intelligence. Admiral Garvie strode across the room and shook the Deep Watch director's hand firmly.

"Good of you to come at such short notice, Sir Robert," the admiral's greeting barked out.

"Your message was far from specific, Admiral. I'm somewhat intrigued by such a mysterious summons to the inner echelons of the security services."

Garvie waved Sir Robert to a seat and returned to his desk. "Rebuke received and accepted," he said gruffly. "To be candid, the matter is hardly one that I could broadcast over public communication channels." He fixed his gaze on Maynard. "You never did find out what happened to your ship last year, did you?"

"The *Aurora*?" Sir Robert sat up. "Don't tell me she's been found."

"Not exactly." The admiral steepled his fingers. "I've asked you here to do a spot of identification." Maynard looked alarmed and the admiral continued hurriedly. "No, no, nothing like that, Sir Robert. There are no cadavers to view, I assure you. However, there may well be a few ghosts," he added mysteriously.

"This morning, a DVD recording airmailed from Marseille, was received by this office. My Chief of Staff and I have already viewed it and we both agreed that you should be asked to see it also." He pressed his intercom button. "Maureen, has the CoS turned up yet?"

"He's just arrived, sir."

"Good show. Ask him to come in, would you."

Garvie introduced him as he entered the room. "My Chief of Staff, Captain Michael Rochester. Chief, this is Sir Robert Maynard, director of the Deep Watch organization. He has a high security clearance through his appointments with the UN and UNESCO, so we needn't worry about what may be said in here. You have the disc?"

"Right here, sir." Rochester crossed to the large viewer set up in the corner of the room while Garvie poured out three large whiskies and handed one to Maynard.

"You will probably need that, Sir Robert. I think you should prepare yourself for a number of considerable shocks during the next thirty minutes. Roll it, Chief."

The half-hour video recording left Maynard speechless. Garvie had said something about ghosts and now he had seen no less than eight of them. Even when the disc had finished its run, he continued to stare at the blank screen, his face seemingly drained of blood.

Garvie gently shook the man out of his state of shock. "Sir Robert, I need to know. The people that you have just seen… are they members of the *Aurora's* crew, as they claim to be?"

Still ashen-faced, Maynard turned to him. "Yes, Admiral, they are. My God, they're alive… but I don't understand. Why have they kept it quiet for all these months? And Calloway… I can't believe it. I met with the man at Wyatt's less than a fortnight ago. I can't conceive of him being involved in something like this."

"We all heard his confession," Garvie said coldly. "In my opinion, it leaves little room for doubt. From what he says, it seems that these Pyramus people have been operating for some considerable time. Surely some hint of their activities must have come through to Deep Watch and other groups. Greenpeace in particular has an accomplished intelligence network of its own."

Maynard nodded briefly. "There was word of an organization engaged in illicit waste disposal. Nuclear and toxic wastes. No one could breach their highly organized defences and anyone who got too far…

"Ten years ago, Greenpeace persuaded the journalist Barrington Hobbes to investigate. He got close. By all accounts, very close.

"I'm afraid we all know what happened. There was a terrible attempt on his life that killed his wife and young child. It forced him into retirement."

Garvie's voice softened. "As you'll know from the newspapers and from the film you've just seen, Hobbes recently resurfaced to resume that investigation on behalf of your crew. Again, the Pyramus Group tried to kill him, this time with a car bomb that got *The Sentinel's* staff reporter Ian

Neale instead. In fact, they finally succeeded in killing Hobbes two weeks ago which brings the death toll on your side to six, by my reckoning: Hobbes, his wife and child, Neale and your crewmen Calvert and May.

"I regret to say that it may not end there. NATO is currently committed to the task of hunting down the *Nautilus* and, frankly, I don't give much for her chances. Where did they get this submarine from, Sir Robert? Is she a Deep Watch construction or, as McKenna claims on the tape, the very boat that Jules Verne wrote about?"

"I can assure you, Admiral, that she has nothing to do with Deep Watch," Maynard said. "However, I've read Verne's book and I dare say you have too. Far-fetched as it may seem, and from my memories of Verne's descriptions, there seems little room for doubt. In fact, I'm convinced. Utterly astonished, but convinced. That is either Nemo's boat or a very good copy of it."

Garvie harrumphed. "Nemo was a renegade, Sir Robert and, from what I read in a report this morning, her present captain has something of a chequered history."

The bland statement surprised Maynard.

"Are you aware," Garvie went on, "that Seán McKenna was once interned for six months in the Maze Prison for an alleged involvement with the IRA?"

"Alleged, Admiral, not proven," Maynard reminded him. "Yes, I know all about it. Seán's always been open about that and about his views supporting a united Ireland, independent of the United Kingdom. He also believes that this should be achieved by peaceful means and not by the bullet and the bomb. He never had any truck with the violence that was been perpetrated by both sides over the years. McKenna is not, and never has been, a member of the IRA or any other paramilitary group.

"Seán had a younger brother, Diarmad. A real tearaway and republican fanatic. He wouldn't even spell his surname in anything other than the Gaelic way, refusing to accept the Anglicized version. Diarmad got into the ranks of the provisional IRA and revelled in guns and explosives. With their parents already dead, and Seán being at sea much of the time—he was then in the merchant navy—Seán couldn't control him. God knows how many deaths Diarmad was responsible for but, in the end, he lost his own life in a shootout with security forces outside Armagh.

"Seán visited Belfast a few months later after returning from sea and was detained for no other reason than the fact he was Diarmad's elder brother. The irony of that situation was that, during his six-month internment, he was actually approached by an IRA recruitment squad. Seán said no, a word one didn't use to the Provisionals in those days, and as a result found himself on their black list. He went back to sea and gained his master's ticket before joining me as a Deep Watch skipper. He has never been back to Ireland.

"It's a tribute to the man's character, Admiral, that Seán has never shown any bitterness or resentment against Britain for his unjust imprisonment, or for the death of his brother. He is not, and never has been, a terrorist. The film we have just seen clearly illustrates his reasons for the actions he has recently taken and, in that, he had the agreement of his crew.

"However, Seán and the crew of the *Nautilus* have, until now, been a mystery and as a result have suffered the oldest form of prejudice. What is not understood is feared and what is feared is often hunted down and destroyed.

"They do not merit this witch-hunt, Admiral Garvie. It must be called off. They should be offered aid and protection."

Garvie looked uncomfortable at that. "It may already be too late, Sir Robert," he said gravely. "Two hours ago, the *Nautilus* triggered a series of sonobuoys laid by NATO anti-submarine helicopters in the eastern Mediterranean. She is trapped off the coast of Egypt with no less than fifteen warships on her tail and nowhere to go.

"I bitterly regret that this day may well see an end to the *Nautilus* and everyone aboard her."

47

Khalig el Tina
Egypt

From the bridge of the *USS Appalachian*, Commander Randall Hayes studied the line of warships strung out on either side of his frigate, some fifteen vessels from five NATO countries. Line abreast and spaced no more than two miles apart, each ship faced the Egyptian coast, visible as a low dark line eight miles to the south.

Hayes turned to his Executive Officer. "You a gambling man, Paul?"

"The occasional hand of poker. Why do you ask that?"

Hayes grinned. "What bet d'ya wanna put on the total number of camel drivers who are crapping themselves over there? Just imagine yourself, sitting on Miami Beach, not a care in the world. Then you look up and see fifteen foreign warships, every one armed to the teeth, staring straight back at you. How would you react?"

Paul Vylander grinned back. "I think I'd most likely crap myself, sir, much like the Egyptians. I gather that the Egyptian President's none too pleased about this himself."

"Can you blame the man? All right, I know he agreed to it but only under massive pressure from NATO, the UN and the President. I'd lay odds that most of the folks ashore don't have a clue what's going down and I don't envy the Egyptian President the job of reassuring them. Especially now that the mad mullahs have resurfaced. You know the kind of thing, Paul… lock up your daughters, the servants of Satan are here. All the usual brand of shit."

"More fool the people if they go on listening to them. How many decades have they spent proving to the world that they're nothing more than a bunch of fanatical fruitcakes? Even so, don't you think there's an element of overkill here? All these warships to flush out one small sub?"

"One small and extremely crafty sub, I'll remind you, Paul. I've been wanting to take a crack at this bastard ever since he damn near sank me with my own torpedo. Not to mention the fact that she's the sole reason our Christmas furlough got cancelled."

"Could I ever forget either one, sir? But it worries me. If she's so damned crafty, how come she's allowed us to pen her into a dead end? It makes no sense to me. We've got her cold and it was all too easy for my liking."

Hayes narrowed his eyes in thought. "That same question's been bugging me for the last two hours," he confessed. He reached for the telephone. "Sonar, this is the captain. Any update on the target?"

"Well, sir, she seems to have quit meandering around," Sonar Officer Emil Garcia's voice came back over the bridge speaker. "Right now, we log her motionless, range two thousand yards, bearing one-seven-five Magnetic. Estimated depth one-fifty feet.

"All ships have been banging active pulses off her every sixty seconds for the past half-hour. She knows we're here and probably how many of us are here. Their ears must be ringing by now.

"Captain, we've been running a playback of her activities during the past couple of hours and the result's interesting. She's been quartering an area about five miles square and, if I had to give a firm opinion, sir, I'd say she's been running a classic search pattern."

"Looking for what, I wonder?" Hayes mused, staring out to sea.

"I couldn't even begin to hazard a guess," Vylander said. "But, if she's stopped, could it be that she's found what she's looking for?"

Garcia's voice floated back over the speaker. "Something else of interest, captain. The bottom hereabouts is of sand and Nile sediment but the target's sitting by a sizeable shelf of rock. The science boys are saying that there's a deep water current flowing from that direction, not a particularly strong one but it's been slackening over the last hour or so."

"We're pretty close to the Nile delta, Emil. Could that be the source of the current?"

"Negative, sir. You'd expect fresh water dilution above the local norm. Instead, samples show that the current's actually carrying water that's a deal saltier than the local background."

"Curious. Okay, keep at it, Emil. Any sign of movement from the target?"

"Negative, sir. Still stationary... no, correction, captain. She's moving again. Dead slow. Her Doppler indicates that she's commenced a turn away from us, towards the south. Still dead slow... *Jesus*!"

There was a long empty pause.

"Sonar?" Hayes said urgently. "You still there?"

Garcia's voice came back, hushed and disbelieving. "Captain, I can't explain this... the target's gone. She just vanished clean off the scopes."

"Any chance of a glitch in the equipment, Emil?"

"No, sir, none."

"What the hell, Paul?" Hayes shot his XO an incredulous look. Vylander got on to communications to patch him through to *HMS Norfolk*.

"Signal already coming in from *Norfolk*, sir."

"Let me guess. Target vanished from his sonar?"

"How the hell—"

"Never mind."

Hayes gave his sonarman a final instruction. "Emil, give me active sonar. Give that whole area a thorough lashing." He waited, breathless, for the result. When it came he was already resigned to the answer.

"Negative result, sir. There's nothing there but a rockface. I have no explanation for this, sir. None at all. One minute she's there, clear as a bell. The next, she ain't."

"Thank you, Emil. Keep on station." Hayes turned to Vylander. "Answer this in your own time, Paul," he said, very quietly. "But can there be a chance, any chance at all, that these guys are not human?"

48

Westminster
London, UK

The House of Commons debate on financing the country's National Health Service was in full, raucous voice. In the midst of the row, an usher entered and, at a nod from the Speaker of the House, moved forward to hand a sealed envelope to the Secretary of State for Defence. Sir Henry Williamson waited for the usher to leave before opening it and scanning its contents.

Around him, barbed comments and catcalls shot from one side of the House to the other, drowning the arguments of the Health Minister and the repeated calls for order from a beleaguered Speaker that were having precious little effect in a debate where feelings were running high.

"She's done *what*?"

Williamson's involuntary cry succeeded in a second where the Speaker of the House had miserably failed. A suddenly hushed, confused House stared at the white-faced Minister of Defence. The Speaker regarded him over half-moon spectacles. Sir Henry leaned forward to mutter into the Prime Minister's ear. The effect was immediate. The Premier visibly blanched. He swallowed hard and stood up.

"Mr Speaker, I am forced to request an immediate recess in order for my Cabinet and I to discuss an urgent matter of security. I wish to convey my apologies to the House for this irregular request, but these are most unusual circumstances."

In spite of the pandemonium and angry protests that raged from the Opposition benches, the Speaker took one look at the faces of the Prime Minister and Sir Henry, their glance at the vacant front bench seat normally occupied by Gerald Calloway, and acquiesced.

A strained atmosphere hung over the hastily convened Cabinet meeting as Sir Henry replaced the telephone and drew the Prime Minister to one side.

"Admiral Garvie's on the way over," he told him. "He's asked for a DVD screen and I've arranged for the stewards to wheel one in here."

The Prime Minister groaned audibly. "I don't like the sound of this, Henry. God knows what the admiral has in store for us. On the other hand, maybe he can shed some light on how the hell something the size of a submarine can simply vanish from the face of the earth."

"All I know," Sir Henry said, "is that off the Egyptian coast are fifteen highly embarrassed and utterly bewildered warship captains asking precisely the same question. One thing's certain. The submarine did not sneak past their blockade. They had a sonar net so tight that an anorexic eel couldn't have got through without them knowing about it, let alone a 230-foot submarine.

"Each ship filed exactly the same report. The *Nautilus* was idling near the sea-bed for a period of time, then set off at dead slow speed. She turned away from the NATO vessels, towards the Egyptian coast, and promptly vanished from every sonar screen in the fleet. Our own submarine *HMS Triumph* and the USA's *Milwaukee* went in for an intensive search and found precisely nothing. It was as if the *Nautilus* had simply dematerialized."

The Prime Minister's shoulders seemed to slump. "I'm beginning to wonder if the sort of science fiction you've just touched upon isn't getting a shade too close to reality. It's uncanny. How can a single non-military vessel continue to evade and confound the world's finest navies and technology? I only hope that Garvie has an answer to it."

Williamson glanced away. "Speaking of which, he's just arrived."

"Let's get under way, then," the Premier sighed.

The eyes of the Cabinet were on the two men as they took their seats at the head of the long polished table. Admiral Garvie was directed to a seat at the opposite end beside which the requested screen had been set up on a trolley.

The Prime Minister started without preamble. "The Secretary of State for Defence has just received a signal from *HMS Invincible* acting as flagship for the combined NATO fleet in the eastern Mediterranean. In view of its potentially serious implications, I felt it necessary to seek suspension of the debate in the House and convene this meeting. Sir Henry will explain further."

It was usual for speakers at a Cabinet meeting to remain seated. Looking weary, Sir Henry felt it appropriate to stand.

"A few hours ago," he began, "the renegade submarine calling itself *Nautilus* was finally trapped off the Mediterranean coast of Egypt by a flotilla of NATO warships. I should point out that, through the good offices of the Prime Minister, the President of the United States and the Secretary-General of the United Nations, NATO received permission from the President of Egypt to enter his country's territorial waters.

"You will all be aware of the recent incident when this *Nautilus* was similarly trapped off the Norwegian coast but escaped by the foolhardy action of running the Maelstrom, one of the world's most lethal stretches of water. On this occasion, no such option was open to her. No less than fifteen ships had her penned into the Khalig el Tina, the old Bay of Pelusium, close to Port Said and the northern entrance to the Suez Canal which was itself blockaded by Egyptian forces.

"You will also know that the Secretary of State for Trade and Industry was outrageously abducted from his home ten days ago. It is strongly believed that he is being held prisoner aboard the *Nautilus*, for what reason we have yet to learn. Certainly there have been no ransom demands, or any other form of demand. It is also likely that the rogue naval intelligence officer, Commander Donall Lindsay," here Williamson regarded an impassive Admiral Garvie over his spectacles, "is himself aboard this submarine, apparently in full collusion with her crew." He paused to take breath.

"I regret to report that the *Nautilus* appears to have achieved the impossible. All fifteen NATO vessels reported that she literally vanished from their sonar screens. A thorough search of the area has come up with nothing. It is inexplicable. It is as though this submarine simply ceased to exist." He let his words sink home before resuming his seat.

The Prime Minister took over. "Admiral Garvie, Director of the Department of Royal Naval Intelligence, has specifically requested to address this meeting. I know no more than the rest of you what he has to say and, at this point, I propose to hand over to him. Admiral?"

"Thank you, sir." Garvie remained in his seat. "This incident is not necessarily without explanation. In fact, I rather think that the French writer Jules Verne had the answer to this particular riddle well over a century ago. If I was asked for an opinion as to the present whereabouts of the *Nautilus*, I would venture to suggest that, at this moment, she is heading south through the Red Sea."

A storm of incredulous voices was quickly quelled by the Prime Minister who frowned down the length of the table at the admiral. "Sir Henry has made it very clear, Admiral Garvie, that she did not, and could not, travel through the Suez Canal which was heavily blockaded by Egyptian forces. Unless this vessel has sprouted wings or wheels, there is no other way that she could have crossed a hundred miles of dry land to reach the Red Sea."

"To use the words of Verne's Captain Nemo," Garvie responded, "not over it, but under it. In his book, Verne describes how Nemo piloted his vessel from the Red Sea to the Mediterranean through a natural passage beneath the isthmus of Suez.

"Geologists will confirm that the Red Sea and its two head branches, the Gulfs of Aqaba and Suez, are northward continuations of the great African Rift Valley, a line of tectonic spread where two plates of the earth's crust are slowly pulling apart. It is geologically feasible for such a passage to exist in the form of a spreading fault.

"According to the NATO flotilla, a deep water current of heavily saline water, easily detectable against the background of Mediterranean water diluted by the outflow of fresh water from the Nile delta, was issuing from the approximate position of the *Nautilus* just before she disappeared. An important point here is that the rate of the current was observed to be steadily diminishing. It is my belief that this salt water current originates in the Red Sea or, more specifically, the Gulf of Suez.

"The *Nautilus* had completed what seemed to be a standard search pattern and waited for a considerable period of time before performing her vanishing act. The reason may be this. Tidal ranges in the Gulf of Suez are not great but they are, nonetheless, several times greater than the nine-inch range in the eastern Mediterranean. When it is high water at Suez, the current flowing through the passage may be too strong, or create too many difficulties, for it to be navigated safely in a southerly direction. At Suez low water, the current will be considerably less, if it does not cease completely. The timing of the submarine's disappearance just happened to coincide with an ebbing tide at Suez."

"And our renegade," the Premier observed, "just happens to have the same name as Verne's boat. An uncomfortable coincidence."

"No, sir," Garvie replied, "and this is perhaps the strangest part of the whole affair. In fact, Commander Lindsay rather hinted at it when he was in front of you recently. Certainly the boat has the same name, for the very good reason that she is the same boat."

"Ridiculous," Christopher Knowles, the Shipping Minister, snorted. "I have heard it all now. Admiral Garvie, for your information, Verne's book was a work of fiction, written well over a hundred years ago and long before there were ever such things as operational, ocean-going submarines. His *Nautilus* was the product of a fertile, indeed brilliant, imagination. Nothing more, nothing less. For heaven's sake, man, we are not dealing with fantasy."

Garvie refused to be flustered. "On the contrary, Minister. I now have overwhelming evidence that Verne's story was solidly based upon fact. I have with me a DVD recording that was received this morning from Marseille. It was addressed to my office and to myself personally. It not only bears out what I have just said but also provides evidence of a more shocking nature. You will find that it goes some considerable way towards vindicating the actions of my officer and explains the entire *Nautilus* affair, including Trade Minister Calloway's abduction.

"It also clears up the mysterious loss of the Deep Watch ship *Aurora* in February last year and, in fact, I have already taken the liberty of showing this film to Deep Watch's director, Sir Robert Maynard. My reason for that will become clear when you view the film. Prime Minister, with your permission?"

The Premier nodded his agreement for the DVD to be screened. Half an hour later, he was almost wishing he hadn't.

44

30 January 2015
Lake Geneva Conference Centre
Geneva, Switzerland

The Chairman of the Pyramus Group paced up and down at the head of the conference table as the delegates argued among themselves.

"Gentlemen." His word secured immediate silence. "We must keep our nerve. Most certainly the situation is serious and there is no doubt in my mind that this *Nautilus* submarine is making for Antarctica in search of our facility. As yet, we do not know the full extent of the information her crew has obtained and I consider it prudent to assume the worst.

"I do not intend to allow this submarine and her crew to jeopardize the years of work that we have put into this project. The Pyramus Group is scarcely short of resources and influence and we must utilize both to ensure that the *Nautilus* never reaches her destination. Our own ship, the *Emperor*, is on her way to intercept should the submarine ever get as far as the Ross Sea and I can assure you all that she carries a few surprises. That, however, is a mere contingency plan. I have every confidence that the *Nautilus* will not even make it across the Indian Ocean. Isao will explain."

Isao Mifune bowed to the meeting. "You will appreciate that certain departments of my country's government hold considerable stakes in the success of the Pyramus Group," he said. "I speak for them when I say that every assistance will be given to ensure that success. Except for our honoured Chairman, none of you will be aware of what we have termed the Honshu Project. It is a secret that has been well kept and its result is currently undergoing testing trials. In my capacity as Japan's Defence Minister, I have arranged the relocation of these trials in the light of our present need and I believe that our Chairman is correct when he says that the *Nautilus* will not complete her voyage."

Congressman Walterson gave out a long sigh. "Isao, with all due respect, you've told us a whole heap of nothing. The Pyramus Group has never operated on bullshit and I don't see the need to start now. So how about you start again, and this time give us all the facts."

Mifune looked to the Chairman for guidance. "Isao," the Chairman said gently, "the Honshu Project will not remain a secret forever. Harvey is quite correct. This meeting should be apprised of the facts, if only to calm a few frayed nerves. You can be sure that nothing of what you say will leave this room."

Mifune bowed again and gave the explanation. Walterson sat back, satisfied that the Japanese minister's claims were correct. Privately, and from the viewpoint of a citizen of the United States, Mifune's revelations had startled and even shocked him. The side issues of national security were immense and, in the future, his own government were going to develop massive headaches in dealing with it. As a member and wealthy beneficiary of the Pyramus Group, his prime concern, he knew that he had no further need to worry.

Isao Mifune was right. The *Nautilus* was en route to an unmarked grave in the deeps of the Indian Ocean.

Buckinghamshire, UK

"Dear God, what an appalling bloody mess!" The Prime Minister of the United Kingdom strode agitatedly across the red Axminster carpet of the private room that lay at the rear of a country pub.

The *Lion and Rose* was a stylish 17th century coaching inn nestling in a wooded fold of the Buckinghamshire countryside seven miles from Chequers. The Prime Minister had a particular liking for the inn, whose oak-panelled conference room he could reserve at a moment's notice. Since he had taken office, the room had seen kings, premiers and princes, and yet patrons of the inn rarely saw anything that was out of the ordinary.

The Premier and his security staff tended to arrive in an unobtrusive Rover saloon. One security man stayed with the car, a second drank convivially in the main bar with the door to the private room in full view, and no one took the slightest bit of notice of the man and woman who walked their dog in the woods behind the inn, keeping the windows of the room under constant surveillance.

"This could be the final straw that brings my government down." The Premier sat down in a leather armchair, hunched as though the entire world lay heavy on his shoulders. "My own Trade and Industry Minister mixed up in this... this filthy business."

The room's only other occupant, Admiral James Garvie, looked up impassively. "Not only mixed up in it, sir, but a senior member of this Pyramus Group," he reminded him.

The Prime Minister gazed mournfully at his glass of Irish stout. "It will be impossible to keep a lid on this, James. The Press already have a sniff of it and the Marshall woman on board the *Nautilus* is the journalist who was partnering Barrington Hobbes, of all people. I don't have the slightest doubt that she will be writing up the whole sorry story. Perhaps a D Notice—"

"Would be out of the question," Garvie finished the sentence. He shook his head emphatically. "This is not a matter of national security that would warrant the issuing of a D Notice, Prime Minister, despite the involvement of naval forces and a British Cabinet Minister. Whichever way you look at it, we're talking international crime. Corruption on the grandest of scales. In fact, sir, I would go so far as to suggest that the best course open to you would be to minimize the damage by taking the initiative."

"I'm open to suggestions, James. My back's to the wall as never before."

"Well, as far as the *Nautilus* is concerned, I'd be inclined to reverse policy. Call off the dogs. We now know the identities of her crew, their individual and collective histories, and I'd say their credentials stand up pretty well. These are no criminals. They're victims of a murder attempt, determined to track down an entire network of evil.

"Certainly my officer's advice would be that we let them get on with it without further hindrance. After all, they're in a better position than anyone else to begin exposing the activities of this Pyramus Group."

"Not to mention the serious apology that's due to them, to Commander Lindsay and your good self, Admiral. Calloway led us all by the nose pretty well, didn't he? Even to the extent of discrediting your own department."

The Prime Minister felt a wave of gratitude at the way Garvie shrugged off the regret, a small, brief gesture of forgiveness. Immersed as he was in a world of political and diplomatic rhetoric and flannel, the Prime Minister felt immensely refreshed by the admiral's straight-to-the-point, no-nonsense approach.

"James, are we any nearer to identifying the man at the head of Pyramus?"

"No, sir, we're not. We have most of the directors' names. Some of them are big names in several governments, including France, Germany, the USA and Japan. I suppose you can take comfort in the fact that your government won't be alone in facing acute embarrassment. A number of world powers are in the same boat.

"The top man's name is the one thing that Calloway wouldn't cough and it seems that he's protected by a cast-iron screen we haven't even begun to penetrate. We don't even know the man's nationality."

"Keep at it, James. You and the other security services. Join forces with those of our allies and anyone else that might be useful. It's vital we get this man."

The Prime Minister changed tack. "This submarine, this *Nautilus*. It scarcely seems possible that she's the very same boat that Verne wrote about. I was far from the only schoolboy to be captivated by that story. In point of fact, she's a schoolboy dream come true. Is it absolutely certain that she is what her crew claims her to be?"

Garvie gave a single nod of his head. "Not much doubt about it. She's the genuine article. My man's filmed tour of the boat was, as you rightly suggest, a fantasy come to life. The saloon, the library… quite incredible.

"As a sailor, what really captured me was her engine room. It's almost embarrassing to learn that a vessel constructed as long ago as 1865 completely outstrips anything we have in both design and capability. Running costs of virtually nil, fuelled from the sea itself… imagine what the Royal Navy could do with that sort of technology."

"Not to mention the colossal saving to the defence budget if all the navy's ships were fitted with similar engines," the Prime Minister said.

"Not very likely, though," Garvie said. "On the film, her crew was adamant about keeping that knowledge firmly within the *Nautilus* herself.

They seem to have identified closely with Nemo himself and are determined to respect his memory by ensuring that no military power benefits from his technology, least of all Britain. Nemo considered himself at war with this country and we had, after all, subjugated his nation and executed his family."

"It could be taken by compulsion."

"It could, but it won't," Garvie countered. "Not in front of the eyes of the world. We are going to need every ounce of international support we can get. In any case, we'd have to catch her first and we haven't exactly done well in achieving that so far. However, sir, if you're at all interested, I can supply you with further details of the boat's history, by courtesy of Dr Melvyn Hunter."

"The naval historian? Sir Henry Williamson's nephew?"

"The same. It seems that he and Barrington Hobbes worked together on identifying the submarine several weeks ago. Some of the documents that Hunter turned up are fascinating to say the least and confirm, beyond any reasonable doubt, that this is the boat that Jules Verne immortalized."

"I'd read those with the greatest interest." The Prime Minister took a deep swallow of his drink. "James, I don't consider that I have any choice left but to follow your advice. As you say, the only clear option is a course of damage limitation.

"In the meantime, I will see to it that the hunt for the *Nautilus* is called off, although I believe that we should continue to track her for entirely different reasons. Where would you say she's likely to be at the moment?"

"Well out into the Indian Ocean. I would imagine. No one got a sniff of her in the Red Sea, not that I'm particularly surprised. There's a deep central trench that runs down its entire length and, if she kept within that, no amount of sonar would have got her. Warm water upwells from the foot of the trench, which would make infra-red heat detection from space well nigh impossible, too. Having said that, to keep a submarine at a steady course and depth against the lift of that warmer water would be a pretty impressive feat."

"Your man Lindsay's a former submariner, isn't he?"

"Yes, sir, and so's McLeish, her engineer. It would appear that they haven't forgotten much. McLeish once served with Lindsay whose apparent loss to the Navy is evidently the *Nautilus's* gain."

"Indeed, James. You told me at the outset that Lindsay's a remarkable man." The Premier sat up as Garvie's words sunk in. "The Navy's loss? Do you believe that to be the case?"

"Who knows? His own employers haven't exactly exercised much faith in his integrity. Things like that can do lasting damage to any man's motivation.

" Commander Lindsay is on a bi-annual contract—all my officers are thanks to Defence cuts and endless attempts at reorganization. He has every opportunity and every right to tender his resignation at the end of all this and, quite frankly, sir, I'll be surprised if he doesn't. We can ill afford to lose a man of his ability."

The Premier stared at the prints that adorned the oak-panelled walls. "They're making for Antarctica. You realize that, don't you, James? They're determined to tackle this Pyramus facility by themselves. If Calloway's summary of its defence systems is anything to go by, they haven't a hope in hell. I wonder, can we as a nation, or as a potential world leader in environmental issues, stand idly by as six men and four women on an unarmed and antiquated boat commit suicide on our behalf?"

He paused as Garvie studied a world-weary face that suddenly seemed to have shed ten years.

"What are you thinking?" said the admiral.

The Prime Minister was seeing a political phoenix rising from the ashes. "We help them," he said simply. "We bring in the best we have."

Chapter 9

Frozen Fire

↞ 51 ↠

8 February 2015
Whitehall
London, UK

The NASA photograph, sent direct to Admiral Garvie by the Pentagon, was astonishing in its detail, particularly considering the fact that it had been taken by a satellite orbiting at a height of 200 miles.

Garvie and his Chief of Staff studied the A3 sized full colour picture, an overhead shot of a highly unusual submarine cruising on the surface of a calm, intensely blue sea that sparkled in bright sunlight. Her peculiar double wake was a distinct feature and even those parts of the vessel that lay below the surface could be clearly distinguished.

"So that's our famous *Nautilus*," Rochester said, his words tinged with an undeniable note of respect. "Just look at the shape of her. That bow tapers right down to a fine point."

"The bit that's done all the damage," Garvie reminded him. "Looks remarkably unbent for all that, doesn't it, Chief? The midships hydroplanes are interesting, too." He peered more closely. "What do you make of those features on deck?"

"Well, that's certainly a boat between those two small items of superstructure. From the lack of shadow, it seems to be sunk into the deck. I can't be sure of that, the sun in those latitudes is almost directly overhead. An open deck hatch just aft of the boat. And people, lying prone by the look of it.

"Might I suggest we use the conference room enlarger, sir? It'll project this on the wall at ten times the size, which might be a useful way of presenting it when the PM and Sir Henry arrive."

At ten times magnification on the white wall of a darkened room, the quality of the satellite photograph was superb, the finest of details being crystal clear. Had a newspaper been placed on the submarine's deck, its headlines could have been read with comparative ease. Enlarged to this size, it was obvious that there were four people on deck; a dark-haired man with a fishing line sitting on the edge of the deck near the boat and looking up at the sky and, unmistakeably, three totally naked women lying on towels, two face-down, the third lying on her back. Dark glasses protected her eyes from the tropical sunlight.

"Absolutely remarkable," Garvie enthused.

"Couldn't agree more, sir." Rochester said. "Natural blonde by the look of it."

"Control yourself, Chief of Staff. I was referring to the bloody boat."

"Of course you were, sir." The heavy irony of Rochester's remark was not lost on the admiral whose full-blooded glare was interrupted by the arrival of the Prime Minister and Sir Henry Williamson.

"Gentlemen, please come in." Garvie waved grandly at the full colour picture projected on the wall. "The *Nautilus*, compliments of NASA and our friends at the Pentagon. Our first good glimpse of her and a remarkably clear one. I'm informed that she accords very closely indeed with the descriptions of her given by Jules Verne."

"Most impressive," the Prime Minister said, staring raptly at the picture.

"Good God above," Williamson exclaimed. "Those are women on deck." He adjusted his glasses. "And a rare trio of beauties they are too."

"Rare indeed," the Prime Minister murmured, peering closer. "A genuine blonde, if I'm not mistaken."

Garvie harrumphed as Rochester turned away to hide an irresistible grin. The admiral consulted a list from an open file on the tabletop.

"There should be four women aboard," he read out. "Deanne Fischer and Dr Carla Schumann, both American, and Madeleine Duvall, French. Those three were members of the original *Aurora* crew. The fourth woman is Karen Marshall, the British journalist who was working with

Barrington Hobbes and who was apparently engaged to the *Aurora's* mate and navigator, a man called Tregenza from Cornwall. From the photographs and descriptions we have, the young lady displaying her charms can be identified as Miss Fischer.

"If you could now turn your attention to the man you see there—"

Williamson broke in. "That's our man. Commander Lindsay. No doubt about it."

Garvie confirmed it. "It is, as you say, sir, our allegedly renegade operative."

"No sign of Gerald Calloway," the Premier observed. "Doubtless confined below decks. Admiral, where and when was this photograph taken?"

"The Indian Ocean, sir. Ten degrees south of the equator, some 300 miles south of the Chagos Islands and heading on a south-easterly course. This was taken yesterday at thirteen hundred hours local time."

"So your theory was undoubtedly correct, admiral. The Suez tunnel truly exists."

"So it would seem, Prime Minister. This picture, by the way, is unique. It's the only occasion the *Nautilus* has been seen on the surface since that debacle off Norway, and the only clear picture yet taken of her. Other satellite scans of the area have turned up blank which would indicate that she's staying submerged for as long as possible in order to remain undetected.

"You'll note the open hatch. I would hazard a guess that they were on the surface to replenish their air supply. The *Nautilus* is limited in that regard. She has to breathe, as it were, every few days, unlike our modern nuclear boats, which can remain submerged without air replenishment for up to eighty days. Even so, this shot is the result of sheer chance and we're particularly fortunate to have it."

"Just look at them," Williamson said, referring to the people on the submarine's deck. "They look as though they haven't a care in the world."

"We shouldn't be deceived by appearances," Garvie countered. "They are certainly on course for the Ross Sea, where their original ship was sunk and probably where this Pyramus facility is located. They seem intent on taking the whole thing on alone, which will most likely mean their deaths if we can't get help to them in time. The problem lies in knowing where to send that help. The Ross Sea coasts of Antarctica cover a vast area."

"What's the present position on that?" the Premier asked.

"Well, I believe they'll go on from here at a fair rate of knots," Garvie informed him. "The risk of doing so is minimal. There are no SOSUS lines and no patrolling warships anywhere between this point and the Ross Sea. We've therefore estimated the arrival of the *Nautilus* in the Ross Sea on or about the twentieth of this month.

"We will have a force waiting at McMurdo Sound for last minute instructions once we've a clear idea where the Pyramus installation is. Satellite cover is singularly unhelpful. Only weather and scientific satellites cross the Antarctic continent. We urgently need a surveillance satellite with high-resolution cameras and, preferably, infra-red facilities. I am trying to persuade the Pentagon to divert one of theirs into a polar orbit."

"Then the protection of the *Nautilus* and her crew is far from guaranteed?"

"I'm afraid that is the picture," Garvie said gravely. "Unless we can locate the Pyramus base. We need that satellite." He gave a long look at the sunbathers and the fisherman on the projected photograph. "Give them their moment of peace, gentlemen. A very grim reality may well be lying in wait for them."

"Perhaps," said the Prime Minister, "I should speak directly to the President of the United States."

52

11th February 2015
Indian Ocean
1500 miles WNW of Perth, Australia

At a leisurely speed of fifteen knots, the *Nautilus* cruised above the Ninety East Ridge on a firm south-easterly course. At McKenna's instruction, she was maintaining a constant depth of four hundred feet, deep enough to ensure that no telltale surface wake would betray her position, particularly in view of the twenty-five knot speed she'd maintained for three full days.

In his cabin, oblivious to these operational facts, Don Lindsay was restless, going over and over in his mind the evidence that had come to light. He was also disturbed by the thought that his mission—if he could still call it that—had gone way beyond his control. He began to wonder if he had ever been truly in control of it, a position that was uncomfortably new to him.

From somewhere beyond his troubled thoughts came a curious sound he couldn't place as part of normality on board the *Nautilus*. Lindsay almost laughed out loud. What the bloody hell was normal on a submarine that wasn't even supposed to exist beyond the pages of a nineteenth century writer's novel?

He glanced at his Seiko watch. Time itself meant little when charging across the oceans of the world, passing from one time zone to another, but he noted that only two hours had gone by since retiring to the privacy and peace of his cabin. He placed his fingertips against the bulkhead—a habit now—and felt the soft vibrations that told him that the submarine had slowed down from her madcap dash across the Indian Ocean. Conscious of a rasping thirst, Lindsay put the wad of photo-copies and computer print-outs aside, swung himself from the bunk and left the cabin.

He groped his way through a darkened and silent ship. Except for the helmsman topside—he knew from the rota that it would be Christian Janssen—her crew slept behind closed doors.

The normally luminous ceiling of the luxurious saloon had also been darkened but the room was lit from outside by the brilliance of the submarine's searchlight rays shining through the open panels. Lindsay was surprised to see a lone figure gazing through the panel on the port side and, as he poured himself a drink, Deanne Fischer was caught unawares by the unexpected clink of glass.

"Don, I didn't hear you come in. Couldn't you sleep?" There was a strange quality to her voice, a hushed, almost reverent tone like that automatically adopted by people entering a cathedral.

He shook his head. "I didn't even try. Too much on my mind, trying to make sense of all that's happened. I found myself trying to come to terms with it all." He gave a short ironic laugh. "I didn't make much headway. I came to realize that we've all become Captain Nemos, fugitives from what we kid ourselves is a civilized world. Now we're dead set on taking that world on, all by ourselves.

"Take what we're doing now. We've a pretty fair idea of what's waiting for us. This Pyramus organization has its roots in corridors of power throughout the world. With that sort of power backing it, and from what Calloway told us, it's obvious that the defences of the Antarctic facility are hardly going to be half-arsed. Does that stop us? Not a bit of it. We're charging in with a boat that has no armaments, nine oceanic gypsies trying to shut down an operation like that. Into the valley of death. You tell me, Deanne, have we all become certifiable?"

She tore herself away from the window, a little reluctantly, Lindsay thought, and joined him as he poured her a glass of sherry. They clinked glasses, smiling.

"Here's to the oceanic gypsies," she said. "All nine of us, however crazy."

He studied the Californian's face, the deep blue eyes and exquisite bone structure. There was no doubt that she was strikingly beautful but she had none of the brashness and exaggerated sexuality of all too many Californian women. Instead, there was a hint of self-consciousness. An air of open honesty completed the picture. What you saw was who she was and Don Lindsay very much liked what he saw.

"I don't believe I ever thanked you for pulling me out of the Atlantic," he said. "It was you, wasn't it?"

She nodded, a flush of embarrassment causing her to glance down at the rich carpet. "I joined Deep Watch as a diver after qualifying five years ago," she said. "It was only by pure chance that we spotted you and I went out on a safety line to bring you in. At first we thought we'd left it too late but Carla saw signs of life and managed to revive you."

"I dimly remember hearing music," Lindsay recalled. "Bach. I'm sure it was Bach."

Deanne laughed. "That would be Ross. You see, none of us enjoy crippling the rogue ships, even though we have to do it to bring attention to what they're doing. Afterwards, we all feel stirred up inside and find it hard to come to terms with what we've done.

"Ross is a wonderful musician. He can play almost any instrument and it was his idea to play calming music on Nemo's pipe organ to settle us down. He calls it music for inner peace."

"I thought it was my funeral lament," Lindsay admitted. "I was pretty far gone. Tell me something, Deanne. Just what is it that drives people like you, McKenna and the rest?"

She gave him a puzzled shake of the head, setting her honey-blonde curls swinging.

"Why do you put your lives on the line for the sake of ecology?" he explained himself. "None of you get anything more than a scratched living. You'd have remained poor for the rest of your days if you hadn't found the *Nautilus*... you didn't know about all the gold she had on board. You and the others had made your choice long before that, to fight against what greed and power is doing to the world.

"On paper, you and Greenpeace are on a hiding to nothing, but the crazy thing is that you're actually winning. You're making the difference. People in the streets are getting up off their backsides to exert their own influence because of what you've done. As a result there's a world-wide ban on whaling, an Antarctic sanctuary, rain forest reserves, a world ban on CFC products, rivers cleaned up all over the planet and, to cap it all, nuclear powers are decommissioning their weapons. You're achieving the impossible but what fired you up to take it on in the first place?"

She gave him a smile that lit up her eyes, took his glass and set it beside hers on a display case by the sparkling fountain that issued from the giant shell in the centre of the room.

"You couldn't have picked a better moment to ask a question like that," she said. She took his hand, a light, tender grasp that sent an involuntary thrill through him. "Come with me."

Still grasping his hand, she led him to the viewing panel and gestured out at the floodlit waters. "Take a look, Don. There's all the answer you'll ever need."

Open-mouthed with shock, Lindsay felt his knees buckle and he held on to the back of a seat for support. He was unable to stop the wordless exclamation that burst from his throat.

It swam on a parallel course to the *Nautilus*, keeping effortless pace with the vessel and just a dozen yards from her side. It was immense, a colossus, the biggest living thing he had ever set eyes on. It was also streamlined, graceful and indescribably majestic. Lindsay judged the titan to be well over a hundred feet long, at least half the length of the *Nautilus* herself.

"The Blue whale," Deanne said softly. "The biggest creature ever to have roamed the earth. Now it's one of the rarest. Before commercial whaling there may have been half a million of them. Now, and solely because of mankind's blind, senseless greed and bloodlust, there may be less than a thousand, scattered across all the oceans. They've been hunted to the very edge of extinction and it may already be too late to save them."

Lindsay saw her blink back a tear before she could carry on. "He's been keeping us company for over an hour now and only twice has he gone up to breathe. He's why Chris slowed the boat down. I've been watching him ever since he showed up. He just slowly swam up, looked us over and moved in alongside."

"Maybe he thinks we're another whale," Lindsay suggested.

She shook her head. "He's far too intelligent to make that mistake. He knows exactly what we are, that we're watching him, learning about him and that we pose him no threat. He hasn't taken his eye off this window in all the time he's been with us. I think he likes to see us here. Maybe we give him some sort of comfort because that is one unbelievably lonely creature."

Lindsay saw no apparent movement in the colossal animal to accompany the sound that suddenly penetrated the double hull of the *Nautilus*. It was a low but plaintive call that raised slowly to a higher pitch, sustained the note for three or four seconds, then descended through the lower registers to a deep, thunderous rumble that faded only gradually. He realized that this was the very same sound he had heard from his cabin. His skin prickled at the haunting quality of the giant's voice.

"He's given out that same call every quarter hour or so," Deanne said. "It'll carry for more than a hundred miles."

"Who's he calling to? He has us for company."

"He needs more than that. He's calling for a mate. The tragedy is that there may not be a female Blue for a thousand miles. She may never hear him. Blue whales are so few and so scattered that their breeding rate can't keep pace with mortality. Protection of the species may have come too late and we're responsible for it. Remember him, Don. You may be looking at the next dodo, the next dinosaur. For all we know, we may be the last ever to see his like again."

"Poor old lad." Lindsay looked through the thick glass into the calm, intelligent eye of the giant, set close to the corner of the closed, gently arching mouth. "I hope he finds her," he said softly.

He felt his hand squeezed gently and looked into Deanne's face as her eyes searched his. "You meant that. You really did mean that," she said.

There was an added warmth to her smile. "I think perhaps you've found the answer to your question."

Don Lindsay gazed at the upturned face. She was right. He was now in no doubt whatsoever why people like her had chosen their particular path. It began to dawn on him that he had found more than just an answer to a question. His mind whirled at the thought.

Like most intelligence agents, he had no immediate family. The hazardous, secretive nature of his profession had kept him shy of deep relationships ever since it had destroyed an all-too-brief marriage. Eight years had passed since then and it still hurt. He could only take comfort from the fact that there had been no children to be damaged by the split.

Now, so much had changed and so quickly. As he had admitted, he was now a fugitive, as much on the run from the authorities that had employed him as were his new companions. Whether he liked it or not, his life had changed, perhaps irretrievably.

He glanced again at the huge whale that had sought the comfort of their company and was convinced he saw a deep comprehension in the great, sad eye.

"He understands, too, Deanne. I'll swear he heard what I said."

A single tear squeezed its way from the corner of her eye. He smelt the sweet warmth of her breath, felt the soft, yielding pressure of her lips and knew that his own long solitude was at an end.

53

12 February 2015
Whitehall
London, UK

Maureen Strangways had taken advantage of a slack day in the office but the careful repainting of her well manicured fingernails was about to be interrupted. The urgent bleep of the telephone sat her up with a start, forcing an unwelcome smear across the width of her finger. The brusque mid-American voice on the line caught her further off guard.

"Admiral Walter Greene at the Pentagon for Admiral Garvie. This is urgent."

"I'm sorry, sir. The admiral's in conference."

"I don't give a damn if he's on the john. He'll talk to me now if he wants his boy Lindsay to go on living."

Maureen stared at the receiver, shocked to the core by Greene's bald statement. "If you'll hold, sir, I'll try to interrupt him."

Greene had less than a minute to wait.

"Walter? Jim Garvie."

"Listen up, Jim," Greene rasped, skipping pleasantries and greetings. "Your boy Lindsay and the *Nautilus* crew are in deep trouble. And when I say deep, I mean deep.

"I hardly have to tell you that Japanese security is one of the hardest nuts in the world to crack but one of our team's just uncovered a real earthshaker. Under our noses, the Japs have been building a nuclear attack sub of their own. Officially, she doesn't exist but, according to our team, she's a slick piece of work."

"Christ, Walter, they're banned by treaty from developing a nuclear capability."

"Sure they are. You know that, I know that and they know it, too. They also know that rules are there to be broken. Hell, Jim, it's been seventy years since the surrender. This had to happen sooner or later. They already have world economic superiority and it was only ever going to be a matter of time before they decided to cut loose and turn their Japanese Maritime Defence Force into a new Imperial Navy."

"Which bloody fool was it who said that the end of the Cold War made military intelligence obsolete?" Garvie observed. "I don't like the implications of this one little bit. Just how far have they got with this submarine?"

"That's just it, Jim. She's already at sea, carrying out trials in the southern Pacific. They've named her the *Honshu*. We've sent one of our boats down there to keep tabs on her."

"God almighty," Garvie breathed. "But how does this affect the *Nautilus*?"

Greene's response was chilling. "Jim, the Japanese come out as major players in this toxic and nuclear waste scam. They have a sizeable stake in the Pyramus Group and its Antarctic development, wherever the hell it is. By the way, I'm sorry to say that the Pentagon and NASA are baulking at the expense of diverting a spy satellite into polar orbit to search for it, but we'll keep putting the pressure on.

"Those people on the *Nautilus* are the only ones who have any idea where to start looking for this facility and I think we're all agreed that's where they're headed. Add to that problem the little matter of some rudderless Japanese whalers and you start to get a picture of some pretty pissed-off plutocrats in Tokyo.

"What our guys found is that the *Honshu* has orders to suspend sea trials, to enter the Indian Ocean and there seek out and destroy the *Nautilus*. This sub is crammed full of the best Jap technology, from computer systems to sensory gear and armaments. I grant you, it's a big ocean but, if the *Nautilus* is there, no matter how quiet she is, the *Honshu's* gonna find her.

"Jim, the *Nautilus* hasn't an earthly against this sub. We know that, apart from her ram, she has no armaments of her own. She's old and manned by civilians. She has to be warned off. Get her to run for the nearest port."

Garvie's heart sank. "Easier said than done, Walter. She's keeping well out of sight. As you know, NATO's called off the hunt but she doesn't know that. One of your satellites did catch her on the surface a few days ago, near the Chagos Bank but that was a one-off. She's generally running deep.

"We only have a rough estimate of her position and, even if we could find her, she has only the most basic of communications and sonar equipment. Unless she surfaces again, we haven't a hope in hell of contacting her. With all the hardware the Japanese will have, the *Honshu* will be on her before she knows what's hit her."

Greene's voice softened. "Between us, we paint a grim picture, Jim. It seems that we're left with only the most basic of strategies."

"Which is?"

"We start praying for the poor bastards."

54

Southern Ocean
1200 miles SW of Cape Leeuwin, Western Australia

It occurred to Deanne Fischer that, for a hundred and fifty years, the *Nautilus* had been a loveless ship. Not in the sense of the love that Captain Nemo had held for his creation and the sea that had given his tortured soul the freedom he'd craved, but of love between people.

There was not a hint, in Nemo's journal or anywhere else, that homosexuality had ever occurred among her former crew members who had all been male. Perhaps that was not surprising, as they lived in the Victorian era when any such thing was not only frowned upon but actively condemned and open to persecution. In fact, that same journal spoke of an island in the southern Pacific whose inhabitants were friendly, still untainted by Western influences and religions, and whose women were extraordinarily hospitable in every way.

On occasions, Nemo had piloted his craft to that island, recognizing the basic human needs of his men and allowing discreet runs ashore, always arriving and leaving under cover of darkness in order to protect the secret of his vessel. Nemo himself had never once partaken of the island women's charms, his love and grief for his murdered wife being so deeply rooted that he could never even contemplate the thought of ever making love to another.

How different it all was now, she thought. Already, one could reach out and almost touch the feelings of love that permeated the vessel. There had been the reunion of Alan Tregenza and the woman who, for nearly a year, had refused to let go of hope, and a special bond had developed between the captain, Seán McKenna and Carla Schumann. Now, against all expectations, it had reached herself.

Deanne basked in the euphoric, dream-like warmth of afterglow, floating high on a plateau of pleasure, filled with love for the man who had brought her to such pinnacles of ecstacy as she had never before experienced.

She was well aware of his profession, that, if necessary, he had the capability to deal out death. To her certain knowledge, Don Lindsay had killed three men and who knew how many more had met violent ends at his hands. The other side of the coin was that these had all been evil men, cold dispassionate killers to whom the sanctity of life meant nothing. Unlike them, Lindsay did not kill for the love of it but because he was faced with no other practical option.

She also knew that, for many months, she had been living aboard a vessel that had itself killed. Nemo, the former Prince Dakkar, had sunk two British warships with total loss of life and, in her new life, the *Nautilus* had killed once more, albeit a boatload of murderous Malay pirates poised to slaughter the innocent crew of an unprotected touring yacht. Deanne knew how much McKenna still agonized over that decision where he had really been given no choice at all.

And this man, in whose arms she lay, had come aboard as an enemy, a threat to their very survival. How much had changed since he had fathomed the full, true story. Since then, and on their behalf as much as his own, he had placed his life and profession on the line and stood up to the most powerful people in his own country. Now she had discovered the real man beneath the mantle of the professional intelligence officer. She marvelled at his tenderness and staying power. Even now, ten minutes after their final, joint peak of joy, he still nestled firmly inside her as she clasped him tightly, almost afraid of letting go.

Deanne recalled with distaste her first sexual experience at the age of seventeen, a rough and tumble affair with a Long Beach surfer whose idea of love had been a rushed, fumbled series of pants, grunts, and thrusts, leaving her feeling unfulfilled and used. Her only subsequent lover had been little better, turning her off the whole idea until now.

Donall Lindsay had been entirely different. With exquisite gentleness, his lips, fingertips and tongue had brought her entire body to electric sensitivity and anticipation until the moment she was ready to receive him. She had reacted to that moment, guiding him into her. Even then, there was nothing of the crude, lust-driven rutting and thrusting she had been subjected to in the past. Every movement had been tender, soft-gentle motions on which she had glided and soared to greater heights of passion than she had ever thought possible. With a sense of wonder, she realized that it was important to him that she should reach fulfillment. She had responded, her body clasping and embracing him, bringing her to her first unexpected peak. She had gasped with its rush of surprise and pleasure from deep within. Several times he had seemed to reach his own point of no return but had somehow managed the control to glide beneath them.

On her third and most eruptive peak, he had released that control to join with her. Both had cried out softly in the spine-arching delirium of a love she had never imagined.

She gently kissed each closed eyelid of the man who, still entwined with her, slept an even sleep. Reaching behind her, she touched the warm metal of the bulkhead as she had seen him do, feeling the faint vibration as the powerful engines of the *Nautilus* took her ever southwards. She did not want to think about their icy destination and the dangers that might yet wrest this man from her.

55

17 February 2015
Southern Ocean
600 miles SW of Tasmania

Japan's greatest secret for more than half a century cruised through the cold waters of the Antarctic circumpolar current at an effortless eighteen knots, maintaining a depth of three hundred and fifty feet. The 300 foot long titanium hull of the *Honshu*, based on the streamlined designs of the Russian *Alfa* and *Viktor* class submarines, bristled with the most sensitive and advanced electronic systems yet devised.

Her complement of five officers and eighteen crewmen was remarkably small for a military submarine of her size and type. The vessel depended heavily on computerized automation but, even so, the technologically geared minds of her Japanese designers recognized the simple fact that machines cannot do it all: that there are no substitutes for spur-of-the-moment human reaction and ingenuity.

Captain Honshiro Takamura was a throwback to the old Japanese military school, dedicated and able, but also ruthless and ambitious. With fifteen years experience as officer and commander of conventional *Uzushio* and *Yuushio* class submarines within the Japanese Maritime Defence Force, his had been the name to emerge at the top of the short-list of officers drawn up for command of Japan's first nuclear powered attack submarine.

Under Takamura's diamond-hard gaze, every officer and crewman was kept on his toes, alert to every signal and command. Chief Sonarman Hideki Kansai was no exception, his keenly attuned ears filtering out the faintest of regular patterns in an acoustic world filled with the sounds of the deep.

"Conn, sonar," he rapped out. "We have a contact, range twelve thousand yards, bearing two-eight-oh True. Extremely quiet." He glanced at the computer display and allowed himself a tight smile. "It is the *Nautilus*, captain. Her signature accords with the data we stole from the Americans."

Takamura nodded curtly. "Good work, Hideki." He was pleased even though he didn't sound it. He had handpicked this crew and knew that if any sonar operator in the world could have picked up the whispering electro-magnetic motors of the *Nautilus*, Hideki Kansai would be that man.

The captain issued orders to quieten the boat and turned to Samu Tsuboi, his Executive Officer. "So we have her, Samu. There can be no better sea trial than this, eh? The British would call this boat a hunter-killer. Well, she has hunted and hunted successfully. Within a few short moments, she will earn her full title. And on her maiden voyage, too. The first vessel of the Imperial Navy to register a kill for seventy years. How does it feel?"

"The *Nautilus*," he continued without waiting for a response, "has repeatedly made fools of the best vessels the western navies have. Her destruction will therefore doubly emphasize the rebirth of Nipponese military strength. Yes, we have her and she is helpless.

"I want all forward tubes loaded, then flood and open the outer doors on One and Two."

"At this range, sir?" The XO risked the query.

"At this range, Samu. Let us be certain we are not heard. Plot me an interception course and slow to ten knots." Takamura's sharp black eyes gazed forward as if penetrating the hull and the waters beyond. "Like the sparrowhawk, Samu, we silently hover and then we swoop."

"Torpedo!" Alan Tregenza clapped his hands to the earpieces of his sonar headset. "Coming in from our starboard side. Maybe a thousand yards!"

Lindsay, doing his stint at the helm of the *Nautilus*, snatched the headset from him and listened. "No pulses," he said. "It's not active just yet. There's no time to head for the surface and hope the surface scatter will confuse its sensors. This has got to be desperate. Say a little prayer, Alan, we're going to need it." He tossed the headset back, signalled full speed and wrenched the wheel hard over.

Tregenza gasped out loud. "Jesus Christ, Don, you're heading us straight at it!"

"That's the general idea. For a start, we present a smaller target. Now, let's just pray that we intercept it before it arms itself." Mentally, Lindsay crossed himself. "No time to argue, just cross your fingers."

The mate studied the sonar display as the sound of the torpedo built in his earphones. "Oh, dear God," he breathed. "It's right on top of us!" He braced himself, eyes screwed tight shut.

Lindsay felt the sweat trickle down the back of his neck, knowing that the convergent speeds of the *Nautilus* and the torpedo left scant seconds before impact. It took every ounce of his willpower to stick to his present course and not veer aside. He took a huge breath and held it.

The torpedo struck the reinforced deck fairing right in front of his eyes. Both men flinched at the force of the collision that shattered the weapon like glass, its fragments whirling past the wheelhouse windows. Lindsay blew out his pent-up breath in sheer relief.

"What the hell happened?" Tregenza wheezed.

"I took a page out of the Russian manual," Lindsay explained. "Their 'Crazy Ivan' manoeuvre. Any British training officer would have slung me in the brig for that but there just wasn't time for anything else. Torpedoes don't usually arm until they're well away from the ship that fired it. I turned us into it before it could do so, but that sort of luck never holds twice. In any case, the bastard that fired it is likely to arm the next one from launch. All we can rely on now is speed and depth, so I suggest we get the hell away from here."

"Let's hope the torpedoes aren't faster than we are," Tregenza said.

Lindsay winced. "There are times, Alan, when your train of thought borders on the downright depressive."

"You'd better put it to the test, Commander. We have another one. Three thousand yards, dead ahead and coming at us like a bullet. What now?"

"We cut, run and go deep." Lindsay swung the submarine hard about to starboard, banking her like a fighter aircraft and angling the planes to send her deep at forty-five knots. The intercom hissed.

"Can someone tell me what the fuck's going on?" McKenna's voice cut through. "I've got people sprawled all over the deck down here. And did we just hit something?"

"No, Seán, something just hit us. We're being used for target practice," Lindsay snapped back. "We have a torpedo up our arse. It must be an attack sub, Christ knows whose. I'm taking her deep, Seán. We might get lucky and find a dense layer that'll confuse its sensors."

"So your boss never got his present," McKenna said sourly. "Or if he did, he didn't listen in spite of everything that was on that disc."

"Pardon the interruption," Tregenza broke in. "Fish at fifteen hundred, closing. She's a fast one. I've a second contact, further away. Presumably your attack sub."

"I'm pushing her as hard as I can," Lindsay replied shortly. "If only we had countermeasure decoys to put the fish off our scent."

"We have," McKenna's voice issued from the speaker. "Hold on while I patch through to Rob in the engine room." He was through to the engineer in a flash. "Rob, when I yell, emergency vent the after air tanks."

"What the bluidy hell for?"

"Don't argue, just do it when I shout." He recontacted the wheelhouse. "What range now?"

"Eight hundred yards," Tregenza rapped out. "Six hundred. Christ, lads, we're cutting it fine..."

In the saloon, McKenna hit the engine room intercom button. "Robbie, now!"

The *Nautilus* pitched sharply as the pressurized air of the after supply tanks powerfully vented out, huge misshapen bubbles erupting from the submarine's stern like a flatulent whale. She banked to port, heading still deeper.

The sonar guidance unit of the Japanese torpedo detected the massive disturbance, adjusting the weapon's course towards it as the *Nautilus* twisted away into the black depths.

McKenna's brainwave gave his vessel valuable seconds but the torpedo, scything through the water at sixty knots, shot through the fragmenting cloud of bubbles. Meeting no resistance, its sonar probed the water for a renewed target.

"I hate to be the bearer of further bad news," Tregenza said, studying the sonar evidence, "but I do believe the bugger's reacquired us." He winced suddenly, tearing the headset from his ears and uttering a gasp of pain.

Lindsay shot a quizzical look over his shoulder.

"Something just went pop," the mate said. "Bloody loud but it wasn't a detonation."

Lindsay was jubilant. He glanced at the depth gauge needle, now passing the three thousand foot mark. "We've gone too deep for it," he said. "The fish imploded under the pressure."

"So we're safe down here?"

"Perhaps," Lindsay said. "Perhaps not. Attack subs generally carry more than one type of torpedo. This one might have a model more suited to deep water."

"And you call my thoughts depressive," Tregenza countered. "You might well be right, though. The depth isn't stopping the sub. She's coming right down after us. Surely she has a limit? What's the submarine equivalent of an aircraft's ceiling?"

"Crush depth," Lindsay said. "I was just wondering about the same thing."

Aboard the *Honshu*, now barrelling downwards at flank speed, close to forty knots, Captain Takamura's jaw was set with a steely determination not wholly shared by his crew.

The titanium-hulled submarine had been designed to a maximum operational depth of 2,500 feet and everyone on board knew the simple formula of multiplying that figure by a safety factor of between 1.5 and 2 to calculate her crush or collapse depth, terms rejected by naval architects who prefer the euphemism 'design depth'. Typically for modern submarines, and for the *Honshu* herself, the safety factor was considered to be 1.75, fixing her crush depth at 4,375 feet.

Already, as the *Honshu* stuck rigidly to the tail of the fleeing *Nautilus*, the digital gauge was approaching four thousand feet. In her control room, sweat-beaded foreheads told their own story. An acrid smell of fear increased at every pop, creak and groan of the hull, now taking the strain of 1,200 tons for every square yard of its surface, and at the captain's counter-productive measure of turning off the depth indicator display.

Takamura had every faith in Nipponese workmanship and in the quality of his vessel, confident that she was well capable of winning the raw battle of nerves against the strange craft she was pursuing into the darkness. His brows drew together as he pondered this curiosity. Could the reports be true that the submarine he was hunting was well over a hundred years old? The concept was improbable at best but, even if it were true, it was inconceivable that such an ancient craft could continue to withstand such crushing pressures.

Had the helmsman of the *Nautilus* but known it, his own vessel was safe from further armed attack. Takamura had no torpedoes that could operate at such extreme depths. His game plan now was to force the old submarine deeper until she was either crushed out of existence, or forced to break for shallower depths where she could be picked off at will. Either way, Takamura had no intention of allowing her to evade him.

Unusually for a submariner, Takamura had never read Jules Verne's famous book. Even though the French author had grossly exaggerated the depths and pressures the *Nautilus* could withstand, she was nonetheless of extraordinary strength. The meticulous logs of the man who had called himself Captain Nemo, still preserved aboard the fleeing submarine, testified that, in 1868, he had taken her down to 12,460 feet in the Atlantic south of Bermuda, roughly the same depth in which the remains of the *Titanic* rested some 2,000 miles north of that spot. Takamura was not to have known that fact.

At 4,300 feet, the *Honshu* had already exceeded the record depth ever achieved by a military submarine. Takamura allowed himself a smile at this achievement, ignoring the increasingly loud protestations of his vessel's hull. He would tell his men of their accomplishment later.

Swallowing hard and noticeably pale, his Executive Officer moved close to his shoulder, speaking quietly. "Captain—"

"Courage, Samu. This is a first class vessel. She can take it and so can we. Already we are deeper than even the Russian boats could achieve and this *Nautilus* must give up soon, one way or the other. By all reports, she's an antique. There is no way she can continue to endure these depths as we can. Any moment now, we will have her..."

Titanium is notoriously difficult to weld. The Russians, pioneers of titanium-hulled submarines, discovered this to their initial and tragic cost until dogged persistence had perfected the technique. Japanese workmanship was no less skilful but, even with the strongest weld, the most resilient of hulls is only as strong as its weakest point.

It could only have been the most miniscule lapse of concentration in the shipyard, for the weak point of the *Honshu* was an area of welding less than a tenth of an inch square. It might just as well have been a square foot.

The initial leak sprayed a needle-thin jet of water clear across the engine room compartment with the cutting force of a laser beam. It was momentarily unfortunate for the *Honshu's* chief engineer who was standing in precisely the wrong spot, the lethal jet severing his right hand from his wrist.

He never felt the pain. Even before the severed hand had hit the deckplates, before the spurt of blood had sprayed the bulkhead, before he or anyone else had even the chance to draw breath and scream, the crew of Japan's first and only nuclear submarine were blotted out of existence.

With no further warning, the *Honshu* imploded, her crushed, fragmented remains tumbling like autumn leaves into the black anonymity of the abyss.

Twelve miles to the west, an American sonarman listened, appalled, to the noise of implosion and the tinkling, breaking-glass sounds of break up. Although he had heard it on headphones, speakers had ensured that the whole episode had been shared by the control room crew of the *USS Denver*, the Los Angeles class nuclear attack submarine assigned to the task of shadowing the Japanese secret.

"Is all that on tape?" her captain asked. Captain Byron Fraser, a bluff man whose greying hair contrasted with his black skin, leant over the sonarman.

"Yes, sir, it is."

"Okay, play it back. In the meantime, give me a run-down of events as you saw them."

"Well, captain, at first we had only the *Honshu* and, as you know, we've had her signature on the scopes ever since picking her up in the Pacific. She never did detect us."

Fraser nodded. In common with others of her class, the *Denver* was designed to be ultra-quiet and he had always kept her well astern of the *Honshu*, in her baffles where the Japanese vessel's engine and screw sounds confounded her own sonar arrays.

"For no reason that we could fathom," the sonarman continued, "she suddenly flooded her tubes and loosed one off. The Doppler showed that she wasn't firing at us. Just then, we picked up a second signature, real faint and mighty hard to pick out from under the sounds of the *Honshu* and her torpedo. Then we got the sound of some sort of collision and minor break-up noises.

"We definitely got two sets of engines accelerating. One was accompanied by coolant circulation—certainly the *Honshu*. There was no such sound with the other one and we couldn't make head or tail of it. Much quieter and an engine sound like nothing I've ever heard. Kinda high-pitched.

"Anyhow, the *Honshu* fired off a second fish. Whoever she was chasing hadn't flooded her own tubes; she was just running. We got a sudden noise of air bubbles—I don't have a clue what that was—and then there was a minor implosion. No more torpedoes were fired and it sounded like the two of them were having a race. After that, sir, the big one. They must have been deep, captain. One of those subs definitely imploded and broke up."

Fraser rubbed his chin, realizing that he needed a shave. "But which one?" he mused. "Just play back the very end bit."

The playback of the implosion was as appalling as it had sounded the first time. Fraser listened through the awful crackle and tinkle of the ship fragmenting. There was something there; he was convinced of it.

"Play it again," he ordered. "Only this time, filter out the break-up."

It was the faintest of sounds, a high-pitched whine, gradually lowering in pitch and volume until it was almost beyond detection. Fraser grinned with delight.

"Well, I'll be damned. The Japanese threat is over, gentlemen. That was the *Honshu* that blew."

His XO, Lieutenant-Commander Ed Martens, glanced at the computer readout that accompanied the sonar reception. "Which begs the question, sir. Who the hell's the other one?"

"You don't know?" Fraser's grin was even wider. "That, my boy, is the famous *Nautilus* we've been hearing so much about. The same one that keeps making mugs of the best ships we have. It seems the Japs can't put one over on her, either. How the hell she got here from the Mediterranean, God only knows."

"Aren't we supposed to be blowing her out of the water?"

"Not any more, Ed. Don't ask me why, but orders have changed. We're to leave her be, even nursemaid her if we have to. Chief of the Boat, take us up to periscope depth. We have news to send out that'll set a load of folks dancing in Norfolk and Washington."

56

20 February 2015
Amundsen Sea
Antarctica

The vagaries of the Antarctic Convergence, that fifty mile wide belt of sea where cold currents flowing northward sink beneath warmer waters, were making life difficult for David Falco. The skipper of the Greenpeace vessel *Atlantis* peered through the wheelhouse windows into a grey murk so thick he could hardly make out his own ship's forepeak.

The mate, Anders Kristenberg, waited for a pause in the wail of the automatic foghorn. "I've never seen it this bad," he commented. "Three days of it now and not a sign of it clearing."

"We're achieving nothing here, Andy," Falco said. His eyes surveyed a radar screeen that remained as blank as it had been for some days now. "What say we go south to clear the Convergence and then aim west?"

"As good a plan as any other," the mate shrugged. "I'm all for it. This fog's a killer on the eyes."

"Not to mention the nerves. We can't relax for a moment." He eased over on the wheel. "Okay, south it is. We'd best signal our course change. I'll do it. Will you take over, Andy?"

Falco went through to the radio shack to relay the change of plan, just about getting through to Greenpeace's Antarctic base at Cape Evans. The conversation lasted three minutes, during which time the skipper was informed that weather conditions south of his position were calm, clear and mild.

He signed off and called through to Kristenberg. "Conditions to the south are good, Andy. Let's face it, if we can't operate in this fog, neither can the whalers, assuming they're anywhere nearby. We may as well head back towards Cape Evans and hope to catch them somewhere along the way…" He broke off as the radio came back to life.

"*Atlantis*. Come in *Atlantis*." The signal was faint.

Falco responded. "Greenpeace vessel *Atlantis* receiving," he said. "Your signal is weak but I hear you. Please identify, over."

"Greetings, *Atlantis*. That you, Dave? This is Deep Watch vessel *Zephyr*."

"*Zephyr*? What the hell are you doing in this neck of the woods? You were in Auckland last I heard."

"Change of plan. We're headed for the Balleny Islands. A plane flying out of McMurdo Sound reckons he spotted a whaling fleet between the Ballenys and Scott Island. Any chance of you teaming up with us?"

"Every chance, *Zephyr*. The Amundsen Sea's so quiet that we're dying of boredom. I can make Scott Island in three days. That any good to you?"

"Suits us just fine, *Atlantis*. I suggest we rendezvous ten miles north of Scott Island. I gather there's a dozen or so vessels involved and, to be honest, we're leery of going in alone."

"Yeah," Falco sympathized. "Makes a lot of sense after what happened to Seán McKenna's boat last year. Same time of year, same area, too. I'm still far from convinced that his loss was any accident. We can put together a game plan when we meet up."

"Good enough, *Atlantis*. See you in three days. *Zephyr*, out."

Falco replaced the handset and pushed a hand through his hair as he wandered back into the wheelhouse. "Did you hear any of that, Andy?" At the wheel, the mate nodded. "I don't understand it," Falco said. "Brian Conran's boat was in Auckland four days ago making ready for a trip up to the Marquesas Islands… apparently our good friends the French are up to something there. But, if that was the case, how come he's within three days of Scott Island?"

Kristenberg shrugged his narrow shoulders. "Since when could you ever describe Deep Watch as predictable, David? We'll doubtless get the answer when we arrive."

Several hundred miles away, in the wheelhouse of a surfaced *Nautilus*, Seán McKenna grinned hugely as he replaced his own radio handset and signalled Chris Janssen, out on deck, to lower the telescopic whip aerial.

57

22 February 2015
Northern Ross Sea
Antarctica

Well wrapped against a keen polar wind, Deanne Fischer and Chris Janssen were already on deck as Lindsay climbed up through the open hatch. Sea conditions were relatively quiet under sullen skies and, here and there, whitecaps glistened briefly. Moving at a moderate pace, the *Nautilus* rolled gently, her creamy wake curving in a great arc. Lindsay studied it thoughtfully.

"What's McKenna playing at now?" he asked. "I've been down in the saloon for the last ten minutes watching the compass needle circum-navigating the dial."

Janssen shrugged. "Search me, Commander. Seán's been steering her in five or six big circles, only he knows why. There's been something on his mind these last few days, something more than this Pyramus thing. I know the man well enough to be sure he does nothing without a reason, and I also know when to leave him alone. He'll tell us in his own good time."

"I hope it has nothing to do with that ship out there." Deanne pointed to the west where, dimly visible, the masts and superstructure of a sizeable vessel punctuated the regularity of an otherwise featureless horizon. "Unusual to see a ship of that size as far south as this," she added. "It's not as if we're exactly on the shipping lanes."

Janssen shaded his eyes. "She's a fair distance away," he said, "but she doesn't have the lines of a whaling factory ship."

Lindsay's own eyes narrowed. Was it his imagination or was the distant vessel altering its course towards them? At that same moment, the *Nautilus* slowed, her screw reversing to bring her to a gradual halt. Within moments, McKenna was on deck.

"I'll be taking her down in a moment," he announced.

"Care to share it with the rest of us?" Lindsay challenged. "Why, for example, have we been going round in ever decreasing circles for the last ten minutes?"

A haunted look clouded the Irishman's face. "A year ago, Commander—a year to the very day—a good ship went down. Murdered, along with two of her crewmen. The rest of us were fortunate to survive at all. Before we got clear, I managed to grab the ship's log in which I'd entered her latest position only minutes before we were rammed and sunk. As near as I can judge," he said, pointing downward, "this is the place.

"Months ago, I swore to get some sort of proof of how the *Aurora* was sunk. We have names for some of the men that ordered it and, with the *Nautilus*, I can get photographic evidence that will help to put the bastards away until they rot. I intend to take care of that job right now."

"Think a minute, Seán," Lindsay interrupted. "There's ten thousand feet of water under our keel. Have you stopped to consider the pressure at that depth?"

"She can take it. According to his own log, Nemo took her down to over twelve thousand."

"A hundred and forty-odd years ago, maybe. Seán, repeated exposure to extremes of pressure will invariably weaken the hull of any submarine and you've never taken her beyond half that depth. You don't have the slightest idea what she's capable of taking now." Lindsay noticed that the entire crew was now on deck and were hanging on every word of the exchange.

"Commander, if we're ever to prove that the *Aurora* was deliberately sunk and that Colin and Paul were murdered, we need that evidence. Okay, I'll agree it's a risk, but it's one I'm willing to take."

"*You* are? What about the rest of your people?"

"I've considered that," McKenna conceded. "I propose we launch the tender and the Zephyr and get everyone into them while I take the *Nautilus* down solo to photograph the wreck. If it goes as planned, all well and good, and I can pick you guys up again. If not… well, I'll be in good company down there with Colin and Paul. The rest of you will have supplies and a VHF radio and, as you all know, I've planned some friendly company for tomorrow. But it's essential that I do this."

"Not without me, you won't," Carla Schumann said stubbornly, clasping McKenna's arm.

"Nor me," Deanne supported her. "If you think for a minute that I'm going adrift in an open boat in these waters a second time, you can damn well think again. I'd rather take my chances with the *Nautilus*. She's never let us down yet."

Lindsay suppressed a smile as each of the crew voiced like-minded opinions. Tregenza summed up the feeling. "Everything we've been through, Seán, we've done together. Why should this be any different?"

McKenna switched his gaze to Lindsay. "Well, Commander? You can see how much authority this particular captain has."

"You're all barking mad," he said. "As for me, risk is part of my job, assuming I still have one. Talk about lunatics running the asylum."

"We took as big a risk in the Maelstrom," Tregenza reminded him. "Which particular lunatic was running the asylum then, Commander?" he added, grinning.

McKenna shepherded them all below, glancing briefly in the direction of the distant ship that, to Don Lindsay's mind, had most definitely altered course towards them.

All hatches and watertight doors were secured for diving. After a momentary discussion with McKenna, Tregenza and Janssen headed for the wheelhouse while the rest gathered in the saloon. Nobody spoke. The nervous tension was almost tangible as each person contemplated the fact that they had consented to dive more than twice as deep than any modern submarine could withstand without succumbing to the pressure. The appalling fate of the *Honshu* remained all too fresh in their minds. It was also twice the depth that they had ever ventured to take the old boat and almost as deep as Nemo himself had taken her. Lindsay found himself peering intently at the interior of the ship's sides.

Sharp intakes of breath accompanied the rush of sound as the ballast tanks beneath their feet flooded. Lindsay's attention switched to the depth gauge among the array of instruments on the forward bulkhead. Deanne pressed close to his side. Rob McLeish and Ross Jourdan were making nervy, ill-considered moves on the chessboard.

Trimmed to dead horizontal fore-and-aft, her hydroplanes set vertically, the *Nautilus* sank straight down into the darkness. Her engines merely idled in neutral so that no power was being transferred to the screw. The depth gauge needle moved steadily. At five thousand feet, the vessel's modern crew were on the verge of venturing into the unknown. Involuntary gasps burst out at every pop and creak of the double hull as it adjusted to the relentless increase of pressure.

Six thousand feet. Sweat began to trickle into Lindsay's eyes but he knew better than to voice the figure aloud. The *Nautilus* sank still deeper, as vertically as any bathyscaphe and still held perfectly level. As the needle swung onto 7,500 feet, the hull let out a long, shuddering groan. Someone uttered the word, "Jesus!" Lindsay felt his heart pounding in his chest.

A gnarled hand patted his shoulder. "Have faith in the old girl, Commander," McLeish said to him. "She'll get us there and back again. Any money you like."

Lindsay refrained from asking how he'd collect if the engineer lost the bet.

"Just how much can she stand, Rob?" he said quietly. "The hull's only steel after all."

"Steel, is it?" McLeish responded. "Now who told you that?"

"In Verne's book, Aronnax described her several times as being built of steel."

The engineer snorted. "He described only what he thought she was made of. She's not a steel boat, Commander. Her hull plates are of some sort of alloy, certainly one part titanium."

"That can't be, Rob. Titanium was only discovered at the end of the 18th century and not obtained in pure form until the 20th."

"That's what the books say, Commander, just as they do about the existence of submarines but, in each case, Nemo got there first. His logs don't use the name titanium, but its older names Manaccanite and Gregorite, but there's no doubt that he perfected the technique of using it, even forming an alloy with it."

"What's the other part of the alloy?" Lindsay pressed.

"I can't be sure," McLeish answered honestly. "But I have a feeling it might be iridium, if that's possible. I'm no metallurgist. Nemo wrote about working with a metal that was iridescent in solution, which hardly describes titanium."

"No wonder she's so well preserved," Lindsay said with renewed respect for the submarine's builder. "And why there's no corrosion on her." He broke off as his eyes caught the depth gauge needle touching the ten thousand foot mark.

By now, the creaks and groans of the tortured hull were almost incessant. McKenna had already set up a camcorder on a tripod and was aiming it at the starboard window as its inner and outer shields slid back. The room darkened as its internal lights were switched off.

Outside, even the powerful beams of the vessel's searchlights seemed to find difficulty in penetrating the stygian darkness but the featureless ooze of the ocean floor could just be made out thirty feet beneath them. There was no sign of any apparent marine life. Lindsay cast a nervous eye on the seals around the thick pane of the window that, to his mind's eye, seemed to be bowing inwards.

"There," McKenna murmured. Lindsay strained his eyes to pick out a formless shape on the very fringes of the light. The *Nautilus* moved closer. The shape resolved itself into the stern section of a ship severed amidships, her masts broken, the bridge and wheelhouse intact. Lindsay noted the shattered windshields and the inward-twisted hullplates at the point of severance on her starboard side. No marine growth obscured any part of the wreck. A grim faced McKenna operated the camera, recording every detail.

Lindsay let out a low whistle. "No doubt, there, Seán," he said. "Whatever hit you was under a full head of steam."

The *Nautilus* swung slowly around the stern of the wreck, the searchlight's rays clearly picking out the words:

AURORA
Kingston-upon-Hull

From the wheelhouse, Tregenza's Cornish tones floated out over the intercom. "Skipper, we have an active-sonar contact, oh-seven-oh degrees. Range two-fifty yards, It must be the bow section."

McKenna's eyes closed for an instant. Lindsay knew he must be thinking of his dead colleagues in the wreck's foc's'le cabin. The Irishman let out his breath in a long sigh. "Roger, Alan. Let's take a look." He glanced up sharply as the submarine's hull gave out another long, drawn-out groan.

The forward section of the shattered *Aurora* loomed out of the abyssal murk, its severed hullplates showing the same evidence of impact as those of the stern section. Like its torn-off other half, the wreck was virtually clear of rust, growth or accumulated sediment, and the ripped edges of its plates gleamed like new under the rays of the searchlight. Not one person averted their eyes from the scene of tragedy, the half-a-ship serving as a dual mausoleum. Every person had gathered behind McKenna and his camera, gazing strickenly at the forlorn wreckage. Most were weeping silently as they said their own private prayers for the dead.

Not even the protestations of the *Nautilus's* hull could disturb their silence until a loud series of bangs from somewhere aft forced more than one to turn their head. Lindsay inspected the glass of the viewing panel, gingerly reaching out to touch one of the seals. His fingertip glistened with moisture as he held it in front of McKenna's eyes.

"Seán, we're pushing our luck. This window alone is holding back over three thousand tons."

"I agree," McKenna said. "We can do no more here and we can't keep asking her to take this kind of pressure." He moved to the intercom. "Alan, take her up but gently, my friend, gently. Do it as though she'd otherwise get the bends. Let the hull readjust nice and slowly."

He turned to his crew, his eyes moist. "Colin and Paul have slept here in peace for a year to the day. It would be wrong of us to disturb their rest any longer."

A new feeling crept into McKenna as he turned back to the window, watching the tangled wreck fade into the darkness beyond the reach of the ship's light. *You will not have died in vain, I swear it.* His silent promise came as he reached out to operate the controls to the panels that protected the window. As they began to slide across, McKenna gave a last look upward towards an invisible surface two miles above him, hearing an inner voice telling him that Nemesis was waiting there.

58

Whitehall
London, UK

Admiral Garvie and his Chief of Staff were burning the midnight oil, examining a high-resolution photograph in minute detail. The phone call from Britain's Prime Minister to the US President had at last paid dividends and an American surveillance satellite was now firmly set in polar orbit.

Taken from two hundred miles up, the photograph centred on an area of the true Antarctic coast on the eastern side of the Ross Sea, several miles east of Cape Colbeck and close to the Sulzberger Ice Shelf.

The terrain appeared to be mountainous but their attention was focussed on a small peninsula, a conical mountain joined to the Antarctic landmass by a low, narrow neck of land. It was surrounded by pack ice and, to the west, a smooth expanse of ice shelf with hints of polynyas here and there, indicating that its thickness was not extensive.

To the north, a curiously ice-free channel, black against the dazzling white of the ice, curved from one side of the peninsula towards the open sea. Garvie tapped this area with his forefinger.

"What do you think keeps this channel open?"

Rochester pulled out a second photograph taken in false colour. "Infrared shows it to be warm water, most likely the outflow of an underground river. The fact that it's warm enough to keep it free of ice probably indicates some volcanic hotspot somewhere inland."

"And these?" Garvie pointed out a pair of elongated shapes in clear water beside the peninsula.

Rochester trained a powerful magnifying glass on them. "Ships, without a shadow of doubt. There's no question, admiral. That peninsula has to be the site of the Pyramus operation. It accords with the details of Calloway's confession and he did state that it was an underground site. The presence of these ships clinches it. There's no other reason for them to be there and I've managed to ascertain that no research vessels are anywhere near this area.

"Unfortunately, Calloway stated that the place has defensive armaments. The photograph shows no sign of these so, presumably, they're well concealed."

"The bloody place is a fortress," Garvie said sourly. "Our Special Forces will have their work cut out for them. Have they reached McMurdo yet?"

"Eight hours ago, sir. They'll be ready to go on our signal."

Garvie nodded approvingly. "Who's in command?"

"Lieutenant-Colonel Byrd."

The admiral looked up sharply. "Vernon Byrd? The man who sorted out that mountain-based terrorist cell in Afghanistan a few years ago?"

"The very same."

Garvie allowed himself a smile. "The Prime Minister did want us to send the best. Brigadier Anderson's choice, I expect. I only wish we had more intelligence to give the man. We have no more idea than he does how to get into the place. I can see no hint of an entrance."

"Nor can I, sir. We do know that there's an underwater loading entrance, probably close to those two ships."

"Speaking of underwater, Chief," Garvie said. "What news on the *Nautilus*?"

"We believe she's entered the Ross Sea, not too far north of Scott Island, although we don't have her precise position. How the hell she got away from the Japanese sub we don't as yet know but intelligence is coming in from the *Denver*, the American sub that was assigned to shadow the *Honshu*. We should know more soon."

"That old antique seems to lead a charmed life, Chief. As we thought, she's after the Pyramus place, but with what plan in mind? The *Nautilus* is the one factor that really worries me. She's a loose cannon that could jeopardize this entire operation. Commander Lindsay has to be warned off but we have no way of contacting him. Damn the man. I need ideas, Chief. We have to get to him somehow."

Rochester smiled. "I think we can manage that, sir."

59

Northern Ross Sea
Antarctica

On the exposed deck of the *Nautilus*, a grim-faced Seán McKenna lowered the binoculars.

"What do you think?" Lindsay asked him.

"There's no doubt about it," McKenna said through his teeth. "It's the *Emperor*, the bastard that killed the *Aurora*. And in the same bloody spot, by Christ. I don't believe in this sort of coincidence, Commander. She's waiting for us."

The remainder of the crew had already gathered on deck, all staring at the approaching ship. The *Emperor* was barely three miles away, a grey, ominous shape in the Antarctic swell. Lindsay took the binoculars from McKenna and studied her.

"She's carrying containers on deck," he observed. "There seems to be some activity, too. I don't think there's any doubt that she's seen us. Strange that she's flying no flag."

"I don't need a flag to know who she is," McKenna growled, "but, by God, I'll show her ours."

The Irishman disappeared below deck, returning a minute later with a cloth bundle. The forward baluster of the starboard deckrail was telescoped upwards and Lindsay realized that it was a jackstaff. McKenna unfolded the flag, attached its guys and hoisted it.

It was the first time since the burial of Barrington Hobbes that Lindsay had seen the flag of the *Nautilus*. Devised by her builder, it was a plain black banner with a single gold capital N occupying its top left quarter. The flag streamed out in a steady, cold north-westerly breeze.

The response was a furious burst of activity on the Pyramus vessel. Figures ran to the containers on her deck, systematically collapsing their sides. Through the glasses, Lindsay took one look at the objects that lay revealed on the *Emperor's* deck and shouted a warning.

"Seán, she's armed! She's a bloody Q-ship, like we had in the Second World War."

A gout of white smoke burst from the deck of the *Emperor*. Lindsay instinctively ducked as the shell roared overhead, the sea erupting in a silver spout fifty yards off the submarine's starboard side. In the same moment, the shattering report of the gun reached their ears.

"Everyone below!"

At McKenna's shout, the crew bolted for the hatch. The Irishman grinned savagely at Lindsay before following him down. "Payback time, Commander. But not here. Not where the *Aurora* lies."

Strike, demented vessel! Shower your useless shot. You will not escape the ram of the Nautilus, *but you will not perish here. I will not allow your ruins to mingle with those of the* Vengeur.

The quote that came to McKenna's mind startled him. It had come from Verne's account of the sinking of a British warship by the *Nautilus* in the Western Approaches in 1868. *God almighty, is history about to repeat itself?* He shook his head clear of the unthinkable as a second shell struck within yards of the submarine's hull, showering him with spray. He vaulted into the hatch behind Lindsay and secured it for sea.

With McKenna alone at the helm, the *Nautilus* moved effortlessly out of range of the *Emperor's* guns. For reasons he himself could not explain, he kept the submarine on the surface. The Pyramus ship altered course, putting on speed to give chase. Her bow wave doubled in height as she powered up to thirty knots. Warming to the task, McKenna began to give her a show of impudence, letting the pursuer get within range and then accelerating away at up to forty knots as the guns opened up again.

In the saloon, where most of the crew had gathered, Lindsay gestured upwards. "What the hell does he think he's doing?" he asked Tregenza.

"Search me, Commander," the mate shook his head. "Why he doesn't submerge and get us away instead of playing silly buggers with an armed ship is beyond me. I can only assume he has some idea in mind."

"That's what bothers me. 'Payback time' was the expression he used on deck. I need to know, Alan—is McKenna capable of sinking this ship?"

"Not in a million years," Tregenza said emphatically. "He saw enough of death with his brother."

"He sank a boat at Krakatau last year," Lindsay reminded him.

"A very different choice, Commander. Those Malaysian pirates were within seconds of slaughtering the crew of an innocent yacht. There was no time to make any other decision. It was the lesser of two evils but it still pained him to have to do it. He brooded about it for months afterwards. This time, though… coming across the very ship that sank us and killed Colin and Paul… I can only hope to hell he isn't starting to crack up."

"What do you mean?" Lindsay demanded.

"He's barred the hatch to the wheelhouse. I can't get in and he won't respond."

Sir, do you intend to sink this vessel?

Monsieur, I intend to sink her.

You cannot do that!

I shall do it and I would advise you not to judge me. Fate has shown you what you were not meant to see. They have attacked and my response will be terrible!

Night was falling when Lindsay ventured back on deck. Rolling in the swell, the *Nautilus* had not altered course but was travelling steadily southward. Deeply uneasy, he stood beneath the black flag and watched the silhouetted vessel, now four miles astern. As darkness fell, the submarine's searchlight was switched on. From the *Emperor*, its brilliance would be only too easy to follow and Lindsay wondered why McKenna had done it. There was no clue from the darkened wheelhouse.

The Pyramus ship was maintaining a speed of thirty knots and McKenna now resorted to baiting her. Lindsay hung onto the deck rail as the *Nautilus* powered up to forty-five knots and raced around the *Emperor* in a complete circle.

At midnight, Tregenza came up and lowered the flag. He and Lindsay went back below and secured the hatch. McKenna had once again allowed the *Emperor* to close in. Her guns opened up in earnest on the brilliant light in the ocean that advertised the submarine's presence. Even from within the saloon her gun blasts could be heard, volley after volley. Shells struck close enough for their impact to heel the *Nautilus* over to one side. Pale white streaks, steeply angled, could be seen in the dark water from the viewing panels.

Lindsay made for the intercom and buzzed the wheelhouse. "Seán? Christ, man, you're inviting her to sink us. Get us submerged and away, now!"

The only response was a strange whining noise from above. Tregenza recognized it and went pale. "Dear God… he's setting up to attack her. That's the hydraulic retraction gear."

"Retraction?" Lindsay queried.

"I mentioned it to you before. He's retracting the wheelhouse, deck rail and lantern housing into the hull. The hydroplanes can be drawn in as well. It's a protective measure in the event of an all-out attack, although we always did it for safety's sake before disabling a ship. In effect, the *Nautilus* turns herself into a streamlined torpedo. Jesus, I hope he's not intending to do anything other than cripple her."

I am the law and I am the judge! I am the oppressed and there lies the oppressor! Through him, I lost all that I loved, cherished and revered—my country, my wife and children, my father and mother. I saw all of them die. All that I despise lies out there. Now, be silent!

The hydraulic whine stopped and the vessel canted over as it swung into a tight turn to starboard at a speed of thirty knots. The hiss of water entering the ballast tanks indicated that McKenna had taken her below the surface. On either side of the saloon, the solid screens closed across the viewing panels as Tregenza made the decision to exercise as much caution as he could. He stared at Lindsay, his face drawn.

"He's started his run. Seán's going for her and I don't think he intends to merely cripple her. We've never done that at this sort of speed."

"Brace yourselves!" Lindsay shouted, reaching for a grab handle attached to the forward bulkhead and, with his free hand, holding tightly onto Deanne. The metal vibrated under his grip as the vessel built her speed up to forty knots.

Lindsay gritted his teeth. *The man's gone insane! He's trying to sink her. Jesus, he's actually attempting to ram this boat through a reinforced steel-hulled ship. The stupid bastard's going to kill us all!*

Sharp cries of fear and the jangling of his own nerves merged with the trembling of the hull and the strong, high-pitched whine of the engines as they reached their maximum revolutions. He could feel her spearing through the water as he blinked away the sweat rolling into his eyes.

When it came, the concussion was both sudden and massive. The *Nautilus* gave a huge convulsive jerk, tearing the strongest grip from its hold and hurling bodies across the carpetted floor like so many rag dolls. At the same time, the vessel swerved sharply, yawing heavily to port. Her screw, suddenly thrown into reverse, gave them a further jolt as the submarine backed hurriedly away and came onto an even keel. Lindsay froze, holding his breath, waiting for the inevitable collapse of the hull and the rush of raging water that would be the last thing any of them would see.

It did not happen. Picking himself up, Lindsay ignored his bruises and the flow of blood from a nose that had slammed into some item of furniture, thankfully without breaking. Everyone else seemed shaken but unhurt. He steered Deanne to a seat and made for the buttons that opened the protective plates over the viewing panels. The sound of them sliding back coincided with the whine of hydraulics signalling the raising of the wheelhouse and searchlight.

The depths of a cold, dark sea lit up as the searchlight came on. Only twenty yards from their port side, a huge black mass was sliding down into the abyss, shrouded by swirls and billowing clouds of densely packed bubbles.

Every person crowded to the window, faces white, shocked beyond all belief. In a strange way, the horrific scene beyond the thick glass seemed almost fanciful, detached from reality as though it were part of a cinema movie screened for their benefit.

On the slanting decks of the sinking ship, doomed specks writhed vainly against the fierce eddies and undertows that drew them down with their vessel. Lindsay stared speechlessly at the gaping, jagged-edged wound in the *Emperor's* side and realized that the *Nautilus* was following the dead ship on its downward path. It was both ghoulish and hypnotic.

A sudden, tremendous explosion rocked the *Nautilus* onto her beam-ends as the *Emperor's* boilers blew up, shattering the ship's decks and reducing the superstructure to tangled masses of twisted metal. For a second time, the submarine's crew were pitched helplessly to the floor before she righted herself and, with a surge of venting tanks, began to rise as the *Emperor* vanished downward into eternal night.

A gentle rocking announced their arrival on the surface. The saloon emptied as every last person, sick to their stomachs, lurched to the central stairwell and made for the deck hatch.

The searchlight illuminated a sea still churning from the *Emperor's* demise. It was littered with floating debris but not a single body could be seen, alive or dead. Slow steps sounded on the companionway below and a pale, weary McKenna appeared on deck. Lindsay immediately swung on him.

"So you went and did it then, McKenna," he said coldly. "You used the *Nautilus* to send a ship and its entire crew to the bottom. You put the lives of your own crew on the line and threw away everything you ever stood for. And for what? Revenge? You tell me, McKenna… how sweet does it taste?"

The Irishman stared uncomprehendingly at Lindsay and at a group of disbelieving, accusing expressions. "Just what the hell are you talking about? You have the wrong end of the stick, Commander… you all have. Damn it all, I didn't sink the *Emperor*."

"Let's try that again, McKenna," Lindsay rasped at him. "We all felt the impact and we all saw her go down… and the poor bastards that went with her."

McKenna took a pace forward, standing eyeball to eyeball with him. "Fuck you, Commander," he snarled. "Those 'poor bastards' as you put it, were trying to do precisely the same thing to us. And for the second time. In any case, there was no collision. The *Nautilus* never touched her.

"Oh, I had every intention of taking her rudder right off. Every intention of leaving her helpless hundreds of miles from any shipping lane, all nice and ready for the authorities to come out and grab her. All right, I went at her fast. I didn't only want to rip their rudder away, I wanted them to know they'd been hit. To really feel it. Sure, I let my anger get the better of me but, at the last minute, I took her wide to miss, throttle down and try again at a more sensible speed.

"I never got the chance. We couldn't have been more than fifty yards from her when there was an almighty explosion. I still don't have a clue what it was, or what caused it. The shock wave hit us like a brick wall. It almost stopped us dead in the water, and that's what you felt. The sea was nothing but foam. I couldn't see a bloody thing, so I backed her away."

"Well, if you didn't sink her," Lindsay said suspiciously, "who the hell did?"

McKenna's attempt to respond was cut short by a sudden, unexpected rush of disturbed water and a strong whooshing sound from some point off the port quarter. The crew swung round, startled. From the darkness beyond the searchlight's rays, a light stabbed out. An amplified voice, unmistakeably American, spoke out in the night.

"Good morning, *Nautilus*. I trust you enjoyed the show. The *USS Denver* is happy to have been of service."

60

23 February 2015
Ross Sea
Antarctica

"No one." From the open bridge wing of the *Atlantis*, David Falco surveyed an ocean empty of anything except the rocky hump of Scott Island ten miles to the south. "Not a ship in sight. Are you sure there's nothing on radar, Andy?"

Kristenberg again studied the 360-degree sweep on the screen in front of him. "Nothing. Not a bloody thing within fifty miles of us and we've been right round the island. I tell you, David, we're the only vessel within miles."

Falco joined him in the wheelhouse. "I don't understand this at all." He swung round as Scott Peterson, his communications man, came through from the radio shack, heavy eyebrows drawn with concern.

"There's something damn funny going on here, skipper," he said. "I've been on to Auckland and, according to them, Brian Conran's boat, the *Zephyr*, is on course for the Marquesas. She ain't within three thousand miles of us and never has been."

"What?" Falco pushed a hand through his hair. "Then who the hell radioed us?"

The mate gave a short, humourless laugh. "Oldest trick in the book, skipper, and I'll put any money you like on it being the whaling fleet. The bastards have decoyed us very nicely out of their way and we totally fell for it."

"Except for one thing, Andy," Falco said. "They knew my name."

Kristenberg shrugged. "Not so difficult. If you remember, we were all over the news after that run-in with the *Izu-shoto* last June."

"Of course," Falco groaned. "They'd have logged me then as the skipper of the *Atlantis*. You have to give them top marks for cunning. You know, I still wish I knew what the hell it was that hit the *Izu-shoto*. In fact, I often wonder if it was the same thing that was creating havoc in the North Atlantic a few months back."

He broke off, grabbing hold of the nearest fixture as the entire boat pitched heavily fore-and-aft. Kristenberg had fallen to one knee and got up quickly to stare out through the windscreen.

"What the hell did that?" Falco was saying.

"David!" The mate was pointing forward.

Falco could see it now, a huge, smooth hump of water, its trailing edge ragged with foam, surging ahead of the *Atlantis*. "My God, it went right under the entire length of us," he said. "It has to be big. Blue whale, maybe?"

"By the surge of the water, it couldn't have been more than ten feet under our keel," Kristenberg observed. "I have a very bad feeling about this, skipper."

"You and me both, Andy. You know, we're in the middle of an empty sea but I haven't been able to get rid of a feeling that we're not so alone out here."

What Falco saw next was an uncanny twist of *déjà vu*. Not more than a hundred yards in front of his ship, a black back broke the surface in a surge of white water. Twin plumes of water and vapour shot high into the air as the thing swung over to port in a three-quarter circle to face their own port side. Falco froze at the size of the creature. Its movements seemed menacingly sinister as though it had sensed an enemy and turned to meet the threat.

It was Kristenberg who caught the sudden flash of reflected light from where he guessed the thing's head was likely to be and brought up his binoculars.

"David! That's no animal. It's a machine, for God's sake, a submarine! I can see her plates."

Falco stared at the long, black shape. "Submarine? Who the hell has a sub like that? Have you ever seen a submarine that looks like that, Andy? Every one that I've ever laid eyes on has a damn great fin… oh, no…"

Half a mile beyond the long low shape of the curious vessel, the tall sail and sail-mounted diving planes of the *USS Denver* rose from the grey waves of the Ross Sea.

Holding his breath, Falco watched as the first, entirely unconventional, craft moved skilfully alongside his vessel and came to a smooth stop, its massive screw in reverse. A deck hatch opened and a tall, tow-haired figure stepped out. He looked up, a lop-sided grin on his face.

"Well, don't just stand there gaping, man. Throw us a bloody line. Oh, and while you're about it, Mr Falco, how about a word of thanks for me saving your crew's asses last June?"

Falco grabbed at the rail to stop himself falling over it. "This can't be happening. McKenna? Seán McKenna?"

"And all bar two of the old *Aurora* crew. I'll tell you all about it later but I've a couple of apologies to make first." He jerked a thumb at the *Denver*. "Sorry about bringing a nuclear sub with us but, you know, needs must when the devil drives. And I also apologize for the fake radio message. I had to take a gamble on that, I hadn't a clue where in the world the *Zephyr* might actually be."

Falco scowled at him. "En route to the Marquesas, you Irish bastard. Now, how about you quit grinning at me, get your nasty carcass on board and get a Bushmills down your neck. Why aren't you dead, McKenna? And just what the hell is that thing you're on?"

"Good man yourself," McKenna said. "Come and raid my stock instead in comfort like you've never seen. Come aboard the *Nautilus*, Dave… and that's no joke, believe me. She's the original *Nautilus*. Without a word of a lie, Captain Nemo's boat. This is a story you have to hear." He watched an expression of total incredulity spread over Falco's features. "I'm also sorry to say that you'll have to rub shoulders with a Royal Navy intelligence guy and," he swept a hand towards the approaching *Denver*, "the captain of that radiation bucket."

"After an invitation like that," Falco said. "How could I ever refuse?"

✦

In the saloon of the *Nautilus*, Falco had to admit that McKenna had not been kidding. He didn't have to be told that he was sitting in a treasure house, or that his own mouth was hanging open in sheer disbelief. A glance to one side showed that Captain Fraser of the *USS Denver* was as visibly awe-stricken as himself.

Both men had taken in the story explained to them by a combination of McKenna and Don Lindsay. For once, Falco stopped admiring the size and splendour of the magnificent room he was sitting in to think about the Antarctic coast to the south, the huge waste disposal facility that had secretly been under construction there for years, right under their noses and in complete disregard of every Antarctic treaty and directive ever signed.

Fraser's response was a pragmatic one. "We're talking about international crime and several cold-blooded murders," he said. "This has nothing to do with one nation acting out of line. Several nations are involved here, including my own. Any number of governments across the world stand to take a real hiding over this.

"I find it amazing that none of them is really trying to hide the truth. Every single one, for perhaps the first time in history, wants this rooted out and stopped even though it's all going to be in the public eye. They have no choice but to come clean. They know they can't keep it quiet and a London newspaper, *The Sentinel*, has already begun running an exposé based on the findings of a journalist ten years ago."

"That would be Barrington Hobbes," Lindsay said.

"Yeah, Hobbes, that was the name. I realize that he's dead. That makes two journalists from that newspaper on the death roll. A third death proved a little too much for the editor who appears to be pretty pissed off. For good reason, I'd say."

"A third death?" Karen Marshall said. She had turned pale, anticipating what was to come.

"I'm sorry, Miss Marshall," Fraser said gently. "Your friend Anne Collinson was found dead at her apartment. She had been shot and by an expert, it seems. Death would have been immediate."

Stunned, Karen sat still, tears silently coursing down her face. Alan Tregenza held her close while Jourdan gave Lindsay a hard stare.

Lindsay understood. "Hans-Dieter Wolf," he said. "So that was the task he was ordered to carry out in London before being sent down here."

Fraser cut across him. "You'll be relieved to hear that the hunt for the *Nautilus* is officially over, if you hadn't already guessed it, and that we have a joint objective—to put this facility and the people who run it out of business.

"It's a rush operation. It's risky in that there are just too many unknowns. In any event, it's being put together by Admiral Walter Greene of US Naval Command and by Commander Lindsay's chief, Admiral Garvie. I have the pleasure of knowing both men and their capabilities. A third man called Anderson, a British army brigadier, is also involved as I understand it."

"As we speak, my boat is in contact with both London and Washington and we should have a very nice satellite photograph coming in at any time. A copy will be simultaneously sent to McMurdo Sound where a British special operations force is already waiting for the signal to go in by air-drop. Those guys specialize in both polar operations and demolitions, so you don't need me to tell you what their orders are as regards the Pyramus facility.

"This photograph will give us the precise location. I'm already informed that a permanently open channel leads to it through the pack ice and that will need to be blockaded to prevent the two ships already in there from getting out and away. That is where you, Captain McKenna, and you, Captain Falco, will come in if you choose to do so.

"Again, we are at a disadvantage in that we're painfully short of details. In particular, where the entrances to this underground base are located. We know there's an underwater entrance, through which most of the waste materials and weapons are taken after being unloaded from delivery vessels like the two we'd like to keep penned in there. We know the place has armed defences but not their precise details. The whole damn place is underground and, thanks to the information collected from British Trade Minister Calloway by Captain McKenna and Commander Lindsay, we know they've hollowed out an entire mountain and excavated down to a considerable depth."

Fraser paused and turned to McKenna. "Speaking of Mr Calloway, London is keen to know his whereabouts."

The Irishman gave him a conspiratorial grin. "Many miles from here, Captain Fraser, and doubtless reflecting upon his many and diverse sins. We considered it too hazardous to risk keeping him on the boat so, instead we thought we'd... er, keep him in the dark, so to speak."

"Fair enough," Fraser said. "I won't press the point." He glanced at his watch. "It'll be a while before we have the complete satellite picture and coordinates, so there's a little time to spare for my next request. Captain McKenna, I would like to beg a little favour, if you'd be so kind.

"I'm an old submariner and, like most of my breed, I grew up on Jules Verne. Now I find myself sitting aboard the very boat he wrote about and staring at an actual photograph of Nemo himself. With your permission, I'd sure like a tour of her. I realize you won't be allowing anyone to dissect your engines but I'd appreciate at least a peek at'em."

Rob McLeish stepped forward, taking both Fraser and Falco by the arm. "That, gentlemen, is my department. As an old submariner myself, it'll be my great pleasure to conduct that tour. Starting, of course, with the engine room."

61

24 February 2015
Whitehall
London, UK

"Admiral Greene has arrived, sir," Maureen Strangways announced. Garvie looked up from his desk. "Show him up to the Ops Room, would you, Maureen, and ask Mike Rochester to meet us there. Oh, and Maureen, would you be so kind as to organize a coffee urn. The biggest you can find. I have a feeling this is going to be a long night."

Garvie took the private elevator from his office to the Operations Room where the small, pugnacious figure of Greene awaited him. Garvie strode forward, extending his hand.

"Walter, you look well. How was the flight?"

"Not as fast as I'd have liked it, Jim. Pity the Concorde was ever taken out of service. Sorry to fly over at such short notice but, with an operation as singular as this one is, I felt it would be best coordinated from one place."

"Glad to have you aboard," Garvie smiled approvingly. "Walter," he added as Rochester entered the room, "meet my Chief of Staff, Captain Michael Rochester. Mike, Admiral Walter Greene of the US Naval Command."

Rochester shook the offered hand. "Good to meet you at last, sir."

"Likewise, Captain Rochester. I gather it was your idea to get our sub to tag the *Nautilus*. It was good thinking. We had no other way of warning her about the operation."

"Thank you, admiral, I'm just glad that it worked out."

More introductions took place a minute or so later with the arrival of the tall, trim figure of Brigadier Neil Anderson. Garvie then went straight into business. "Walter, Neil, we're in direct contact with our special forces at McMurdo Sound and with the US submarine *Denver* which, thanks to Mike here, has teamed up with the *Nautilus* and also with a Greenpeace boat. Don't ask me how that came about. Captain Fraser of the *Denver* has kept me fully up to date. Comes across as a first rate officer."

"I can assure you he is, Jim," Greene cut in. "He doesn't know it yet, but he's in line for promotion to Rear-Admiral at the next review. He'll get it, too."

"He was happy to give me one piece of good news," Garvie said. "We no longer have to worry ourselves about the Japanese nuclear attack submarine. It would appear that she went after the *Nautilus*—just as you warned me, Walter—and came off second best. I have no idea how the *Nautilus* pulled that off, bearing in mind that she carries no armaments of her own."

"I can fill in the missing pieces there, Jim," Greene told him. "I've already seen Fraser's report. The *Denver* picked up the whole thing on sonar. To cut it as short as I can, the *Honshu* loosed off two torpedoes. The *Nautilus* somehow evaded the first one, then went deep enough for the second to implode under the pressure. The Japanese boat went down after her but the *Nautilus* just kept going deeper still.

"I don't believe the Japanese captain had the slightest idea what that old sub is capable of. He probably thought to bluff it out and play chicken until the *Nautilus* either went too deep and caved in, or was forced to come up. She did neither. The *Honshu* must have exceeded her own crush depth… she imploded."

"After your signal, and Captain Rochester's suggestion, the *Denver* then kept on the *Nautilus's* tail and, a couple of days ago, a second incident happened. Fraser had a periscope view of most of it.

"The *Nautilus* surfaced and there seemed to be some sort of discussion on deck. He counted eight or nine people, three of them women. They went back below and the sub dived. Fraser stayed where he was and, according to his sonarman, the *Nautilus* went straight down and all the way to the bottom. That, gentlemen, is ten thousand feet.

"Now, here's a thought for you. The position was precisely that radioed in by the Deep Watch ship *Aurora* just before she was lost, and it was a year to the very day since that occurred."

"And now we know that the people on the *Nautilus* are the *Aurora's* survivors," Rochester said. "They claim they were deliberately rammed and sunk by a Pyramus vessel steaming north from Antarctic waters, and that the ship in question was named the *Emperor*. I wonder if they went down to record the evidence of how the *Aurora* was sunk so that they could get the *Emperor's* captain charged with murder?"

"The *Emperor*, by God," Greene said strangely. "You'd better hear the rest of this. When the *Nautilus* resurfaced an hour or so later, she found herself under heavy fire from a merchant ship carrying concealed weaponry."

"Like the old Q-ships in the last war?" Garvie observed.

"Quite so. Now, hear this. The attacking vessel was the *Emperor*. Fraser got the name clearly through the periscope.

"The *Nautilus* acted real strange here. Instead of diving and getting the hell away, she stayed topside and started playing tag, letting the other ship chase her. At times she'd let the *Emperor* get within firing range, then go charging off. According to Fraser, she has one hell of a turn of speed.

"She kept this up until it got dark then, of all the fool things to do, the *Nautilus* switched on that damned great light of hers, deliberately letting the *Emperor* know exactly where she was. Fraser had a hell of a job keeping up with all this but he says that, at one point, the *Nautilus* was physically running circles around a ship that was itself doing thirty knots. Craziest behaviour I ever heard of.

"Fraser reported that she then slowed down until she was well within range. The *Emperor's* guns really opened up at that point. Shells were impacting all round her, and then she submerged. The *Denver* heard the *Nautilus* powering up and concluded that she was initiating a ramming run. She was only a fathom or so under the surface, still with her searchlight on to begin with. The *Emperor* just kept right on firing, at which point Fraser decided that enough was enough. He couldn't fire torpedoes for fear of hitting the *Nautilus* so, instead, he banged a pair of tube-launched Harpoon anti-ship missiles into the *Emperor*. She went down like a rock."

Garvie pursed his lips. "That old submarine seems to have more lives than a yard full of cats," he commented. "In the end, though, it seems that justice might well have been done."

He broke off as the door opened for his secretary to admit the Prime Minister and Sir Henry Williamson. "Sorry to breeze in unannounced," the Premier said. "Sir Henry advised me that things were about to come to a head so, as we were passing on our way to an all-night sitting in the House, I thought we might drop by and keep ourselves up to date."

The admiral introduced Greene and gave a brief summary of events, embellished by additional information from the American. The Prime Minister and Sir Henry listened intently to both men.

"Admiral Greene," the Premier said. "You say the *Denver's* captain has actually been aboard the *Nautilus*. Was there any sign of Gerald Calloway?"

"No, sir. He wasn't aboard. McKenna apparently said something about keeping him in the dark to repent his sins, whatever that means. I assume they locked him up somewhere en route. I would suggest some location in the Mediterranean. The *Nautilus* didn't go in there purely to take her short cut into the Red Sea. She was there at least two days longer than she needed to have been, but nobody yet knows why. She called in somewhere, that's a sure bet."

Garvie turned to Rochester. "Let's see the satellite picture, Chief."

The latest photograph showed an area just fifteen miles square. Projected on the wall to a huge size, it was clear enough for fine details to be picked out. Using a pointer, Garvie indicated the likely site of the Pyramus disposal site within its mountain peninsula and the clear water channel that led to it through the pack ice.

"This channel," he instructed, "is just over ten miles in length and varies from six hundred to eight hundred yards in width. A third of the way in is this pinch point just two hundred yards wide.

"Now, as it stands, the plan is for the *Nautilus* and this Greenpeace ship to form a blockade at the pinch point to deny exit passage to these ships." His pointer tapped at the pair of cargo vessels moored against the side of the peninsula. This will leave the *Denver* free to carry out the underwater surveillance that I'll come to in a moment.

"The airdrop is due to take place at 0900 local time, or 2000 GMT, a little over two hours from now. Lieutenant Colonel Byrd and his men will be taking off from McMurdo Sound in roughly an hour's time and I must say I don't envy their HALO jump from fifteen thousand feet in polar temperatures."

"HALO?" the Prime Minister queried.

"High Altitude, Low Opening," Brigadier Anderson explained. "It's a hazardous technique, to say the least. The plane needs to be high to minimize detection, the men freefall for thousands of feet, not opening their chutes until the last possible moment."

"Good Heavens, rather them than me."

"I quite agree, sir, but all these men have done this before. The selected landing site is here." His pointer tapped a snow covered area inland from the Pyramus site. "It's a flat plateau at twelve hundred feet above sea level, but less than one mile from the target."

Williamson interrupted at this point. "Why not the ice shelf adjacent to the peninsula? It looks flat enough to me."

"We're uncertain of its thickness and stability, sir," Garvie replied. "The picture shows it to be pretty seamed and these darker areas are what we call polynyas, areas of thin ice and even open water. There do seem to be areas of solid thickness but the possibility of katabatic winds rushing down the slope from the plateau would make landing accuracy far too hazardous. If just one of our men got blown into one of those polynyas, he'd freeze to death in minutes."

The Minister of Defence nodded his understanding.

"The object of the operation," Garvie continued, "is to secure the Pyramus facility, arrest its personnel and seal it permanently with explosive charges in such a way that its shafts will collapse and render it totally unusable. Colonel Byrd's men are particularly talented when it comes to demolition. Later, it will be essential to seal the site properly to ensure there is no leakage from the materials stored inside"

"And the problems?" the Prime Minister asked.

"Twofold. We have detected no clear signs of any surface entrance and Byrd's men are going to have to locate it by themselves. As for the underwater entrance, it is the *Denver's* intention to go in under the ice, use its full range of sensors to locate it and then she will use torpedoes to destroy and seal it.

"Secondly, we have Calloway's testimony as to the sort of defences that Pyramus has put in place here. We do not have specific details but the gist of what Calloway said is that they are not to be taken lightly. With these disadvantages, gentlemen, I regret to say that we may well suffer some casualties before we can shut this place down."

"It would surely be easier to destroy the place with a well-placed nuclear missile," the Premier observed.

Greene shook his head emphatically. "No, sir, for good reason. There are nuclear warheads stored within that facility. These would not and cannot react to destruction by conventional explosives but a nuclear strike could well ignite a sympathetic detonation. In that case, even a low-level nuclear strike could create a holocaust taking everything out within a twenty mile radius, including your men and our vessels, and poison a large part of the Antarctic continent for centuries.

"Technically, we are breaching the Antarctic Treaty simply by having a nuclear powered boat there at all. Now, we believe that small indiscretion will be forgiven once weighed against the greater evil. The cooperation of the Greenpeace boat confirms that much. If, however, we used nuclear weapons down there, the world at large would never, ever, forgive us."

"So it's effectively one warship and a handful of men against a fortress," the Prime Minister said gloomily. "I don't like the odds, Admiral. I don't like them at all."

62

Southern Ross Sea
Antarctica

"Goddammit!" Byron Fraser, gazing out from the top of the *Denver's* sail, was far from pleased. "Goddammit all to hell and back!"

On the bridge wing of the *Atlantis*, ten feet below him, David Falco looked up in mild surprise. "What a thing to say," he commented. "And on such a beautiful morning, too."

It was, as he said, a beautiful beginning to the day. The low sun shone from a cloudless sky of eggshell blue. Between the dazzling ice sheets, the clear water of the channel was a deep ultramarine. All three vessels, the *Atlantis* and the two submarines flanking her, one of them a spanking new, hi-tech giant, the other a miracle of nineteenth century engineering, lay outside the pinch point of the channel. Six miles away, the rocky cone of the peninsula concealing the Pyramus site formed a small mountain rising seven hundred feet above the flat icy wastes, its white-coated sides seamed with black streaks of exposed rock. Beyond its low, narrow isthmus, the terrain swept steeply upward to the inland plateau.

"And a lousy fucking morning for a war," Fraser growled as the combined crews of the *Atlantis* and the *Nautilus* gathered on the deck of the Greenpeace vessel. "Goddamned weathermen. Just look at it, will you? Crystal clear visibility for us, and just perfect for the other side. The element of surprise blown all to hell. Those British guys will be dropping out of the sky at any moment and the people in that base will have a front-row view of them, just as they have of us.

"I know you people tend to be pacifists. Well, it might surprise you, coming from an old warrior like me, but in essence, so am I. I don't drive this boat for the purpose of blowing the world to kingdom come. I drive it to ensure that other people don't do it. I wanted this operation to be a simple matter of going in, shutting the damned place down and rounding up the people in it. The smoother, the cleaner, the less blood spilt, the better."

He shook a fist at the clear sky. "We wanted fog. The goddamn forecasters said we'd have low-level fog. Guaranteed it, damn their eyes. Now, none of us can go in unseen and those guys over there are gonna hold out for all they're worth. It's going to be bloody and there's no way of avoiding it."

"Bloody's the word," Lindsay said. "The Pyramus people will be led by one of the worst butchers on record. Hans-Dieter Wolf. Remember that name, captain? The Linden Wolf?"

"The *Stasi* guy? Is that bastard still alive?"

"Still alive, still killing. He just has new employers. Pyramus moved him down here to head up their security a few weeks ago."

Fraser said something unintelligible and trained his binoculars on the Pyramus mountain. "Looks to me like those two freighters are preparing to pull out," he said. "They'll try to run our blockade. If they get within two miles I'll give a single radio warning. If, after that, they fail to stop, I'll have no choice but to put a torpedo into one of them. I'll keep it to low charge, just enough to make them reconsider.

"There's going to have to be a change of plan, Commander. The underwater topography hereabouts is mostly unknown. We've put a full sensor array onto it and we find there's a deep, steep-sided canyon under this channel that looks to be too constricted for us to safely manoeuvre a boat the size of the *Denver*. Nevertheless, I have to know if there's a clear field of fire to the facility's underwater entrance.

"Added to that is the fact that those two freighters are bigger than we originally thought. If they wanted to break out, they could roll right over the *Atlantis* and the *Nautilus*. They couldn't achieve that against a boat of this size, particularly as she has teeth.

"You told me that the *Nautilus* can be piloted solo, Commander. I'm going to need her to go in and scout out the terrain. She's not much more than half the length of my boat and a damn sight more manoeuvrable..."

Fraser broke off suddenly and checked his watch. "Right on time." He pointed high to the south. The score of white specks drifting lazily down above the plateau were clearly visible against the cloudless blue of the sky. There was neither sight nor sound of a plane and Lindsay guessed that it had been a HALO jump.

The American submarine captain resumed his briefing. "You'll have to drive the *Nautilus*, Commander—"

"Now, wait just a damned minute," McKenna broke in angrily. Fraser cut him short.

"I appreciate that she's your boat, captain, but I can't risk civilians on a military operation. We don't know what defences they may have under the surface. Lindsay knows submarines. He's still a serving officer of the Royal Navy. You were prepared to risk your boat alone until we showed up. I'm asking you to let us do this if you want that place shut down."

The Irishman looked furious. Lindsay laid a hand on his shoulder. "Don't fret, Seán. I'll take good care of her. In any case, you wouldn't see a thing from down there. Here, you have a grandstand seat. You've waited a whole year for this. Come on, Seán, let me do this."

All attention was on Lindsay. Fraser and McKenna. No one saw the figure that slipped over the *Atlantis's* opposite rail onto the deck of the *Nautilus* and into the submarine's open hatch.

McKenna bit his lip. "Very well, Commander, but I don't like the idea of you going in alone."

"It's what I do, Seán."

"Commander Lindsay," Fraser barked from his perch on the *Denver's* sail. "Any problems and you get out fast. Is that clear?"

Lindsay glanced across at the snow-clad mainland, spotting the first of the paratroops making his landing approach under the wide parasail. *There's no time to waste. God, this has all the makings of a bloody shambles.*

"Clear, sir!" he shouted, turning away quickly to board the *Nautilus*. He vaulted onto her deck, cast off the mooring lines and entered the hatch, securing it firmly before making his way to the wheelhouse. As usual, she handled like a dream as he skimmed her away across the glassy waters of the ice-free channel and took her down under the ice.

Byron Fraser watched the ancient submarine slide effortlessly below the surface. *Old she may be*, he thought, *but that is one fine boat.* He glanced down at the *Atlantis's* deck, taking in the drawn, worried faces of McKenna and his colleagues. *And a fine set of people, too.*

Don Lindsay only had to take the boat down to a depth of sixty feet to clear the deepest reaches of the icefield. The water was crystal clear, giving him a good field of visibility without the need to use the searchlight. The sunlight diffusing through the ice above him gave the water a translucent turquoise-green hue, indescribably beautiful, but Lindsay had no time to admire the effect.

A check of the echo sounder told him that the water was deep under his keel, more than 450 fathoms, while side-scan sonar picked out the walls of the submarine canyon, little more than three quarters of a mile wide at this point. Logically, he thought, it would narrow towards the coast.

There was no visible sign that the channel had been mined but he had no way of knowing if a passive sonar array was picking up his approach. He would just have to risk that possibility. He gave himself the chance to do a quick all-round look out of the wheelhouse's four view ports. Brighter light to starboard gave him the position of the open channel and certainly, this far at least, there were no outcroppings that would prevent Fraser's torpedoes a clear run at the facility's underwater entrance. Now it was a matter of finding that entrance, letting go a single active sonar pulse to give Fraser the exact bearing, then getting to hell out of it.

Lindsay made the decision to play it as safe as he could and make his approach from under the landward ice shelf, the direction from which any intruder might be least expected. He estimated that there was little more than a mile and a half between himself and the Pyramus mountain.

He veered the submarine to starboard, throttling down to ensure near-silence. At his touch, the *Nautilus* skimmed beneath the open channel and under the ice on its far side, her engines carrying her silently at under five knots. Here, even the keenest of sensors would receive only confused echoes from the uneven underside of the ice, and the endless growling and cracking as masses of ice ground against each other. The *Nautilus* would now be as completely concealed as it was possible to achieve.

An unexpected voice broke into his thinking. "Need a helping hand, Don?" Startled, Lindsay twisted around as Deanne Fischer climbed up into the cramped wheelhouse.

"You little fool," he gasped. "What the hell are you doing here?"

She gave him the sweetest of smiles. "It's the least a girl can do. If you thought for one moment that I was about to let you do this alone, you were very wrong. In any case, two heads are better than one."

The glare that Lindsay gave her was hollow. For good or ill, this was a girl who was ready and willing to be at his side, no matter what. *You lucky bastard*, he told himself.

"Damn it, Dee," he said. "Get yourself into the other seat and strap in tight. This little jaunt could turn rough at any time."

She did precisely as he told her and peered out through the thick view ports. "This ice is almost transparent," she observed. "How thick would you say it is?"

"At a guess, twenty feet or so," he answered. "Thin enough for sunlight to penetrate."

"Well, something up there isn't transparent," she said, pointing upwards through the starboard port.

Lindsay craned his neck to look up. He quickly caught sight of what she had seen, a large oblong shadow crawling across the surface of the ice above them. At the same time, the sound of muffled explosions penetrated the water and the submarine's double hull. He felt the hollowness of tension in his stomach.

"It's started," he said.

With a considerable amount of relief, Byron Fraser saw that the two cargo ships had heeded his radio warning and come to a halt two miles away, clearly unwilling to challenge the 360-foot, six thousand ton nuclear attack submarine that barred their way.

His grin of satisfaction didn't last long. White bursts of smoke, tinged with orange flame, erupted in unison from the base of the Pyramus mountain. A brace of shells roared towards his vessel, crashing into water and ice a quarter mile short.

From the *Atlantis*, Falco shouted up to him. "We're under fire, captain! What do we do now?"

"I stay put and do nothing, Mr Falco. However, I'd advise you to take your vessel back a mile or so. It's my guess that we're marginally out of range, although I wouldn't care to put money on it. This could be a ploy to scare us into backing off in order to give their two vessels a better chance of getting past us in the wider part of the channel. I'll warn them again that if they try it, I'll put both of them on the bottom without hesitation."

"Well, if you're taking the risk, captain, I might as well stick around as well. I'll hide behind you if necessary."

Fraser gave Falco a grin of appreciation and trained his binoculars on the foot of the mountain. There was some kind of movement there. He steadied the glasses against the coaming, concentrating his gaze on the massive shape that was crawling across the surface of the ice shelf. From this distance, it looked like a caterpillar-tracked vehicle on the Sno-Cat principle, but a good deal larger. Above its elevated cab, he could make out a clustered arrangment of tubes that were being raised to line up with the slope leading down from the plateau.

My God, they have a mobile ground-to-ground missile launcher! Fraser's blood ran cold as he realized that, however good Byrd's men might be, they would stand no chance against that sort of firepower on an exposed hillside. He turned to his Executive Officer.

"Get Byrd on the radio. Warn him off, and for Christ's sake make it quick."

The XO disappeared down the hatch and Fraser raised the glasses to scan the mountain once again. Something was now happening near the top of the cone-shaped outcrop. A square black opening had suddenly appeared and an object was rising slowly from within. To Fraser, it looked horribly like a further array of missiles which were slowly turning his direction.

He sucked in his breath. *Now, that we surely didn't know about, and it makes for a whole new ball-game.* His immediate orders over the bridge telephone were brief, clear and precise before raising the binoculars once more, this time rather more anxiously. *How long before that thing's up and ready to launch? Sixty seconds? Ninety? My guys need to break all known records if we're gonna be faster to the draw.*

"I have a nasty feeling," Lindsay said, "that these bastards have got themselves a mobile missile launcher. Judging by the direction it's going, I have an even nastier thought that it's after the paratroops."

Deanne went cold. "If you're right, they won't have a hope. Not against missiles. Is there nothing we can do?"

"Nothing short of smashing through the ice under him but, if it's thick enough to support his weight, it'll be too thick for us to break through it."

The brilliant flash was so sudden that Lindsay and Deanne recoiled too late to prevent being dazzled. A thunderous noise shook the hull of the *Nautilus*. Huge blocks of ice cracked off from the ragged underbelly of the ice shelf, sinking slowly before rising again to bump against the solid ceiling.

"Hell, Deanne, he's fired one off!" Lindsay took a deep breath as his eyes began to readjust. "We have to think of something. How are your eyes?"

"Clearing."

"Look out for a polynya. Thin ice, open water, I don't care which. The closer to that bastard the better and we need to find it fast."

Alone in the cabin of the mobile missile launcher, Hans-Dieter Wolf allowed himself a leering smile as his first missile impacted and exploded on the icy slopes above him. His binocular viewfinder revealed a flurry of activity on the hill, distant, ghostly figures barely discernable in their polar whites, scuttling for what scant cover there was as fragments of rock and ice rained down on them. Wolf's pale, cold eyes picked out a limp figure, either wounded or dead, being dragged into shelter and the German's thick lips stretched into a grin of pure malevolence.

He judged his first shot to have been acceptably close but, if anything, too far to the left. At the very least, it had pinned the assault force down and there was at least one of them who would play no further part. They were going nowhere, especially in view of the fact that his giant vehicle held another eleven missiles, all fully armed and awaiting the mere touch of a button.

Just half a degree to the right. Wolf carefully made the adjustment, knowing that he had no need to rush it. His range had already proved to be perfect. Now, he thought, perhaps a full salvo to finish it. A sledgehammer to crack a nut, maybe, but there was nothing like being certain.

Wolf's thumb flipped open the guard over the firing button and hovered half an inch above it.

"Thin ice!" Deanne was pointing directly ahead at a point where the sunlight's penetration of the ice was noticeably stronger. Lindsay moved the boat closer.

"It could be good. It doesn't look to be more than a foot or so thick."

"Can we surface through it?"

"Not in the conventional sense," Lindsay said. "We're not going to stop him by simply popping our heads up. That would only give him another static target."

Deanne's expression turned to one of sheer horror, realizing what Lindsay meant to do. Lindsay could see that she had latched onto his crazy idea.

"There's no choice. This has to be drastic," he defended. "The only way to stop this bastard is to take him out. Make sure your straps are tight and adjust the headrest for the maximum possible protection. There could be one hell of a whiplash effect from this."

"Don, you're not serious about this?"

"Never more so. Every second we waste could cost lives. Those guys on the hill are totally defenceless against a missile attack. Now brace, Dee, and brace hard!"

Lindsay peered out to locate the telltale shadow of the launcher, taking careful note of its bearing and distance from the centre of the polynya above him. He steeled himself to the task in hand and took the *Nautilus* deeper, powering up her engines as he did so. At a depth of two hundred feet, he turned her tightly, banking her round and bringing her nose up to a steep angle pointing directly at the centre of the area of thin ice that was easily visible even at that depth. The acceleration to full speed slammed them both back in their seats.

The tremble that carried through every part of the submarine's hull could be felt in every fibre of their bodies. Already, Deanne's eyes were tight shut, her breath held and her hands gripping the armrests until they were chalk-white.

"Three seconds!" Lindsay's voice was hoarse as the underbelly of the ice, now looking to him like solid concrete, raced at the sharp prow of the *Nautilus*.

"Mister Falco!" Telephone in hand, Fraser called down to the *Atlantis's* skipper, who glanced up sharply. "I said that I don't drive this boat to blow the world to blazes. Sadly, my friend, there are times when you just don't have a choice. Keep your heads down right now!

"Tube Five... LAUNCH! Tube Six... LAUNCH!"

Startled, Falco saw a violent burst of bubbles at the *Denver*'s bow, then a twin burst of spray as the two TLAM Block IV Tomahawks broke surface. Immediately, their rocket motors fired, accelerating the missiles to flight speed with roaring tails of fire. Within seconds, the rockets cut out for the turbofan engines to take over, propelling the two twenty-foot cruise missiles on an almost silent six-mile flight that would take them just forty seconds to complete.

Hans-Dieter Wolf's thumb still hovered steadily over the bright red firing button as his free hand lowered the viewfinder to his eyes. The section of snowy hillside, with its sharply contrasting streaks of black rock where the assault troops lay helpless, was at dead centre of his sights.

His evil grin of triumph froze on his face.

Just fifty yards in front of him, the smooth unblemished surface of the ice erupted like a frozen volcano. Immense, razor-edged shards of ice a foot thick were blasted into the air from a billowing cloud of snow and ice fragments.

A dark, huge shape burst from the blindingly white cloud at tremendous speed, airborne for an instant, then bellying onto the surface of the ice field with a stupendous crash. The entire ice shelf shook with the impact of sixteen hundred tons dead weight, as the hurtling *Nautilus* crashed onto it.

Wolf's involuntary paralysis of shock, as the massive shape of the ancient submarine skidded uncontrollably across the ice towards him, saved lives on the hill and claimed his own.

Even as the stranglehold of stupefaction loosened its grip, he had no time to take evasive action, no time even to scream as the sharp ram of the *Nautilus* exploded through the windshield of his cabin and Wolf's own torso, virtually severing the German in two and pinning his mutilated remains to the back of his seat and the bulkhead behind him. A scarlet fountain burst inside the cramped cabin space.

The sheer force of the collision slewed both the massive launch vehicle and the *Nautilus* around in a half circle, spraying snow and ice high into the freezing air as the dead man's thumb, in a reflex of death, clamped onto the firing control.

All eleven missiles streaked away in a thunder of smoke and flame.

On the hillside a mile or so away, Lieutenant-Colonel Byrd's special forces found themselves occupying a grandstand seat. Six hundred feet below them, billows of snow, ice, smoke and fire swirled over the ice shelf as the missiles shot away on erratic courses.

Two of them converged, collided and blew up in mid-flight with a thunderclap of sound and flame. The remainder, falling, rising, twisting in flight, slammed into the mountainside above the Pyramus complex at 400 mph in a series of ear-splitting blasts.

In the same moment, the *Denver's* two Tomahawks, streaking in at 550mph just half a second and ten feet apart, speared into the missile array opening, their 1000lb warheads exploding within feet of its arsenal. White-hot flame, gouts of fire-tinged smoke and chunks of rock the size of houses burst outward with stunning force. Inside the complex, searing incandescence shot along shafts and tunnels at lightning speed, instantly incinerating everything and everyone in its path.

Under the mountain, eight thousand conventional high-explosive warheads stored and stacked in the higher levels, erupted in sympathetic detonation. Beneath a stupendous, rolling billow of fire, the mountain disappeared.

On the opposite hill, Lieutenant Colonel Vernon Byrd watched in rapt fascination as the appalling destruction came to completion. The echoes of explosion after explosion clapped and resonated around the mountainous Antarctic terrain until, at last, an uneasy silence descended, broken only by the rumbling of distant avalanches set off by the same shock waves that had, for a moment, deadened his own hearing.

Byrd and his men looked down at the ice shelf. The snowcloud was beginning to dissipate, revealing the slender, exposed shape of the stranded *Nautilus*, heeled halfway onto her port side, her sharp beak embedded in the tangled remains of the huge rocket launcher. In front of their horrified gaze, the surface of the ice around the two forcibly locked craft starred like the shattered windscreen of a car, cracking and splitting apart with sounds like volleys of gunfire.

The wreck of the launch vehicle went through first, dragging the trapped submarine nose-first behind it into the black depths beneath. Byrd saw the vessel's stern rear vertically into the air before plunging through at frightening speed, leaving nothing on the surface but a jagged, foam-filled hole, dotted with bobbing blocks of ice.

Donall Lindsay moved fast, fighting to stave off the stunning effects of the collision as the huge weight of the missile launcher dragged the *Nautilus* through the ice. Suspended by the straps that bit into him as she began her nose-first dive, he frantically tried and tried again to restart the engines, which had stalled upon the initial impact with the ice. He needed those engines, needed them desperately, for the power of reverse thrust to either shake them loose from the doomed launcher or to slow their descent sufficently to minimize the collision with the sea floor sixteen hundred feet down.

The engines stubbornly refused to respond.

Lindsay punched the ballast tank vent controls to drive every last drop of water from the tanks. For a moment, their headlong descent seemed to slow but it was not nearly enough. His heart pounded against his ribs as he stared out through the forward port, through a dark red cloud and straight into the dead eyes and horribly contorted features of Hans-Dieter

Wolf. Then, thankfully, the darkness of the rapidly increasing depth blotted out the awful vision.

There had been no sound from Deanne. A quick glance round at the mottled contusion on the hairline of her temple showed that she'd been stunned by crashing into the back of his own seat. Suspended facedown as he was, he had no way of telling if she had suffered any further injury. Not that it mattered now. At least she would have no awareness of the end when it came.

The depth gauge needle was moving alarmingly fast. Lindsay gritted his teeth.

Dear God in Heaven, this is not good news…

Just as the words came into his thoughts, the missile launcher and the *Nautilus*, still locked firmly together, slammed into the ocean floor at sickening speed.

For Lindsay, there was only a flash of light, followed by utter darkness.

63

25 February 2015
Downing Street
London, UK

Britain's Prime Minister rose from behind his desk as a weary looking Admiral Garvie was shown into his office.

"James," he greeted, shaking the admiral by the hand. "What news?"

Garvie sank into a seat. "Well, the upshot is that the Pyramus facility no longer exists," he said.

"You mean it's destroyed? Everything went according to plan, then?"

"To be brutally honest, sir, not a bloody thing went to plan."

The Prime Minister eyed him with concern, appreciative of the fact that the ageing admiral had not slept for at least thirty-six hours.

"I've received any number of encrypted signals from the *Denver*," the admiral went on, "the American submarine on the scene. To cut a long story short, sir, it was every bit of a bugger's muddle from start to finish. The fog that was so confidently forecast failed to show up so that the entire surprise element was not only shot to pieces but had the effect of giving every advantage to the other side.

"The *Denver* and the Greenpeace boat were blockading the entrance channel. They found themselves under threat from a missile array on the mountaintop after being kept at distance by a gun battery. At the same time, the Pyramus people used a mobile missile launcher against Colonel Byrd's troops. I regret to say that they sustained one dead and two injured and it could easily have been a sight worse than that.

"At that point, Commander Lindsay and a member of the *Nautilus* crew, a woman by all accounts, decided to take things into their own hands. At Captain Fraser's request, they'd already gone in to scout out the underwater approach and then the missile launcher opened up against Colonel Byrd. Lindsay crashed the submarine up through the ice from below and rammed the launcher. The force of the collision knocked the launcher askew, its entire battery of missiles went off, straight into the Pyramus complex and blowing it to blazes. Two cruise missiles launched from the *Denver* hit simultaneously. It seems that all the conventional HE already stored there went up as well. The mountain effectively collapsed into itself and there's literally nothing left."

"What about the decommissioned nuclear warheads that were stored there as well?" the Premier asked, horrified.

Garvie shook his head. "They would not have reacted at all. They're still there, buried under millions of tons of rock and totally out of reach."

"So your man Lindsay came good in the end," the Prime Minister said. "He justified your own faith in him."

"Yes, sir, he most certainly did." Garvie paused, looking strained. "The two Pyramus vessels were boarded and are being escorted away by the *Denver* as we speak. Their crews are confined in the holds under the armed supervision of Colonel Byrd's men. Ships of the New Zealand Navy are on their way to intercept and take them into proper custody. The wounded are being cared for in the *Denver's* sick-bay.

"The Marshall woman, the journalist that partnered Barrington Hobbes before his death, is at present on the Greenpeace ship along with the rest of the *Nautilus* crew. Reports say that she is rounding off a complete story for the Press."

"Oh, my God." The Premier looked crestfallen. "I can't say that you didn't warn me about this."

"She can't be stopped," the admiral said.

The Prime Minister sat down in his chair. "James, this whole affair implicates government ministers and senior industrialists in a dozen major countries. When this story breaks, it's bound to create instability in international markets and politically, too. Stock markets will collapse and galloping global recession will follow as sure as eggs are eggs. Once these things start, there's no stopping them. They snowball until there's total chaos. Prices will spiral out of control and wages will not be able to keep pace. Then we'll get industrial unrest and strikes. All the work that went into the economic stability we have now will go belly up overnight. It's a nightmare, James, and I happen to be in the chair when it breaks. History will blow my reputation to pieces."

Garvie felt a twinge of pity for the beleaguered Premier. "I can't say that I've ever envied you or your predecessors in this job, sir," he said. "Prime Ministers tend to get bogged down and stifled by policies, doctrines and the outdated conventions that surround them. I've mentioned before that, in this instance, you do have an opportunity to break that mould."

"You could be right, James." The Premier regarded the admiral with respect. "The normal reaction of any government to the culpability of its own members has been to bury as much of the story as humanly possible and issue official denials until the public is sick of hearing about it.

"I intend to buck that trend. The civil servants and several others will go apoplectic but I do not intend to change my mind. I will go on the air before the Marshall woman's story breaks and come clean about the entire affair. I will hide nothing.

"Furthermore, I have decided to take the lead in setting up a world environmental summit. This will consist of world leaders and of experts from both scientific fields and from the various pressure groups. I see their experience and first-hand knowledge as essential in formulating international policies that could, for once, have a chance of working."

Garvie nodded his approval. "You could do worse than to publicize that as well, sir. *The Sentinel* in Fleet Street will have the world exclusive on Miss Marshall's story and its editor, Tony Saunders, has a solid reputation for responsible journalism. If I could perhaps suggest a chat with him?"

The Premier smiled for the first time that day. "I'm grateful to you, James. Not only for your advice but also for your guidance throughout this whole sorry affair. I'm more than grateful. Tell me, has my former Minister for Trade and Industry been located yet?"

"I'm afraid not. We have no idea where he was incarcerated."

The Prime Minister reflected. "Perhaps it would be for the best if he was never found." He gave the admiral a meaningful glance.

Garvie shook his head emphatically. "With the greatest respect, sir, my service is not an assassination squad. My operatives may, from time to time, be forced to kill under life-threatening circumstances but none of them would ever consent to carry out an execution in cold blood. Nor would I ever issue any such order."

"No, of course not," the Premier sighed. "I'm sorry, James. Put it from your mind."

"In any case, sir," Garvie said quietly. "The only one of my officers who would even know where to start looking for Gerald Calloway was Commander Lindsay."

The Premier's eyebrows drew together sharply. "You said 'was'."

Garvie drew a long breath and, again, the Prime Minister could see the lines of fatigue in his face. "As I understand it, the *Nautilus* was locked fast to the missile launcher after the collision. The ice gave way beneath them and both went down in an uncontrollable descent. There is something like sixteen hundred feet of water in that spot and they would have hit the bottom at lethal speed.

"Nothing has been heard from Commander Lindsay since then. The place in which this happened is a narrow underwater canyon too restricted for a boat the size of the *Denver* to have entered and searched safely. Nonetheless, she fired in signal after signal, sonar pulse after sonar pulse. There has been no response of any sort.

"I deeply regret to say, sir, that both my officer and that wonderful old submarine are irretrievably lost."

64

26 February 2015
Southern Ross Sea
Antarctica

In the wardroom of the Greenpeace vessel *Atlantis*, David Falco placed a mug of strong coffee in front of Karen Marshall. Surrounded by paper and sat in front of Falco's own computer screen, she was red-eyed through overwork, lack of sleep and grief at the loss of the *Nautilus* and of Anne Collinson.

Falco gestured at the mass of paper. "How's it coming?"

"I've just about finished," she said wearily.

"Well done. You can put it out just as soon as you like," Falco said. "We have everything you need right here on the *Atlantis* to get it to *The Sentinel* via satellite relay. No expense spared. It can all be on the front pages within twenty-four hours."

"I can't," she smiled weakly. "Not yet. Not until we know what's happened to Don and Deanne on the *Nautilus*."

Robin McLeish, looking lined and older than his years, placed a fatherly hand on her shoulder. "Face it, lass, they're gone. Yon Colonel Byrd saw her go down, nose-first and straight to the bottom. The *Denver's* sonarman heard the sounds of impact and break-up on the bottom. Nothing could have survived that. In any case, there's been not a sound since." The engineer's voice began to break up and he blinked back tears. "We just have to face up to it. We've lost two brave wee souls and the best bluidy ship ever built."

Karen patted his hand. "You loved that boat every bit as much as Captain Nemo did, isn't that true, Rob? You said it yourself, she is the best ship ever built. She's survived a volcanic eruption and a hundred years in the ice. She's defied the Maelstrom twice. She took us to ten thousand feet under the sea. What's to say she can't survive this, Rob? You can't just lose hope, and I won't." She looked from McLeish to Falco. "Give them another day, please."

Falco ran a hand through his hair. Other members of both crews had come into the room, each of their faces telling him what decision he should make. "Okay," he conceded. "You win. We're the only ship left in the area now and it won't hurt to stick around a while longer. Twenty-four hours it is."

"Thank you, captain," Karen said, greatly relieved. McKenna simply went up to his old friend and shook Falco's hand gratefully. Karen got to her feet, flexing her cramped joints painfully. "I need a stroll on deck to loosen up before I seize up completely," she said.

Alan Tregenza went with her. Above the *Atlantis*, the sky was darkening, a deep blue flecked by wisps of cirrus cloud tinged with pink by a low red sun. The ship rolled gently on a soft swell and, in spite of the sub-zero cold and the sadness, it was still a good evening to be alive. The thought shattered at the memories it triggered: Don Lindsay and Deanne Fischer, Barrington Hobbes, Ian Neale, Anne Collinson and, before them, people she had never met, Hobbes's wife and child, Paul Calvert and Colin May of the sunken *Aurora*. All of them dead.

She leant back against a ventilator fairing. "Alan, is there really any hope for Don and Deanne? Or am I just clutching at any straw that comes along?"

"I only wish I knew," he said quietly. "Rob's right, though. The *Denver's* sonar guy told me he'd heard them hit the bottom with a hell of a crash. He reckoned nothing could have survived it. On the other hand, you were right, too. We have every reason to know that you can't write off the *Nautilus* lightly. With her, anything's possible, even miracles. All we can do is wait and hope."

They both felt the bump against the ship's opposite side. Tregenza glanced out over the stern at a stretch of water littered with ice floes.

"Falco really ought to be keeping a watch out for those," he said. "Some of those growlers weigh tons and can do this boat a lot of damage if he's not careful."

Karen wasn't listening to him. A movement at the starboard rail caught her eye. She wanted to scream but the breath jammed in her throat as a face, grey with weariness, dark with two days growth of beard and with a jagged cut in the forehead, rose slowly above the gunwale. The apparition spoke.

"Don't just stand there gawping." The hoarse voice was Lindsay's. "Give us a hand."

There was no hiding the grin of sheer delight on Seán McKenna's face. "So what the hell kept you?" he said lightly.

Wrapped in blankets and with four stitches freshly inserted in the gash above his right temple, Lindsay took a gulp of his coffee and grinned at Deanne's black eye.

"Oh, this and that," he said. "When we smashed into the bottom, the missile launcher hit it first and took the brunt. Half of it disintegrated and we just jammed even deeper into the half that was left. We were locked solid. Deanne and I were both laid out for a couple of hours during which time we'd heeled over so that the boat was lying on her side, stern up because I'd emergency vented the tanks on the way down. It was the only way of putting the brakes on that I could think of.

"I'm sorry to say that the radio and sonar gear are smashed to hell. We could hear the active sonar pulses coming in, which had to be the *Denver* looking for us, but there was no way we could signal back. We did try hammering on the hull but obviously weren't heard. The ice-growl on the surface probably drowned us out.

"We figured that the only way of getting ourselves free of the launcher was to get the engines going and use full reverse power. It took us until half an hour ago to get the bloody things to cooperate." He picked out McLeish in the sea of faces around him. "Sorry, Rob. The best I could do was a patch-up job."

"Don't worry yourself, Commander," the engineer grinned back. "I've seen the damage. It isnae that bad. The old team of Jourdan and McLeish will have her back to normal in a matter of hours. As for the radio and sonar, we can always pick up replacements in Auckland if Seán will agree to breaking out another gold bar. What aboot structural damage?"

"As far as I can tell, her nose is a bit scarred up and there's a problem with the starboard diving plane. Internal, I think. I checked her right through and there's no sign of any hull breach, which is more than a blessing considering the beating she took. After you and Ross have sorted her out, she'll probably be good for another hundred years."

"So will you two after a good night's sleep," McKenna said, looking pointedly at their cuts, bruises and abrasions. "You'll probably be needing an ice-pack apiece."

Lindsay winced. "Please don't mention ice, Seán. I've seen enough of the bloody stuff to last me a lifetime. I'm only sorry I had to risk the boat like that. Call it sheer desperation but it was the only way to take out the missile launcher. The boys on the hill would certainly have died otherwise. Still, I did manage to kill two birds with one *Nautilus*."

"In what way?" McKenna asked.

"The driver of the missile truck was Wolf. The bastard's dead. The ram of the *Nautilus* went straight through him. Cut him in half. There'll be no more victims of the Linden Wolf."

"So it's over."

Lindsay gave McKenna a keen look. "Not quite," he said.

65

28 March 2015
La Roque del Fuego
The Canary Islands

The white heat of volcanic eruptions that had raged centuries ago had given expanses of black basalt a mirror-like smoothness. Other minerals had melted and rehardened into volcanic glass, producing highly reflective surfaces that glittered and gleamed in the pure intensity of the electric searchlight, turning the vaulted interior of the hollow mountain into a wonderland of light.

The *Nautilus* floated on the still surface of the underground lake that reflected the sparkles of light to amplify the Aladdin's Cave effect. It tended to belie the fact that, at all other times, the interior of La Roque del Fuego was a place of darkness, as cold, stark and silent as the tomb it had become.

Expressionless, Seán McKenna gazed at the corpse. The dead man lay on his back amid a scatter of wooden crates, thankfully concealing the fact that much of the back of the head had been blown off by the bullet's passage through the roof of the mouth. A lake of blood beneath Gerald

Calloway's shattered skull had congealed and hardened to a dark brown mat.

"So Ross got his wish," he muttered.

"What was that?" Lindsay had caught only half of what the Irishman had said.

"He wanted to lash Calloway to a boulder and drop him in the lake," McKenna explained. "He can do that now, if he wants. We can't leave him like this."

Around and about the dead man lay evidence that crates had been broken up and piled together to build fires. About half the food had been consumed and McKenna estimated that Calloway had been dead for about a week.

The arms of the corpse were flung wide and the Browning automatic pistol lay on the bare rock surface near the curled fingers of the right hand. McKenna picked it up and examined the empty magazine before tossing both into the lake and giving Lindsay a keen, penetrating look.

"One gun and a single bullet," McKenna said softly. "Now who, I wonder, could possibly have been bastard enough to leave the man with an option like that?"

Chapter 10

The Last Words of Captain Nemo

66

4 April 2015
Plymouth
Devon, UK

Karen Marshall's story, put out under the names of herself and Barrington Hobbes, and the Prime Minister's own painfully revealing revelations in the Press and on live television, had by now reached most of the world.

Environmental issues, so prominent during the nineteen seventies and eighties had, through political and commercial chicanery, led to public apathy in the nineties. Now, fifteen years into the new millenium, it blossomed anew as the existence of the *Nautilus* and the exploits of her modern crew were brought to public attention, and as the people behind the Pyramus Group were systematically arrested, hounded from public office, or both. No less than three of these, in addition to Gerald Calloway, had since committed suicide.

As a result of the Prime Minister's initiative, new or reformed governments in industrial nations were making new pledges to place the earth's ecology at the forefront of internationally agreed policies coordinated by the United Nations. That and his own unprecedented political honesty had saved the British Prime Minister's bacon.

Only time would tell if, this time, the promises would be kept.

The arrival of the legendary *Nautilus* in the territorial waters of Britain—her traditional enemy—out in the open and no longer a hunted ship, could hardly be termed a homecoming but the strength of her reception gave every impression of it being so. McKenna could not help but wonder what Nemo would have made of it.

The first indications of the reception that was waiting had come when the old submarine had risen to the surface of a gently rolling Channel ten miles south of the Eddystone Light. Press-chartered helicopters were out in force, already circling in wait. Cameras pointed from every available orifice for the first sight of her long, black, reptilian shape and creaming wake.

Closer to Plymouth, the Royal Navy frigate *HMS Broadsword* and the Brittany ferry *Quiberon* blasted their horns in a deafening salute that forewarned the waiting crowds ashore. The decks of both ships were awash with people crowding the rails for their first glimpse of the craft that had captured the public imagination. The sudden blast of sound had also acted as a signal for the huge flotilla of smaller vessels that lay in wait outside the Breakwater at the mouth of Plymouth Sound. Hundreds of boats seemed to be crammed together, each of them eager to escort a legend into harbour.

Thousands upon thousands of people lined Plymouth Hoe, the Cornish heights of Mount Edgcumbe and, on the Devonian side, Mount Batten, Wembury and Staddon Heights. The blare of car horns and cheering filled the air.

Even from within the double-skinned wheelhouse of the *Nautilus*, Seán McKenna could hear it. He shrugged to himself and decided to enter into the spirit of it all, taking water into the submarine's ballast tanks and venting it back out with all the force of the vessel's pumps. From the outlet valves, situated on either side of the deck fairing just aft of the wheelhouse, the twin plumes jetted more than a hundred feet into the air. The applause was tumultuous.

By the end of the day, McKenna felt completely washed out. The dockside had been crowded all evening and, as midnight approached, hundreds of people remained to goggle at the nineteenth century miracle of achievement and in the hope of getting a glimpse of the crew whose courage was now global news.

Steadfastly refusing to allow people on board, McKenna had fielded endless questions from newspaper, television and radio journalists from more countries than he cared to count. In the end, his eyes could no longer stand the relentless flashlights and he retired below deck.

One request that he had been delighted to answer had come from a representative of the Musée de Jules Verne, inviting the *Nautilus* to officially visit the Breton port of Nantes, Verne's birthplace and the home of the museum that celebrated the great author's life and works. This had been the only man that McKenna was prepared to invite aboard and the ecstatic Frenchman had spent hours inspecting, exploring and photographing every inch of the vessel. McKenna had firmly resisted the Frenchman's suggestion that the *Nautilus* become a permanent exhibit of the museum at Nantes, but promised to consider the man's second notion that the submarine be registered at the Breton port if she was to remain operational.

As he relaxed below, Seán McKenna felt the mental surge of sudden release from the tensions of the past year. No longer a 'dead' man, no longer a fugitive cocooned for over a year in a metal cylinder beneath the sea, unable to emerge into the world he knew. Had it really been so bad? Nemo had existed in precisely that way for eighteen years.

Tearful reunions had brought a particular stress of their own, not only from the families of his crew, but also the unexpected arrival of Madeleine Duvall and her parents. There was also a young American couple named Reynolds who swore they owed their lives to the *Nautilus*. McKenna remembered the yacht he had saved from Malay pirates at Krakatau but had never, until now, seen the faces of the *Greyhound's* crew. Susan Reynolds's father, Brian Challoner, had been given a new resolve by the incident. Not only had he survived his cancer to see the young couple married in Hawaii as he had hoped, he had even lived just long enough to see the arrival of his first grandson. McKenna knew nothing of this, but had been profusely thanked for it just the same.

By one o'clock, those who were due back to the *Nautilus* had returned. Rob McLeish had been as good as his word and overdone it in true Caledonian style in the Barbican pubs where he'd been royally treated as a homecoming hero. He was now sleeping it off in his engine room bunk. Don Lindsay and Deanne Fischer, now none the worse for their Antarctic ordeal, had returned from a Greek restaurant and retired, Carla Schumann had remained aboard with McKenna.

Of the remainder of the vessel's crew, Ross Jourdan and Christian Janssen were on their way to Heathrow to catch flights to their respective countries but both had pledged to rejoin the *Nautilus* within the month. Tregenza and Karen Marshall had hired a car and driven down to St Ives but would be back in the morning in time for the arrival of the VIPs.

Inwardly, McKenna shuddered at that prospect but there was no avoiding it. The Prime Minister himself would be coming aboard, along with Sir Henry Williamson and Lindsay's chief, Admiral Garvie. Sir Robert Maynard, Deep Watch's director, and Dr Melvyn Hunter, who had done so much to help Karen and the late Barrington Hobbes, were also due. The only member of the Press that would be permitted on board was to be Tony Saunders, editor of *The Sentinel* in which Karen's exclusive had blown the entire affair to the world. Rumours of a royal presence were also rife.

At ten past one in the morning, McKenna decided to take a turn around the deck. Crowds still ogled the *Nautilus* and a strong police presence deterred any prospective souvenir hunters from leaping down onto the submarine's deck. It was all too much. The Irishman smiled weakly, gave a tired wave to the crowd, cast off the moorings and retreated below.

The night, he decided, would be more peacefully spent on the sea-bed off the Eddystone Light.

67

5 April 2015
The English Channel

It was a tense McKenna that studied the entourage of spellbound guests assembled in the saloon of the *Nautilus*. The Prince—the rumours had been true—the Prime Minister and Sir Robert Maynard were minutely examining and discussing the priceless works of art displayed on its walls. Tony Saunders sat with a laptop on his knee entering reams of notes. Dr Melvyn Hunter, having explored every nook and cranny of the vessel since coming aboard, was in a rapturous world of his own, unconcerned with the close discussions going on between Lindsay, Admiral Garvie and the Minister of Defence. In a corner of the room, Deanne and Carla sat with Madeleine Duvall and her parents. With Ross Jourdan and Chris Janssen on their way home, the only people missing from the room were Alan Tregenza, presently at the submarine's helm, and Rob McLeish, nursing his precious engines like a mother hen.

The uncomfortable captain was grateful for the buzz of the intercom. "We've arrived, Seán," Tregenza's voice came through quietly.

"Okay, Alan," McKenna replied. "Hold us at thirty feet from the bottom, as gently as you can."

The Prince turned aside from a stunning example of Rembrandt's work. "Captain, this vessel is incredible," he enthused. "I can't get over all this space. So different from the cramped conditions of so many submarines that I've seen. No mazes and tangles of pipes and ducts either. Quite apart from her origins and the wonderful things she contains, I've felt no sense of motion. Her engines are unbelievably quiet."

McKenna acknowledged the praise. "They certainly are. Gave NATO all kinds of problems," he added cheekily. "You might be interested to hear that, since clearing Plymouth Breakwater, we've been maintaining a steady rate of thirty knots." He indicated the photograph of Captain Nemo. "To be fair, the credit is entirely his."

"Captain McKenna's being a little modest, sir," Lindsay cut in. "It was he and his crew who stripped her down and got her running again after she'd been blown out of a volcano and then spent a century in the ice. Not to mention having to do it again after I crashed her into the ocean floor."

Melvyn Hunter joined the conversation. "It is humbling to think that this was the world's first fully functional ocean-going submarine. In many respects she's still superior to the best the modern world can offer. I rather think that her recent exploits have demonstrated that rather well."

"Indeed," the Prime Minister said. "The *Nautilus* and her modern crew have little left to prove. Captain, where are you taking us?"

"We're already there," McKenna said simply, glancing at the wall-mounted instruments to check that the vessel was maintaining her depth and trim as instructed.

The panels had remained closed since leaving Plymouth. McKenna touched the controls, steeling himself for the inevitable gasps of surprise as the lights dimmed and the panels slid back to admit their view of the depths lit by the brilliance of the submarine's searchlight.

On either side, the oblong windows looked out onto a scene from a nightmare. For as far as the powerful light could penetrate the Channel's murky waters, the floor of the sea was obscured by an endless tangle of rusting, leaking canisters, spent missile casings, torpedoes, mines and high explosive shells.

The guests stared out in sober silence.

"The Hurd Deep," McKenna announced. "In reality, a shallow valley in the floor of the Channel twelve miles north of Alderney. We are at a depth of sixty-seven fathoms—four hundred feet. Peanuts in oceanic terms.

"What you see out there is the result of decades of indiscriminate military dumping by Her Majesty's Government. If you care to look closely, you will also see containers bearing radiation warning labels.

"Your own eyes will tell you that a great many of those canisters are leaking, spreading lethal toxins throughout the marine environment and the entire food chain, right down to your own dinner tables. Can you now still wonder why it is that human sperm counts have halved in the last fifty years? Or why cancers are more prevalent among the population than ever before? This site is no isolated example… you can find the self same thing on the floor of the Irish Sea and a hundred other places around the globe.

"For those of you in government and positions of power, this is your legacy. This is what you and your predecessors have let loose upon the world.

"If what I've told you already isn't bad enough, you can take it from me that the explosives down here are in a highly unstable condition. By bringing you here, I've placed us all at considerable risk, nothing new to my crew, but a very new experience for many of you. In my opinion, that's a risk well worth the taking in order that you see for yourselves the damage that has been done.

"Please feel free to take a good long look and, on the way back to Plymouth, perhaps you'd care to consider how to call a halt to this sort of practice and how to put it right, not just here but in the rest of the world as well. You owe that to yourselves and to future generations that have to live on the planet you leave them.

"In the meantime, we'll move away. Very, very gently. Make no mistake, this place is now so volatile that one wrong vibration could cause the entire site to go up, taking everything within ten miles straight to hell."

68

Plymouth
Devon, UK

The *Nautilus* had once again tied up in Plymouth and, with her engines shut down, her crew had joined the guests in the saloon. Glasses of wine were filled and handed round. McKenna himself offered a glass to the Prime Minister who stood, grim-faced, in a corner.

"How did you enjoy the trip?" McKenna asked lightly.

The Prime Minister turned slowly to confront him, furious. "Enjoy the trip? How dare you, McKenna? How dare you place our lives in danger. You were even prepared to jeopardize the Prince. What gave you that right?"

"Necessity, now that you come to ask. And let's get something straight here. I owe neither you nor the Prince any allegiance whatsoever. In fact, and I speak for myself, not for my crew, I renounced all nationality years ago. My allegiance lies solely with the oceans of the world which, thank God, are not governed by politicians."

The exchange silenced all other conversation in the room. Every ear was turned towards McKenna and the Prime Minister as the Irish captain said his piece.

"People like us have sounded off about places like the Hurd Deep until we're blue in the face, and what response did we ever get from the likes of yourself? Nothing, but patronizing platitudes. Your policy, like that of every one of your predecessors, has been 'out of sight, out of mind'. There was only ever going to be one way of getting you to even envisage the problem, and that was to rub your nose in it. Today, we had the perfect chance to do just that and we all agreed to take it."

The Premier's mouth dropped open but McKenna was well into his stride. "Well, we achieved that much and, quite honestly, I don't give a damn for your sensitivities. Until a few hours ago, you had no idea of the powder keg that had been created out there, and that's just one example. Whether you like it or not, we need the seas for our survival, every man, woman and child on the face of the earth.

"We have no choice but to safeguard the oceans and the environments of the world if we truly want our children and their children to have a world worth living in. You people in government have every opportunity to seize that chance but, instead, you choose to protect profits and the greedy.

"That is why we, Greenpeace, Friends of the Earth and all the other groups exist. To try and achieve what governments have a duty to do, but never even try, and to make you realize just what is at stake here. That is what the *Nautilus* has fought for, not only during this past year but from the very day she was launched.

"Think what you like of Nemo, but he spent years of his life studying the world's oceans in order to understand them and gain the essential knowledge of how best to protect them. He achieved results our modern oceanographers haven't even got close to. All that information is here on this boat and that's the one secret she holds that we are willing to share."

McKenna peered intently into the Prime Minister's eyes. "In lending us your aid against the Pyramus Group, Prime Minister, you actually made a start. You took a step in the right direction. Wouldn't it be poetic if the very nation that Nemo rightly despised became the first to embrace his dream and take the lead towards making it a reality? The conservation of the oceans. You could do far worse and, besides, you might even begin to make amends for what Britain did to that man. In short, we don't need the politics of greed but the politics of care."

The Prime Minister had noticeably cooled own, somewhat deflated by the stark truths of McKenna's onslaught. "Your point is taken, captain," he said. "and I do take some pride in the fact that the destruction of the Pyramus Group has removed at least one major threat to the environment. All its key personnel, in various countries, have been arrested, eliminated or otherwise removed from the picture."

"All except the top man," Admiral Garvie reminded him. "He's still at large and still unidentified."

"As a matter of fact, Admiral," McKenna said. "I was just coming to that. There have been a few hints and clues here and there, and I thought it might be worth a few minutes putting them together and seeing what we have.

"On a black night in February last year, my ship, the *Aurora*, was rammed and sunk by a Pyramus vessel. This, we know, was no accident. The ship in question was the *Emperor*, the very same that attacked us recently using concealed armaments that turn out to have been newly installed in Japan. Probably for our benefit. This was also the same ship that got herself sunk by the *Denver* after attacking us.

"The *Emperor's* master, one Captain Franz Schiller, knew very well that the *Aurora* had no operational radar. He may well have heard us bitching about it over the radio but it's just as likely that he was forewarned. Schiller made sure we knew nothing about his approach by extinguishing every light on his ship.

"Now, the *Aurora's* radar was a brand new installation, supposedly the best available. Perhaps it was, but its complete breakdown after just a few days at sea was no accident. It had been specifically programmed to do so. And, you'll never guess, but its manufacturer turns out to have been a Pyramus subsidiary.

"We'd been told that this same radar system had been installed on another boat but when we asked Marcel Duvall here to do his bit of computer hacking, we entered files that told us she'd had no such installation. We found that particularly interesting, so we chased down her registration where she's entered under her previous name, the *Adélie*. Her registered owner was, of course, a branch of the Pyramus Group.

"An amended registration confirmed that the *Adélie*, a luxury yacht by the way, had been renamed. She's now the *Lady Sibella*. Now here's a curious coincidence," McKenna's eyes, now ice cold, turned towards Sir Robert Maynard. "That's the same name as your boat, Sir Robert. In fact, same boat."

A shocked roomful of eyes stared at Maynard as McKenna pressed on. "How long is it since you founded the Pyramus Group, Sir Robert? Twenty years? Your UNESCO and UN appointments gave you every opportunity to recruit from the powerful and greedy of the entire world. What better cover could you conceive than to found and direct an environmental pressure group like Deep Watch, a highly publicized and applauded move when, in fact, you were putting together an international web of murder, deceit and corruption, designed to rape the very environment you were being seen to champion?"

Maynard said nothing, maintaining silence as his eyes stared unblinkingly at McKenna.

The Irishman shrugged his shoulders. "Ten years ago, you ordered the murder of Barrington Hobbes who was getting just a tad too close to your activities. He barely survived the attempt to kill him, but his wife and five-year old daughter did not.

"It was you, Sir Robert, who recently ordered the deaths of Hobbes and Karen over there. The first attempt killed the reporter Ian Neale. The second, on the cliffs down in West Cornwall, at last succeeded in killing Hobbes but, thanks to Commander Lindsay's intervention, your operatives failed to get Karen. A bad mistake that, for she knew everything that Hobbes knew.

"You used your position and influence to gain the complete trust of government ministers like Sir Henry and then to cleverly manipulate them. In that way, you and Calloway could even influence NATO chiefs into a policy of hunting down and destroying the *Nautilus* which, you'd realized, had latched onto the activities of your ships. And all the while, you maintained the illusion of being the environment's great white hope.

"You concealed yourself well. Your associates loyally protected your identity. Of course they would. You were making them extremely wealthy men, the carrot if you like. But there was a stick, too, wasn't there? Those who failed you died, like Senhor Valdera in Lisbon. You were employing, as a professional killer, a certain Hans-Dieter Wolf, a former *Stasi* torturer and murderer on the wanted list of a dozen nations. That alone was enough to keep any mouth quiet. Happily, thanks to Commander Lindsay, he is now the late and unlamented Linden Wolf."

McKenna calmly lit a cigar and blew the smoke out in a long steady stream. "It must have been the hell of a shock to discover just who the crew of the *Nautilus* were. You totally believed that you had eliminated us aboard the *Aurora*, simply because we happened to be in the wrong place at the wrong time. You couldn't prevent us from patrolling the Ross Sea, and it would have looked mighty peculiar had you tried. You couldn't risk us seeing what we weren't supposed to. It would have raised some bloody awkward questions if we'd reported a sighting of the *Emperor* steaming north out of Antarctica when she was supposed to have been on a Sydney to Valparaiso voyage. So, before we sailed, you insisted on the radar changeover and effectively sentenced us to death.

"Once you knew it was us aboard the *Nautilus*, you redoubled your efforts to get us removed from the equation, hence our little problems with the *Honshu* and a newly armed *Emperor*.

"You, Sir Robert, are directly responsible for the deaths of Paul Calvert and Colin May, of Ian Neale who died in the car bomb explosion intended for Hobbes. You ordered the deaths of Hobbes, Anne Collinson and the attempt to kill Commander Lindsay on board the *Noordzee Marquess*. You can add to that all those who died on the *Honshu* and the *Emperor*, the men who lie inside the wreck of your Antarctic disposal facility, of one of Colonel Byrd's men and even your friend Calloway who, incidentally, took his own life. All those deaths, and Christ knows how many more, lie at your door and you will not escape justice. Not while I live."

Maynard rose to his feet, adopting a dignified stance and straightening his suit. He removed the rimless glasses and tucked them neatly into an inside pocket as he scanned the horrified faces around him.

"A masterful piece of deduction, Seán," he said calmly. "I congratulate you. You are, of course, correct in every detail and I don't intend to stoop to pointless denials. We are, I take it, speaking of a considerable penal sentence?"

Admiral Garvie glowered from beneath beetling eyebrows. "If you consider life imprisonment considerable," he said coldly. "If the death penalty had still been available to us, Sir Robert, I would have no hesitation in recommending it. Alas, it is not."

Very few people in that room had ever stared down the barrel of a gun. They now knew exactly what it was like, not that it was a very big gun, just a compact, small-bore Beretta pistol that the cut of Maynard's suit had concealed. Big or small, at a close enough range, any gun will kill as effectively as the next.

Maynard was calm and professional enough to ensure that the gun was held close to his own body. He backed away to the door leading from the saloon to the library and, ultimately, the boat's central stairwell so that he could see everyone at a glance and cover them all by a simple quarter turn of his upper body.

"You are, of course, entitled to your opinion, Admiral," he said evenly," but I didn't come this far without applying a modicum of intelligence and forward planning. The gun, for example. I regret having to produce it but it was a necessary precaution. Once I'd discovered who had hacked into my files it was fairly obvious that my chairmanship of the Pyramus Group was not going to remain a secret forever. I did have a notion that it might be today."

"And now you believe that you can get away," Garvie grated.

Maynard smiled condescendingly. "I'm assured of it, Admiral. My wealth has already been discreetly redistributed among banks around the world, under a variety of pseudonyms, one of which may be my future name. I have also arranged a course of minor surgery—facial, fingertips, even the larynx to alter my voice pattern. Within weeks, I could engage any one of you in conversation without you having the least idea to whom you are speaking.

"I now propose to leave the *Nautilus* and trust that none of you—particularly you, Commander Lindsay—will be foolhardy enough to follow. I will have no compunction about putting a bullet into anyone who tries. None of you are armed and, as I understand it, your famous electric guns are stored somewhere aft. In the time it would take you to reach one, I shall be long gone. I shall simply melt into the considerable crowd on the quayside and disappear. From that moment, Sir Robert Maynard will cease to exist."

He cast a long look around the luxurious expanse of the saloon and again sought out McKenna's gaze.

"She really is a wonderful boat," he said. "I don't regret not having sunk her. If I had, I would never have seen her. Goodbye, Seán. I shall be of no further concern to you. Just go out and save those whales."

Maynard backed away into the adjoining library and through to the dining room on his way to the central stairwell. The gun remained steadily trained on the saloon doorway.

McKenna made a move forward. Lindsay barred his way. "No, Seán," he said softly. "Stay clear of this. It's still my job. Keep everyone in this room for their own safety."

By the time Lindsay reached the door that led into the stairwell, Maynard had almost reached the upper landing.

"Sir Robert!" he shouted up. "Give it up!"

Maynard twisted and fired down at the naval man as he dived away under the first flight of metal stairs. The sound of the shot and its impact on the deckplates was deafening in the confined space. There were cries of fear from the saloon.

"I'm all right. Stay put," Lindsay called through.

He looked around him, desperately seeking for what he knew was somewhere close by. Captain Nemo, the submarine's builder, had installed an ingenious security device designed to deter unwanted intruders. Lindsay found it, just an arm's length away, a simple calibrated knob set into a bulkhead niche. On the few occasions it had ever been used, the system had never been turned higher than a fraction of its full potential, the intention having only been to sting and repel.

Lindsay looked up. "Maynard!" he shouted. The man was on the high landing, only needing to climb the last short flight of rungs to the deck hatch. He turned and squeezed off a second shot. Lindsay flattened his body to the bulkhead as the bullet flattened itself on the deckplates uncomfortably close to his feet. He quickly examined his right boot where the bullet had taken a sizable chunk from its heel.

"You're wasting your time, Commander." Maynard turned away, pocketed the gun and grasped both handrails to haul himself up the final ladder. Lindsay used the opportunity to lunge for the control, twisting the knob as far as it would go.

His eyes clamped shut against the brilliance of the blue-white flash that lit up the entire stairwell as the huge store of electrical power contained in the vast array of the boat's fuel cells transferred itself to the handrails. Maynard's body arched back in a spine-cracking convulsion, hair standing on end, his eyes bulging from their sockets and his mouth open in a scream that never reached it. The stairwell filled with a withering hiss and crackle, and reeked with the sickly smell of roasting flesh.

Lindsay turned off the power. Above him, the body crashed to the expanded metal catwalk and lay still. The naval agent climbed the stairs wearily and gazed down, dispassionately, at the smoking corpse.

"Do mind the stairs, Sir Robert," he said.

69

The English Channel

Just as on the previous evening, Seán McKenna took the *Nautilus* out from her berth in Plymouth and set her on the bottom off the Eddystone Lighthouse to get a night's respite from the crowds that still thronged the quayside. Those same crowds were still buzzing about the earlier gunshots heard below deck, the corpse that had been removed by armed police in a sealed body bag, and the white, haunted faces of the distinguished guests as they left the vessel under protective escort. Those same faces, with shock etched into every line, would be all over the front pages in the morning. The crowds would double in size.

Shutting down the engines and leaving the wheelhouse, he went below to the saloon and opened the panels to gaze out on the waving fronds of kelp that sparkled reflections from the ship's searchlight. It was well past one in the morning but McKenna was both weary and restless, unable to believe that the ordeal was finally over. He poured himself a stiff drink, selecting his favourite Bushmills whiskey, and settled himself on a divan with the great weight of Captain Nemo's journal on his lap.

His eyes managed just ten minutes of the clear, neat, calligraphic script before their drooping heaviness persuaded him to bunk down for the night. He tossed what was left of the Bushmills down his throat, took the journal back into what had once been Nemo's own cabin and went off to his own. Carla was deep in sleep. McKenna slid in beside her as gently as he could and was asleep almost immediately.

Perhaps the whiskey was to blame, but McKenna dreamt vividly that night. He saw himself sitting in the saloon of the *Nautilus*, every detail of which was clearly imprinted on his sleeping mind, and he was not alone.

A tall figure stood by the open port side panel, gazing out into the floodlit depths of the sea and he was not one of McKenna's own crew. The man wore sealskin boots and loose, flexible clothing. From beneath a cap of sea-otter fur, satin-black hair, traced with grey at the temples, flowed over his wide shoulders.

The stranger turned away from the window and gazed analytically at the Irishman. The neatly bearded face was a handsome one, with nobility set into its features. The forehead was broad and high, the nose straight and finely chiselled. His calm, jet black eyes were widely set, giving the man an unusually wide angle of vision, and their large lids seemed to close in around them, concentrating the gaze to one of piercing intensity.

McKenna felt as though the man was looking, and could clearly see, into his very soul.

Then the expression relaxed. The stranger's finely formed mouth, stern in repose, smiled briefly, giving McKenna a glimpse of perfectly even teeth.

He could never afterwards recall whether the man in his dream ever spoke to him but he was in no doubt who he was. The man was standing directly under the portrait of himself that graced the saloon's forward bulkhead. In both hands he held a large, heavy book—his own journal, which he then laid down on a table, its pages open…

The touch of warm lips on his forehead roused McKenna from a confused sleep. He rubbed his eyes, looked into Carla's face and noted with relief that he was still in his own cabin.

"What time is it?" he mumbled.

"Oh-seven-hundred," Carla said. "Give or take a minute or so."

McKenna kissed her in return and struggled out of bed. "Best freshen up and put back into Plymouth," he said. "More bloody Press calls and I suppose I'd better let that TV crew aboard, if only in the interests of good public relations. I'll be glad when we can put back to sea."

He dressed himself and made his way into the saloon, peering round suspiciously. No tall, bearded figure awaited him. McKenna smiled ruefully at his own idiocy.

Carla had followed him in. "So we will be going back to sea, then?"

"Damn right we will, girl dear. Same crew, too. Ross and Christian have signalled to say they're cutting their leave short and will be back at the weekend. Maddy's coming as well. Even Don Lindsay—he's taken a month's leave to consider his own future. He reckons that a sea voyage might do him some good!"

Carla laughed. "I don't suppose for a minute that Deanne will object to that."

McKenna glanced towards the after saloon door as Tregenza and Karen walked in. "We'd better start choosing some wedding presents, too," the captain said.

He turned to look out of the port panel and, for a moment, his blood froze. Nemo's journal lay open on a table, precisely where the figure in his dream had left it. Fully aware that, on the previous evening, he'd returned it to the desk in Nemo's cabin, McKenna stared wordlessly at it before moving slowly to pick it up.

It had been left open at the very last page of entry, a page that McKenna had yet to read. The hand in which it was written was not the bold script of earlier pages but shaky and laboured, the lines none too straight. The dying Nemo had evidently summoned every last ounce of his remaining strength to write his last words:

16th October 1883

Harding and his companions have, at my request, withdrawn, granting me a few hours to make my peace with God, reflect upon my life and to make this, my final, entry. By morning I shall be dead and I will die content. I have warned Harding of the volcano and the terrible threat it poses. I can only pray that the precautions I have already taken on their behalf will deliver these brave, honest and resourceful men from the cataclysm that will surely come, for I can do no more for them.

I have given Captain Harding my final instructions. It is impossible now for my remains to be placed beside those of my companions who rest in the coral cemetery beneath the Java Sea and, therefore, I must remain here. I have told him that my wish is to be sealed aboard my Nautilus. *He will then open the external cocks that will fill the ballast tanks and submerge the* Nautilus *into the considerable depths of this cavern. I am fully confident that he will obey my instructions to the letter.*

I cannot dispel the thought that this grave may not be a permanent one. When the sea breaks through to the volcano's heart there will be such an explosion that I fear this island will cease to exist. Both Nature and Fate are capricious creatures. Will they contrive to restore the Nautilus *to her rightful place as a traveller in the deep?*

I have the strangest premonition that the life of my vessel is far from over. For a score of years she has been a refuge, a home, a laboratory of researches and learning. I did not intend that she become a weapon of destruction and yet, on two terrible occasions, I used her as such to destroy vessels of war belonging to those who occupied and oppressed my native land; those who had put my loved ones to torture and the bullet. I will defend those actions, and my right to have carried them out, unto my last breath.

The integrity and dedication of Harding and his men have given me the gift of renewed hope for the future. If men such as this exist in the world, there may also be others among whom will be those who will care for the oceans as I have done. Should this be so, and if Fate decrees that the Nautilus *is freed to roam the seas once again, I have the most curious, perhaps irrational, notion that she will seek them out, almost as though I believe her to have a life and will of her own. Perhaps those same people will discover my mortal remains and lay them beside the loyal few with whom I shared my submarine existence. Perhaps, too, in the right hands, the* Nautilus *may serve as the flagship of a new dawn.*

To those unknown people, I bequeath my Nautilus *and all that she contains. Should they ever read these words, let me say that I shall keep vigil, for I go to my rest in the certain knowledge that, wherever my mortal body may lie, my eternal soul can never leave this vessel.*

Fate will ultimately decide and I must be content with that.

"*I bequeath my* Nautilus*… my eternal soul can never leave this vessel…*" The words seemed to stand out from the page.

"Did I hear you say we're taking the *Nautilus* back to sea?" Tregenza's question broke into McKenna's stunned concentration.

"Could you ever doubt it, Alan? After all, she's our boat now."

He laid the open book almost reverently on the table and ran his fingertips over its last words. "She's ours by right."

The End

Also available from

Evertype

Twenty Thousand Leagues under the Seas
Translated by F. P. Walter, 2009

Cuairt na Cruinne in Ochtó Lá
Around the World in Eighty Days in Irish,
Translated by Torna (Tadhg Ua Donnchadha), 2008

Adro dhe'n Bÿs in Peswar Ugans Dëdh
Around the World in Eighty Days in Cornish,
Abridged and translated by Kaspar Hocking, 2009

A Concise Dictionary of Cornish Place-Names
by Craig Weatherhill, 2009

www.ingramcontent.com/pod-product-compliance
Lightning Source LLC
Chambersburg PA
CBHW020942310726
48980CB00001B/22

* 9 7 8 1 9 0 4 8 0 8 4 0 4 *